The
Group Trip

Also by Audrey Ingram

The River Runs South

The
Group Trip

◆ A NOVEL ◆

AUDREY INGRAM

alcove
press

Published in the United States by Alcove Press, an imprint of The Quick Brown Fox & Company LLC.

Alcove Press and its logo are trademarks of The Quick Brown Fox & Company LLC.

Library of Congress Catalog-in-Publication data available upon request.

ISBN (paperback): 978-1-63910-869-5
ISBN (ebook): 978-1-63910-870-1

Cover design by Sarah Brody

Printed in the United States.

www.alcovepress.com

Alcove Press
34 West 27th St., 10th Floor
New York, NY 10001

First Edition: August 2024

10 9 8 7 6 5 4 3 2 1

To Jenn, Maria, Meagan, and Sara,
for two decades of epic group trips

PROLOGUE

THE SKY IS BLUE, the sand is white, and the water is a shimmering green. That's how this stretch of beach on the Panhandle of Florida gets its name: *The Emerald Coast.* In the exclusive town of Seaside where Chloe is vacationing, the beaches are private. This strikes her as unnatural, limiting access to something that should belong to everyone. There are a handful of public access points, but mostly you need a key if you want to touch sand. Long boardwalks provide peeks of the ocean, but at the end there's a gate. And only the select few who pay enough to belong can enter this shoreline. Of course, when you're staying in an oceanfront house, this isn't an issue.

Chloe doesn't complain. After all, she's spent six days soaking in the sun on teak lounge chairs arranged each morning by a concierge service, sipping frozen cocktails delivered by a catering team, and watching the sunset on cushions surrounding a beach bonfire while nibbling crab and corn fritters.

She likes the space this privilege affords. She can swim in the ocean without bumping into another body. She can whisper secrets about the night before without the family on the next towel overhearing. She can walk up and down the empty beach and wonder how it's possible to love and hate the same person.

If this were any other year, Chloe and her friends would have to shout over laughter, they'd be exhausted from staying up all night talking, and her cheeks would ache from the constant smiling. But this trip is different. And that's mostly Chloe's fault.

If she has discovered anything over the last six days, it's that her best friends are full of secrets. And no matter how hard she tries to fix the mistakes she's made, she fears that they may have grown too far apart.

She glances at her watch. They're supposed to gather for another beachside dinner, but everyone else is already thirty minutes late.

They scattered today, her friends venturing in opposite directions, dispersing to the various beach towns that neighbor Seaside. Rosemary Beach with its European-style village, and Alys Beach with its white stucco buildings. The surfers gather in Grayton Beach, and the nature lovers congregate in the towns with the biggest dune lakes, Blue Mountain and Watercolor. The area is called 30A because that's the county road that winds along the coast, connecting one village to another.

A cluster of beach towns, each with its own unique personality, not unlike Chloe's group of friends. This trip is supposed to bring everyone together. But if tonight is anything like the last few nights, someone will get too drunk, someone will cry, and they'll all spend the night wondering what went wrong. Again.

The catering crew has set up a circle of tiki torches and low tables covered with food: heirloom tomatoes topped with cracked pepper and blue cheese crumbles, fried oysters with caper aioli, grilled grouper with creamed corn and basil vinaigrette, a key lime pie with graham cracker crust. She is the only one on the beach, and she adjusts the straps of her blue gingham dress as she stares back at the house full of her friends.

From her chair, she can see familiar bodies moving around the oceanfront mansion. The silhouettes of two women, fingers pointing. Are they shouting again? A door closes and a tall figure emerges onto the back deck. She knows who it is by the limp in his gait. The way he carefully leans against the railing so as not to jostle his bruised body.

There's a seagull chirping, a car door slamming, and then silence. She turns away from the house and all its chaos and pain. The five people she loves most are inside. How do friends that became family turn back into strangers?

Chloe stands and walks to the edge of the ocean. The waves lap against her bare feet, and she watches as her toes sink into the sand. She takes one step into the water and then another. She flings her dress over her head, revealing the bikini that has barely left her body this week and dives under. Immediately, the cool water erases any lingering traces of hot Florida sun. The whirring silence of being underwater is a welcome break from the constant echo of shouts. She swims out as far as she can and when she finally surfaces, it's the smell she notices first.

She doesn't think much of it, assuming it's another one of the elaborate bonfires being set up. Or maybe a spill of kerosene from the tiki torches. But when she hears the shriek, Chloe knows something is wrong.

She turns around and sees flames on the back deck. They spread quickly, the entire back of the house soon engulfed. She swims to shore, her heart and breath in a competition to see which one is going to give out first. Her eyes scan the shoreline, trying to count the friends running out of the house.

It happens so fast. Chloe thinks that a whole home shouldn't burn so quickly. But it does. Giant clouds of gray smoke billow up into the sky as she hears sirens approaching.

When she finally reaches the sand, she's grateful for the first time this week that they've gathered close together. The water beads on her bare skin as she joins her friends, their eyes focused on the flames. Everyone's breath is ragged. No one is speaking, paralyzed by shock and fear. She counts. One. Two. Three. Four.

Sloane.

Alden.

Marianne.

Wyatt.

When the house explodes, the flames having reached the propane tank in the basement, Chloe's eyes dart back and forth from the house to the beach, scanning for another person.

"Luke!" Chloe screams. But no one answers.

♦ 1 ♦

Last Year

CHLOE'S FACE TILTED UPWARD. The brightness of the sun made everything seem orange through her shut lids.

"What are you doing?" Luke asked.

"I'm photosynthesizing."

He laughed. "What does that mean?"

Chloe's lids fluttered open. She glanced toward her boyfriend, wondering when the edges of embarrassment had started creeping into Luke's laughter.

"I'm soaking in the sun," Chloe plainly explained. "Winter felt unbearable."

"You always say that."

"Because it's always true," Chloe replied, turning her face back toward the sky.

"What happened to your shoes?" Luke picked up the leather sandals Chloe had kicked off moments earlier.

"It's called grounding. One of the artists at the gallery was talking about it. It's good for our bodies to be barefoot."

"I don't know how you deal with those crazy artists." Luke handed Chloe her sandals. "Maybe you could test this theory somewhere other than Central Park? There's no telling what happened on that patch of grass. At a minimum, it's full of dog piss."

Chloe stared at her feet, the fresh spring grass poking between her toes. Luke was probably right. But it wasn't like she had other options. She suffered through the unbearably cold winters surrounded by dirty snow and too much concrete. She needed warmth and fresh air and nature. And for one perfect March day, New York had delivered. It was a tease. Next week, she'd be bundled in a parka and the weather report would threaten snow. But New York always gave Chloe one warm serotonin-boosting day, and she wasn't going to waste a minute of it.

She reached for her sandals, slipping them back on her feet as Luke wrapped his arm around her waist. Her wavy blonde hair trailed down her back, brushing against Luke's forearm. "Where to next?" Chloe asked.

Luke had planned an entire day of birthday surprises. He had woken her that morning with a deep kiss and a gleam in his eye, vague on details but full of promise, instructing her to "get ready for the best day of her life."

That was Luke. Everything was going to be the best, and he was usually right. So far, the day had been pretty perfect. They had eaten at their favorite breakfast spot. Not one of the pretentious brunch places that were more of a scene than a meal, but the diner that made the crispiest hash browns and the fluffiest waffles. Then he took her to a small pop-up exhibit of an artist she'd been wanting to see for months. Luke even attended the partner yoga class Chloe asked him to join each weekend. After a quick shower, they made their way over to Central Park to soak up the sun.

"This is our final spot," Luke replied, a nervous shake to his voice. "Does it remind you of anything?"

Chloe nodded. "Yeah. It reminds me of freshman year, lying on the quad, pretending to study."

"Me too," Luke replied. "There was this one day, Wyatt was giving you shit for being late to class."

"That was every day," Chloe said as she and Luke began walking through the park, finding an empty path to explore.

Luke smiled. "Yes, but this day you poured a bottle of water over his head and told him he was going to be late to his next class."

"I did do that," Chloe winced. Luke's best friend Wyatt had a way of pushing her buttons. "Except he wasn't late." Her eyes fluttered at the memory. "Wyatt went to class soaking wet." Chloe and Luke had crouched at the door to Wyatt's English literature seminar, watching him shake the water out of his hair as he shouted to Chloe that there was never an excuse for being late.

"That's when I knew," Luke said, stopping at a bend in the path.

"Knew what?"

"That I loved you," Luke said.

Chloe's eyes darted away, focusing on the blooming daffodils instead of her boyfriend's face. "You didn't love me for another year, Luke." Like many couples who met in college, Chloe and Luke had skirted around commitment—perhaps even longer than most.

Luke shook his head. "It might have taken me a year to say it out loud. But I knew way before then. When you poured that bottle of water on Wyatt's head, I knew. And I was terrified." He swallowed slowly. Chloe noticed how he seemed to hesitate before speaking again. "Who meets their soulmate at nineteen?" Luke said quietly.

Chloe focused on the bend in the path ahead. "You don't believe in soulmates."

Luke reached out, cupping her face and turning it toward his. He stared into her eyes as he said, "Yes, I do. Chloe, you are my soulmate. I've known it for nine years."

Chloe held her breath, afraid to make any movement that might alter the moment she'd spent almost a decade anticipating.

"I never should have made you wait. I never should have made you doubt that you are the single most important person in my life. There's no one like you, Chloe." Luke's face beamed in a bright smile as Chloe heard footsteps approaching.

Chloe turned around and found herself surrounded by their best friends. Marianne, with her swollen belly, tears falling down her cheeks. Sloane with her hand so tightly linked with Alden's that Chloe could detect a slight wince cross Alden's face. And Wyatt, with his hands shoved deep into his pockets, a small grin even he was unable to hide. Her heart raced as she saw a bottle of champagne in Alden's hand, a nervous energy bouncing among the friends who had become her family.

"What are you guys doing here?" Chloe stuttered.

Alden and Wyatt began to hum a familiar tune. Sloane immediately elbowed Alden's side. "You two are such idiots. That's the commencement song, not the wedding march." Sloane's hand flew over her mouth, realizing her mistake.

Marianne's eyes narrowed. "Do not ruin this moment. I've waited nine years to see Luke beg."

Chloe's eyes widened. Her breath shortened to tiny puffs as her heart beat faster. When you're twenty-eight and you've been dating the same boy for the better part of a decade, you start to wonder whether it was a forever kind of love. Most of the time, Chloe felt like life with Luke was inevitable, and yet their big commitment was missing.

Chloe turned toward Luke and rubbed her palms along the sides of her blue floral dress. Of course she would have sweaty palms and unmanicured fingers on this day. Luke didn't seem to notice. He reached for her hand and slowly bent onto one knee, his eyes never leaving Chloe's.

Chloe focused on Luke's bright blue eyes sparkling against his perpetually golden skin. He reached into his pocket, strands of wheat hair falling across his forehead. Luke retrieved a small black box. His voice was clear and confident as he asked, "Marry me?"

Chloe's eyes filled with tears. This was a moment Chloe and Sloane and Marianne had giggled about for years. When and how Luke would finally propose, because everyone assured Chloe it was as certain as the sunrise.

But as the years had passed, Chloe's confidence faltered, especially when everyone else's lives seemed to advance. She watched her friends get married, first Marianne right after graduation, now expecting her first child. Then two years ago, Sloane and Alden got married at the most lavish party Chloe had ever attended. Wyatt was still single, but relationships were never Wyatt's priority. He was married to his writing.

As Chloe approached her thirties sometimes she felt frustrated, waiting on her forever. She wasn't the type of person to issue relationship ultimatums. But she had been ready and wondered why Luke wasn't.

Despite her insecurities, Chloe knew there was no love like Luke's love. He could change the energy of any room he walked into, immediately drawing a crowd with his playful confidence. When he focused on Chloe, while the rest of the room was focused on him, Luke's attention became a drug she could never stop using.

They had survived the jealousy of young love. Stayed together through new jobs and new cities. They had fought and made up and daydreamed about a future together. Chloe believed in soulmates. She thought she'd met hers as a college freshman, but Luke was too sensible to admit the same. Until now.

On this warm spring day, Luke's practicality and Chloe's faith were finally aligned. Maybe it was the promotion he had gotten at his investment bank earlier in the week, or maybe it was the new moon rising, or maybe after nine years together Luke finally realized that Chloe was a once-in-a-lifetime kind of love. A love he could lose.

Luke stayed on his knee, a confident smile directed at Chloe as he waited for a response to a question he should have asked years ago. He cleared his voice and asked again, "Will you marry me, Chloe?"

Chloe looked at the sky, taking a deep breath as she readied herself to shout the answer she'd waited years to deliver.

Luke placed the ring on the tip of her finger. Chloe's eyes drifted to the perfect vintage setting, an emerald surrounded by a circle of diamonds, exactly like she'd always wanted. Luke was right. This was the best day of her life. For years, she'd joked about a drive-through Vegas wedding or a courthouse lunch break. Luke's response was always, *We're going to do it better than that.* And that's exactly what he was doing, giving Chloe a better proposal than she'd ever wished for.

She didn't want to forget a single moment, her mind replaying the morning she had spent with Luke leading up to this proposal in front of their closest friends.

In between flashes of Luke kissing her awake to the way he had nervously rolled his shoulders on the walk into the park, one seemingly insignificant interaction hitched in Chloe's brain. She didn't know why it bothered her or why it was the most vivid memory of the day. But it triggered dominos of memories Chloe couldn't ignore.

A wave of unease rose in her body. Maybe everyone has doubts in these important life moments, but that wasn't Chloe. She had a fearless approach to life, one of her many lovable qualities. After so many years together and so many years of longing, Chloe's answer should have been an easy yes.

She looked over her shoulder, the blur of her friends waiting to celebrate. When her eyes turned back toward Luke, nothing about the moment felt easy. Her body panicked, a result of her heart and gut clawing against one another. That's when she pulled her hand back, the ring falling to the ground. She couldn't see the confused faces behind her, but she could hear Sloane gasp.

Chloe's lips quivered. She shook her head as she whispered, "No."

Then Chloe ran away.

♦ 2 ♦

This Year

"LEAVE. IMMEDIATELY."

Chloe looks up from her desk and finds Sylvia standing in her doorway, disappointment flooding her face.

"I told you no one works on their birthday," Sylvia continues. Chloe shifts nervously. As the director of the Wick Collection and Chloe's boss, Sylvia is used to making demands that are immediately satisfied.

"Your presence here today is unacceptable," Sylvia says, pushing the bold green frames of her glasses upward. "You only turn twenty-nine once. Leave the gallery and go get drunk."

Chloe glances at her watch. "It's ten in the morning."

"A perfectly acceptable time to get drunk on champagne."

"On a Tuesday?" Chloe laughs.

"If your birthday falls on a Tuesday, then you drink on a Tuesday," Sylvia replies.

Chloe smiles, remembering her twenty-first birthday. They were all taking the same geography seminar required for graduation, and the professor counted attendance as 50 percent of the grade. Instead of skipping class, Sloane made Chloe a thermos of mai tais and insisted Chloe chug every time the professor said "topography." Luke had to carry Chloe out of class. Then Marianne drove everyone to the swimming hole off campus. While Alden and Wyatt spent hours on the rope swing, performing more elaborate cannonballs into the water, Chloe dozed in Luke's lap, thinking that it was impossible to feel that happy.

Sylvia's piercing voice brings Chloe back to the reality of how different this birthday is going to be. She won't be surrounded by her friends. She won't fall asleep in the arms of the man she loves. She will be alone. Because last year, she said no, and it changed everything.

"You are too young to spend the day with an old woman like me," Sylvia says, her silver bob swinging in the art gallery's perfect light. "At a minimum, go sleep with a stranger. That's the best part of your twenties. You're single. In your prime. But you're acting like a sad sack."

"Maybe," Chloe says, not really meaning it. "Stranger sex is hard to achieve in the daylight. I don't mind working today." She takes a breath and continues. "I'd like to work today." Chloe knows the day will move too slowly without work.

"Fine." Sylvia sighs dramatically. "Bring me the color swatches for the new Sandersen exhibit," she says, walking away.

Chloe gathers her portfolio, grateful for the distraction of this task. It will take hours to debate the wall colors for their newest exhibit. As head of installations, it's Chloe's job to select every aspect of how the pieces will be displayed, from their order on the walls to the best background color to highlight the work. Sylvia always has final approval, so Chloe gathers her portfolio, relieved for once to spend the morning discussing shades of olive.

She spends the rest of the day at her desk, handling the never-ending logistics associated with locating, transporting, and delivering priceless artwork. Chloe works with a small team, but today she doesn't do much delegating. She wants to bury herself in the work.

When Chloe walks out of the gallery just after six, she's surprised to find someone waiting. Wyatt is sitting on a bench, legs crossed casually as he studies the novel in his hands.

"Hey, Chloe," he says, standing and walking toward her.

It's a busy sidewalk, commuters focused on after-work activities with little patience for Wyatt's disruptive crossing. But he weaves through the sea of people with ease. That's true of much of his life. No matter what is happening around him, Wyatt walks confidently in his own direction, unfazed by the expectations or reactions of others.

He brushes the edge of a woman's shoulder and raises his hand in apology. Chloe watches as the woman stops, starstruck by the brief interaction. This woman hesitates for a moment and then continues down the sidewalk, but twice she looks over her shoulder at Wyatt. Of course, he doesn't see any of this. It's not that Wyatt is oblivious to female attention. Over the years, there have been dozens of women who have earned his focus. But these types of everyday reactions are constant, and maybe that's why he's unaffected.

Chloe understands the passing woman's reaction. To a stranger, Wyatt is a tall mystery, so attractive it's almost intimidating. Brushing against his muscular shoulders or watching his midnight hair fall across his forehead as he casually pushes it aside—it's swoonworthy. At least that's the echo Chloe and Sloane and Marianne have heard through the years. Women always seemed mystified that Wyatt is just a friend, as if his sex appeal renders platonic relationships impossible.

But the broad smile he delivers as he reaches her side immediately puts her at ease. Wyatt takes a step back, raises his phone, and snaps a picture.

"What was that?" Chloe asks.

"Proof of life," Wyatt says. "Sloane is freaking out."

"I was going to call her as soon as I got home," Chloe fibs. "I was swamped at work." It's not that Chloe is ignoring her best friend, it's just that conversations with Sloane are stressful. At least these days they are. Sloane is incapable of having a single discussion without asking for explanations Chloe is unable to formulate.

Wyatt texts Sloane the picture. "That should satisfy her," he says.

"Sorry you had to come all the way over here." Chloe shifts uncomfortably. When she ended things with Luke last year, there was an unspoken division among their friends. Luke got Wyatt, obviously. And ever since then, she can't help but feel guilty every time she sees her ex's best friend. Even though Wyatt is her friend too, it feels disloyal somehow.

"You know how it is when Sloane issues orders," Wyatt says. "Plus, I wasn't going to let you spend your birthday alone, Chloe."

"How do you know I don't have plans?" she asks defensively.

Wyatt raises his eyebrows, seemingly confident in his prediction that Chloe is planless and alone.

"Fine. You're right. But I want to be alone."

"Really?"

She nods, and it must convince Wyatt because he grabs his phone and quickly types another message.

"What did you tell Sloane?" Chloe asks.

"That you're alive and you're smiling. That's all we care about."

Chloe can feel the tears fighting to surface. She's not sure how she managed to find these friends who have stuck by her through so many years. Especially after last year and the disaster she caused, they still seem to care.

"Where are you going?" Wyatt asks.

Chloe takes a deep breath, using the time to settle her emotions. "Home," she says.

"Can I walk with you?"

"It's out of your way." Chloe lives about ten blocks from the gallery, in a fourth-floor apartment of an old townhouse near Embassy Row. When she abruptly moved to Washington, DC, after leaving New York last year, it was available and in her budget. The stairs are a hassle, but they are worth it for the light that floods into the living room each afternoon.

"I like walking through the fancy neighborhoods once in a while," Wyatt says. His apartment is in Petworth, close to the office of *Granite*, the online magazine where he's worked for years. The downtown neighborhood has become one of the trendiest areas to live, filled with renovated lofts and newer condos. Chloe prefers the tree-lined boulevards of upper Northwest, but her life there is far from fancy. After last year, she needed to wash away the past. She's content with her simple new beginning.

"I'm fine. I promise," Chloe says as she starts walking. When Wyatt places his hand on her back, guiding her through the busy crowds, she knows she doesn't need his company but she still feels happy to have it. Despite their constant bickering, Wyatt has always been one of her favorite people.

"Tell me about your plans while I walk you home and then I'll leave you alone," Wyatt says.

"I'm just going to do some stuff in my apartment," Chloe says.

"Does it involve facials and chocolate?" Wyatt asks.

Chloe eyes Wyatt suspiciously. "No."

"Okay." Wyatt reaches for his phone again and types another message.

"Who are you texting now?" Chloe asks.

"Marianne."

"Things must seem bad if Marianne is also giving you orders."

"She occasionally checks in on the *Chloe Death Watch* text thread."

Chloe groans. "I'm disturbed to know that text thread exists."

"You ghosted everyone for months. It became necessary." Wyatt continues typing on his phone as Chloe processes his statement. She didn't mean to cut off communication, but after the breakup, it became impossible to give anyone answers when she was still searching for them herself.

Wyatt looks up from his phone. "Marianne says I have to make sure you aren't crying into a bottle of wine with a face mask and a pound of chocolate because"—Wyatt reads Marianne's message—"*'Face masks make Chloe break out, especially the cheap sheet masks, but she never remembers this, and if she only eats sugar, she gets jittery by midnight and can't sleep. Don't let Chloe be a pimpled zombie on her birthday.'* Those were my instructions," Wyatt relays.

"She's really mastering this mother thing." Chloe tucks her hair behind an ear, knowing that Marianne is exactly right. "How is she doing?"

"Sometimes she's harder to get in touch with than you. The baby is always napping or about to nap. But she seems happy. Teddy is a very chill baby." Wyatt's simple observation makes Chloe flinch. She hasn't spent enough time with Teddy to know.

"We missed you last week," Wyatt says.

Luke, Alden, and Wyatt spent Easter at Marianne's house. Alden dressed up as the Easter bunny while Luke and Wyatt had a stupidly competitive egg hunt. Marianne said she found a plastic egg in her yogurt container. Chloe skipped the reunion, promising to visit soon, which was probably for the best because Sloane got stuck on a work crisis and couldn't make the trip. Somehow Chloe had successfully avoided Luke for over a year, but that also meant avoiding her friends too.

"Marianne's an excellent mother," Wyatt says. "She's definitely meant for it."

Chloe feels guilt wash over her. She shouldn't be getting updates from Wyatt. She should know this. Marianne had a baby six months ago and Chloe's been to visit twice. She could say that life's been busy, with a move and a new job, but that's not the truth. If everything hadn't changed last year, Chloe would have been dyeing eggs last week and visiting constantly. It's what they'd always done for each other.

Each time Chloe has seen Marianne she has apologized. Marianne says she understands. Marianne even attempts to ease Chloe's guilt by claiming that Chloe is doing her a favor because it's so much easier to keep up with everyone over the phone now that she has a baby's nap schedule to navigate. Which, based on Wyatt's comment, might be accurate. But Chloe knows she needs to do better.

"I don't deserve them," Chloe says. She swings her bag to the opposite shoulder as she and Wyatt continue walking up Connecticut Avenue. "Everything feels different now. I broke us."

Wyatt stops walking, reaching for Chloe's shoulders. "You didn't break anything."

Chloe looks up at Wyatt, surprised by his answer. After Chloe and Luke broke up, it fractured their close-knit group.

Chloe assumed everyone blamed her, but maybe that wasn't the case.

"Stop punishing yourself," Wyatt says. "You shattered someone's heart. Who hasn't?" Wyatt shrugs, his eyebrows raised, and Chloe realizes how much she's missed his quips over the last year.

"Are you giving out lessons?" Chloe asks.

"You really nailed it your first time." Wyatt puts his hands in his pockets and leans back on his heels. "Maybe you should be the instructor in this scenario."

"Breaking someone's heart was never my intention," Chloe says as she stares down at the sidewalk.

"No. I know it wasn't," Wyatt says.

"Do you think Luke knows that?" Chloe asks, her voice as small as her heart feels.

Wyatt opens his mouth and hesitates. He finally says, "I think that's a question for Luke."

Chloe nods. If only she could be brave enough to ask him.

"Here." Wyatt hands her a small wrapped package.

"Sloane is making you deliver her gifts too?"

"It's not from Sloane. She said you should be receiving a link," Wyatt shrugs.

Chloe knows that Sloane loves giving gifts, but they usually come via email and with a side of judgment. Last year Chloe received a gift certificate to Rag & Bone along with a note that said: *Skinny jeans are out. Can't wait to see how you update your wardrobe!* Chloe wonders what Sloane thinks she needs this year. Therapy, most likely.

She eyes the small package Wyatt holds. Her heart swells for a moment. "Did he ask you to give me something?" She doesn't need to say his name. The *he* in her life is always Luke.

Wyatt looks away as he shakes his head. "This is from me."

"Oh," Chloe says, a mix of shock and embarrassment. Of course Luke wouldn't give her a birthday gift. But in the ten years of their friendship, Wyatt has only given Chloe a handful of presents, usually when Sloane mandates some kind of holiday gift exchange.

"It's nothing really. I just figured you should have something to unwrap," Wyatt says.

"Thanks." Chloe holds the box, nervously turning it in her hands.

"Go ahead," he says. "Open it."

Chloe crosses the sidewalk to a bench and sits as she carefully unwraps the package. She peels open the box lid and laughs loudly.

"It reminded me of you," Wyatt says.

She holds up a bobblehead hula dancer, long blonde hair swinging down its back.

"It even looks like me," Chloe says. "Except the boobs. These are obscene."

Wyatt swallows. "No good can come from me discussing your boob size." He reaches for the doll, changing the subject. "This is why it reminds me of you." He holds up the hula dancer as its hips sway back and forth, Chloe's signature move.

"I'm an excellent dancer," Chloe states.

"You really are," Wyatt says as he clears his throat.

She holds the gift and smiles. "Thank you, Wyatt. I needed to laugh today."

They lean back on the bench, the warm spring air brushing against Chloe's skin and making her feel, for a moment, like life is good again.

"Have you heard from him?" Chloe timidly asks.

"Today? No." Wyatt shakes his head. "But I'm sure Luke's thinking about you."

"I doubt that," Chloe replies.

"He still thinks about you. He still misses you, Chloe. I know that for sure."

Chloe places the bobblehead doll back in the box. "He hates me."

"No one hates you," Wyatt says with more generosity than Chloe thinks she deserves. "But an explanation might help." Wyatt is probably referring to Luke, but Chloe knows that her friends want an explanation too.

Chloe and Luke haven't spoken since the proposal. She tried, but it was a disaster. When she ran away from Central Park, her friends swooped in. Chloe showed up at Marianne's hotel room, and Sloane came over to join them for room service. The three of them sat in silence as Chloe pushed cold French fries around her plate and held back tears. When Alden stopped by later that night with a bag of Chloe's things and a message from Luke that he wanted her to move out as soon as possible, the dam broke. Chloe started sobbing and didn't stop until Marianne and Sloane forced her into bed.

She understood Luke's hurt and embarrassment that flamed those initial days. But after a week, she asked him to meet at their favorite diner. His usually friendly demeanor was erased. All Luke wanted to discuss were the logistics of Chloe leaving his apartment and the division of their things. Chloe thought their history was deep enough for a more open-ended conversation. She hoped the damage was fixable or at least open to discussion. But Luke's mind was clear. Their end was a judgment Chloe wasn't allowed to debate.

Chloe left the diner more confused than the moment of the proposal. She sent unopened text messages, left unreturned messages, and finally realized that Luke never wanted to speak again. Which made spring break complicated.

The six friends always took a spring break vacation together, a tradition that started in college. The location changed over the years, but everyone's attendance was nonnegotiable. The year of Luke's proposal, they had already booked a vacation home in Costa Rica. When Luke insisted that he couldn't be in the same room as Chloe, she agreed to stay home. Then Marianne decided that she didn't want to travel outside the country while she was pregnant. And Sloane said she didn't want to tag along on a boy trip. It was the first time in their nine years of friendship that they hadn't spent spring break together.

And the birthdays and births and moves since then hadn't brought them together either. Chloe's heart broke again. Because the consequence she feared was losing her friends along with the love of her life.

When her relationship with Luke ended, when she told Luke no, Chloe knew that she was saying no to the entire world they had built together. Every time the group discussed getting together, Luke refused to see Chloe. It wasn't fair to ask him to stay away. And it wasn't fair to ask her friends to choose. So instead, Chloe got used to being alone.

"What are you really doing tonight?" Wyatt asks, bumping his shoulder against Chloe's.

"It's private."

"Battery-operated private?"

Chloe rolls her eyes. "You wish."

"So, Chloe has a secret," Wyatt says, leaning back on the bench.

"Maybe," Chloe shrugs. "Maybe I have lots of secrets."

"I have no doubt about that." Wyatt turns toward her, his long legs folding under the bench so that their faces meet. "But the question is, are you going to share this one with me?"

Chloe hesitates. After years of sharing her life with Luke, it feels good to have something for herself. Actually, it feels necessary.

But something about Wyatt tonight makes Chloe feel safe. Maybe it's the stupid gift or maybe it's the fact that their conversation has helped ease the guilt mountain she has built over the last year. Because, finally, she feels like she doesn't have to be alone all the time.

"Fine. You can come over. But not a word to anyone, Wyatt. This is between us."

"You can trust me, Chloe." Wyatt doesn't need to say it because Chloe already knows it's true.

♦ 3 ♦

Ten Years Ago

THE DUFFEL BAG SAT on her bed. It was her second attempt at packing. The first time, she couldn't get the bag to zip and took that as a sign that it was the wrong decision. But she folded better this time, and when the zipper smoothly connected, she knew she was leaving.

She had tried. She went to class. She ate in the dining hall. Maybe she could have made an effort to meet more people, but nothing felt natural here. Chloe hated forced.

Moving across the country to the bucolic campus of Mayfield College was supposed to be an adventure. Her parents thought she was crazy. But something about the small, southern town nestled in the mountains of Tennessee had called to Chloe. She thought it was where she was meant to be.

But she was wrong. Maybe it was too small. Everyone seemed to know someone or have a distant cousin in common or have gone to the same summer camp. She had finished the first semester, but it was time to admit defeat.

She'd take a few months off and then register for Berkeley next year. It was closer to home and she'd be surrounded by friends.

A group of students walked down the hallway, their laughter drifting past her open door. A sense of longing hit Chloe. She missed laughing. She missed belonging. She was definitely leaving.

A guy Chloe had seen a couple of times around campus hesitated outside her room. "I'll catch up," he yelled down the hallway to his friends.

He lingered, his hands holding on to either side of her doorframe as he leaned into her room. "Hi," he said.

Chloe was immediately struck by how much this person belonged at Mayfield. A bright white smile offset by tanned skin and sandy hair; add a college sweatshirt and he could have been the cover model for the school's admissions handouts.

"Hi," Chloe said, adding her duffel bag to the pile of her luggage by the door.

"I've seen you. At the student center."

Chloe nodded. "Makes sense, me being a student and all."

"I'm Luke," he said, walking into her room. "I make very obvious observations so that I can talk to beautiful girls."

"I'm Chloe." She was unaffected by his compliment, preoccupied with deciding whether she should ship her bedding back or donate it somewhere.

Luke crossed his arms. "That's all I get? No embarrassing declarations?"

"I don't embarrass easily. Sorry."

"Hence the prominently displayed poster of a children's book."

Chloe looked at the wall. She had a poster of *Where the Wild Things Are* hanging above her bed.

"Maurice Sendak was a brilliant illustrator. I have no shame in my love."

Luke laughed loudly and then flopped onto Chloe's bed, immediately comfortable in an unfamiliar space.

"What's with the bags?" he asked, pointing toward Chloe's pile.

Chloe shifted, unsure how she felt about this stranger in her room but bored enough to keep talking. "I'm leaving tomorrow morning."

"Where are you going?"

"Home."

Luke sat up and leaned forward. "Winter break doesn't start for another week. You're going to miss all the fun."

"I'm leaving early," Chloe quietly explained.

"Homesick?"

Chloe stared at Luke. Then she smiled, grateful not to hear a hint of judgment in his voice. "Something like that," she said, not explaining more.

"Where's home?" Luke asked.

"California. Monterey."

"Never been." He picked up a candle that she'd smuggled into her dorm and gave it a sniff, smiling, seemingly satisfied with the salt and sandalwood scent.

Chloe perched on the edge of her desk chair. "It's pretty much the opposite of this place."

"So, it's horrible?" he asked.

"No, Monterey is perfect. At least for a lot of people it is. I thought . . ." A shout of Luke's name echoed down the hallway. "Never mind." Chloe stood up and walked toward the door. "You were on your way out. I don't want to hold you up."

"Come with me," Luke said, his hand grazing against her elbow. "Finish your thought."

Chloe shook her head. "I can't. I have an early flight."

"Well, maybe after winter break we could grab some breakfast? I'll find you. Now that I know where you live." Luke winked, and for some reason it looked good on him.

Luke started to walk away. Chloe could have let him. But she didn't. She quickly said, "I'm not coming back. I'm transferring after this semester."

Luke stopped. It looked like he was going to say something, but he hesitated. Chloe waited for some variation of the same refrain she'd heard dozens of times over the last week about how she needed to stay and give Mayfield a chance. But instead, he walked up to her, their faces inches apart, and his eyes danced as he said, "Then you absolutely have to come out with me tonight. What if we're soulmates?"

Chloe looked up. "Not possible."

"Why? You don't think you can fall for a classically good-looking, brilliant athlete?"

Chloe took a step back, eyeing Luke inquisitively. "What's your sport?"

"Flag football," Luke said confidently.

"That's an after-school activity. Not a sport."

Luke's shoulders shook in amusement. "Okay. Maybe I'm not an athlete. But everything else is true."

"The truly brilliant never feel a need for labels," Chloe pointed out.

Luke had a giant smile as he said, "You're not debating that I'm good-looking."

"No," Chloe plainly replied. "You've clearly heard that description too often for me to waste time debating."

Luke slipped his hands into his jacket pockets. Chloe caught herself staring, marveling at how this guy oozed confidence with even his smallest movements. He leaned in and whispered in her ear, "I think you might fall for me, Chloe."

Chloe stared, batting her eyelashes before whispering in his ear, "Unlikely. I don't fall for arrogant, delusional boys."

Luke clutched his chest. "How have I made such a terrible first impression?"

But he hadn't. After their brief conversation, Chloe was almost sad she wouldn't see him again.

"You've got to let me fix this. Come out with me tonight." Luke coaxed. "Let's go have breakfast now."

"It's eleven at night. There's no breakfast."

"Oh yes there is," Luke said, grabbing Chloe's hand. "We'll go to Waffle House."

He pulled her out of the room, and she barely had time to grab her jacket. Luke held her hand the entire walk off campus, and even though she wasn't used to it, she followed him easily. When they arrived in front of the bold yellow and black sign, Chloe saw a few other college kids inside the restaurant. Luke seemed to know most everyone's name, but instead of joining any group, he found a table toward the back and slid into one of the hard plastic booths. He pulled Chloe in beside him.

"What's your order?" he asked.

Chloe shrugged. "I've never been here."

"How is that possible?" Luke questioned. "Well, if you're a Waffle House virgin, do you trust me to order for you?"

"Is this another one of your many skills?" Chloe teased.

Luke laughed and as the waitress appeared he ordered, "Two waffles. One order of hash browns, scattered, smothered, covered." The waitress nodded and left.

"What was that? Some secret code?" Chloe asked.

"Kind of."

"What did you order?"

"Waffles, obviously. And potatoes with onions and cheese," Luke explained.

"Luke!" Chloe heard the shout across the diner and looked up to see a group coming their way.

"Hash browns, chunked and covered," a boy shouted his order on his way to join them.

"Decode that for me?" Chloe whispered to Luke.

"Hash browns with ham and cheese."

Chloe shifted closer to Luke as a girl slid next to them in the booth. "Hi. I've seen you in Pulaski's art history seminar. Your hair is amazing. I'm Sloane. You're smart too."

The ham and cheese hash browns boy sat on the opposite side of the booth. "You just added the smart thing because of your feminist studies class," he said to Sloane.

Another girl plopped down, and all of a sudden Chloe was surrounded by Luke and his three friends. She had thought she was going to have another quiet night alone in her dorm, but this was the opposite. Luke wrapped his arm around Chloe's shoulders as he leaned in and whispered, "That's Alden," pointing across the table just as the waitress dropped off Alden's order of ham and cheese hash browns along with Luke's order. Chloe looked at the waitress in shock. It felt like magic, the food came out so quickly.

"Sloane already introduced herself," Luke continued whispering. "And that's Sloane's roommate, Marianne," gesturing to the girl sitting next to Alden. She had smooth brown hair cut into a perfectly even bob and not a trace of makeup, a rarity among Mayfield's female student population. When Marianne enthusiastically waved at Chloe, even though they were only two feet apart, Chloe liked her immediately.

Sloane reached across the table and plucked a piece of ham off Alden's plate. "You're absolutely right, Alden. I'm trying really hard to reprogram the patriarchy out of my daily interactions. But she is smart," Sloane said, pointing toward Chloe. "She knows way more about Manet than the professor."

Sloane's strawberry blonde hair fell in front of her face, and she immediately pulled a rubber band off her wrist and created an effortless updo that looked like it took way more time than the seconds she spent. Unlike Marianne, Sloane's makeup was expertly applied, not a single imperfection in her kohl eyeliner and peony lips, even though it was the end of the night when everyone tended to look a little smudged.

"It's Monet. Not Manet," Alden said, pulling his plate out of Sloane's reach.

"No, you idiot," Sloane scoffed. "There are two of them. Claude Monet and Edouard Manet. Maybe if you took classes outside the Engineering building, you'd know that."

"But Engineering is my cozy home. I will never leave," Alden said without a drop of embarrassment.

Sloane narrowed her eyes and Alden sat up straighter.

The friends were all so familiar with one another, sharing bites of food and teasing each other about the party earlier that night, that Chloe should have felt uncomfortable. She was the outsider. But she didn't. Chloe would always remember feeling like she instantly belonged.

"But seriously, Chloe, how do you get your hair to look like that?" Sloane asked. "Do you use a one-inch barrel?" Sloane leaned closer. "Tell me about the products involved."

Chloe ran her fingers through her long blonde waves. "I don't think you're going to like this answer," she said. "I wash it. Maybe twice a week. And I use conditioner. That's it. I let it do its own thing."

Sloane leaned back against the hard restaurant booth. "Ugh. It's going to be very hard to restrain my jealousy around you."

Chloe took a bite of the crisp and sweet waffle and then dug into the hash browns. Everyone ate as they laughed about a disturbingly detailed review that had just been posted online about one of their professors. Chloe managed to snag a menu and studied the different hash browns options and the coded words used to describe each order. She wished she'd found this spot earlier in the semester.

"Who brought her?" an unfamiliar voice asked.

Chloe looked up and immediately recognized the boy standing in front of them. His stare made her shift uncomfortably. He was hard to miss on campus, taller and more intense than most. More than once, Chloe had let her imagination run wild, inventing stories about what this mysterious guy was really like.

"I believe what you mean to say is 'Nice to meet you. My name is Wyatt,'" Marianne suggested.

Sloane was blunter. "Honestly, Wyatt, for an English major, you have a poor grasp of the use of language."

"Don't worry, Wyatt. The extra face is only temporary. Chloe's leaving tomorrow," Luke said. He looked at Chloe, his eyes begging her to disagree. "Right?"

Chloe stared at Luke, their bodies pressed close together, a welcome consequence of his friends crowding the booth. "Right. I'm leaving tomorrow," Chloe said after a silence that lasted too long.

"For good?" Sloane asked loudly.

Chloe nodded. "Yeah, I'm going to take the rest of the year off and then transfer to Berkeley next fall."

"No. We just met. You can't leave yet." Sloane said.

"That's exactly how I feel," Luke said for seemingly different reasons.

"Let's break this down and determine whether you're making an informed decision. Why did you pick Mayfield?" Alden asked.

"Yes. I'm all about this plan." Luke leaned forward. "Let's help Chloe remember why she picked our school and then maybe she'll stay."

Wyatt was sitting at the end of the table, having found a spare chair. "It's a top college. Who wouldn't want to go to Mayfield?"

Chloe smirked because Wyatt's assessment may have been accurate for residents of the South, but if he wasn't so moody, he'd probably admit that Mayfield's reputation wasn't necessarily nationwide. Chloe was one of the few students from the West Coast.

Chloe didn't feel the need to defend her decision, but something about Wyatt's voice made Chloe feel like she'd been issued a challenge she wanted to meet. "Lily Drake. That's why I picked Mayfield."

"Who's that?" Luke asked. "Is she a senior?" Luke looked across the table and Alden shrugged in response.

"I'm embarrassed on their behalf," Sloane said. "Lily Drake is one of our most famous alumni. She was a painter in the 1960s."

"I'm pretty sure there are no Drake buildings on campus," Luke said. "She can't be that famous."

"She never got the kind of fame that can buy buildings," Chloe said quietly. "But I love her paintings. I figured if this place inspired her, it would work for me too."

"You want to be a painter?" Wyatt asked, never looking up from his coffee cup.

"I don't know if I'm good enough to be a professional artist. But that's the dream."

"You're definitely good enough," Sloane said.

"You haven't seen any of my paintings," Chloe laughed.

"No, but I've heard you in class. You have an excellent eye. You must be amazing," Sloane replied confidently.

Chloe shrugged. "I love art. I want to be a painter, but I'll settle for any job that will surround me with beautiful paintings. That's why I'm leaning toward an art history major. Seems like a safer choice."

"Aren't we a little young to be making safe choices?" Wyatt interjected.

"She's not getting an accounting degree," Sloane said defensively. "I think it's a smart idea, Chloe. I'm thinking about doing the same thing."

Alden narrowed his eyes. "Sloane, your stick figures have misplaced body parts. I don't think *artist* was ever really an option for you, but I applaud your camaraderie."

Sloane replied with a stuck-out tongue.

Chloe couldn't stop thinking about Wyatt's comment. Maybe eighteen was a little too young for backup plans. When she looked across the table and saw Wyatt staring intently at her, she shifted in her seat, unsettled by his gaze and his insight.

"Why do you love art?" Wyatt asked, earning an elbow in the side from Marianne.

"Give her a break, Wyatt," Marianne said.

"I'm just going along with the plan," Wyatt replied. "Trying to figure out why she's rejecting our school without ever really giving it a chance."

"Art makes life less lonely," Chloe said, feeling an uncharacteristic defensiveness as she tried to answer Wyatt's question. "Connecting with a painting allows me to understand a stranger's experience. There's nothing else that powerful." Chloe took a bite of waffle before she continued. "And I did give Mayfield a chance. Sometimes you don't need years to know that something is a wrong fit."

"Books provide the same connection," Wyatt said. "And a few months spent sitting by yourself and hiding in your dorm room isn't giving something a chance."

Luke laughed. "Wyatt, I have to drag you out all the time. You're in no place to judge someone for staying in their room."

Chloe smiled at Luke, grateful for his defense, and then turned her attention back to Wyatt. "Art and books aren't the same. There is a specificity to novels that limits the audience. Artwork has the potential for universal connection. It's much more powerful."

"That's ridiculous," Wyatt said.

Luke leaned back in the booth. "Let the battle begin. Art history versus English literature, which dorky major will reign triumphant?"

"I'm certain the economics major cannot call anyone dorky," Sloane said. "Well, except maybe the engineering and computer science guy." Sloane pointed toward Alden. "You also need to limit your computer lab time. Your skin is translucent."

Alden looked at his arm and sighed. "You're right."

"*East of Eden*," Wyatt interrupted. "Steinbeck. Universal discussion of good versus evil." Wyatt's eyes were focused on Chloe, clearly wanting to continue their debate.

"Are you serious?" Chloe scoffed. "You think a portrayal of women as evil, tempting the good out of men, has universal appeal? Maybe for that end of the booth." Chloe pointed at Luke and Alden.

"Burn," Marianne said, high-fiving Chloe.

Chloe leaned forward as she whispered, "But the *Mona Lisa*'s smile? Who hasn't known a woman with a secret?"

Wyatt shrugged. "But the painting will never tell you what she's hiding. That's where books will always win."

Chloe shook her head. "Not all secrets are meant to revealed."

Wyatt stared at Chloe, his standard intensity somehow elevated. He raised his eyebrows. "Maybe," he said.

"Are you giving up that easily?" Luke asked Wyatt.

"I'm too hungry to fight," Wyatt said. "I'm going to order some food. Anybody want anything?"

Wyatt didn't wait for an answer as he walked toward the counter, but everyone seemed satisfied with what was already on the table.

"I still don't get why you're leaving," Sloane prodded in between bites of waffle.

"It didn't fit. I guess I couldn't find that Lily Drake inspiration," Chloe tried to explain.

"Don't be ridiculous," Sloane said. "You can find inspiration anywhere."

"Even in an empty Waffle House at midnight?" Alden said, raising his eyebrows.

Chloe looked around. Most everyone had left. Their table was the only one occupied. Chloe had been so focused on Luke and his four friends that she hadn't noticed.

"If that isn't a song title it should be," Sloane said.

"Someone check the jukebox," Marianne added.

Luke hopped over the back of the booth. He held out his hand and Chloe accepted.

"Come on," Luke said, drawing her toward the ancient jukebox in the corner. "Let's find some inspiration."

Chloe ran her finger across the old-fashioned peg buttons as she scanned the catalog. It was mostly country, but in the bottom left she found the perfect song. She slipped in a quarter, pressed E-5, and turned back toward the group. As the song started, she found herself half walking, half swaying back to the table.

"Fleetwood Mac," Luke whispered in her ear. "Pretty fitting. A captivating blonde woman mesmerizing her bandmates."

Luke wrapped his arm around Chloe's waist as their bodies swayed together to the music. "I think you could find lots of inspiration here. Are you sure you want to leave?"

Chloe stared into his eyes. "This isn't the place for me."

"How do you know?"

Chloe swallowed and answered truthfully. "Because I never worried about fitting in until it became obvious that I didn't."

Luke eyed Chloe skeptically. "Maybe you're just like Wyatt," he said, gesturing across the room at Wyatt bent over a plate of eggs and bacon. "Giving up too easily."

"Maybe," Chloe echoed. And for the first time that night, she second-guessed her decision.

Luke grabbed Chloe's hand and spun her in a circle under the fluorescent lights of Waffle House. Chloe could feel his tall body pressed against hers. He shook his sandy sun-streaked hair away from his eyes as his arms wrapped tighter around her.

Chloe felt the focused attention of Luke's friends and spun out of his arms and toward the table. She reached for Sloane's and Marianne's hands. "Come on," she beckoned.

Chloe stepped up onto the table and Sloane followed. Marianne shook her head, but immediately Chloe and Sloane were grabbing her arms, pulling her up to join them. The three of them began singing along, eventually screaming the lyrics as they coordinated ridiculous dance moves. Feeling every beat of the music, Chloe closed her eyes, and when they opened, she was met with Luke's gaze and his beaming smile.

Wyatt spun around on the counter stool, arms crossed, and shook his head, but Chloe detected a grin. "You three look ridiculous," he shouted.

"You look jealous," Sloane replied.

Chloe, Sloane, and Marianne continued dancing, stomping on the tabletop to the rhythm of Fleetwood Mac, the sound of their laughter weaving with Stevie Nicks's voice.

Then all of a sudden, the music stopped.

"Get down," their waitress yelled as she held the unplugged cord of the jukebox.

Luke held out his arms and Chloe jumped in. Marianne immediately snaked her body back into the booth and tried to sit normally. Sloane continued standing in the middle of the table, hands on hips.

"Out! All of you!" the waitress shouted. "Dancing on tables like a strip club. This is Waffle House." The solemnity with which she named the restaurant made all six college students erupt in laughter.

"We're leaving," Wyatt said, discreetly leaving a twenty dollar bill on the counter.

"We are so sorry," Marianne added, unable to make eye contact.

They filed out of the restaurant, trying to look contrite, but as soon as the door closed and the waitress walked back to the kitchen, they all exploded in laughter.

"Chloe, you just got us kicked out of a Waffle House," Alden said with a mix of shock and pride.

Chloe winced. "Sorry about that."

"Do not apologize," Sloane said. "People pass out in Waffle House booths for hours and still don't get kicked out. What we just achieved is legendary."

"We should have taken off our shoes before we got on the table," Marianne added.

Marianne seemed concerned, and Wyatt wrapped his arm around her shoulders as they started walking back toward campus. "Our shoes are not the dirtiest things those tables have seen," he said.

"Where to next?" Alden asked.

"Chloe has an early flight in the morning," Luke said. "I should probably walk her back."

She nodded, feeling sorry for ending the night.

"I want to stay out," Wyatt said, walking a few steps ahead of the group. "Anybody else?"

"Yes," Sloane said on a drawn-out exhale, looping one arm through Marianne's and one through Alden's. "You lead the way, Wyatt. There's got to be a party on campus somewhere."

The four of them walked away, leaving Chloe and Luke alone. Their footsteps slowed, maybe both hoping to extend the walk to Chloe's dorm as long as possible.

"I'm sorry I got your friends kicked out of your hash browns supplier," Chloe said.

"Worth it. You are forgiven," Luke replied.

"If you want to join them, I'll be fine walking back on my own."

"I'm exactly where I want to be," Luke said.

"Okay." Chloe smiled, not hiding how happy Luke's statement made her feel. But she did try to hide how much her boots were killing her feet. She paused and lifted her foot slightly, trying to relieve some of the pressure.

Luke looked down and noticed Chloe's strange movements. "Feet hurt?" he asked.

"Yeah. I must have danced a little too hard. I'll be fine," Chloe said, but with each clumsy step, sharp pains shot up her leg. She paused, waiting for her feet to recover.

Luke stood by her side. "Okay, two options. One: we ditch our shoes and run back to campus barefoot."

Chloe tilted her head. "You shouldn't have to suffer for my poor choices."

Luke shrugged. "I'm a gentleman. You go shoeless, I go shoeless."

"You're really working hard to fix that first impression," Chloe commented. "What's the second option?"

"You can hop on my back and I'll give you a ride." Luke's eyebrows wiggled and Chloe's stomach fluttered.

"Door number two sounds like more fun," she said.

"That's the one I was hoping you would pick." Luke crouched and Chloe hopped onto his back. He held on to the crook of her knees as he jogged back to campus, occasionally bumping Chloe upward, and constantly making her laugh.

She checked in a few times to make sure his chivalry wasn't more ambitious than his stamina. "Chloe, I'm fine," he said, making her feel weightless.

Then he let go of her knees and Chloe slid down his back, grasping for a more secure grip around his neck. "Do not let me fall," she giggled.

Luke's broad hands immediately reached around. A round butt cheek in each palm, Luke pushed her up his back until she was no longer falling.

"That was a middle school–level move, Luke."

"Yep. Worked then. Works now," he said without embarrassment. Chloe tightened her arms around his neck, her chest pressing into his back. She could smell the eucalyptus scent of his shampoo.

"How's the view up there?" Luke asked.

Chloe looked around at the night sky, edges of hazy purple mountains visible in the distance, and clear, crisp air all around them. "It's perfect here," she said. And she meant it, for the first time since arriving at Mayfield.

Luke stopped at the entrance to her dorm. Slowly, carefully, he spun Chloe around so that she was no longer on his back, but instead they were face to face, her legs still wrapped around his waist.

"Think you can walk now?" Luke asked.

Chloe's breath disappeared as she managed a tiny nod.

Luke lowered her to the ground, hands trailing up the sides of her body as their mouths finally met.

Sometimes, there's a fumbling at the beginning of a kiss, mouths finding positioning, noses getting in the way. But not this kiss. Luke's mouth covered Chloe's like it was molded to match hers. The only thought in her mind was the electrifying sensation of his perfect lips.

Luke pushed Chloe toward the dorm building, hands on either side of her body, pinning her against the wall as their mouths searched for more of the other. His hands moved up her shirt, around to the back, eventually clawing into her long hair as their faces pressed closer together. In between ragged breaths, Chloe nipped at his lower lip before diving back into his mouth.

"I can't believe you're leaving tomorrow," Luke groaned.

"I know. But we still have the rest of the night," Chloe said shyly. She'd never see him again. Maybe that's why boldness triumphed over the uncertainty bubbling in her stomach. "I think you should come inside," Chloe whispered.

Luke pulled back, eyes widening, surprise then amusement on his face. He nodded twice and then said, "That sounds good."

Chloe's heart raced as she swiped her campus keycard. Luke pushed the door and they both tumbled inside, hands never leaving each other's bodies as they frantically skipped down the hallway to Chloe's room.

She fumbled with the lock on her door, and within seconds they were stumbling past Chloe's bags and toward her bed.

She froze for a moment, still unsure what she was doing. This tall boy she'd met only hours earlier was inside her room. His fingers trailed over her skin, slipping under the waistband of her jeans as Chloe sucked in air.

Her hand hovered over his, stopping him from moving it down any further.

"What's wrong?" Luke asked.

Chloe wanted to be the girl who said nothing. For one night, she wanted to act and not think, and forget about college transfers and consequences. For a brief moment outside, she thought she could do it. But no matter how comfortable Luke made her feel, she barely knew him. And she wasn't experienced enough to pretend this was her typical behavior.

"I don't usually get naked with strangers," she said.

He glanced at the clock beside her bed. "We've got hours before your flight, right? Plenty of time to get to know each other better."

Chloe laughed. "Luke, I'm leaving. We're never going to see each other again."

"I'm still hoping you're going to change your mind about that."

Chloe shook her head. "Not likely," she said. But even as the words came out of her mouth, she wondered if they were true. How could a few hours make her question a decision she'd spent weeks contemplating? At this moment, time seemed as infinite as Chloe's confidence. She was unaccustomed to uncertainty.

Luke made her question so many things. Should she give Mayfield another chance? Would she ever feel comfortable in a place that felt so foreign? Should she keep kissing the strange boy who made her heart race and her head dizzy?

"I don't have a problem seeing strangers naked, but I fully respect your boundaries." He cupped her head in his hands. "There's a lot we can do with our clothes on. Or I can leave. Up to you."

Luke's eyes pleaded, but she didn't feel any pressure. She genuinely believed what he said. What happened next was completely within her control.

"I like creativity." She didn't think it was possible, but he grinned even bigger. "What kind of fully clothed scenarios did you have in mind?"

Luke erased all the space between their bodies as he said, "Let's see if I can find some other things you like."

★ ★ ★

When Chloe's alarm went off at six in the morning, she rolled over and found the other side of the bed empty. She wasn't surprised. After all, she had told Luke to leave, reminding him about her early flight as she drifted to sleep, her lips raw from kissing his for hours.

She stretched her still fully clothed arms over her head, memories of Luke's body filling her mind. She could still feel the weight of him on top of her, the way they had fumbled together, laughing when his fingers got tangled in her hair. Luke had kept his promise. He had very creatively respected Chloe's boundary, exploring and teasing her body through too many layers of denim and cotton. Chloe was the one who had tried to erase the previously established limits, but Luke was firm. "I'm not going to be on Chloe's list of Mayfield regrets," he had said. She already knew that he would be her favorite memory of the entire Mayfield college experience.

She rolled out of bed and changed into fresh clothes for the airplane. While she was packing her headphones into her backpack, the door crept open and Chloe gasped.

"You're up," Luke beamed.

"What are you doing here?" Chloe questioned, her heart still racing.

The giant smile never left his face. Luke took two broad, comfortable steps into Chloe's room. "I figured you could use a coffee. And maybe a ride to the airport?"

"I was going to take the bus," Chloe mumbled, still surprised to see someone she thought was a distant memory.

"With all of that luggage, my car will be a lot easier."

Chloe shook her head. "You don't want to spend your Sunday driving a stranger to the airport."

"After last night, we definitely aren't strangers." He stared at the floor as he softly said, "And spending an hour in the car with you sounds like an ideal Sunday."

"Are you sure?" Chloe tentatively replied.

"I brought bagel sandwiches too." Luke held up two egg and cheese sandwiches, wrapped in the blue and white paper of the town's deli.

Maybe that was the moment Chloe started falling for Luke. Knowing that he had woken up before the sun to secure the best breakfast option for the girl he'd spent the night kissing.

"You might be the perfect guy," Chloe said.

"Why do you say that like it's a bad thing?" Luke asked.

"Because it's hard to leave something so good," Chloe admitted.

★ ★ ★

Once Chloe got home for Christmas break, her rehearsed explanations about leaving Mayfield seemed harder to deliver. She sat on the kitchen counter as her mother cooked their holiday paella, prepping the dozens of ingredients that would fill their home with the exotic smells that had perfumed Chloe's childhood. Chloe hadn't traveled much, but her mother loved experimenting with new cuisines, calling their nightly meals "food vacations."

"You can change your mind, you know." Rhonda chopped onions and garlic as she tried to coax a discussion out of her daughter. "A million times if that's what it takes to figure out what you want."

Her father piped up. "Do you think I'm made of money? Changes cost money."

"We're out a plane ticket, Walter," Chloe's mother shouted across the room. She waved her hand in the air and mouthed *Ignore him*. "Are you happy there?" she asked as she toasted the rice in her beloved paella pan.

Chloe shook her head. "I wasn't. But maybe I didn't try hard enough. Maybe I could be happy there."

Chloe wanted to chase the dream of being an artist like Lily Drake. She wanted to be brave enough to explore a whole new life at Mayfield. And she hated giving up when there was a chance of something working out. Up until that last night, she hadn't seen a possibility of happiness at Mayfield. One night shouldn't have changed her mind, but somehow it had.

"It's your choice," her mother said. "You can live here and go to school closer to home. You can try Mayfield again. You can join a traveling circus if that's what you want."

"Nope," her father shouted from the couch. "No clowns allowed. They creep me out." Chloe's mother threw her kitchen towel across the room, thumping his head.

"I don't know what to do." Chloe plucked an olive and a slice of cheese from the platter her mother had prepared. "I'm sorry."

Rhonda set down her knife, resting her elbows on the counter and leaning forward. "Why are you apologizing?"

"Because I keep changing my mind. Ezra would never do anything like this. I'm the flaky one. Again." Chloe's older brother Ezra was spending his first married Christmas with his wife's family, and although she missed him, it was nice to have her parents' undivided attention. Ezra's perfection seemed to magnify Chloe's flaws. They were polar opposites, responsible Ezra attending Stanford and getting married to his college sweetheart. Irresponsible Chloe, who tried three different instruments before abandoning music for dance classes and then finding painting. Her mother called her *well-rounded* while her father muttered about the expense of all those talents.

"You and Ezra are different." Rhonda walked around and squeezed her daughter's hands. "It's not a competition. I'd rather you change your mind than stick with something that makes you miserable."

Chloe hugged her mother, got another slice of cheese, and joined her father on the couch.

"Kiddo, do you know what will help?" Walter wrapped his arm around her shoulders and pulled her close.

"Please don't say a James Bond movie marathon," Chloe sighed.

He reached for the remote control and smiled. "A James Bond movie marathon," Walter replied solemnly.

Chloe closed her eyes and shook her head.

"Sean Connery can help. Maybe even a dash of Daniel Craig. I will not subject you to Roger Moore. James Bond has all the answers to life's problems."

Chloe's father started the movie, and eventually Chloe's mother joined them as dinner simmered. Chloe was flanked by her parents and snuggled under the fur blanket that was only necessary because her mother had opened all the windows in the house to create some holiday atmosphere. She would have preferred to watch anything else, but seeing her parents happy was worth it. It was easy to make little sacrifices when they brought joy to someone you love.

Sometime between *Goldfinger* and *GoldenEye*, Chloe realized that feeling comfortable wasn't enough. She wanted more. And it wasn't fair to give up on Mayfield and her dreams just because home was easier.

★ ★ ★

When Chloe returned to Mayfield for second semester, her father seemed relieved and her mother seemed cautious. When they asked what had changed her mind, she said it was a lot of things. The first semester at Mayfield had felt lonely. It seemed impossible to chase a dream in a place where she didn't belong. But one night in a Waffle House had given Chloe the hope of fitting in. And she had faith that everything else would work itself out.

Chloe hadn't come back for Luke. Or at least that's what she told herself. She never wanted to be the type of girl who would change her life for a boy. And it was partly true.

Because when classes started and Chloe sat next to Sloane in Italian Renaissance painters, and Marianne showed her the bizarrely delicious combination of peach cobbler and cornbread at the dining hall, and Wyatt and Alden convinced her to join their kickball team, she knew she'd made the right decision. Luke wasn't the reason. Or at least he wasn't the only reason she had changed her mind. It was all of them. She had found her friends. It never occurred to her that she could lose herself.

♦ 4 ♦

This Year

CHLOE REACHES INTO THE break room fridge, pulling out the salad she packed this morning. She debates throwing it in the trash and walking down the street for a slice of pizza, but she sighs and does the grown-up, responsible thing and picks up a fork instead.

"Check your email," a familiar voice commands.

Chloe turns around and smiles at Wyatt. "Stop stalking me," she says.

In the month since her birthday, Wyatt has met her almost every day. Sometimes they'll grab a drink or he'll walk with her for a bit and head back to his apartment. Chloe often wonders how much Sloane must be guilting him into these daily check-ins. And what Wyatt is telling the rest of their friends, Luke especially.

Chloe sits at the break room table, an interior room at the back of the gallery, behind several doors clearly labeled *Employees Only*.

"How did you get back here?" Chloe asks as she takes a bite of her salad.

Wyatt joins her at the table. "I have credentials. I can get in all kinds of places."

"Your press badge doesn't work at the Wick." Chloe takes another bite.

"Your boss likes me," Wyatt says, smiling too widely.

"She wants to sleep with you."

Wyatt moves his head from side to side, as if considering this possibility.

"Wyatt, Sylvia is at least thirty years older than you," Chloe whispers.

Wyatt smirks. "She's aged well."

"If you value our friendship, please do not detonate the professional bomb of sleeping with my boss. Sylvia will describe your penis in detail. She may even paint it."

Wyatt laughs. "I'm not going to sleep with Sylvia. Although I do find her interesting."

"The world finds Sylvia interesting. Why are you here again?"

Wyatt reaches across the table and pulls the fork from Chloe's hand. "Because you need to check your email."

"Why?"

"Hurricane Sloane has landed."

Chloe pulls out her phone as Wyatt runs a hand through his dark hair. Chloe's stomach sinks as soon as she sees the subject line, "Spring Break."

"She's out of her mind," Chloe says. "There's no way the trip is happening this year."

"Why?" Wyatt asks flatly.

"Because Luke won't speak to me. Luke won't be in the same room as me. Which makes sharing a house for a week kind of impossible."

"I think not speaking is mutual," Wyatt says. "At some point, you two are going to have to work that out. Or do you think it's better that we all stop being friends?"

"No," Chloe says immediately. "That's not a question. We are going to work this out. But spring break is not the solution."

Wyatt leans back in the hard plastic chair, a creak escaping from his long body. "We've waited a year for you guys to figure it out on your own. I'm not always a fan of Sloane's plans, but I have to admit she's right this time."

Chloe studies Sloane's email. She's planned every detail of the trip, leaving no room for Chloe to manufacture an excuse. There's even an airplane ticket in her name.

Sloane and Alden moved to the beach last year after the sale of Alden's company. A week in Florida, soaking in the warm sun, does sound appealing, but Chloe knows that no amount of ocean air can ease the tension with Luke.

"I can't go," Chloe says.

"I didn't want to do this. But I'm going to." Wyatt reaches for his phone and dials a number. He puts it on speaker and within moments, Sloane's cheerful voice is filling up the Wick Collection break room.

"Did she say no?" Sloane asks.

"Of course I said no," Chloe replies. "I'll come visit. I promise. Maybe in June. You guys have a good time together."

Sloane exhales so loudly Chloe can't help but lean away from the phone. "You broke us, Chloe."

Even though Wyatt is shaking his head, indicating that he does not think Chloe did any breaking, Chloe knows that Sloane is saying what everyone thinks.

Sloane continues, "Get on that plane. You need to fix this."

"Having me there isn't going to fix it. If anything, I'll make it worse."

"No. False," Sloane declares. "We need everyone together. That's the way our friendship works."

"She's right," Wyatt adds. "Alden's Internet freedom lectures are only bearable with Luke dancing in the background."

Chloe can't help the smile that creeps across her face as she remembers long nights filled with laughter. They were right.

Luke's charm was a necessary balance to Alden's logical nature and Wyatt's intensity. Just as Chloe's spontaneity balanced Sloane's planning. Marianne provided a safe place for them all to land. They were the best versions of themselves when they were all together.

At least that's the way it used to be. Chloe's smile disappears as she focuses on the present. "There's no way Marianne is going," Chloe tries to argue. "She has a baby at home."

"Marianne is thrilled to go," Sloane says decisively. "Noah is staying behind with the baby."

Chloe's face is full of surprise. "She's okay leaving Teddy?"

"Why wouldn't she be?" Sloane quickly replies. "Mothers go on vacation all the time. You don't give up your life and your friends just because you have a baby. There is so much more to life than children. Surely you know that."

Chloe and Wyatt exchange glances, both surprised by Sloane's uncharacteristic defensiveness.

Chloe says, "I just thought maybe she'd have some reservations about leaving Teddy for the first time."

"I'm sure she does," Sloane says, softening. "You should talk to her about that."

Chloe looks away, echoes of her discussions with Wyatt and the guilt Chloe still can't erase seeping in.

Sloane takes a deep breath before continuing. "I know what you're doing. You're trying to get out of the trip and use Marianne to create some domino situation like last year. It's not going to happen."

Chloe's voice is small as she asks, "Will Luke be there?"

"Of course he'll be there. Besides, Alden is his biggest client these days. It would be irresponsible of him to turn down a client's invitation."

Chloe shakes her head as she stares at the table and her half-eaten salad. "That's what we are now? Clients and financial advisors? Strangers?"

"No. We are best friends. We have been best friends for a decade, and I'm not going to let anything break that up."

"Luke doesn't want me there," Chloe shouts at the phone.

"I'm going to tell you the same thing I told him. Get over yourself and get on the plane," Sloane shouts back.

"I can't, Sloane. I'm not ready."

"I'm sure you aren't," Sloane says softly. "It's been a year. Marianne had a baby. Alden and I . . ." Sloane trails off. "Alden and I miss you. We miss us. I will see you Friday night."

"I love you, Sloane. I'd do anything for you. But I can't spend a week with Luke."

"Why?" When Chloe doesn't speak, Sloane fills the silence with her assumptions. "Because you still love him and you're afraid of what's going to happen. Tell him you're sorry. Explain. Your. Feelings. This can be fixed. You can get him back. He's your soulmate."

"It's not that simple," Chloe whispers. "I'm not coming," she says with complete resolve.

"Take me off speaker," Sloane orders.

Chloe reaches for the phone and holds it up to her ear. Sloane's voice is firm and clear as she reiterates all the points she's already made. Then Chloe hears Sloane's voice break in a way she's never heard in their decade of friendship.

Chloe's heart sinks as Sloane tells her why she needs this trip. Her face moves through a dozen emotions as she processes Sloane's confession, ultimately settling on guilt. It turns out the last year has felt lonely for them all. Chloe can see Wyatt watching their conversation.

"Okay. I'll be there," Chloe says, and hangs up.

She hands Wyatt his phone, his face full of confusion. "What master manipulation did Sloane inflict to achieve this miracle?"

"That's between us," Chloe says as she walks over to the trash can to throw away her lunch. She walks back to the main gallery and Wyatt follows.

"We never used to have secrets," Wyatt says to the polished wooden floor.

"We've always had secrets, Wyatt. We just haven't let them tear us apart."

Wyatt nods. "So you're really going? A week in Florida with Sloane and Alden and Marianne and Luke."

Chloe notices how Wyatt hesitates on the last word, as if saying her ex-boyfriend's name is forbidden language. She elbows him in the side. "And you."

Wyatt smiles. "Let's go shopping."

Chloe glances at her watch. "I have about thirty minutes, but I don't think there's any amount of retail therapy that is going to prepare me for this trip."

"You'll be fine. You have us," Wyatt says.

Chloe isn't sure. Nothing about seeing Luke again feels fine.

Chloe and Wyatt walk outside into the brisk air of early spring. Chloe knows that she'll experience three seasons of weather over the next few weeks, the tease of warmth never lasting long.

"Where do you want to shop?" Chloe asks. "There are a couple of stores on Wisconsin Avenue that have swimsuits already."

"Nah," Wyatt points across the street. "Much more important shopping."

Chloe laughs as they walk toward the liquor store. "Are we really doing another spring break in Florida?"

"The last one was pretty fun," Wyatt says. And Chloe remembers, it really was.

♦ 5 ♦

Nine Years Ago

THE FLOOR OF MARIANNE'S minivan was a dumpster. Cheetos, bottles of Dr. Pepper, and countless Skittles wrappers littered the floor. Luke and Alden played an unsuccessful rainbow toss game where they tried to simultaneously throw different colored Skittles in each other's mouths. Chloe was in the front seat with Marianne, shielding her from stray candy.

"How much longer?" Wyatt moaned from the third row. "This drive is taking forever."

"Maybe if someone drove above sixty, we'd be there already," Sloane said. "It's not my fault we are off schedule."

Sloane had planned most of the spring break trip and seemed to take every comment about the adventure as either a personal attack or a compliment. Sloane's intensity was 90 percent asset, 10 percent annoyance.

"My parents will kill me if I get a speeding ticket," Marianne said, hands gripping the steering wheel in the same position they'd been for the last six hours.

"You're doing great," Chloe said encouragingly. "It was really nice of you to drive everyone."

"No, she's not. Let me drive," Sloane said.

"No way," Alden shouted with a mouth full of candy. "Sloane, you're a terrible driver. I don't want to die today." He studied Sloane's face and must have realized how much his comment pissed her off. "Plus, we can't afford to wreck Marianne's van," he added. "We need it to get off campus."

They drove past a sign and Chloe pointed. "Look, only ten more miles. We're almost to Panama City. Hold it together, you guys."

Luke seemed to ignore Chloe's instruction when he unhelpfully added, "It's the first day of spring break, Sloane. Schedules don't matter anymore."

Sloane narrowed her eyes. "With that attitude, it's no wonder you're getting a B in our anatomy class."

Luke turned and whispered to Alden, "That class is not what I thought it was going to be, by the way."

"Seriously," Alden replied.

Wyatt shook his head, unbuckled, and leaned forward to turn up the radio.

"Wyatt, put your seat belt back on." Marianne nervously glanced between the rearview mirror and the road.

Chloe leaned back in her seat, trying to enjoy the music filling the car. It was a country station and some song about your toes in the sand filled the minivan and created a cease-fire.

The trip had been a last-minute plan. Chloe was supposed to fly home to California, but then her father got called away on a business trip and her mother decided to tag along since she'd never been to Paris before. Chloe's mom had already sent a dozen blurry selfies in front of the Eiffel Tower. When Luke heard that Chloe was going to stay on campus, he bailed on his fraternity trip to stay back with her. It was Marianne who initially suggested that they go to the beach. Since her boyfriend Noah was going on a trip with his friends from college, Marianne wanted to have her own trip to even things out. Sloane jumped at the idea and by the next day had emailed everyone itineraries. Alden and Wyatt said they were up for anything, as usual.

Chloe stared out the window, her leg bouncing up and down in anticipation. She had never been to Florida before, and she could already tell it was so different from the beaches where she grew up. There seemed to be a very high demand for T-shirts and souvenirs. Every other shop in those final few miles of the drive seemed to advertise airbrush designs. She'd never seen so many store entrances designed to look like open shark mouths.

And even though it was April, it already felt like August. She tried to roll down the window so she could smell the salty air but was immediately greeted by a series of groans from everyone else in the car about how she was impacting the air conditioning.

"Turn left," Sloane directed. As soon as Marianne made it through the traffic light, Chloe could finally see the ocean. It was a giant stretch of flat, white sand, covered in tourists spread out on brightly colored towels, and Chloe could not wait to join them.

"How much further to the hotel?" Chloe asked.

"It's right there." Sloane pointed.

The motel was across the street from the beach, but it seemed like lots of people were willing to dash across a highway. Marianne had to slam on the brakes twice to avoid groups of teenagers darting across traffic.

When Marianne parked, Sloane directed everyone to stay in the car. "We're only supposed to have four people in a room. You guys stay here and I'll go get the key."

"Are we shoving Marianne and Chloe in suitcases?" Alden asked.

Marianne looked horrified and Chloe laughed.

"No. I don't think they check," Sloane said. "I'm sure we'll be fine. I'll ask for a room toward the back of the building."

Minutes later, Sloane skipped out of the registration office, waving plastic key cards over her head. "There was a slight mix-up with our room, but they're going to give us a discount."

They were all too excited about an influx of cash to ask what exactly had changed about their reservation. They grabbed their bags and walked up two flights of stairs. The concrete outdoor hallway led around the back of the building to the room Sloane had booked. As soon as they opened the door, the mix-up became apparent. They were supposed to have two queen beds and a sleeper sofa. But instead, there was one king-size bed and a carpeted floor, full of sand and probably a thousand bacteria particles that Chloe refused to think about.

Chloe dropped her backpack and walked straight for the sliding glass door to a balcony that overlooked the highway. She stepped outside and craned her neck enough to make out a slice of the beach.

"It's perfect, Sloane," Chloe said. Everyone joined Chloe and nodded their heads. In reality, it was way too small to fit all six of their bodies; the price, even with a discount, was already a stretch for them even though they were splitting the cost; and there was a high likelihood they'd get kicked out by the end of the week for violating some occupancy code. But as they stared out at the ocean and thought about the fact that they had an entire week away from classes and grades and cranky professors, none of those things mattered.

"We call the bed," Luke shouted as he pressed his mouth over Chloe's lips.

Sloane shook her head. "First, we need to set some ground rules about this porn star lifestyle you two have adopted. We get it. You like each other. There's some sex happening. Clearly. But. We. Don't. Want. To. Watch."

"I'm not entirely opposed to watching," Alden stated.

Marianne and Sloane's faces pulled into matching grimaces while Chloe punched Alden in the shoulder. "No one is watching anything," Chloe said.

"There is only one reasonable solution," Sloane declared. "The girls get the bed. The boys get the floor."

"What happened to your feminist studies seminar?" Wyatt asked.

"Feminism has its limits," Sloane said, unpacking her bag.

That night, they ordered pizzas and took them to the beach, eating dinner on the sand. They watched the sun set and swam in the ocean before stumbling back to the hotel room, sandy and exhausted. Thankfully, the boys brought sleeping bags, so they were fine on the floor, although several times Wyatt threatened to sleep in the bathroom if Alden didn't stop snoring.

The next morning, just as the sun was rising, Marianne bounced up and down on the edge of the bed. "I'm ready to go to the beach."

"Someone punch her," Sloane moaned as she rolled over.

Wyatt was more diplomatic. "It's too early, Marianne."

Chloe glanced at the clock. It was just after eight, and after staying up playing Truth or Dare, it did feel ridiculously early. But once Chloe was awake, she couldn't get back to sleep.

"I'll go with you," Chloe groaned. She slid out of bed and hopped over the boys in sleeping bags. Her bathing suit was drying on the shower curtain rod, so she slipped it on and met Marianne in the hallway.

"Sorry I woke you up," Marianne whispered. "I'm just too excited to sleep."

"It's fine," Chloe said, jealous that no one else seemed to have any trouble falling back asleep. "Besides, I like walking on the beach in the morning."

"Me too," Marianne said.

"But we need doughnuts and coffee first," Chloe suggested.

"Absolutely."

Moments later, Chloe was sipping iced coffee and nibbling the glazed peach fritter that they'd bought at the coffee shop down the street from their motel. The food was one of Chloe's favorite parts of the South. The unexpected surprises, like roadside gas stations with the best pulled pork sandwiches and foods that had no business being fried, like pickles, that somehow became addictive favorites. The peach fritter was soft and cakey in the middle, with hints of cinnamon around the juicy peaches, and drizzled in a creamy vanilla glaze around the crisp exterior. It made the early hour bearable.

Chloe noticed Marianne ignoring her doughnut and focusing on her phone. "Have you heard from Noah?" Chloe asked.

"No. But it's fine," Marianne said unconvincingly. "The boats leave so early in the morning. And then they sleep in the afternoon. Our schedules are all out of sync. We'll talk next week."

Chloe knew that Noah was on a fishing trip in the Keys with a few of his friends from school. Initially, Noah and Marianne were going to spend spring break together in their hometown, but when he was invited on the trip, Marianne told him to go. It was one of those things you don't pass up, when someone else's parents pay for you to have an experience you've only dreamed about. Spending a week in suburban Virginia shopping at Target and eating dinner with your parents was nowhere near as much fun as deep-sea fishing. Still, Chloe knew Marianne missed her boyfriend, and maybe a part of her wished Noah thought home with Marianne rivaled the Florida Keys.

Chloe and Marianne found a quiet spot on the beach and spread out a towel to continue eating their breakfast.

"Are you having fun?" Chloe asked.

"I miss Noah. You don't get it because you have Luke here." It almost seemed like Marianne was trying to justify her feelings.

Chloe tilted her head, careful in her response. "First of all, Luke and I are nothing like you and Noah." Chloe laughed as she said, "I have no idea what Luke and I are. But it's not serious. We're having fun." She remembered last night and Luke's attempt to sneak into the bed and Sloane's drunken fury and promises to lock him on the balcony if he didn't stay in his sleeping bag.

Chloe looked at Marianne, her hands mindlessly playing in the sand as she stared at the ocean. "You and Noah should be having fun. If you aren't, you should think about that."

"Please," Marianne said, holding up her hand. "I hear this lecture enough from Sloane. I'm not going to break up with Noah just because long distance is hard."

"I wasn't going to say that. You and Noah could make it. There aren't instructions on when you're supposed to fall in love. But you can't spend the next three years making each other miserable."

"I'm not miserable," Marianne protested.

"Can you have fun without him?" Chloe pushed. When Marianne didn't respond, Chloe continued. "It doesn't mean you love him any less. The fact that you can have friends and adventures and enjoy life and then come back together may even make you love each other more."

Marianne leaned back on the towel. "It's not fair that you have good hair and good advice." Marianne poked her side.

"And what do you mean you and Luke aren't serious? You stare at each other all the time. I think you love him."

"We stare at each other because we love seeing each other naked. There are no baby names doodled in my notebooks."

"Do not tell Sloane. That teasing will be unbearable."

Chloe mimed a zipper over her lips and then pointed at the sky. "What's that?"

"A plane pulling a banner."

"But why?"

"It's a beach thing. You'll see them all day. They don't have these in California?"

"They probably do, but I've never seen one," Chloe said, squinting to make out the name of the business advertised. "Oh, we have to go there tonight."

Marianne laughed. "No way."

"I was the only one who would accompany you on this disturbingly early morning beach adventure. You can't deny me this."

As the plane flew out of view, Marianne said, "You really want to go there?"

"Yes. It's a cultural experience. I cannot leave spring break without going."

"Fine. But it's going to take a lot of convincing to get everyone else on board."

"On board with what?" Chloe and Marianne turned around to find Luke and Wyatt standing on the beach. "We came to join you guys. Alden's snoring was ridiculous." Luke took a giant bite of Chloe's fritter. "Do you have more of those?"

"I will, when you go buy me another one, you breakfast thief," Chloe jumped up and immediately Luke's arms were around her waist, swinging her in the air.

"Where do you want to go tonight?" Wyatt asked. "We have to minimize our time in that hotel room."

"We're going country line dancing," Chloe stated.

"No," Wyatt said and turned and walked away.

"Wait," Chloe shouted. "You didn't even let me pitch the brilliance of this outing."

"I'm getting breakfast." Wyatt kept walking.

"Get more doughnuts," Luke shouted. "I'll pay you back."

Chloe kept her arms wrapped around Luke's neck as she asked, "Will you dance with me, Luke?"

"I'll do just about anything with you, Chloe," Luke said with mischief in his eyes.

"Quit talking about sex," Marianne complained.

"So you'll go?" Chloe excitedly asked.

Luke shrugged. "Why not?"

"What about everyone else?" Chloe asked.

"I'm sure I can convince them." Luke winked.

"Even Wyatt?" Chloe pointed down the beach where Wyatt was walking toward the coffee shop, a tall, dark figure against the bright colors of the beach boardwalk.

"Let me worry about Wyatt," Luke said.

★ ★ ★

Later that night, after a morning spent swimming in the Gulf, an afternoon napping on the beach, and a carefully orchestrated schedule of showers in the increasingly small hotel room, everyone was walking to Pier Park for a night at the country western bar. Chloe was practically skipping, and Wyatt was trailing behind, but Luke had somehow managed to convince everyone that it was worth the sacrifice to see Chloe's reaction.

When Chloe walked inside the bar, she beamed. It was better than she imagined. There were state flags hanging from the ceiling and the walls were covered in dollar bills, some decorated with elaborate designs, while others were signed with an equal number of declarations of love and promises of greatness. The dance floor seemed to be made of plywood, and it was already full of sweaty bodies.

"This place is perfect," Chloe said, kissing the air.

"This place is terrible." Sloane tugged on the bandana Chloe had tied around her hair like a headband. "But you're adorable."

Chloe had dressed for the occasion in cutoff denim shorts and a tight white tank top. Wyatt teased her about the *Dukes of Hazzard* cosplay, but Chloe loved embracing a theme.

"Let's go dance," she squealed.

"No," they all shouted in unison.

"Drinks first," Luke instructed, pointing Chloe toward a dark wood bar with black leather stools.

Luke used his fake ID to order Chloe a cocktail called the Spray Tan. It came out smelling like coconut and was an unnatural shade of blue. But when she took a sip, it tasted like a melted popsicle in the middle of summer, and Chloe thought it was the best drink she'd ever had.

The boys downed a round of shots, and when the band announced "Cotton Eye Joe," Luke slapped his hands on the bar and solemnly said, "It is time."

Chloe hopped off the barstool and laced her fingers with Luke's as she pulled him onto the dance floor. Everyone else followed with much less enthusiasm.

None of them knew what they were doing. Alden's efforts were the most genuine and the most disastrous. Even Wyatt couldn't stop laughing, the music and energy of the room contagious to even his grumpy attitude. Marianne and Sloane linked arms and invented their own more elaborate steps. Every time Marianne smiled, Chloe felt her own happiness increase, especially after their conversation on the beach that morning.

For the next hour, they danced and laughed and Chloe watched as her friends' reluctance disappeared into a haze of joy.

"I'm so hot," Chloe shouted over the music into Luke's ear. The tank top she wore clung to her body, and blonde hairs escaped from her ponytail, sticking to the back of her neck. "I'm going to sit the next one out. You keep dancing."

"You sure?" Luke asked. Somehow, Luke knew the majority of the dances, and Chloe wondered whether he'd been secretly line dancing behind all of their backs. At one point, he was leading a huge group of women in the cowboy cha-cha. It was one of the things Chloe liked most about Luke, his ability to connect with almost anyone.

"Of course." Chloe kissed his cheek and started to walk away. Luke pulled her back, their bodies slamming against one another before he dipped her low and kissed her deeper. Chloe was laughing as he pulled her upward, and for a moment the rest of the crowded room disappeared.

"Does that mean you're going to miss me?"

Luke's answer was more of a groan as Chloe walked toward the bar. She could feel his eyes on her body the entire time.

Chloe ordered a glass of water and sat on a stool, her back to the dance floor.

"You caught on fast," Wyatt said, sliding onto the barstool next to her, his tall body struggling to fold within the tight space.

"I love to dance. You know this," Chloe said, eyebrows raised. Wyatt frequently liked to tease Chloe about how her dancing had gotten them kicked out of Waffle House, which later turned into a two-week ban when the waitress saw them try to come back after winter break.

"You looked good out there," Wyatt said. Chloe was surprised by the compliment. Out of all their friends, Wyatt kept the most distance from Chloe. She suspected he wasn't a fan of the way she consumed Luke's time.

"Luke could make anyone look like a good dancer. How does he know all of the steps?" Chloe asked.

"He's full of surprises," Wyatt muttered into his drink.

Chloe smiled, agreeing completely. The last few months of being with Luke had been the best surprise. Luke could make going to the school bookstore feel like an adventure, and he was happy almost all the time, but especially when he got to see her naked. And Chloe really loved being naked in front of Luke—the way his eyes got big and he rushed to touch every part of her skin. They were still figuring each other out, but he already seemed to have a map of her body burned into his brain. Chloe took a slow sip of her ice water, grateful to cool off when everything about her felt hot.

Wyatt cleared his throat. Chloe had forgotten he was there and blushed at the realization she'd been silently daydreaming for too long.

"Are you going to try another dance?" Chloe asked. Wyatt had mostly sat out after the first group dance, but he seemed happy enough chatting with different groups of people around the bar.

"This isn't my scene," Wyatt said.

"And what is your scene? Coffeehouses with cigarette-smoking brunettes who sneak off with you into the bathroom?"

"One time. That happened once, Chloe."

Chloe laughed, remembering how red Wyatt's face had turned when Luke and Chloe had caught him at a local poetry reading in their small college town last month. Luke had been reluctant to attend, but when they saw Wyatt making out with a senior lit major in the hallway between the kitchen and the bathrooms, Luke had claimed that the night wasn't a total loss.

"Well, thank you for going along with us tonight," Chloe said. "Even though your body seems to be rebelling against this place."

Wyatt was scratching his neck. "I got a little sunburned."

Sloane and Marianne joined them at the bar. "Wyatt, Alden needs your help picking up those girls," Sloane said, motioning toward where Alden was awkwardly chatting with another group of spring breakers.

"Duty calls," Wyatt said, hopping off his barstool.

When Sloane claimed Wyatt's seat, Chloe leaned in and asked, "Did Alden really ask for help?"

"Of course not. But it's obvious he needs it. And I needed Wyatt's seat," Sloane said.

"Where's Luke?" Marianne asked.

"Oh, he's still dancing," Chloe answered. The three women spun around on their barstools and scanned the dance floor. It was easy to spot Luke. His sandy hair towered above most everyone else, especially the crowd of women around him.

The bar was full of college students on spring break, crammed onto an already packed dance floor, all in search of memories that washed in and out like the tide. It was an energy Chloe loved. Even when the guy she was kind of seeing, kind of falling for, was surrounded by a group of girls who looked like they were all hoping to make a memory with Luke that night.

There was one particularly persistent girl who kept asking Luke to dance. And he seemed happy to oblige. The dress she was wearing kept creeping higher the faster she moved. Plus, she had the type of body that required more time in the gym than Chloe would ever willingly devote. She was unquestionably hot.

Luke twirled the girl around. She wrapped her arms around his neck, clinging tighter as he spun her in the air. When he gently put her back on the ground, her hands lingered against his chest, their eyes connected for seconds longer than any casual dance move required.

When Chloe looked back and forth between her friends, it was clear that Marianne and Sloane had seen it too.

Chloe turned around on her barstool, her back now facing the dance floor.

"Does it bother you?" Marianne asked, her voice soft in the loud room.

"Not at all," Chloe said.

"It would bother me," Sloane said.

"He's allowed to dance with whoever he wants. We don't own each other."

"So if he went home with that girl tonight, you'd be fine with it?"

"No," Chloe quickly said. "I'd be annoyed. Although we would have more space in the hotel room without Luke there."

"You really aren't jealous?" Sloane asked as if challenging her.

"I don't have anything to be jealous about. First of all, he's dancing. That's it. Second, we haven't defined anything."

"If that were Noah, I'd be losing my mind," Marianne said. "Wait, do you think Noah is dancing with other girls like that?"

"No," Sloane quickly replied. "Noah is a horrible dancer. And Noah's game is about as strong as Alden's," she added, gesturing to where Alden and Wyatt were standing. Wyatt was in his element, leaning against the bar and captivating a girl with some story. Whereas Alden was at his side, piping in with commentary that only Wyatt seemed to find amusing.

"Noah has excellent game," Marianne said, smiling. "But you're right. He'd never dance with a bunch of other girls. No offense, Chloe."

"None taken," Chloe said. "Either Luke realizes what we have, or he loses it. Being jealous is only going to make me miserable." Chloe raised her glass of water and clinked cups with Marianne, who smiled and rested her head on Chloe's shoulder, then pulled out her phone, disappointment filling her face when she saw no messages from Noah.

"Marianne, put your phone away," Sloane instructed. "Let him have fun. Let yourself have fun."

"I know. I'm going to," Marianne said reluctantly. "I just miss him. I'm glad I'm here, but I wish I was there too. Haven't you ever felt that way?"

"No," Sloane said. "I live in the moment, and at this moment, I want to do more stupid dances with you two." Sloane downed the rest of her drink and pulled Chloe and Marianne back onto the dance floor.

The three of them made their way to the center of the floor, cutting through the crowd of patrons who were still trying to line dance in an increasingly packed bar.

Chloe brushed shoulders with a man and reflexively apologized. He caught her elbow and said, "No worries. I've been trying to bump into you all night."

His voice was smooth and slow, drenched in a heavy southern accent. Chloe laughed and tried to keep walking toward Sloane and Marianne, but he held on to her arm. "Wanna dance?"

Chloe bit her lip. He was significantly older, probably somewhere in his late twenties. Judging by the size of his belt buckle, he was familiar with line dancing, and Chloe really wanted to learn the dance that was just starting. His grin suggested that he'd be a fun teacher.

"Are you good?" Chloe asked.

"My name's Clint," he said, as if that was a sufficient explanation. He wrapped his arm around Chloe's waist and immediately guided her toward the center of the dance floor.

"Where are you going?" Sloane shouted.

"I'm dancing with Clint," Chloe replied, pointing to the tall man in front of her and shrugging.

Chloe had no idea what she was doing, but she immediately realized she was having fun. She caught on fast. The steps were easy, and she moved in sync with Clint, laughing as he twirled her in circles and gently nudged her in the direction of the changing choreography. At one point, she was laughing so hard at the way Clint effortlessly tucked his thumbs in that giant belt buckle while his feet seemed to float across the floor that she had to stop moving to catch her breath.

It was around that time that Luke must have noticed Chloe on the dance floor. She saw him walk across the room and she was excited for him to join in, until she noticed his face.

Luke grabbed Chloe's wrist and pulled her toward him. Minutes earlier, she'd felt the same reach from Clint. Another man pulling her in a new direction.

"Hey," Clint said calmly. "We're dancing."

"This is my girl," Luke shouted, slurring slightly. His arm swung around Chloe's shoulders.

Chloe was shocked, not only by the force of Luke's statement but also by the content. They'd never had any discussion about being exclusive. And although a tiny part of her liked being wanted, the larger part was furious at this assumption.

Chloe reflexively shrugged away Luke's possessive arm and took a step to the side. There was a foot of space between Chloe and Luke, and he seemed gutted by her action.

Clint smirked. "Dogs and horses are property. Not women." Clint extended his hand toward Chloe. "Wanna keep dancing?"

Chloe swallowed, unsure of her decision. Alden and Wyatt seemed to sense the mounting tension and started to make their way toward Luke.

"She's not dancing with you," Luke said, shoving Clint in the chest.

Clint barely moved as he said, "That's her decision."

Wyatt stood beside Luke as he asked, "Everything okay?"

"No," Luke said. "Everything is not okay. This idiot is hitting on Chloe."

Chloe finally spoke up. "We were dancing, Luke. That's it."

"She's right," Clint said. "We were just dancing. I hadn't gotten to the hitting on her part yet." Clint winked, and that seemed to send Luke over the edge.

Luke lunged for Clint. "Hold me back, Wyatt." Maybe it was an instruction meant to intimidate, as if Luke's rage needed to be restrained and Clint would somehow fear this moment. But Luke's comment had the opposite effect. The whole thing was embarrassing.

Clint chuckled as he put up a strong arm to stop Luke's advance. "You're out of your league here, kid." It was an obvious statement to everyone but Luke. Clint towered over him, both in size and maturity.

Instead of holding him back, Wyatt gently placed a hand on Luke's shoulder. "This is unwise, Luke. He's got fifty pounds and ten years on you. You're going to lose this situation."

"He's hitting on my girlfriend." Luke probably meant to sound justified, but instead he sounded whiny.

Chloe stepped in front of Luke and pointed her finger at his chest. "I am not your girlfriend. You are embarrassing me and yourself. Walk away."

When Luke didn't respond, Clint stepped forward and grabbed Chloe's hand. "Let's keep dancing. I haven't showed you my best moves yet."

That was all it took. Luke lunged forward like a small cat and swung his fist. Clint seemed to anticipate this move and leaned backward. Luke's wild swing managed to connect with the edge of Clint's jaw but sent Luke so off balance that he fell to the floor. Clint lifted his booted foot and firmly pushed Luke down as two bouncers ran to the dance floor.

"You okay?" the bouncer asked Clint with familiarity.

"Oh, I'm fine. He just got a little graze in," Clint said, rubbing his jawline as he continued stepping on Luke's back.

The bouncers lifted Luke off the ground and immediately dragged him to the exit.

"Okay, so looks like we're leaving," Alden said. "I'll go tell Sloane and Marianne."

Wyatt looked upward and mumbled to himself. He lifted a hand apologetically in Clint's direction and then looked at Chloe. "What are you going to do?" Wyatt asked.

"I'm not leaving with him," Chloe said, pointing toward Luke and the door.

"Understandable," Wyatt said. "Are you okay?"

Chloe looked around at the crowd slowly returning to their dances but still staring in her direction. "I can't believe him, Wyatt."

Wyatt looked over his shoulder and then back at Chloe. "I'm not going to defend him. But he did have too many shots, Chloe. Luke is going to be full of regret when he sobers up."

Chloe looked across the bar. Luke was already outside. Alden was making his way to the door, and Sloane and Marianne were walking in the opposite direction, toward Chloe.

"I'll be fine. You guys go ahead," Chloe told Wyatt. "We'll meet you back at the hotel."

Wyatt hesitated before he left.

Sloane joined Chloe and shouted, "Did you cause a bar fight? You are truly a living legend." Based on the volume of her voice, it was likely Sloane had had too many shots as well.

"I didn't cause anything. That was Luke's fault." Chloe turned toward Clint. "I'm sorry about my friend."

"You aren't the one that needs to apologize." Clint extended his hand. "Ready to dance?"

Chloe shook her head. She was frustrated that Luke had ruined such a fun evening. And even though she knew she had no reason to feel guilty about dancing with Clint, she did. "I think I've had enough dancing tonight. We should go."

"Alright," Clint shrugged. "Thanks for the dance." He walked away, as if fist fighting and finding new dance partners were as common as Bud Light.

Sloane was twirling around the dance floor, oblivious, but Marianne studied Chloe's concerned face. "Are you okay?" she asked.

"I don't know," Chloe said. "Can we go?"

"Should we find the boys?" Marianne suggested.

"No," Chloe quickly replied. "Luke needs to sober up, and I need to cool off."

"Okay. How about a walk on the beach?" Marianne proposed. "Sloane might need to sober up too." Marianne and Chloe turned to look at their friend, who was now involved in an elaborate dance with the cement column in the middle of the dance floor.

"Great idea," Chloe said.

They managed to drag Sloane outside, and the three of them made their way down to the beach. The moon was full, creating a dusk-like lightness across the sand even though it was well into the night. As Chloe and Marianne chatted about the frustration of boys and the pitfalls of relationships, Sloane did cartwheels up and down the sand. The next day Sloane would complain of a mysterious shoulder pain, suggesting that there was very little of the night she actually remembered.

By the time they made it back to the motel, Chloe hoped the guys would already be asleep. But as they approached the door, she could hear Alden and Wyatt bickering through the paper-thin motel walls.

Sloane went in first, going straight to the bathroom. Marianne followed while Chloe lingered in the hallway. She leaned against the wall. Even after dissecting the night with Marianne, she still wasn't sure how she felt.

"Is she coming back?" she heard Luke ask. The slur in his voice seemed to have disappeared.

"Yeah, she's outside," Marianne replied.

Chloe took a deep breath and entered the room.

"I'm sorry, Chloe," Luke said as soon as the motel room door opened.

Alden and Wyatt looked up from their card game, eyes shifting nervously around the room.

"I'm willing to have a discussion with you outside," Chloe said to Luke, gesturing toward the glass slider onto the balcony.

Marianne turned on the radio, providing some noise to muffle their discussion through the flimsy door, and Chloe was grateful for the slice of privacy.

Luke looked like shit. He leaned over the balcony railing and pushed his sandy hair off his forehead. Bloodshot eyes stared at Chloe, pleading for forgiveness before he even opened his mouth.

"I really messed up, Chloe. I'm so sorry."

She wanted him to apologize a thousand more times, and at the same time she was so annoyed by the apology. Luke hadn't just ruined her night, he'd ruined everyone's night. It seemed selfish that she was the only person hearing about his regrets.

Chloe stood in front of Luke, her voice low as she said, "I'm not into jealousy. At all. This thing between us stops now if you can't get over the fact that we are our own people. We have to trust each other."

Chloe expected protests and excuses. She was surprised when Luke plainly replied, "You're right. I was out of line."

"What were you thinking, Luke?"

"I wasn't. I looked across the bar and saw you with that guy and I lost my mind."

"You really did," Chloe replied.

"It won't happen again, Chloe. I promise. That's not who I am."

"I think I know that," Chloe said. "That's why I was so surprised." Luke was pacing on the small balcony and Chloe reached out her hand to stop his movement. "Do you want to talk about it?"

Luke winced. "What exactly?"

"Us. Do we need to define what we're doing?" Chloe asked.

Luke exhaled. "We've only been hanging out for a few months. You didn't want a relationship."

That's what Chloe had said. Because when she had returned to campus after winter break, she had wanted to be clear that she wasn't coming back for Luke. And immediately jumping into a relationship with him would have made that point hard to argue. So she had told him it was casual. She had told him it was fun. And they had both played along with that story. But they both knew that wasn't the complete truth.

Luke continued, "I trust you, Chloe. But I don't want to watch you dance with other people." Luke swallowed nervously before he said, "I only want you to dance with me."

The edge of Chloe's lips broke into a small smile. "Okay. I can handle that."

"Good." Luke exhaled.

Chloe took a step closer, erasing the space between their bodies. "But that means you don't dance with other people either, Luke. I'm not okay with a double standard."

"Of course," he said too quickly.

Chloe's eyes focused on his. "Your flirting seems to be uncontrollable. Do you think you're ready for only one person?" Her tone reflected the earnestness of her question.

Luke pulled her close. "I'm ready for you, Chloe. Despite my stupidity tonight. I really don't want to mess this up."

"Good. Don't be an idiot again and we should be fine." She wrapped her arms around his neck.

"Man, my girlfriend is so intense," he said as he trailed kisses across her shoulder.

A wide grin spread across Chloe's face. It was fun hearing him call her that. "Only because her boyfriend drives her crazy," she replied.

The curtains in the motel room moved, and Chloe and Luke looked into the room to see their four friends lined up at the door, ears pressed against the glass.

Alden slid open the door. "Did you guys make up?"

"Yes," Chloe laughed.

"Good," Marianne said. "I hate tension."

"We are never dancing anywhere again," Wyatt declared. "We're cursed. We always get kicked out."

The six of them gathered on the hotel bed, joining in Alden and Wyatt's competitive game of Go Fish and belting out the lyrics to the songs that had been playing on repeat in the bar. Eventually, they abandoned the cards for dancing, trying to re-create more and more elaborate and ridiculous moves until the hotel manager knocked on the door and threatened to throw them out because of the noise complaints. The boys hid in the bathroom while Sloane promised the manager that they'd be quiet and they finally, reluctantly, fell asleep.

Chloe would remember so much from that first trip together. The piles of Alden's clothes that drove Sloane insane. The smell of sunscreen and rum that perfumed the motel room. Days spent playing competitive games of beach volleyball and floating on cheap inflatables in the Gulf. Dinners of McDonald's fries spread out on beach towels before they spent the night hopping from one bar to the next using the fake IDs Luke had gotten from his fraternity brother. They all drank too much at night and got sunburned during the day.

But mostly, Chloe remembered waking up each morning, clinging to the edge of the bed because Marianne always managed to sprawl in the middle, Luke asleep on the floor, his hand extended from his sleeping bag and wrapped around Chloe's. His girlfriend. Each morning, Chloe looked around at her sleeping friends and felt like the luckiest person in the world.

◆ 6 ◆

This Year

"THIS IS NOT THE same," Chloe says as she steps out of the car Sloane arranged to pick them up at the airport. Chloe and Wyatt arrive together because they took the same flight from DC. Marianne would be arriving later. Maybe Luke is already here—Chloe isn't sure, she hasn't asked.

"It's an upgrade from that motel for sure," Wyatt says, eyeing Sloane and Alden's new home. Chloe smiles, thinking about their first spring break trip to Panama City. Unquestionably, this house is nice. And unquestionably, Chloe would rather sleep in a cramped, musty motel room if it meant avoiding Luke this week.

"Sloane and Alden's whole life is an upgrade," Chloe states.

Last year, Alden sold his company for a stupid amount of money. At least, that's how Alden described it. Sloane was a little more modest, saying they were *very comfortable*.

But when you have enough money to be *very comfortable* for the rest of your life, regardless of whether you work or not, Alden's description is probably more accurate. Chloe agrees that it's stupid to have that much money at twenty-nine years old.

Alden plans on investing in other tech start-ups while Sloane continues her interior design business, just being more selective with clients. Sloane has always wanted to live near the beach and now they have enough money to do that.

Chloe and Wyatt hesitate outside the entrance, a giant white oak panel that seems too heavy to actually function as a door. It's weathered to look like it's survived decades of sea winds even though the house was built last year.

Chloe feels a welcome breeze as she stands immobile. After years of living in the South, Chloe knows that for most of the year it's too hot to be outside unless you are submerged in some body of water. But in April, there's an occasional breeze, especially if you're close to an ocean, and there's no more perfect feeling. Every part of Chloe's body wants to stand still, to delay entering this house and facing Luke and the past, and the perfect weather isn't making it any easier to step inside.

Wyatt raises his fist to knock on the beautiful front door, and Chloe wants to tell him to stop, because it's too nice to knock on and there has to be some gong-like bell to ring. But also because she wants one more moment of peace.

Before Chloe can speak, Sloane flings the door open and squeals, "You're here!"

"We are!" Chloe says, trying to mimic Sloane's enthusiasm.

"That was not convincing," Wyatt whispers. "Your happy voice needs some work, Chloe."

Sloane waves her hand, dismissing Wyatt, and walks inside, immediately describing tiny details about the design of the herringbone floors and the exposed wooden beams in the two-story living room. But it's hard to focus on those details because all Chloe sees is ocean and all she feels is panic.

"Anyone else here?" Chloe asks.

"Yes," Sloane states. She crosses her arms and narrows her eyes. "Luke is here. He got in this morning. He's with Alden on the beach right now."

Chloe's eyes dart over to Wyatt, who shrugs, seeming to reply *You knew this.* Chloe has imagined various scenarios for when she will see Luke for the first time, and she's still unable to predict how he's going to react. A part of her wants to complain that it is unnatural to have to see an ex again. That's why you break up. You end the relationship. Except Luke isn't just an ex. He's part of her family. And she's put off seeing him for long enough.

Sloane stares at Chloe and says, "You have the house to yourself for thirty minutes. That's how long I'm allowing you to act awkward, and then you need to put on your big girl panties and handle the mess you created."

"Please don't say panties, Sloane." Wyatt carries their suitcases inside and drops them on the floor.

"Go find the boys on the beach," Sloane instructs.

"Nah. I want to watch Chloe act awkward," Wyatt says.

"You got Chloe for the last three hours on the flight. I get her now. Leave." Sloane points toward the wall of glass that opens to merge the living room with an expansive deck.

"Alden's skin will blind you. He should be easy to find," Sloane says.

"How can Alden be pale if you guys are living at the beach?" Chloe asks.

"Because he still loooves his computers," Sloane drawls. "It's a wild world of computer programming, and his exploration cannot be restrained."

Chloe laughs and is instantly comforted by the dichotomy that is Sloane and Alden's relationship. They've always been an unlikely pair, except that they are equal in their fierce devotion to each other. It's something Chloe has always envied.

Wyatt walks over to the fridge and gets a beer. "I'll see you guys later," he says and turns toward Chloe, mouthing *Good luck.*

As Wyatt closes the door, Chloe wonders how far he will have to go to find Alden and Luke. Are they somewhere up the beach, a safe distance away? Or, more likely, will he find them quickly, a rush of half hugs and easy banter as the trio is reunited? And then Luke will know that Chloe is here, the timer set on a reunion they both would rather avoid.

Sloane gives Chloe a tour of the downstairs, delaying the conversation Chloe knows is coming. But it is obvious that Sloane is proud of this house, as she should be. The kitchen with its grand marble island, deep gray veining matching the woven rattan barstools. Oversized pendants with accents of brass highlighting the fourteen-foot ceilings.

There's a bowl on the kitchen counter overflowing with lemons. Too many lemons for any person to ever use at one time. Other than that one pop of yellow, everything else is neutral. Shades of sand and driftwood and sea glass that feel so grown up compared to the thrift store furnishings that make up Chloe's apartment. The calm surroundings of Sloane's house fail to mitigate the chaos Chloe feels in her mind.

Sloane hooks her arm around Chloe's and leads her upstairs. "This is your room," she says, pointing to the end of the hall-way. All Chloe can see is the giant king-sized bed stacked with fluffy white pillows and linen bedding. She wants to dive in and hide there for the rest of the week. When Chloe walks into the room, Sloane following, she takes in the bright white plaster walls, the chaise lounge in the corner, and the giant window overlooking the Gulf.

"It's stunning," Chloe says, before spinning around and seeing a familiar bag in the corner.

Chloe spots Luke's leather duffel, and then the sleeve of his blazer hanging in the closet, and her eyes narrow.

"Sloane, you're insane. Luke has clearly already put his stuff here."

Sloane shrugs. "There are only four bedrooms. Two of you have to share."

"Then Marianne and I will share a room. Obviously." Chloe turns and immediately walks out of the room, Sloane trailing closely behind. "I know you, Sloane. Please don't do this. It's a big enough deal that Luke and I are both here this week. Don't try to force us together."

"I think the problem is that I haven't been doing enough forcing. It's been a busy year, and I've been thinking of other things, but now my focus is back where it needs to be. Getting you and Luke back together."

"Don't push your luck. Being in the same house is a big enough step." Chloe shifts her bag and asks, "Which room is the farthest from Luke's?"

"Go down there," Sloane sighs, pointing Chloe toward a room at the opposite end of the hall.

They pass a primary suite that looks straight out of a magazine and then the room where Wyatt is staying, the walls painted a warm chocolate.

Sloane points to the room with two twin beds, a perfectly logical sharing scenario and sighs, "This will have to do." It's the fanciest place Chloe has stayed this year.

"This is perfect." Chloe drops her bag at the foot of the bed, surveys the adjoining bathroom and the lush ivory carpet that she hopes she doesn't stain. "I like sharing with Marianne. It gives us more time to talk."

Sloane rolls her eyes. "I need to move some things around since you're messing up my room arrangements."

"I'll help," Chloe says, trying to appease her friend, an impossible task. Sloane is never happy when her plans are disrupted. Usually it's not worth the fight, but in this instance, Chloe will suffer the consequences. She's not sharing a room with Luke, even if it means upsetting Sloane.

They step into the hallway and Chloe notices a closed door. "What's in there?"

"That room is not finished," Sloane says.

"I love seeing your projects." Chloe steps forward and opens the door just as Sloane tries to block her entry. For someone who's been rattling off the names of paint colors and furniture sources for every room, Sloane seems strangely private about this space.

When Chloe looks inside, she understands why. It's not unfinished. Every detail is precisely planned, from the over-sized teddy bear propped in the corner to the rattan rocking horse under the window. Chloe walks into the room and takes it all in—the closet full of baby clothes, the muslin blanket draped over the crib, the changing table stuffed with tiny diapers.

"Oh, Sloane." Chloe looks over her shoulder at her friend lurking in the doorway, somehow unable to step foot in a place that she's clearly spent hundreds of hours designing.

Sloane shrugs. "I like to be prepared."

"It's going to happen," Chloe says, mustering every ounce of positivity she can find.

Sloane's eyes start to fill and she bites her cheek, stopping the tears before they fall. She nods her head, and that seems to be the only response she's capable of making.

"Do you want to talk about . . ."

"Absolutely not." Sloane ends the sentence and leaves the room, shouting over her shoulder. "Don't bring it up again. That's not what this week is about."

Chloe sighs and gently closes the door to the nursery. She isn't sure what this week is supposed to achieve, but they've already succeeded in ignoring their problems. Sloane used to tell her everything, and now there's an even thicker wall around her friend's heart.

Chloe knew things would be awkward with Luke, but she isn't prepared for Sloane awkwardness. Five minutes into the trip and Chloe already feels like she's walking on eggshells. She wants an honest conversation with the best friend she misses like a phantom limb, but she knows better than to push someone in pain. Instead, she waits, sitting in a room alone, worried she's going to use the wrong towels when she washes her face. They should be discussing the hundred ways their lives have changed over the last year. Chloe fears all those changes stole away their comfort with each other.

Chloe hears Sloane opening and closing closet doors, her friend's movement the only sound echoing in the giant house. She looks out the window. The water is emerald green, and she can't help but think about the engagement ring that was almost on her finger. She looks down at the powder-white sand beach and sees three figures walking toward the house. Wyatt's jeans are rolled up because he didn't bother changing before joining Alden and Luke. Sloane was right about Alden, his skin does seem to reflect the sunlight in a disturbing manner, but seeing his lanky stride in the outfit Sloane clearly bought for him is a familiar comfort.

And then Luke. It's unfair that, even after everything, he still has the power to pause Chloe's functioning. She reminds her heart and lungs that their operation is required, forcing herself to inhale deeply and slow her racing heart.

It shouldn't be so easy to remember the feeling of her head resting against Luke's chest. How his palm would rub circles on the small of her back as they stood in conversation with others. Those memories should have been erased along with their relationship, and yet Chloe can't suppress the haunting comfort of her ear absorbing his heartbeat.

She pulls the curtains closed tight and shakes her head. She needs a glass of wine and a game plan for surviving this week.

A familiar female voice shouts, "I'm here!" and Chloe smiles. Marianne. Many times in their friendship, Chloe has known that Marianne is the solution to all of their problems. Practical, joyful, and steady, the balm of Marianne's presence is exactly what she needs at this moment.

Chloe runs downstairs and finds Marianne standing in the entryway, her arms loaded with bags. She snakes her arms around Marianne's waist, forcing her to drop the luggage and hug her friend in return.

"I have missed you so much," Chloe sighs.

Marianne leans her head back and exhales. "Me too. You have no idea how nice it is to hug a human being without them trying to bite your nipple."

"I'm sober now, but watch out later tonight." Chloe shimmies her shoulders as Marianne laughs.

Chloe takes a step back, examining her friend. Marianne's hair is longer, her usual chestnut bob replaced by a ponytail at the nape of her neck. Her petite frame is softer than before, but Chloe knows they're all softer as they've gotten older. And Marianne is the only one of them who has actually grown an entire human being in her body.

Mostly, Chloe sees exhaustion in Marianne's eyes and bliss across her face, and for the first time Chloe thinks that maybe this week isn't a complete mistake. Because she can't wait to spend the night catching up with Marianne.

"You're stuck with me this week. We're roomies," Chloe says.

"That's okay. I was hoping we'd get to share. Plus, I've already taken a bath in the big tub," Marianne says.

"Huh?" Chloe asks.

Sloane walks over and kisses Marianne's cheek. "Marianne and Noah came for a long weekend right before Teddy was born," she explains.

"Oh," Chloe says, wishing she had already known that.

Sloane seems to sense Chloe's discomfort. "It was the week you moved to DC. I knew you couldn't come. Besides, she was such a horny pregnant woman there are things my ears can never unhear. Trust me, it was good you missed that trip."

Marianne points her finger in Sloane's direction. "Just wait. You'll see what it's like when there are so many hormones running through your body" She puts her arm around Chloe's shoulders. "I've missed you as much as I've missed sleep."

"I've missed you too," Chloe says, leaning into Marianne's side so tightly she can smell her coconut shampoo. "Show me pictures. All of them."

Marianne laughs. "We don't have that long. My entire phone is full of pictures of Teddy."

Sloane is not a hugger, but even she can't seem to resist the reunion. She grabs both of their hands and says, "I can't believe we're finally all together again. I've missed my girls."

"Let's go upstairs and unpack. You can show me the pictures of Teddy while Sloane criticizes our wardrobe," Chloe says.

"Let's look at pictures later," Sloane says before she quickly adds, "when we have enough time for Marianne to tell us everything . . ." Sloane trails off and Chloe notices her friend flinch slightly. Marianne stares at her phone and misses Sloane's face. "We have to get ready for tonight," Sloane says.

"Okay," Chloe replies. "What's first on the agenda?"

"They're almost set up on the beach," Sloane explains.

"For what?" Marianne asks.

"Dinner," Sloane says. "As soon as the boys get back, we'll move down to the beach for dinner. I've set up a welcome bonfire."

Chloe walks over to the window and sees a crew setting up chairs and tables on the sand. "That's for us?"

"Of course. It's our spring break kickoff dinner. Why don't you change into that white Reformation dress?" Sloane says, walking upstairs and leading Chloe and Marianne into their bedroom.

"I don't have a white Reformation dress," Chloe says absently.

"Yes, you do. I'm almost done moving your things since you insisted on changing rooms." Being friends with Sloane requires a certain level of going along with things that they have learned to accept over the years. A few minutes later, Sloane returns with full arms and starts hanging items in the closet.

Chloe walks over and sees a beautiful white silk dress. It is practically backless, with thin straps that would cross over her shoulder blades. As Chloe pulls the dress out of the closet, the thigh-high slit flaps open.

"I can't wear that. I'll freeze," Chloe says.

"It's eighty-four. You'll be fine," Sloane says.

"Okay. I can't wear that for other reasons," Chloe says.

Sloane crosses her arms, waiting for Chloe to elaborate. When she doesn't, Sloane says, "You are a guest in my home and have been gifted a stunning, chic welcome outfit. Try. It. On."

Marianne tries to muffle her laughter but fails. Sloane spins around. "I wasn't sure what size you'd be so I got you shoes instead of a dress. You look phenomenal, by the way. And I have an eye mask that will take care of those dark circles."

As Chloe goes into the bathroom with the dress, she sees Sloane handing Marianne a sheet of paper. Marianne smiles and immediately tucks it into her bag. Sloane's face is full of smug satisfaction. Whatever was on the paper made her friends happy, erasing the tension that seemed to be building with Sloane. Chloe closes the bathroom door and decides she'll wear the dress. After all, Sloane has gone to so much trouble.

"I'm going to check in with the caterers," Sloane says through the bathroom door. "I'll see you downstairs in ten minutes." There's zero trace of question in Sloane's voice.

Chloe looks at herself in the mirror. As much as Sloane can be controlling, she's also very good at knowing exactly what's right for someone. It's an overbearing personality born from accuracy. And in this case, the dress is perfect on Chloe. It falls over every curve of her body, and the smooth fabric feels electrifying. It's the kind of soft white that pops against her skin and highlights her light hair. She decides to sweep up the blonde waves, partly because the humidity at the ocean is unbearable and partly because the back of this dress is too good not to show off.

It doesn't matter what she looks like, these are her best friends, she lies to herself. But when she sees her reflection and likes what she finds, she's relieved. Sloane must have known that Chloe needed to feel good the first time she saw Luke. It's impossible to look bad in this dress.

Emerging from the bathroom, Chloe hears a repetitive whirring sound and finds Marianne holding a breast pump with one hand and unpacking her suitcase with the other. "You weren't kidding. Even the machines are biting your nipples these days," Chloe jokes.

"The most horrific part, I can barely feel them. And I used to be a big fan of nipple play."

"Who doesn't like nipple play," Chloe says uncomfortably. It's jarring to think about someone's sex life while their boobs are attached to a baby-feeding torture device.

"Hopefully the sensation comes back," Marianne says seriously.

"Keep me updated on those developments." Chloe tries her best to be supportive. She doesn't know anything about breastfeeding or pumping or postpartum nipple sensation, but if this is what is important to Marianne, then it's going to start being important to Chloe.

"That dress is phenomenal," Marianne says.

Chloe's hand skims the silky edge that opens to the slit down her side. "Too much?" she asks.

"Of course it is. But I kind of think that was Sloane's goal."

"Do you have a sense of Sloane's other goals for this week?" Chloe asks.

"You mean the typed itinerary she distributed to each of us detailing the ways in which we are supposed to force you and Luke together?" Marianne reaches into her bag and pulls out a paper with surprising dexterity given she is doing everything one-handed and topless.

"She didn't," Chloe sighs.

"Of course she did."

Chloe points at the paper Marianne is now reading. "Are you going to share that with me?"

"Of course not." Marianne's eyes widen but never leave the page.

"Marianne."

Marianne tucks the paper back into her suitcase. "I'm just as scared of Sloane as the rest of you. Plus, I have a feeling this is going to be entertaining to watch."

Chloe looks away and fidgets with the strand of hair that's already escaped her ponytail.

Marianne adjusts the breast pump and then seems to notice Chloe's silence. "You okay?"

"It's not entertaining," Chloe says softly. "I know I messed up. I know I ruined the group. But none of this is entertaining for me."

Marianne switches off the pump. "You're right. I shouldn't have said that."

"I don't want to lose you guys," Chloe says with a crack in her voice.

"I thought joking about it would ease the tension. Clearly, I made it worse."

Chloe shakes her head. "You didn't. It's impossible for this situation to get worse."

"I have to admit, you're kind of jumping into the deep end. Everyone hasn't been together for over a year. Since . . ." Marianne trails off. "A week in the same house was an intense choice."

"It wasn't exactly a choice. You said it. We're all scared of Sloane. And she presented convincing reasons that made it hard to say no."

"What did she say?"

"You should ask her," Chloe answers.

"Okay. Secrets and threats on day one. Seems pretty Sloane-typical. How can I help you get through this week?"

"Never leave my side," Chloe says intently.

Marianne restarts her breast pump. "I'm currently tethered to a wall outlet with plastic suction cups attached to my chest. We are going to be separated this week."

"I can be your pump assistant."

"I actually look forward to the alone time of pumping."

"That's depressing."

"Yep. Motherhood decimates all of your standards." Marianne seems to shake off whatever thought she was about to share. "How about this. Anytime you need a break, shout *nipple*. It will be our code word."

"Could you come up with a less awkward code word?"

"My life is kind of single-tracked these days. It's all nipples and butt stuff."

Chloe is afraid to ask, but she does it anyway. "Butt stuff with Noah?"

"Negative," Marianne frowns. "Butt stuff as in diaper cream and explosive diarrhea. Would you prefer *blowout* as the code word?"

"No, *nipple* is good," Chloe replies.

Marianne finally turns off the pump and begins a complicated process of wiping and detaching all the various parts that were just attached to her body. "I'll meet you downstairs. There's no reason for us both to be late and double Sloane's wrath."

Chloe shifts. "I don't mind waiting. I'm sure Sloane will understand."

"Rip off the Band-Aid, Chloe. He's been your friend for ten years too. It's always worse in your mind."

"Is it? Because I'm hyperventilating thinking that maybe I have underestimated Luke's fury."

Marianne puts down the bottles of milk and comes closer. "Do you remember that first trip we took? To Panama City?"

"Of course." Chloe smiles.

"Do you remember what Luke did after the line dancing night?"

Chloe nods. Luke had gone back to the bar the next day, leaving an apology note for Clint, after the bartender confirmed that he was a regular and promised to pass along the message. All week, Luke worried that he should go back and apologize in person, but Wyatt kept reminding him that when he dropped off the note the bartender told him he wasn't allowed to come back. It was one of the many times when Chloe realized she was falling for Luke. Everybody makes mistakes, but few people are capable of admitting and taking responsibility for their actions.

Marianne's right, Chloe thinks. Luke hates conflict as much as Chloe. It's possible that he will be trying just as hard to make this week work. And maybe if he'll give her the chance, they can both admit the mistakes that got them to this place.

Chloe carefully closes the door to the bedroom and makes her way downstairs. She can hear her friends before she can see them.

When she rounds the corner, Alden adjusts his glasses and his voice slurs adorably as he screams "Chloe!" Clearly, beer has been consumed.

"Hey, Alden-O," Chloe says as she walks toward him and is enveloped in a tight hug. "This place is amazing. Thanks for having us."

"What's the point of a big house like this if it's just for Sloane and me, right?" Alden must want to make everyone feel welcome, but Chloe notices Sloane fumble her wineglass.

Before she can check in on her friend, Wyatt is at Chloe's side whispering, "Nice dress. Very bridal-y."

Chloe's eyes narrow as she whispers back, "Sloane picked it out."

"That tracks," Wyatt says, chuckling at the floor.

Chloe scans the room, but there's an empty space on the couch where Luke should be. Maybe he's hiding in his room. Maybe he's as nervous as Chloe.

But when a voice in the kitchen says, "Hey, Chloe," her entire body clenches in response. She'd know the low rumble of Luke's voice blindfolded in the dark. When she slowly turns around and sees him emerge from the kitchen, she struggles to find the ability to use her own voice.

"Hey, Luke," she manages to reply.

"They spoke! They spoke!" Alden says and the room erupts in applause.

"What did I miss?" Marianne says, coming downstairs with a small cooler and going to the fridge to store her milk.

"Chloe and Luke just spoke to one another and now we're all staring at them to see what happens next," Wyatt says.

"We're going to be fine, right, Chloe?" Luke says. He seems so relaxed and comfortable as he flops on the couch next to Alden. His light-blue button-down and khaki shorts blend perfectly with Sloane's décor, almost as if she hired Luke to be the model in a photo shoot.

Chloe tries to look away, but she can't, her eyes studying the tiny differences in his appearance after a year of separation. His hair is cut shorter on the sides, and the strands that fall over his forehead are lighter. Chloe wonders if he's been outside more, which seems unlikely because Luke always spent long hours in his office. But maybe he has a new hobby. Maybe he has a whole new life that Chloe knows nothing about. Her heart pauses at the thought.

"Mm-hmm," is the only response Chloe can manage.

She sits in a chair across from the couch. It's too soft and she slumps backward, but then she's worried her boob is going to slip out of the ridiculously skimpy dress Sloane bought. She wants to lean forward but knows the shifting will show Luke just how uncomfortable she is, which is accurate and yet not the impression she wants to make. So instead she slowly leans to the side, pretending she's reaching for a coaster on the side table, but somehow manages to drop it. The crack of the gilded agate coaster and the sudden focus of every eye on Chloe immediately creates a pool of sweat in her armpits. Chloe looks at the broken coaster and then across the room at Marianne and mouths *nipple*.

Marianne shakes her head and mouths back *too soon.*

Sloane walks over and picks up the broken coaster. "I didn't love these anyway."

Chloe stares at Marianne, pleading, but Marianne keeps shaking her head.

Sloane looks back and forth between her friends. "What are you guys talking about?" Sloane asks.

"Nothing," Marianne and Chloe say at the same time.

"Let's go down to the beach, then," Sloane says. She drops the broken coaster in the trash and walks outside. Everyone follows like schoolchildren lining up at the cafeteria.

Chloe can't help looking over her shoulder at Luke. But he's deep in conversation with Alden and Wyatt, something about a boat Alden is renting, or maybe looking to buy, and their plans to go deep-sea fishing later in the week.

Sloane is rambling about how many different catering teams she had to test before she found one that's reliable, delicious, and aesthetically pleasing, a trifecta of standards Chloe doesn't completely understand. Chloe's only frame of reference is the difference between the burrito bowls at the two different Chipotles downtown. It's worth the extra walk for the good salsa, but Chloe doesn't think those are the standards Sloane applies to her catering services.

Marianne starts talking about how no one is reliable anymore. The substitute teacher who took over her math class while she's on maternity leave keeps playing *Good Will Hunting* instead of actually teaching. "These teachers straight out of college have no work ethic," Marianne complains.

"Marianne, you're only twenty-nine. You're acting like the sub is from a different generation," Chloe says.

"She is! She sends me emails about the *vibes* of the classroom. I don't care about *vibes.* I care about whether the students understand Euclidean vectors."

"Really?" Sloane asks. "Because I have no idea what Euclidean vectors are, I have never once used them, but *vibes* can be critical to someone's life."

"Well, Euclidean vectors are critical to math teachers."

"Maybe get some perspective about everyone else," Sloane snaps.

Marianne rolls her eyes. "You are lecturing me about perspective? As you complain about the standards of your catering teams?"

"It's important to me." Sloane enunciates every word.

Marianne's eyes narrow. "And what about what's important to me?"

Chloe steps in between her two friends. It's a position she's familiar with. Sloane and Marianne are polar opposites, but most times their differences bring them closer. There's no competition, the hindrance to many female friendships. But something about this exchange feels different. Fragile. Chloe looks back and forth between her friends and sees their growing divide. Marianne's exhaustion and Sloane's quest to create a perfect vacation has put them on edge. But Chloe knows there's deeper pain bubbling beneath the surface.

"The vibes of this dinner look immaculate, Sloane," Chloe says, hoping to defuse the tension.

"Totally," Marianne says, not even trying to hide her sarcasm. She heads down the beach and pulls out her phone to call Noah. Sloane walks in the opposite direction toward the catering crew. Chloe stands alone, staring at the purple and coral streaks in the sky as the sun sets over the ocean.

Chloe's toes burrow into the powdery white sand, and the Gulf breeze tingles her bare arms. She tries to make herself relax, but that seems like an impossible task when she's navigating silly squabbles and an ex who may or may not want to fling his dinner in her direction this evening.

Luke and Alden walk past her toward the table set up by the caterers. Luke seems totally unaffected by her presence, which is more annoying than him being blatantly combative. Alden is discussing an IPO and shareholder dilution, and it's the last conversation Chloe wants to join, but she wonders if she should try.

Thankfully, Wyatt stops at her side, and she's relieved to see his friendly face. "Hanging in there?" he asks.

"Barely," she answers honestly. "He seems fine," she says, subtly gesturing toward Luke.

"That's just because he's a better liar than you." Wyatt leans toward Chloe and whispers, the warmth of his breath tickling her ear. "Luke changed his shirt three times."

"That makes me feel so much better," Chloe sighs.

"Wanna play a game tonight?"

Chloe genuinely smiles for the first time since seeing Luke. "Absolutely," she tells Wyatt.

"We drink every time we feel poor," Wyatt says.

Chloe shakes her head, laughing. "I do not have a tolerance strong enough for that game. Look at this place." Chloe uses one arm to motion at the beachside dinner arrangements and the other to point out Sloane and Alden's house in the background.

There's a rectangular table covered in a white tablecloth with a burlap runner down the center. Hurricane glasses with votive candles flicker down the middle next to silver mint julep cups filled with pale pink roses. As Chloe steps closer, she finds blue and white china, antique silverware, and seafoam-green napkins that match the water. In the center of each place setting is a printed menu for the evening.

In Chloe's mind, dinner on the beach involves takeout containers and maybe a blanket. Not this. It's a whole room that's been created outside, and somehow Sloane ordered even the weather to behave appropriately. A little breeze, enough to cool your skin but not enough to disturb the candle-induced ambience.

Chloe picks up a menu and reads about the foods she will eat while trying to make small talk with the man whose heart she broke. Crostini with goat cheese and peach preserves followed by shrimp with stone-ground grits, and then bread pudding with whiskey cream sauce for dessert.

Her stomach grumbles because breakfast was airport yogurt, and lunch was a bad decision iced coffee that only made her more anxious. Chloe's dinner is usually a couple of scrambled eggs and maybe some popcorn, both of which she eats in front of her laptop while she watches Netflix. The difference between her norm and Sloane's makes Chloe feel like a toddler.

Next to the dinner table, there is a bonfire being lit, with teak lounge chairs arranged in a circle and tufted cushions on the side, providing too many seating options for a group this small. There's also a basket with graham crackers, marshmallows, and chocolate bars. And long sticks. Sharp objects seem like the only planning mistake Sloane made.

It's overwhelming, the amount of effort and extravagance Sloane has put into this dinner. Chloe would have been fine with sandwiches on the kitchen island, and she suspects the rest of their friends feel the same. But she'd never tell Sloane. Over the years, Chloe's learned that it's important to celebrate what matters to those you love. And it's clear Sloane needs to be in control of hosting the perfect dinner. So Chloe is going to work hard to make sure that happens. Even though she feels like a child sneaking into her parents' party.

"Is all of this for us?" Chloe asks Wyatt. "It seems like a lot."

"And this is day one," Wyatt comments.

"I would have been fine with Waffle House takeout," Chloe replies. "Ever miss Waffle House days?"

"All the time," Wyatt says, dragging out each word. "Especially those two weeks you got us banned."

"Biggest mistake of my life," Chloe quickly replies.

Wyatt turns, an amusing gleam in his eyes as he asks, "Really?"

"Well, next to . . ." Chloe stops herself. "Never mind. The last thing I want to do is dissect all of my mistakes tonight."

"Good plan," Wyatt smirks. "So about this drinking game. You up for it? Because Sloane's temporary outdoor dining situation makes my apartment look like squalor. I figure we need to start chugging now."

"Same," Chloe sighs. "Apparently, over the last year Sloane and Alden turned into grown-ups. How did that happen?"

"Millions of dollars."

Chloe sighs, "I'm going to be a child forever."

"You say that like it's a bad thing," Wyatt comments. "Your thrift store couch is very comfortable, and your face doesn't look like that when you're about to eat dinner."

Wyatt points across the beach to where Sloane's face is pulled in a disgusted expression as she examines a plate of food the chef has prepared.

A waiter walks over with a tray of cocktails and offers Chloe a glass. She quickly accepts and takes a long sip.

"Game on," Wyatt says, reaching for his own glass.

"How many of my poor choices are you going to encourage this week?" Chloe asks Wyatt.

"Hopefully? All of them." Wyatt kisses Chloe on the cheek and walks away. And somehow, she feels better.

Chloe takes another sip of the cocktail and asks the waiter, "What is this?"

"It's a Bushwacker," the waiter answers.

Chloe holds up the frosty glass and eyes the milky coffee-colored drink inside. "What's in this thing?" she asks, gulping down more.

"Rum, Kahlúa, coconut, and ice cream," the waiter explains.

"Say less," Chloe holds up her hand. "I will have a second." She grabs another glass and makes her double-fisting way over to the table, sipping her adult milkshake.

She finds the place card with her name next to Marianne. As Chloe sits down, Marianne whispers, "I switched your seat. You are no longer next to Luke. You're welcome."

"Nipple, nipple, nipple," Chloe murmurs. Everyone except Wyatt seems too focused on the flurry of waiters delivering food to hear her.

But Wyatt clearly does and puts an arm on the back of her chair as he asks, "Are you playing drinking games with someone else or do you have some new interests you'd like to share?"

"It's my safe word. With Marianne."

"That answer applies to both scenarios I described. I need more information," Wyatt says.

"Marianne said she would help me escape if I was feeling overwhelmed. *Nipple* is the code word she suggested, and I've said it at least a dozen times and I'm still here. She's an awful crisis buddy."

Marianne leans over. "You are overusing our code word. It only works if it's used in true crises. Not every single uncomfortable moment. And if you tell everyone about the code word, it kind of defeats the purpose."

Sloane finally stops chatting with the caterer as they drop off plates and joins everyone at the table.

Chloe watches as Sloane's eyes focus in her direction and immediately narrow.

"The Bushwackers are supposed to be served with dessert," Sloane says. It looks like she's about to make a waiter cry. Chloe's mind reels on how to fix this situation because she doesn't think she can handle any additional conflict.

"I couldn't wait to try one," Chloe says, trying to keep Sloane at the table. "This is the best thing I've ever put in my mouth."

Wyatt starts to speak, but Chloe cuts him off. "Don't make that joke."

Marianne swallows down whatever resentment was bubbling earlier and helpfully adds, "Everything looks amazing, Sloane."

"Well, the chef put cilantro on the appetizer, which is a disaster. And the Bushwackers were served too soon. It looks like I'm going to be looking for a new catering crew. But at least everyone is here. So let's enjoy." Sloane sits and raises a glass of champagne.

"I like cilantro," Chloe says in between bites of the crostini.

"Don't be ridiculous. It tastes like soap," Sloane says as she picks off every green speck on her plate.

Maybe it's the second Bushwacker Chloe dives into or the decade of friendship that gives the group the ability to pick up and talk about anything or nothing with equal comfort, but somehow Chloe starts enjoying herself. The food is delicious: tangy goat cheese with juicy peaches; creamy grits dotted with ham served alongside blackened Gulf shrimp. It feels like she's playing pretend at a fancier life as they eat dinner by candlelight to the sound of soft waves in the background.

And between Sloane and Alden's stories about living in Seaside juxtaposed with Marianne's anecdotes about motherhood, there's not a moment of silence, everyone talking over one another, hungry for more information about these new lives they've missed.

Everyone, that is, except Chloe and Luke. They're careful to make sure that their voices never overlap. They don't speak to each other, directly or by accident. They seem to navigate around questions about their lives and volley between discussions to make sure they aren't ever involved in the same chat.

Chloe keeps looking over at Luke. Not once do their eyes meet. She keeps expecting him to say something—yell at her or cry or scream *Why, Chloe?* like some heartbroken movie hero, but he doesn't do any of those overly dramatic things. He seems fine. Actually, he seems happy. He's laughing with Alden about some golf story and he's asking Marianne whether Teddy is eating solid foods and he's telling Sloane that the shrimp are perfectly cooked.

The fact that he's basically ignored Chloe since their initial exchange is even more devastating than any of the anger Chloe expected. Because maybe that means her absence isn't as devastating as his.

When they've finished dinner, and Wyatt has made Chloe chug yet another cocktail when Sloane mentions that she and Alden took a quick trip to France to source the wooden table in the kitchen, and Chloe can feel the bread pudding sinking into her stomach but she still roasts two marshmallows because she feels obligated to utilize every aspect of this elaborate dinner, Alden suggests that they go back to the house and change into swimsuits. Apparently, there's a hot tub on the roof deck.

The thought of putting on a bathing suit when she's consumed three solid pounds of food this evening is the least desirable thing Chloe can imagine.

Until Luke shows up at her side.

"How about we go for a walk?" Luke asks.

Chloe chokes on her marshmallow. Wyatt slaps her on the back. Twice. By the time Chloe swallows and tries to tell Wyatt that a third slap is unnecessary, Marianne has joined the conversation.

"What's happening? Do we need to talk about our nipples, Chloe?"

Luke looks horrified and Wyatt nods. "Yes, you two go talk about your nipples."

"What's wrong with your nipples?" Luke reluctantly asks.

"Nothing," Chloe quickly says, staring daggers at both Wyatt and Marianne. "I'd love to go on a walk with you, Luke."

"You would?" Wyatt and Marianne ask together.

"Yes." Chloe reaches for Luke's arm and pulls him away from the bonfire before Marianne can embarrass her more.

But as soon as her fingers touch his skin and feel the velvet warmth of his tense forearm, she pulls back. It's hard to stop your body from doing the simple things it's done without thinking for years.

Chloe and Luke are quiet for the first few minutes, but once they are far enough up the beach, out of listening distance of the crew of spies that they call their friends, Chloe turns to Luke and says, "Thank you for talking to me." She takes a deep breath as she continues, "All I want is for us to be friends, Luke."

Luke stops walking and bends down to pick up a shell. "I have no idea how to be your friend, Chloe." Luke turns the shell back and forth between his hands, never looking into her eyes. "But I figured if we're going to make it through this week, we need to talk."

"I know," she says. "And maybe we can figure out the friendship thing this week. At least, I hope so." She knows she sounds stupidly optimistic.

"Dinner was painful," Luke says.

"Really? I thought it was so great. Sloane's gone to so much trouble and it was so much fun to be back together . . ."

"Cut the shit, Chlo."

"You're right. It was painful. I was worried all night about upsetting you."

"You never seemed to care about that before," Luke says to the sand.

"I've always cared." Chloe says. Then she takes a deep breath and rips off the Band-Aid, trying, again, to have the conversation she wanted to have at the diner a year ago. "I know I hurt you."

Luke clears his throat and loudly says, "I don't want to talk about that. All I meant is that you've always said what's on your mind. You're acting weird. And it's making me feel weird. And everyone else is already acting weird."

"I don't know what's normal anymore. None of that," Chloe says, pointing back at the dinner setup, "is normal in my life."

"I know. We're all getting used to having friends who are millionaires. Even Sloane and Alden are still getting used to it. He wants to buy a boat, and when I sent him his budget, he thought I'd made a mistake."

"Why?"

"Because his boat budget is bigger than most people's house budgets."

"Why does anyone need a boat that costs as much as a house?"

"No one needs this much money. But once you have it, it's a hard adjustment figuring out how to spend it."

"And that's what you're doing now? Telling Alden how to spend his money. Isn't that weird?"

"I think when your life changes this much this quickly, it's helpful to have someone you trust. I didn't ask to be his advisor. But he came to me after we handled the sale of his company. I'm just trying to help a friend."

Chloe nods. "Of course. You're right. He's lucky to have you."

"Thanks." Luke keeps walking down the beach and Chloe follows.

"It's not just the money that's so different," Chloe says as the waves cover her feet. "I don't know how to act around everyone now that I'm not your girlfriend."

"I don't think any of us know how to navigate this situation," Luke says.

"Do you think it's possible?"

"What?"

"Still being in each other's lives? Still sharing the same best friends?"

"Honestly? No. But Sloane and Alden seem to think so. I guess that's what this week is about."

"How did Sloane convince you to come?" Chloe asks tentatively.

"She didn't."

"Was it Alden?"

"Not exactly. Sloane called my secretary with flight details. I told my secretary to cancel. But my boss overheard. It's complicated because the sale of Alden's company was one of our firm's biggest deals. I can't turn down networking opportunities because I want to avoid run-ins with my ex."

Chloe winces. She hates that a trip with friends is now a networking opportunity. She hates being called Luke's ex. An accurate label, but it feels painful to reduce their past to such a tiny word.

Luke continues. "Basically, between my boss and Sloane, they're equal on the scary to disappoint scale. So here I am." Luke looks over his shoulder and shoves his hands in his pockets. "Why are you here? You've stayed away for a year, but then Wyatt calls me and says you're coming. Why?"

Chloe stops walking. "Because Sloane needed me." She doesn't elaborate. Before he can ask more questions, Chloe continues, "And because being without your best friends for a year is a long time. I've missed my friends. All of my friends," staring intently into Luke's eyes.

"It's harder to see you than I thought it would be." Luke swallows, the lump in his throat distracting Chloe's focus. "And I knew it was going to be hard. But I'm having to remind my hands that they don't touch you anymore. And I'm having to remind my mouth not to laugh at your jokes."

Chloe's breath pauses, unprepared for the impact Luke's words have on her body. "Well, if it makes you feel any better, my hand feels itchy not holding yours." She steps forward, but Luke takes a step back.

"Stop. You ended it. And I can't handle you saying things like that to me."

"I didn't end it, Luke. I said no. But you're the one who refused to talk to me. Who packed up all my things. You're the one who ended us."

Luke stares at the sky as he shouts, "You wanted to get married. You'd been saying that for years. Was it a game?"

"Of course it wasn't." Chloe can't hide the way her voice cracks.

"You crushed me, in front of an audience of our best friends. You wasted a decade of our lives. No warning. Not a single indication that you didn't want to spend your life with me. I will never understand you, Chloe."

"Luke, we have so much to talk about . . ."

"I don't want to talk," Luke shouts. "Not now and not then, because there's nothing you could say that would fix what you did to us."

Chloe feels disappointment wash over her. She hoped a year would dull his anger, but if anything he seems even more upset now. "What do you want, Luke?"

"We get through this week. Bare minimum of contact."

"I think that's going to be harder than you think. Sloane has some mastermind plan for forcing us together."

"I know. Alden told me." Luke turns around and starts walking back to the beach house. "I'm going to pretend that I can handle being in the same room as you. We'll do our best to get through this week. But after that, I need to be completely done, Chloe."

"No. We can't do that to our friends. We have to find a way to work this out."

"No. We don't. I can't be your friend."

"Well, too bad," she says. "We share best friends. We are going to see each other again. I'm sorry I hurt you. But you hurt me too."

Luke whips around and Chloe is convinced that this is the moment he's going to explode. This is the moment she's been waiting for all night. Except he doesn't. Instead, he closes his eyes, his jaw pulsing as his face tilts upward and then he walks away.

"Luke, where are you going?" Chloe shouts after him.

"Back to the house," Luke says, seemingly unfazed.

Chloe runs after him. "We need a plan for this week and for everything. I don't want to keep our friends in the middle of this."

"You created this problem, you figure it out. I'm going to the hot tub." All emotion in Luke's voice has been erased.

Chloe stands still while Luke walks away, seemingly unbothered. That's the problem. Chloe can feel every drop of tension, every twitch of discomfort among her friends. She wants to fix the situation. She wants things to go back to the way they were, but Luke seems perfectly content to stew in their silence. Which means nothing will ever change. Chloe will always be left out, partly because it's easier for everyone else and partly because Chloe hates being the problem.

Maybe Sloane's scheming is exactly what she needs, enough time alone with Luke so that he forgets his hurt and remembers that, at the end of the day, even if they aren't married, they're still best friends.

When Chloe finally makes it back to the house, she can hear the laughter coming from the roof deck. They are all together, lounging in the bubbly hot water, likely drinking something delicious prepared by the caterers Sloane will never hire again. And Chloe is alone. Again.

She hangs up Sloane's dress in the closet. She washes her face and brushes her teeth. She slips into the crisp, cool sheets and pulls them over her head, turtling into the makeshift shelter of very expensive bedding. When Chloe closes her eyes, it's the same image she sees every night. Luke and their friends, walking away, while she stands by herself.

♦ 7 ♦

Eight Years Ago

CHLOE STOOD ON THE cliffs near her home. This stretch of the California coast was so wild and untamed that she felt free to be any version of herself she desired. As a child, she pretended to be an explorer, a captured princess, a lost bird, the ocean tides crashing with varying intensity seeming to encourage changing roles. It used to be her favorite spot, but she wondered whether she'd ever feel safe in this place again.

Her brother's voice echoed in her head, his childhood stutter returning as he stumbled out words about a car accident. Ever since that moment one week ago, Chloe felt like it was impossible to take full breaths.

As she stood on the high overlook of the Pacific Ocean, she forced herself to breathe the air of a world in which her parents were no longer alive.

Her parents loved their dog, a rescue puppy that had the face of a German shepherd and the body of a beagle. They took her everywhere, on car rides especially. A sudden jump. That's what the police officer described. The dog must have jumped, startling her father, who swerved across three lanes of traffic. They didn't suffer, the officer said. They died instantly.

Chloe knew it was supposed to bring comfort, but it didn't. To be alive one moment and gone the next. No time to think about who and what mattered in life. No time to reflect on a well-loved and well-lived life. Chloe couldn't imagine anything more tragic.

Last week, Chloe had been complaining about finals, and how much she was going to miss everyone over the summer. Wyatt was going to be interning at the town paper, and Sloane and Marianne were working in the alumni office along with Alden and Luke. Sloane told Chloe that she could get a job too. Five students seemed like too many students to staff a tiny office and make phone calls asking for donations, but somehow Chloe knew Sloane could make it happen. But Chloe's parents convinced her to spend the summer in California, promising road trips up the coast visiting different galleries and introducing her to all of their local artist friends. As much as Chloe loved campus, she needed the recharge of her parents and a summer without humidity.

It was the end of sophomore year. And next summer, the year before graduation, would be the time to focus on internships and their future. This summer, her parents had argued, was the summer to play.

They had called her together. Chloe's parents always did that, each speaking on the phone over each other, excited to tell her about tiny mundane details of their day. They were describing a new restaurant in town when Chloe cut them off. She said she needed to get back to studying. But she would see them next week, she had said. Her mother was describing a new granola she'd discovered at the farmers market. She'd pick some up when Chloe was home. Chloe had mumbled, "Sounds good," and hung up the phone. Those were the last words they spoke. Maybe she said, "You too" when her parents said, "We love you" as the phone disconnected.

Did it matter that Chloe got to read her notes on Surrealist painters one more time? Not when she could have heard about her mother's latest knitting project. Or the vintage Ford her father was restoring. Or the watercress salad they ate at lunch. Instead, Chloe prepared for her exams while her parents took a spontaneous drive down the coast. For the first time in her life, Chloe wished they were less adventurous. Boring, but still alive.

She'd been in bed with Luke when her phone rang. She saw her brother's number and ignored the call. But when he called back, once and then twice more, she answered, pulling on Luke's T-shirt and swinging her feet over the edge of the bed. Luke was kissing her shoulder, slipping his arm around her waist, fingers trailing lower, trying to distract her. It was working, her mind barely registering her brother's voice. But when her body froze, when she swatted away Luke's hand and screamed into the phone, Luke wasn't sure what to do. After the moment when Chloe's brother relayed the horrifying news, Chloe knew nothing would ever be the same again.

As she stood on the cliffs in Monterey, her fingers rubbed back and forth over the necklace her mother had given her on her sixteenth birthday. Chloe needed to get back inside the house to help her brother, but all she really wanted was a few quiet moments to imagine that her parents were still alive.

Chloe felt Luke's presence before he said a word. As he extended his steady arms, she felt herself collapsing into his chest. From the moment she had received her brother's call to this moment before the funeral, Luke had barely left Chloe's side. She never asked. He just showed up.

"Sorry I skipped out of there," Chloe said.

"You aren't obligated to do anything, Chloe," Luke whispered.

Chloe fidgeted with the hem of her dress. A thread had come loose and she pulled, making the whole thing unravel. When she looked down, she saw that half of the bottom had come undone. It looked as ragged as she felt.

"I'm ready to go inside," Chloe said.

"Are you sure? We can stay out here all afternoon."

"I don't want to leave Ezra alone," Chloe said. But she knew her older brother wasn't really alone. Ezra was married, and their newborn had been a welcome source of distraction over the last week. It was the longest stretch of time Chloe had spent with her nephew since he was born while she was away at school. Ezra lived only twenty minutes away from her parents, and his wife seemed more comfortable in Chloe's childhood home than she did.

There were little things that were different. Her mother had changed the pillows on the living room sofa. The pantry was reorganized, and Chloe couldn't find the oatmeal. It was in a drawer now, Ezra's wife showed her. It was a strange, untethered feeling she'd experienced all week. Tiny differences in a house shouldn't matter because home was wherever her parents were. Except they were gone. And in their absence, each tiny difference made Chloe feel like there was no place she now belonged.

"Let's go back inside," Chloe said, walking up the pathway toward her parents' house. But halfway up the steps, she stopped.

She stared at the four people approaching, her eyes narrowing at the mirage. But when she looked at Luke, who smiled sheepishly and shrugged, and then back to the faces approaching, she felt overwhelmed by emotion.

Sloane, Alden, Marianne, and Wyatt were waiting at the top of the stairs. And when Chloe finally got over her shock and climbed to join them, she was immediately surrounded and hugged so tightly that it muffled her tears.

"What are you guys doing here?" Chloe stuttered.

"We want to be here for you," Sloane said.

"We insisted," Marianne added.

Chloe looked at Luke, her face full of questions.

"They want to help" was Luke's simple answer.

Chloe had told her friends to stay at Mayfield. It seemed like too much hassle for four people to fly across the country for two strangers' funerals.

"You're missing finals," Chloe tried to argue.

"You're more important than all of that." Alden said the words, but Chloe knew it wasn't true. Alden obsessed over every single quiz grade. She couldn't imagine him bailing on finals.

"Sloane got us all extensions," Wyatt explained.

Chloe laughed. For the first time in a week, she laughed at the undeniable negotiating power of her friend. "Of course she did."

"We still would have come," Marianne added. "We're your family too."

Most friendships are fun. Parties and inside jokes and brunch discussions of bad outfits over poorly poached eggs. Those friendships are important, but many times, friendships never move below that joyful surface.

In that moment, when they showed up for Chloe, it moved their friendship deeper. Because when she walked into her childhood home, wrapped in the five of them, she didn't feel so alone.

The next few days were a blur. Somehow, Sloane and Ezra's wife coordinated food for everyone. Alden helped Ezra access passwords and login information for her parents' accounts on her dad's laptop. Marianne was a baby whisperer, never once complaining even when she was covered in spit-up. Wyatt sat down with Chloe and helped her with the obituary.

It was a task Chloe hadn't anticipated being so difficult, but reducing two whole lives into two simple paragraphs seemed impossible. Wyatt sat as Chloe talked for hours about her parents and everything she thought the world should know about them. And somehow, Wyatt managed to write the most beautiful words about people he'd never met. When Ezra broke down in tears reading the obituary, Chloe was even more grateful to have Wyatt in her life.

Luke did everything else. Ezra and Chloe struggled with the logistics; the list of tasks seemed overwhelming for the siblings. But Luke handled all of it. Finding the will, contacting the insurance company and the bank, and filing all the offensive paperwork the federal government required to prove the people you love most are actually dead. Luke was a college student. He shouldn't have known how to handle a situation no one is prepared for. And yet he called his mother to ask all the legal questions about notifying Social Security and filing for a death certificate. He handled all the phone calls from people expressing condolences, sentiments Chloe couldn't bear to hear. Luke didn't even know these people, and yet he listened as they grieved and said all of the things. He kept a list of who sent flowers and even wrote thank-you notes, something Chloe would have forgotten even if she was able to hold a pen without crying.

He gave Chloe a list each morning of things she needed to do and things he was going to handle, and then at night he studied for his exams because they still had to finish their sophomore year.

They all stayed for an entire week. Chloe barely remembered those days, except she knew her friends were by her side.

"You should transfer," Ezra said once everyone had left and they were back in an empty house. Chloe didn't have to return for finals. Her professors said they would give her a grade based on her work earlier in the semester. "You can live in Mom and Dad's house," Ezra said.

Chloe shook her head. She knew that her parents would want Ezra to raise his family in this home. No matter what the will said, there was no way she was going to sell a place that meant so much so that she could split money she didn't need with her brother.

It turned out her parents had life insurance that would cover the rest of her college tuition and give her a cushion better than most new graduates had. To Chloe, the house was an extra she didn't need. But having her brother live in this place, so that the memories could stay in their family, was something she desperately wanted.

"You and Jillian and the baby are going to move here. You're going to raise that adorable hellion in the same backyard we played in, not some rental house across town."

"We don't need this much space," Ezra tried to argue, but it was pointless. Chloe could tell that Ezra wanted it just as much as she did. "You could live here with us."

Chloe shook her head. "I love you. But I can't wedge my life into yours."

"You need family, Chloe. You can't go back to that school all by yourself."

"I'm not. I have my friends," Chloe said.

It took some convincing, but eventually Ezra got on board with Chloe's return to Mayfield. Chloe suspected that Jillian had played a role, persuading her husband that living with a baby was not an ideal situation for a college student.

When Chloe called Sloane and asked if she could get her a summer job in the alumni office, Sloane squealed and said, "Consider it done."

When Chloe came back to campus that June, she was a mess. There were weeks when she struggled to get out of bed.

But Sloane was there each morning. Some days she pushed, forcing Chloe to put on clothes and walk outside. Some days she sat at the end of the bed so Chloe wasn't alone. In those early, heady days of grief when most people flee because it is uncomfortable to be surrounded by so much pain, Sloane showed up. She pulled Chloe out.

And when Chloe was finally able to wake up on her own, to start a day, Marianne was there to help her fill it. They got very into adult coloring books. There was something almost meditative about filling in the designs as they monitored the alumni office phones. And doing it together made Chloe feel less alone.

Chloe pushed Luke away. But he never left. For most of that summer, Chloe told Luke she wanted to be alone. She cried too often, at the most inopportune times—when she saw a family taking a campus tour, when she saw her father's favorite pen in the campus bookstore, when she burned toast in the cafeteria, a trait directly inherited from her mother.

Her relationship with Luke still felt too young and too new for him to witness these emotions. She built a wall around her heart and her body and locked him out.

Anyone else would have given up. There's only so much distance young love can take. But Luke kept coming back. He sat outside her dorm door for two hours every night, just to be there until she fell asleep. In their year of dating, he'd had a few phone calls with Chloe's dad, mostly leading up to parent visits and how the school's football season was going. So Luke wrote down every word he could remember about those conversations. And he'd slip those stories under Chloe's door so she could read about other people's memories of the parents she loved.

Luke called Ezra every afternoon to update him on how Chloe was doing. And he sent a birthday present to Ezra's wife Jillian, an occasion Chloe forgot about and then panicked.

But mostly, he was there for Chloe. When she needed him and when she didn't. He made himself available, without expectations and without questions. Outside of the hours he was at work, he was otherwise within eyesight of Chloe. If she wanted to talk to him. To hug him. To yell at him because the anger at having her parents stolen sometimes diverted to whoever was closest. Luke was there. He had started telling Chloe he loved her in March. But it wasn't until the end of that summer, a summer filled with so much heartache, that Chloe knew he really did.

And by fall, when Chloe was ready to cry herself to sleep on Luke's chest instead of in an empty bed, he was still there.

◆ 8 ◆

This Year

THE FIRST MORNING IN Sloane and Alden's beach house, everyone follows Sloane's instructions: *Be ready by ten and wear a swimsuit.*

They all climb into Sloane and Alden's Range Rover, Chloe and Marianne sitting in the third row like middle schoolers on the way to soccer practice. There's a bag of towels in the back of the car, and Chloe wonders why they aren't spending the day on the perfectly manicured, snow-white beach in front of the house. The beach where they can spread out and avoid awkward conversations instead of the tightly enclosed vehicle where everyone's hangovers and resentments swirl.

"Where are we going?" Chloe shouts from the back of the car.

Alden is driving, and Luke is in the front passenger seat. Sloane had tried to force Luke into the middle row, claiming she gets terrible carsickness these days. Luke argued that his legs were too long to be cramped in the middle, to which Wyatt shrugged and said, "I think you can suffer through." But he wouldn't. Luke and Sloane stood in an awkward

standoff for five minutes, fighting over seats in a car like siblings, until Alden said, "Either get in the car or walk." Sloane
huffed as she climbed in the middle next to Wyatt, mumbling
about how her plans were already going off the rails.

Sloane turns around, giddy as she answers Chloe's question. "Stand-up paddleboarding. It's so much fun."

"In the ocean?" Luke asks.

"No. We're going to a dune lake," Sloane says.

"What's a dune lake?" Chloe asks.

"I'm getting carsick," Sloane says. "I have to turn around.
Google it."

Marianne whispers out of the side of her mouth. "I have a
guidebook. There's a chapter on dune lakes." Marianne reaches
into the diaper bag she's using as a purse and hands a book to
Chloe.

"I didn't know they still printed these," Chloe says, flip-
ping through the glossy pages.

"I checked it out at the library," Marianne says. "They
have a baby story hour. I'm there a lot. It's a social activity."

"Sitting around with a bunch of infants at a library is not
social," Sloane says, staring out the car window. "Don't let
your entire life become about a baby."

The entire car is silent. Everyone knows Sloane, that her
good intentions are often lost in overbearing delivery. But this
statement seems to have gone too far. And Sloane's lack of
awareness makes it worse. Chloe looks at Marianne and sees
her jaw moving back and forth.

"Teddy," Marianne says, swallowing slowly. "My son's
name is Teddy. And I am completely fine with him being my
whole life right now, Sloane."

"You're right. I apologize." It sounds like Sloane means it,
but she doesn't elaborate and rolls down the window, the outside wind hopefully easing her motion sickness and blocking
any further discussion.

"What's with her?" Marianne asks, leaning over and whispering in Chloe's ear.

"She's cranky. Maybe Alden forgot to feed her this morning?" Chloe tries to joke away the tension. But it only seems to make things worse, Marianne retreating into silence along with the rest of the car.

Chloe spends the next few minutes reading Marianne's guidebook. The coastal dune lakes along this stretch of beach in Florida only occur in four other places in the world. They form over time when fresh water fills depressions in the dunes, creating unique habitats for fish, turtles, birds, and the occasional alligator. They're also calm, perfect for paddleboarding.

When they pull into the sand and gravel parking lot next to the dune lake, everyone jumps out of the car as soon as it stops moving.

The dune lake is beautiful. Tall grasses surround the border, with peek-a-boo views of the Gulf and water pathways that wind around the sand. There's a small shed set up off to the side with paddleboards and kayaks propped between wooden slats.

Luke is the first to take a life jacket and one of the long boards. He fidgets with the buckles as he's given a few brief instructions, and then he pushes out into the water.

When Chloe came downstairs this morning and fixed herself a bowl of yogurt topped with fresh mango and papaya, homemade granola, and coconut flakes from the buffet Sloane had arranged with the morning catering crew, Luke left the kitchen. He muttered something about getting ready. Except he was already dressed and this outing didn't seem to require any advance preparation. It's obvious Luke simply wants to avoid Chloe.

Chloe's never been paddleboarding before, but a few friends from her yoga studio rave about it. Knowing she has decent balance, she's not too concerned. But she still listens intently as the rental guide goes over the best spots to explore and carefully attaches the paddleboard strap to her ankle.

Chloe pushes off and sees the rest of her friends standing on the edge of the lake. "Are you guys coming?" Chloe asks.

"I forgot my credit card," Sloane yells out across the water. "I need to head back to the house. Alden's going to give me a ride."

"I'm getting sunburned," Marianne says. "I'm going to head back too and grab more sunscreen."

"They sell sunscreen right there," Chloe says, gesturing to the rental desk and almost losing her balance in the process.

"It's not my brand," Marianne lies, not even trying to make it sound convincing.

Luke must hear the shouting because he paddles over to see what is going on.

"Why isn't anyone else in the water?" Luke asks Chloe.

"This is a trap. A Sloane trap. What's your excuse, Wyatt?" Chloe asks, catching on to the blatantly obvious trick their friends are playing.

"Sloane is scary," Wyatt shrugs. "Sorry, guys. You two have fun out there."

Chloe and Luke stand in the middle of the lake, balancing on their boards, as their four friends pile back into Sloane and Alden's car and drive away.

"What are we supposed to do?" Luke asks.

"Stand here like idiots," Chloe says. She looks over at Luke. His normally confident posture has been altered to wobbly baby giraffe legs. He's terrible at paddleboarding, and Chloe tries hard not to point this out.

"Do you think they'll come back?" Luke asks with a hint of panic.

"Eventually." Chloe paddles farther out.

"Wait. Where are you going?" Luke asks.

"To explore. Might as well enjoy this paddleboard kidnapping." Chloe looks forward, dipping the paddle into the water and pulling it backward as she skims the lake's surface. There's no one else on the lake, and although she's annoyed with Sloane's scheming, there are worse places to be abandoned. It's almost meditative, and Chloe can use all the calming exercise possible this week.

Chloe looks over her shoulder and sees Luke, immobile. He's having trouble balancing, and the way his head is moving back and forth suggests that he has no idea where he is going to go. He stares at the sky, and Chloe takes pity.

She circles back toward him and asks, "Are you okay?"

Luke tries to shake his head, but even the subtle movement seems to impact his balance. "Can we stick together?" Luke asks.

"Why?" Chloe knows that Luke would never willingly ask for time together.

"I don't really know what I'm doing," Luke manages to say in a stilted voice. "I kind of rushed through the instructions. I figured Alden could fill me in when he got out."

"Stand. Paddle. Those were the instructions," Chloe says suspiciously.

Chloe starts out on the route the guide recommended. The dune lake is open at the beginning, but then narrows as it gets closer to the Gulf. There's a hill of sand in front of them blocking the ocean, and winding water pathways that seem to go on for miles. Chloe loves how the terrain expands and contracts, creating a secret escape from the more well-traveled beach.

Even though it is still early, the sun is hot, and Chloe is grateful for her wide straw hat and the sunscreen she remembered to apply, unlike Marianne. Allegedly. She looks over her shoulder and sees Luke following, wobbling on the board, his feet shifting as he constantly tries to maintain his balance.

"Tighten your stomach," she instructs. "It makes it easier."

Luke must have listened to her instructions because the next time she looks back, he seems more comfortable. There's a calming rhythm to the way the board glides over the water and the paddle propels her forward, silent motion as the landscape slowly changes. Chloe wishes her mind could feel as peaceful as her body.

They are silent for too long, an awkwardness building because there is no one else out on the water and there's nothing but the sound of seagulls filling the air. Chloe pushes her paddle in the opposite direction, stopping the forward momentum so that Luke can catch up.

He looks uncomfortable. That's probably because he is, Chloe thinks. But she is unclear as to whether it's the wobbling paddleboard or her that is the primary source of discomfort.

When she can no longer tolerate the silence, she says, "This is nice."

"No, it's not," Luke shouts. He must see Chloe's face fall because he quickly adds, "Lakes freak me out."

"They're too calm and peaceful?"

"On the surface," Luke says. "But you never know what's living underneath all of that calmness."

"You fish all the time," Chloe points out.

"In. A. Boat," he states through gritted teeth. "There's no protection with these boards." Luke points across the lake to the rental stand. "Can we go back to the beach?"

"I want to explore a little bit first," Chloe says. "Hang out and I'll get you on my way back."

She paddles off, but she quickly hears rough splashes behind her. When she turns around, she sees Luke slapping the water with the paddle as he tries to follow Chloe.

"Are you coming with me?" Chloe asks, unable to hide her shock.

"Better than the alternative of staying here alone," Luke says.

Chloe continues paddling. "Your fear of a fish-related death is stronger than your fear of me?"

"Yes," Luke quickly replies. "And I'm not afraid of you. I just don't . . ."

"Want to talk to me?" Chloe offers. "Want to see me again?"

"I don't know, Chloe. It's hard to know what I want when it comes to you."

Chloe doesn't respond. Even though she wants to. Even though she wants to ask why Luke seemed so unsure so many times in their relationship. And the one time she expressed any hesitancy, he interpreted that as the end. But instead, she saves those questions for later, when he tells her that he's ready to have a real conversation. And right now, it doesn't seem like they are ready for much more than basic attempts at civility.

"Well, if we're going to be paddleboarding buddies this morning, I want equal protection," Chloe says. "If an alligator comes at me, I expect a rescue attempt."

Luke hesitates for minute and asks, his voice barely a whisper, "Are there alligators in this lake?"

"How am I supposed to know? I didn't have time to finish reading Marianne's book. But in general, I think alligators like warm wetland situations." Chloe gestures around the lake, to the marshy forests around the edge that are so thick it is hard to see where the lake ends and land begins.

Luke is silent and when Chloe turns around, she sees that his face has gone white.

"They wouldn't let people rent paddleboards in alligator lakes," Luke says, sounding like he's trying to reassure himself.

"This is Florida. Not exactly the same safety standards as Manhattan, Luke."

He starts looking around nervously. "Oh my God, Chloe. I don't want to die like this."

"No one is going to die." She starts laughing, thinking Luke is joking but stops when she sees the seriousness on his face. "When did you become so afraid of alligators? How did I not know this?"

"How many alligator interactions did we have in our relationship?"

"Zero. But it seems like something I should have known."

"All reasonable people are afraid of alligators," Luke says defensively. "We have to go back." He tries to turn his board around, but his balance is already questionable. He bends down, trying to squat his giant man-body on the board, when there is a rustling at the edge of the lake. "Did you see something move over there?" Luke's voice has now moved past panic into terror territory.

"Yes," Chloe says slowly, trying to calm this person who is acting so unlike the Luke she's always known. "It's probably a snake. An alligator would make more movement."

"A snake is not better," Luke says through clenched teeth. "This is some Romeo and Juliet bullshit. Sloane's trying to get us to die together."

"I'm sure this is safe," Chloe says, trying to hide any hint of laughter in her voice.

All of a sudden, a crane lands on the edge of the lake. But because the bird lands behind Luke, he doesn't know it's just willowy, long-legged poultry. He must assume the worst because he turns abruptly, holding his paddle in the air, ready to use it as a weapon.

The sudden movement makes Luke lose his balance, and, predictably, he falls in the lake. But he also manages to fall with such force that his paddleboard flies away into the murky reeds at the edge of the water.

"Chloe, help," Luke screams as his head bobs in the water.

"Why wasn't your paddleboard attached to your ankle?" Chloe asks, slowly paddling in his direction.

"I don't know!" Luke says, gulping in water and then trying to spit it out.

Chloe would find this amusing, except in his panic, Luke seems to have forgotten the basics of how to swim. She bends down and tries to help him up on her board, but they both fall in the water in the process.

"Is it coming toward us?"

"What?"

"The alligator?"

"It was a crane, Luke. You tried to wallop a beautiful bird. Now get up on the board first and sit in the center."

Luke does as he is told, but he can't even manage to sit. Instead he lies on his stomach and grips the edges of the board. Chloe hands him the paddle. "Do not drop this. It's our only way back."

Luke seems to debate Chloe's instruction, eventually loosening his grip on the board and reaching out for the paddle's handle.

Chloe treads water, resting one arm on the side of the board. "You are the worst paddleboarder ever," she says.

"I kind of freaked out. Did you see where my board went?" Luke doesn't raise his head to look, seemingly afraid to make any sudden movements.

Chloe points to the edge of the lake. Pushed into the tall grasses and already covered in a layer of algae is Luke's board. "Let's go get it," Chloe says.

"Absolutely not. I will pay the replacement fee. If there is an alligator or a snake in this lake, that's its little home over there, and I'm not going near it."

"Luke. Don't you think you're overreacting a bit? You were right earlier. If they knew there were deadly creatures in this lake, they wouldn't set up a paddleboard business here."

"I'm not risking it."

"Well, how are we going to get back?" Chloe asks, thinking that the reverse *Titanic* situation isn't going to work much longer. Chloe is holding on to the side of the board, but it is too far for her to swim, and Luke seems incapable of basic functioning.

"We'll share your board," Luke says, and he moves two inches to the side, hardly enough room for another person.

Chloe can't think of another option. "Fine. Try to stay still." She slowly pulls herself up on the edge of the board, instructing Luke to shift sideways and distribute the weight. All of her yoga strength pays off at the same time all of Luke's obsessive neuroses come to light. The more Luke flails, the more likely they will both end up in the water, so Chloe spends equal amounts of energy trying to position herself and to settle Luke's jerky movements.

Chloe manages to get one leg up on the board and wrap one arm around Luke's waist, but the board tilts toward the water.

"Stop moving," she tells him, but it seems like a pointless instruction because Luke's eyes are shut and he is mumbling to himself something that sounds like a motivational mantra.

Slowly, she pulls her second leg out of the water and scoots toward the center of the board. There isn't enough space for two normal-sized people, and with Luke's long muscular body, there is nowhere for Chloe to put herself except practically on top of him.

It's not exactly an unfamiliar position. How many mornings did they wake up exactly like this, Chloe wrapping herself around him as his eyes slowly opened and his hand swept her blonde hair out of her face? Except now, with every brush of their bodies, the warmth of his skin feels unfamiliar and terrifying.

When Luke finally opens his eyes and sees Chloe next to him, he seems to realize that maybe there are more dangerous things than alligators in lakes. Dangerous things like exes pressed up against one another, lips mere inches apart, and a wobbly board that requires bodies touching whether they like it or not.

Chloe feels Luke's arm wrap around her waist, pulling her closer. His eyes never leave her face, staring with intensity. She can't decipher whether it's directed toward her or the situation. But when he reaches up and brushes a strand of her wet hair off her forehead, a motion he's done a million times, Chloe's eyes flutter closed. It's a strange sensation, her body debating whether she wants to freeze time or teleport away.

When her eyes open, Luke whispers, "You're here."

She can barely manage a nod, the electricity of his body pressed against every inch of hers, his hand still cupping her face, as she wonders what will happen next. As she wonders what she wants to happen next.

Chloe swallows and sees Luke's face moving forward. For a moment, it seems like he's forgotten his anger. He's forgotten that the person lying next to him is the person he claimed he never wanted to see again. It seems like he is just as drawn to her as he's ever been. And despite the words they exchanged a year ago, their bodies remember the decade before and the magnetic pull they've never been able to deny.

Chloe is frozen as Luke's lips hover above her own. But then, just as quickly as the moment came, it disappears, and Luke's face whips away, creating the few inches of distance they can manage wrapped together on this single paddleboard.

Chloe takes a deep breath and finally says, "I'm going to stand."

"Okay," Luke murmurs in the other direction.

"You can sit," she suggests. "I'll handle the paddling."

"That's probably a good idea." His words are mechanical, and immediately she knows that whatever happened, or almost happened, is over. For now.

Chloe stands and Luke hands her the paddle. After some maneuvering, they find their balance together. But she can't quite manage to paddle without feeling like her ass is directly in his face, making this situation even more awkward than it already was. She decides sitting is better.

She mumbles an excuse about having more leverage when she's on her knees.

Immediately her head whips around and Luke is fighting back a laugh.

"Don't say it," Chloe instructs.

"I wouldn't dare," he says through muffled laughter.

Luke sits with his legs spread in a wide V and Chloe is in the middle, her back to Luke's stomach as she tries to paddle forward without leaning too much into his body. But they can't help but brush against each other. And every time Chloe feels the firmness of Luke's chest against the strings of her bikini top, she feels the unconscious tugs of memories of what he used to do in these situations.

The way his fingers would trail up and down her bare skin.

The way he would wrap his arms around her body, holding her close enough that the murmur of his heartbeat filled her ear.

The fact that he always made her feel safe in a fragile world.

Thankfully, Luke can't see Chloe's face and the redness creeping up her neck.

"This is torture," she admits for more than one reason. It's difficult to paddle two people, especially when the other person is almost twice your size.

"I know. Who would paddleboard for fun?" he says, his voice even, annoyingly unaffected by this situation.

"I'm not talking about paddleboarding, Luke."

She lays the paddle in the middle of the board and carefully turns around, her face now inches apart from his.

"We have to talk. Now."

Luke tilts his head sideways. "But then Sloane wins."

"I wouldn't be surprised if she'd planned every bit of this," Chloe says. "She's probably been subconsciously feeding into your hidden fears of alligators knowing we would be stranded on a single board."

"Unlikely." Luke's eyes narrow, seemingly annoyed by Chloe's reference to his obvious phobia. "But the fact that there is even a chance of that happening is credit to Sloane's overall mastermind. Do you think any part of her life has ever gone off plan?"

Chloe hesitates before answering. "If it did," she says, "I'd imagine it would be very difficult for Sloane to manage."

"That's an understatement."

Chloe doesn't say more. Instead she asks, "Can we talk about us?"

"There is no *us*," he states.

"I want to be your friend, Luke. I miss you, but I also miss everyone else."

"Well, you should have thought of that."

Her eyes narrow. "I should have accepted your proposal so I wouldn't lose my best friends?"

"If you lost them, then maybe they weren't your best friends," Luke says.

This is the sinking moment she's been trying to avoid. Because what he said is her worst fear vocalized, from the person who probably understands the situation the best.

"Is that what you think, Luke? Honestly. Sloane and Alden and Marianne and Wyatt don't really care about me? They just pretended to be my friends for ten years because I was your girlfriend?"

Luke stares at Chloe, seeming to understand his comment's impact on the person sharing a slender floating board in the middle of a lake. "A part of me wishes it was true," he admits.

"Why?"

"Because it would make this thing between us easier."

"What thing?"

"I don't know what we are anymore, Chloe. We were never really friends. We were always more than that. Now I'm supposed to be in your life in some demoted role? I don't see how that works."

"And if I was just gone? If I lost every person that matters the most to me?" She barely whispers the words.

"It would make it easier for me. Yes. And I know that makes me an asshole."

"It doesn't make you an asshole." Chloe adjusts herself and the board tips slightly. There's panic on his face. She smiles. "It kind of makes you an asshole."

"What do you think we should do?" Luke asks. It sounds genuine, but Chloe thinks maybe he's just so desperate to get out of the lake.

"Other than talking about what happened last year?" she asks.

"You said no. That was all the talking that was required."

"You don't want an explanation? Everyone else is asking for one."

He shrugs. "Then explain to them."

"I'm not talking to our friends about something you and I haven't even discussed. Everyone's too involved in each other's lives."

"They need the explanation. I don't."

"Why not?"

"Are you happy, Chloe?"

"What do you mean?" She looks away. When she turns back, she finds that Luke's eyes haven't left her face.

"If you're happy without me," he says, swallowing before he continues, "then that's all the explanation I need."

She thinks about the last year. Leaving New York was scary because all she knew was her life with Luke. She was willing to follow him wherever he wanted to go. No adventure seemed out of reach with him at her side. Moving to New York, finding themselves wrapped up in the world of his investment banking job and all of the wealth and privilege and rules that world encompassed.

It wasn't until she left that she realized the neglect of her own adventures.

"I'm trying," she finally says. "I think I'm getting closer to happy."

The side of his mouth turns up. He can't manage a full smile. And Chloe doesn't blame him. Because it's not good news when someone tells you they're happy without you.

Luke clears his throat and manages to reply. "Good."

"What about you?" she tentatively asks. "Are you happy?"

"I'm working on it," he says.

"If I hurt you, I'm sorry. That was never my intention." She reaches for his hand and he lets her hold it, for a brief moment, before pulling back.

"I think I know that. Somewhere very, very deep inside." Luke rubs his hand along his jawline. "Give me another year or so to fully realize it."

"And until then?" Chloe asks, begging for an opening, some pathway forward.

"I don't know. We get through this week and then agree to some sort of separate custody arrangement? Honestly, I think everyone else feels as awkward as we do. They'll probably be relieved."

Chloe looks away. "I don't think Sloane will be relieved. And I don't want separate custody." Her brows furrow and her lips purse as her fingers trace the logo in the center of the board. When she looks up, Luke is imitating Chloe's face, pursing his lips in an exaggerated fashion and squinting his eyes. She can't help but laugh, the same way she'd always react when Luke would point out that Chloe is incapable of hiding her emotions.

She smiles as she says, "I think there's a better solution."

Luke smirks. "What's that?"

"You said it earlier," she points at his chest. "We were never just friends. We kissed the first night we met."

"I tried to do a lot more than that." Luke grins.

"I know," she says as she pushes away the memory of that first night in her dorm, focusing on their current situation. "We need to start over."

"How does that work?"

"At the beginning. We do the things that friends do. When they first meet. And we see if we can't salvage something out of this disaster we've found ourselves in."

"Any ideas of where to start?"

"Friends tell each other things," she says.

Luke eyes her suspiciously. "Like what?"

"Why are you afraid of alligators?"

He shrugs. "No reason. Reasonable people fear alligators."

She shakes her head. "This isn't a normal fear. You're completely freaked out in a very un-Luke way. Pretend I'm your friend. I just asked you a question. Tell me about your irrational fear of alligators."

"No. I'm not telling you."

"Why not?"

"Because it's embarrassing."

"Why does that matter? I know millions of embarrassing facts about my friends. You don't have to pretend with me. There's no chance of us sleeping together. Tell me the embarrassing thing."

"I see what you're doing."

"Good. I'm being pretty obvious about it." Chloe waits for Luke to respond, but he sits in silence. "Tell me your embarrassing story," she says in earnest.

"Fine. Promise not to laugh?" he asks.

"I don't think I can make that promise," she says. "But I promise to keep the reasons for your deep-seated fear a secret. I'm very good at keeping everyone's secrets."

As they paddle back to the rental stand, Luke tells Chloe about his childhood trip to Disney World, the terrifying Jungle Cruise ride, and the months of bedwetting alligator nightmares that followed before Luke's mother made him see a child therapist whose experimental aversion therapy treatments seemed to only make the fear worse.

Chloe feels a ton of sympathy for child-Luke and cannot stop laughing at adult-Luke.

When they finally reach the sandy shore of the lake, Luke hops off the board, barely letting his feet touch the water before he unbuckles his life jacket and throws it on the ground.

As Chloe returns the paddle at the rental stand, the employee says, "Your friend arranged for a car to pick you guys up. It's waiting over there."

"Thanks," Chloe says, smiling. Sloane is a manipulative mastermind, Chloe thinks, but sometimes all that planning works out. Because when Chloe looks over at Luke as he is nervously scanning the edge of the lake, and he sheepishly smiles in her direction, she thinks maybe this is a step in the right direction. Maybe Luke is finding a way to replace all that anger with something else.

When they get back to the house after a mostly silent car ride, four sets of eyes are focused on their entrance as they step inside. Sloane, Alden, Wyatt, and Marianne hesitate to speak, waiting to observe the dynamic between Chloe and Luke.

Chloe's arms quiver as she drops her towel near the door. She knows she's going to be sore the rest of the week and her eyes narrow in on Sloane.

"How did it go?" Sloane asks.

Luke steps forward. "After you abandoned us? After you left us alone in an alligator-infested lake?"

"You saw an alligator?" Sloane's voice pierces the air.

"No. We did not," Chloe quickly replies. "Luke was just afraid that there could be alligators in the water."

Wyatt shrugs. "Seems like a legitimate fear. It is Florida."

Chloe purses her lips. Through gritted teeth she says, "That's not helping, Wyatt."

"I told you, Chloe," Luke says with confidence. "That was dangerous. And you were swimming in that lake."

"You swam in the lake?" Sloane has a look of disgust on her face. "That wasn't a smart choice."

Chloe throws her hands in the air. "Paddleboarding was great," she says. "I loved being in the water. But now I'm going to go take a shower."

Chloe starts to walk away, but Sloane blocks her exit. "Wait. How did things go between you two?" Sloane gestures to Luke and Chloe. "You look less murder-y."

Chloe looks at Luke and waits for him to speak. He stares at the floor before saying, "We're fine." His eyes meet Chloe's as he says, "We're friends." She nods as he continues. "At least we're trying to be."

Chloe goes upstairs and Sloane follows. "No lake sex?"

Chloe rolls her eyes. "At the public lake? On a paddle-board? With my ex who hates me? No, Sloane. There was no lake sex. And if there was, why would I tell you, you manipulative ditcher?"

"You and Luke always hid away the good stuff. You're too private," Sloane says.

Chloe raises her eyebrows, and Sloane waves her hand dismissively.

"Okay, no sex," Sloane says. "But a friendship is a start, right?"

"It's a start," Chloe says as she heads toward the shower.

Even though she's the one who suggested it, Chloe wonders if she can be friends with Luke. Because in the past, they've loved each other and they've hated each other. And there's never been an in-between.

Seven Years Ago

THERE ARE MOMENTS THAT happen in slow motion. That's how the entire night felt for Chloe. She knew Luke's fraternity was having a big party. She didn't want to go. She had a threshold for the smell of spilled beer and sweaty bodies, and it had already been met that week.

Instead, Chloe and Sloane spent the night in Marianne's room, watching rom-coms and eating popcorn with M&M's for dinner. When Noah called Marianne to say good night and Sloane had already fallen asleep on the couch, Chloe snuck out and walked across campus toward her apartment. She could see the lights and hear the laughter from the party. She thought, maybe, she'd find Luke in the sea of bodies and then they could sneak away into a dark corner or back to Chloe's room. Stolen moments with Luke had become her addiction.

Their entire junior year they spent more time together than apart, bouncing between Luke's room in the fraternity house and the apartment Chloe and Sloane shared off campus. Alden and Wyatt were in the same upper-class dorm building as Marianne, three floors apart. There were Sunday dinners at Chloe and Sloane's apartment. Sloane attempted meals that were too ambitious, both for their budget and her cooking skills, but it became a weekly tradition. Other nights, they texted plans about meeting at various dining halls, happy hours after class, football games in the fall, and baseball games in the spring. But whenever plans were made, Chloe and Luke were a pair. If one couldn't make it, the other usually stayed behind. Sloane and Marianne moaned about the lack of girl time, which was one of the reasons why Chloe had been excited for their movie night. Except now here she was doing the thing Sloane and Marianne complained about, running to Luke at the end of every night.

When she opened the door to Luke's fraternity house, she was overwhelmed by the thickness of the air. A cloud of steam rose off the room packed with bodies, pressed against one another, as music played so loudly it was impossible to hear anyone's voice.

No one was having private conversations. There were no discussions of classes, or passions, or plans for next year. There was the sound of shouting along with song lyrics, the occasional call of someone's name, and strangers' lips crushing into each other.

Chloe almost went home. In the sea of people, she'd have to search for Luke for longer than her patience would last. And maybe if Luke wasn't so tall, she would have left. She wouldn't have seen the wisps of his blond hair peeking above the room of crushed bodies. She would have gone back to her bed and woken early, like usual. And he would have knocked on her door with their traditional Sunday breakfast sandwiches in bed.

But that's not what happened. She spotted his tall head in the crowd. At first, she just saw him. But as she walked across the room, her body pulled toward Luke's like some kind of magnet, she saw that Luke was not alone.

There was a girl. In a purple dress. Chloe wouldn't remember many other details about this other person. A person who cracked her life apart. But Chloe remembered thinking *not many people can pull off purple* as she watched this stranger with her arms around Luke's neck, their tongues twisted together for so long that Chloe wondered when they would come up for air.

And when they did, and when she saw an almost invisible line of saliva still connecting their bodies, it was the first time that night Chloe thought she might vomit.

"C-C-Chloe?" Luke stuttered.

He was so drunk. And at first Chloe was relieved. He probably wouldn't remember this night. And maybe that meant she could forget it too.

"Yeah. It's me" was the only response Chloe could manage.

"Who's that?" the strange girl giggled as she dove back in for more of Luke.

By this point Luke seemed to gather awareness of his surroundings. Almost as if he was surfacing from under water, he pushed the stranger away, her purple dress sweeping against Chloe's arm.

"That's my girlfriend," Luke said.

"Ick," the girl replied and walked away, happy to find more fun and less drama elsewhere. Leaving Luke standing in front of Chloe.

He could have been a stranger. This wasn't the Luke she knew, who smelled like eucalyptus and held her tightly when she woke up in the middle of the night and drew letters on her back when she couldn't fall asleep. This person had red-rimmed eyes and his breath smelled of stale beer and there was a sheen of sweat across his forehead that made him look like he was recovering from a stomach bug. This person disgusted Chloe.

"I messed up," Luke slurred.

Chloe didn't want to hear any of his words. She turned and walked away, weaving through the crowd despite Luke's pleas to stop and shouts from friends to come dance. She kept walking until eventually she was moving faster, pushing people out of her way, needing to escape a room with no air left for her to consume.

Before she got to the door, she stopped. Not because Luke finally caught up. He was too sluggish and Chloe too determined. She stopped because out of the corner of her eye, she saw someone lurking in the corner, his eyes focused on Chloe.

Wyatt tilted his head to the side, beckoning her over. His gesture felt like a refuge, a friendly place for Chloe to land in the midst of chaos.

But when Wyatt scanned the crowd, his eyes zeroed in on a stumbling Luke and he quickly glanced back in her direction, and his face changed. Chloe noticed it immediately and her stomach sank. Because Wyatt had no reason to feel guilty, and yet the way he looked up at the ceiling and let his eyes briefly flutter suggested that he had some unexplained regrets.

"Hold up, Chloe," Wyatt shouted.

She shook her head, the tears that should have been directed at Luke, now falling in front of Wyatt. "Did you know?" she shouted over the party noise. "Did you know he was here, making out with someone else?"

"Let's go outside," Wyatt suggested, tilting his head in Luke's direction.

"No. I don't want to talk to him," Chloe said, holding her hand up to create distance as Wyatt stepped closer. "And I don't want to talk to you either."

"I'll tell Luke to back off. Wait for me outside." Wyatt pushed into the crowd toward Luke.

Chloe ignored Wyatt's instructions and ran outside, not stopping as she distanced herself from that awful fraternity house. Tears clouded her vision as she tried to navigate the campus pathways in the direction of her apartment. After a few minutes, she was crying so hard she couldn't see to keep walking. She found a bench and sat down, pulling her legs up and hugging herself tightly.

She tried to piece together what had happened. Four hours ago, Luke had handed her a bag of yellow M&M's, her favorites because they were obviously the most cheerful. Luke had bought every bag of M&M's at the Circle K and picked out only the yellows for Chloe's movie snack. He gave Chloe her snack, kissed her goodbye twice, and then left. Sometime between then and now, he had apparently consumed all the alcohol available and found a purple-dress girl to slide against his body as he mistook her mouth for Chloe's.

Her breath came in ragged bursts, her head swimming in loneliness and anger. She reached for the safety net she relied upon too often and brought her phone to her ear.

Replaying a message from her parents that Chloe had saved from years ago, she let their departed voices fill her ears as they laughed about a disastrous shopping trip involving tapered sweatpants for her father. "I'll text you the picture," her mother had laughed. "They look like leggings on him." Her father's protests in the background ended the call. Chloe listened to the message one more time and felt her breathing slow.

She missed them all the time, but in moments like these, all she wanted was to hear her parents' voices, to temporarily trick herself into thinking that her problems could be solved by calling her mom instead of being left by herself. To think that no matter who broke her heart, her father would always be there to love her best. Sometimes it worked, and sometimes, like this time, it made her feel more alone. Knowing she once had love like that and now it was gone.

Chloe shoved her phone back in her pocket and hugged her legs tighter, burying her face in her knees. She let herself cry, hoping the tears would help wash away the betrayal.

She didn't look up, but she felt the warmth of his body as Wyatt sat down on the bench next to her.

"You didn't wait," Wyatt said softly.

"I didn't feel like following instructions," she mumbled, not looking up.

"What happened, Chloe?"

His question was stupid. They both knew it. Chloe raised her head, wanting to see Wyatt's face when he tried to lie for his friend. Or worse, defend him. "I think you know exactly what happened, Wyatt."

"He was drunk—" Wyatt tried to say, but Chloe quickly cut him off.

"You knew. And you didn't stop him?"

Wyatt shifted uncomfortably as he tried to formulate his answer. "I'm not his babysitter."

"Are you his alibi? If I hadn't walked in, would you have told me?"

"I don't know. This is between you guys." Wyatt ran a hand through his dark hair, staring in the opposite direction from Chloe.

"Screw you, Wyatt," she said, hitting his shoulder. "And screw Luke. When he sobers up, pass along that message."

She stood up and started walking away, but Wyatt was immediately at her side. She felt his hand reach for her arm, but she batted it away, walking faster as fresh tears fell down her cheeks.

"Has he done this before?" she asked.

"He loves you. He's just stupid. They had some drinking competition earlier tonight. He won't remember any of this."

"I will."

"I know," Wyatt said with desperation. He put his hand on her shoulder, and this time Chloe stopped walking. They stood there, seconds of silence filling the air.

"I can't believe you would lie to me too," she said.

"I didn't lie, Chloe," Wyatt quickly replied.

"I know you don't like me. But I don't deserve this."

"What are you talking about? I like you. I . . ." Wyatt trailed off and Chloe quickly filled in.

"You hate us together. You're always complaining when I come to softball."

"That's just because you're bad at softball,"

"I'm not bad."

"You can't catch the ball."

"That's not my fault. It's too big for my hands."

Wyatt bit back a smile.

"It's not just softball, Wyatt. You leave the room every time Luke and I sit together. It's like the sight of us disgusts you."

"I'm giving you guys privacy."

"When we're studying for behavioral psychology? The class all three of us have together?"

"I've never been a group study guy, Chloe. It's not you. I promise."

"Whatever," she said. "I can tell you don't like me. You don't like Luke and me together. Fine. But you made me feel like an idiot tonight."

"Hold on a second. I didn't do anything to you. That was Luke."

"Yes, but you knew. And I don't know how much more you know. Or if you'll even tell me the truth, but it makes me feel like there's some secret everyone knows except me. It makes me feel like even more of an outsider."

"You're not an outsider, Chloe."

"I'm Luke's girlfriend. That's what I am to you and Alden and even Sloane and Marianne."

"That's not all you are to me," Wyatt said to the ground. "I should have stopped Luke. You should never have to be hurt like this." He reached out and put his hand on her shoulder.

"I can't believe he did this," Chloe whispered.

"Me either," he said, never looking away. Chloe found herself leaning into Wyatt's chest, and he wrapped his arms tightly around her body.

If everything had gone differently, she'd be standing in Luke's arms. But instead, Chloe found herself in this unfamiliar place, closer to Wyatt than they'd ever been. Chloe tended to keep her distance, assuming that's what Wyatt preferred. But at this moment, his hug was a cushion for Chloe's shock.

She couldn't help but categorize the differences between Wyatt and Luke. She was used to Luke's arms, staring up into his light-blue eyes. Wyatt's dark eyes blended with the night sky, an intensity that made Chloe look away. Whereas Luke smelled like crisp eucalyptus, Wyatt's scent was more like worn leather. It made Chloe think of her favorite chair on the second floor of the library, and immediately his unfamiliar arms felt safe.

"I don't know what I'm going to do," Chloe said through hiccupped breath. "Without Luke, I'm so alone."

Luke wasn't just Chloe's boyfriend. After her parents died, she leaned on him for too much. She spent Thanksgiving with his family so that she wouldn't have to fly home for such a short break, which then turned into Luke asking about Chloe's family traditions. He couldn't cook, but he did find a Spanish restaurant an hour away from campus so that Chloe could have her holiday paella that December. He'd even hum "Moon River" when Chloe was nervous before a test because Chloe told him that was the lullaby her mother had sung. Luke tried to fill the hole her parents had left and Chloe gladly let him.

Wyatt squeezed her shoulder. "Delay the big decisions. For now, let's get you home."

She pulled away from his body. She shouldn't have felt better, but somehow Wyatt's comfort helped.

"I'll see you later," she said.

Wyatt tilted his head. "I'm walking you back to your apartment. Luke would kill me if he knew you were this upset and alone."

Chloe turned and walked away, shouting over her shoulder, "Luke doesn't care about upsetting me."

They were silent for the short walk to her apartment, but Wyatt stayed by her side, keeping whatever promise to himself or Luke to keep Chloe safe.

When they went inside her building, Chloe turned toward Wyatt. She hated the look on his face. Pity, mixed with something else. Maybe concern. It made Chloe stand straighter and pretend that she was fine. She hated being pitied by anyone, especially someone like Wyatt.

"I'll be fine," she lied.

"Chloe, I need to say something." Wyatt ran his hand through his hair again, sweeping away the dark strands that fell over his forehead. His face was pulled tight, and Chloe waited to hear whatever additional bad news he was about to deliver. Because whatever Wyatt was going to say, he looked pained to say it. Wyatt took a deep breath and continued, "It's not the best timing, I know, but . . ."

Wyatt was cut off by the sound of Marianne and Sloane's voices flooding the hallway. "Chloe!" they shouted as they ran toward her.

"We've got this, Wyatt," Marianne said.

"Does everyone know already?" Chloe asked.

Sloane shook her head. "Wyatt called us from the party."

Chloe looked toward Wyatt. "I knew I wasn't what you needed," Wyatt said. "But I figured they were."

"Thanks," Chloe said softly. Sloane was already pulling her toward their apartment, but Chloe stopped and turned back toward Wyatt. "What did you want to tell me?"

"Another time," Wyatt said, shoving his hands in his pockets. "Take care of her," he said to Sloane and Marianne, tilting his head in Chloe's direction. And then he left, leaving Chloe standing in the hallway before Sloane and Marianne flanked her and wrapped their arms around her waist, leading her into the apartment.

As soon as the front door closed, Chloe felt their eyes on her body, seemingly waiting to see if she would fall apart or start throwing things. She settled somewhere in the middle, her sadness slowly morphing into rage.

"What did Wyatt tell you?" Chloe asked.

"Luke made out with someone at the Sigma Chi party," Marianne said quietly.

"He's such a dick," Sloane cried. "I will never forgive him. I cannot believe Luke would cheat on you."

"It doesn't seem like him at all," Marianne added.

Sloane quickly whispered, "That's not helpful."

Chloe sat on the couch. "But it's true. Unless we didn't know him at all."

In the two years Chloe had known Luke, she'd never questioned his loyalty. If anything, Luke was the jealous one. Chloe often noticed how he seemed to find her at parties, especially if she was having a conversation with a new guy. Luke would suddenly appear, slinging his arm over her shoulders, marking his territory. But she never minded, because he was always the person she wanted to talk to most.

Luke was often surrounded by a group of people, the center of attention, while Chloe was more comfortable off on the sidelines. He was energized working a room, chatting up any-body and everybody about easy topics like football playoffs and more obscure topics like their favorite restaurant back home. It never felt to Chloe like he was crossing a line, but maybe that's what other people saw. How many times had a group of girls come up to Chloe after hearing one of Luke's epic stories and sighed about how lucky Chloe was to be his girlfriend? Maybe they didn't really think she was lucky. Maybe they thought she was pathetic for being blind to Luke's flirtations.

In that moment, all of Chloe's insecurities bubbled to the surface. How could she have ever thought that someone like Luke would be captivated by only one person? They were young and their relationship became too intense too quickly after Chloe's parents died. Chloe's lips trembled as she realized that maybe it wasn't love, it was obligation. Or even worse. Maybe Luke pitied Chloe too. He needed an escape, and tonight it had come in the form of a purple dress.

"Everybody makes mistakes," Marianne said, joining Chloe on the couch. "Maybe this was one very stupid mis-take." Chloe looked up at her friends, swallowing slowly as Marianne continued, "He's such a good guy, Chloe. You and Luke are meant for each other."

Sloane nodded her head in agreement, but her eyes darted around the room and seemed to say something different.

Chloe wanted to believe that this was Luke's one stupid mistake. But at the same time, she felt like only stupid girls give out second chances. So the next morning, when Luke showed up with breakfast sandwiches and a giant apology, with the audience of Sloane and Marianne, because her friends refused to leave her side, Chloe told him to leave.

But Luke refused. He sat outside her apartment door all day, begging for a chance to explain himself. With Luke's painful hangover, his hallway vigil was a sacrifice, a point

Alden tried to argue but Sloane dismissed immediately. Sloane and Alden then devolved into a debate about what would be an adequate punishment for Luke's behavior, and all of Sloane's ideas involved naked public embarrassment. It was the first time Chloe laughed in twenty-four hours, and she vowed to never get on Sloane's bad side.

Sloane, Marianne, Alden, and Wyatt hung out in her apartment all day, and at the end of the day, Alden took Luke home. But the next morning, Luke was back again. Chloe still refused to speak to him, so instead he wrote her letters. Every morning, he slipped them under her door.

By the end of the first week, even Sloane commented that Luke's dedication to his apology tour was impressive. But Chloe wouldn't budge.

Eventually she opened the door and told Luke how she felt. She was embarrassed and she didn't trust him and she didn't need any more pain in her life. She told him that he was causing her pain and she needed him to leave.

But Luke kept begging. For five weeks, Luke apologized with words and grand gestures. He left flowers and more notes at her door each day. He kept trying. He kept showing Chloe that she was worth all the effort.

And finally, after all that time, Chloe let herself believe him. After all, it was just a kiss. It was something she could move past. It was something she had to move past, so that they could go back to Sunday dinners with Sloane's burnt chicken and Wednesday nights playing drinking games with reality shows. Chloe fell back into Luke's life. And that also allowed her to fall back into the family her friends had created.

Because while Luke was banished to the hallway, everything shifted for the six of them. It became clear that they each played a special role and with one person missing the dynamics weren't the same. Luke wasn't there to kick off Peak and Pit, the game they played to describe the best and worst parts of their week. It was something Luke's mother made him do at the dinner table, and he made them start their own version. In Luke's absence, Alden started describing a *peak* coding discovery in the computer lab and Wyatt threw a frozen roll at his head. None of them tried to play again after that. And, of course, no one held Chloe's hand on the couch during movie night. Even Sloane complained that it took so much longer to get their drink orders at happy hour without Luke charming the bartenders.

So when Chloe caved, and told Luke to come back into the apartment, everyone seemed relieved. When Chloe and Luke started holding hands again, her head finding its resting spot on his shoulder, no one moaned about their displays of affection. And when Chloe finally admitted that they were back together, she wasn't surprised to hear her friends yell "Finally!" and deliver a round of applause.

Chloe had to trust Luke because her life was better with him in it. Forgiving Luke for one mistake seemed like a small sacrifice to make for an entire lifetime of love.

But Chloe never forgot how she felt that night. Or the way Wyatt looked away when Marianne kept claiming Luke was a good guy. Because Chloe knew that good guys only get so many chances before they change sides. And best friends always know more than they admit.

♦ 10 ♦

This Year

CHLOE WAKES BEFORE THE rest of the house. The night before, they sat in the rooftop bar of Bud & Alley's and watched the sunset as they ate smoked Gouda pimiento cheese, crabcakes with arugula and fennel salad, and drank a steady stream of watermelon margaritas. After dinner, Marianne needed to go back to the house to pump, and Chloe quickly joined her. She was happy to leave as everyone else was debating where to grab drinks. Wyatt wanted to stay at Bud & Alley's because it was easy. Sloane wanted to take everyone to Neat for their custom craft cocktails. And Alden and Luke wanted to go to some hidden bar in a gas station. Chloe had skipped the argument, using Marianne as an excuse to escape and go to bed early.

But now she's awake while everyone else sleeps off their hangovers. Except Marianne, who's been asleep for ten hours and seems to be stockpiling rest while she's away from her baby.

Chloe throws on her yoga pants and a sports bra and takes one of the mats Sloane stores under the stairs. She plans on heading out to the beach to stretch before the sun is too high, but she sees a steady stream of people walking toward the amphitheater in the center of town and her curiosity wins. She leaves the mat propped by Sloane and Alden's front door, grabs her bag, and follows the growing crowd.

It's a giant farmers market, full of locals and tourists moving from one stand to another. Chloe smiles as she moves between the stalls. Jars of pickled green beans and boiled peanuts are next to homemade soaps, the scents of lavender and rosemary tickling Chloe's nose.

She samples the plump strawberries and juicy peaches and buys some of both to take back to the house. The sun beats down on her skin, but she's cooled by the breeze coming off the Gulf of Mexico.

At the end of the market, there are several artists selling their work, mostly beach scenes and wooden bird carvings. Chloe shifts her produce purchases from one shoulder to the other as she navigates between the artists' booths, surveying their work.

She stops at a booth of oil paintings, mostly unframed canvases hanging from metal hooks on the rails of a pop-up tent. The paintings are of the same location, a beach scene, but the colors subtly shift from one canvas to the next. As Chloe examines the paintings, she realizes she's watching the sun rise as she moves around the tent.

"What do you think?" a woman asks, approaching Chloe.

"Are you the artist?" Chloe asks.

The woman extends her hand. "Ashley Tyler."

She's at least a decade older than Chloe, dressed in loose linen overalls splattered in paint, with tanned arms and dark hair pulled into a simple ponytail.

Chloe shakes Ashley's hand and turns back to the painting in front of her. "Your brushwork is so delicate," Chloe says. "The way you created the cloud line mirroring the ocean. It's really perfect."

"Thanks," Ashley says, beaming. "Are you an artist?"

Chloe shakes her head. "I just really like paintings." Chloe wonders why she still feels a pain in her chest every time she admits that she's not an artist. "I work at a gallery," she says, taking a deep breath and trying not to dwell on major life regrets while shopping at a farmer's market. "It's called the Wick, in Washington, DC."

Ashley's eyes widen. "Yeah, I've heard of the Wick," she says, nervously laughing.

"I just work in installations. But I could pass along your name to the director. If you'd like."

"Are you kidding me?" Ashley quickly grabs a business card and shoves it in Chloe's direction.

"I'm serious," Chloe laughs.

"I'm selling a couple of paintings at a farmers market that I did during my kid's nap time, and you want the director of one of the best galleries in the country to take a look at them?"

"Yep," Chloe says, smiling at Ashley's card. There's a splatter or paint on it and Chloe doesn't think it's intentional. "I can't make any promises. Our exhibits are usually more established artists. But if my boss Sylvia likes your work, she'll connect you with the right people."

"This feels like a prank," Ashley says.

"It's not. Do you have another card?" Chloe asks, knowing that Sylvia can be unfairly judgmental.

"Of course. You can have all my cards." Ashley starts reaching deep into a giant, messy bag.

"Just one will do." Chloe takes the clean card and slips it into her bag before waving goodbye.

"Thanks for stopping by," Ashley says.

Chloe winds her way back through the vendors. She buys a smoothie and heads toward the house. But she's not ready to talk to her friends yet. And she also doesn't want Sloane catching her with outside, unapproved food when there is likely some elaborate breakfast planned.

Instead, Chloe makes her way to the beach to enjoy the quiet.

Even though she's been there for two days, she's still surprised by how private the beaches are. It's still early, but Chloe basically has the sand to herself, with the exception of one runner jogging along the shoreline. She sits on the beach and runs her hand through the fine-sugar sand, drawing letters with her finger, just like she used to as a girl.

She keeps thinking about the artist from the farmers market and how Ashley said she created those paintings in stolen moments during her daughter's nap time. It's a comforting thought for Chloe. That maybe dreams can be dormant and come back to life when they are needed most.

The jogger, with his steady gait, veers away from the water and starts heading in Chloe's direction. As he gets closer, it's clear who it is, even behind his dark sunglasses. He's covered in sweat, his bare chest glistening in the morning sun, and Chloe holds up her hands as he approaches.

"Do not stink up my square of beach with your cardiovascular efforts, Wyatt."

Wyatt tosses his phone next to Chloe, turns around, and runs into the ocean, diving under the waves. He surfaces and shakes his dark hair like a shaggy dog and walks back up to Chloe.

"All clean," he says as he plops next to her on the sand.

"I thought I was the only one up," she says.

"Nah." He leans back on his elbows and digs his feet in the sand. "I saw you head out this morning and gave up on trying to sleep."

"Is the bed too fancy for you?"

"Something like that." Wyatt doesn't elaborate and Chloe doesn't pry. Her head is already full of too many secrets.

"Where did you guys end up drinking?" she asks.

"Where do you think?" His mouth pulls into a half smile.

"Wherever Sloane wanted you to go."

"Correct. We went to Neat. The drinks were very good and very fancy, and after Alden spilled half of his down the front of his shirt, it was easy to convince Sloane that we needed a more casual place for the rest of the night. We ended up at Redd's Fueling Station and closed the place down."

"How are you up running?"

"I stopped drinking early." Wyatt shrugs as he continues. "It looked like there might be some babysitting needed. Plus, I got some excellent footage of Alden and Luke singing with the band. Want to see?"

"Absolutely."

Wyatt hands Chloe his phone, and she scrolls through the videos and pictures he took the night before. Alden and Luke were in prime form, re-creating their signature moves from senior spring karaoke sessions. Chloe almost wishes she'd stayed out.

"Did you and Marianne have a wild time with her pumping machine?" Wyatt asks.

"Crazy night. You really missed out."

"Maybe I did," he says earnestly.

She leans over and elbows his side, the salt water and sand from his body now lingering on her own.

"Where have you been this morning?" he asks.

"There's a farmers market in town."

"Get anything good?"

She hands him her bag of fruit and he reaches for a peach and takes a bite, the juice dripping down his chin. He wipes his mouth with the back of his hand, rotates the peach and finishes it off in a second bite. "Delicious," he says.

"There was an artist there," Chloe says. "She was pretty good. She painted this whole series during her daughter's naps."

"If you care about something, you make the time," Wyatt says.

"I know."

"How is your series coming along?"

She looks over her shoulder. "That's supposed to be a secret."

He leans back on the sand and laughs. "There's literally no one else out here. How is your painting going, Chloe?"

The night of her birthday, Chloe had invited Wyatt back to her apartment and showed him what she'd been doing for the last year. For the first time since college, she was painting again. She wasn't sure why she'd picked up a paintbrush, but once she did, she found it hard to stop. Her painting kept her company on nights alone, and then her painting became more exciting than the idea of any night out.

"It's going well," Chloe understates. Because the truth is, her latest series of watercolors is quickly becoming the most important thing in Chloe's life. But that isn't an admission she's ready to make. "Please don't bring it up around anyone else," she whispers.

"You can trust me, you know that," Wyatt says.

Chloe nods because, despite the ups and downs in their relationship, Wyatt is right. He's always been trustworthy.

"Why are you scared to tell everyone?" Wyatt gently asks. "You should be proud."

"Because it's a hobby. Not a job."

Wyatt's eyes narrow. "I'm pretty sure your entire job is based around other people taking their artwork seriously."

"I mean for me. I handle installations. I'm not a painter."

"Who told you that?"

"Everyone. My entire life."

"Liar. You grew up in California. Surrounded by artists."

"Yes, but this life," Chloe says, motioning around, "the world I entered when I went to Mayfield, is not like home."

"You let the Mayfield bubble dictate how you spent your life?" Wyatt asks.

"I was already different enough. I wanted to fit in," Chloe admits to Wyatt, and maybe to herself too.

"How does giving up something you love help you fit in?"

Chloe takes a deep breath, reflecting before she answers. Then she tells Wyatt a story. One she hasn't told anyone else, not even Luke.

"Do you remember when Luke's parents came to visit for homecoming junior year?" Chloe begins.

"Yeah," Wyatt says. "They took us out to that ridiculous tasting menu. Alden was puking red wine the next day."

"And Luke's mom had to leave twice to take conference calls," Chloe adds. Luke's mother is a top litigator at an Atlanta firm, and despite almost a decade with Luke, Chloe never fully relaxed in his mother's presence.

"There was a painting on the wall by the restroom at that fancy restaurant," Chloe says. "I was studying it and bumped into her."

"Did she say something?" Wyatt asks.

"She asked if I liked it. I said something about the perspective of the horizon line. Then she asked me if I painted." Chloe closes her eyes, remembering a moment that seemed to shift so much in her life. "I naïvely said yes and started rattling off dreams about life as an artist."

"You were twenty, Chloe. You should have been full of dreams. You should still be full of dreams."

Chloe shrugs. "Luke's mom said there are two types of people in life. The ones who create the art and always wonder

if anyone likes it. And then the people who never have to wonder. Because they have the money to buy the art they like.
'Never underestimate the power of money, even in matters of
creativity,' she said."

"That's bullshit," Wyatt quickly replies.

Chloe turns and faces him, her legs crossed and her body
leaning toward his face. "Is it?" She starts tracing letters in the
sand again. "There's a lot of truth in what she said. At least
that's been my experience."

"What are you talking about? You're around artists every
day."

"Yes, but all of them have made it. I'm not around artists
like the woman at the farmers market."

"So if you're not successful, then there's no point in creating something beautiful?" Wyatt asks as he turns and faces
Chloe. Their faces are inches apart, their bodies tense.

"I wanted to be a part of Luke's life," she claims. "But Luke's
life is cocktail parties and entertaining clients. Showing up in
T-shirts splattered with paint is not conducive to Luke's life."

But really, it started before the move to New York, subtle
shifts so that Chloe could make herself more palatable to Luke's
world. She wanted a close relationship with Luke's parents, and
Luke's mother expected perfection. Chloe changed the way
she dressed, and she spoke less about her own projects and
more about art as an investment, a topic Luke's mother enjoyed.
It was easy and Chloe was good at playing the role. She justified those changes as small sacrifices to make for love, but
when she stepped back, she realized that all those tiny shifts
added up to leaps away from where she began.

"Well, you aren't a part of that life anymore," Wyatt says
defensively. His face pulls in a grimace and then softens.

"You're right," Chloe says, swallowing. "I'm not."

"So are you going to keep painting?"

"I've spent the last year trying to figure out what I thought was expected and what I actually wanted. They're not always separate."

"I think you're making this harder than it needs to be," Wyatt says. Chloe wonders whether he's only referring to her artwork. Or if he's talking about their friendship too.

"Yes. I'm still painting," Chloe says. "But I'm not talking about it yet. Because I'm not ready to wonder if anyone likes it. It's just for me."

"I like that life motto," Wyatt says proudly.

"Me too."

"And by the way, you don't have to wonder with me. I like it. You are incredibly talented, Chloe." He reaches out and brushes his hand over hers.

She looks down and sees their fingertips lightly touching as the rest of her body buzzes. "What do you even know about art?" she says in a breathy whisper.

"Maybe not much. But I know passion."

She rolls her eyes. "Oh, that I believe."

"I'm serious," he says, drawing his brows together in a mock scowl that Chloe knows has elicited sighs from more than one woman. "Hear me out."

"Okay, I'm trying to keep my serious face."

Wyatt pulls his hand away from Chloe's and rubs his jawline. She immediately misses his touch, even though she knows she shouldn't. "Do you remember the first night we met?" he asks.

"At Waffle House?" she says, trying to focus on the conversation and not his body.

"Yeah. What do you remember about that night?"

"I remember fighting with you."

"About art. You loved it so much you were willing to fight with a stranger about it."

"It's easier to fight with strangers." Chloe sighs.

"Is that what happened? You didn't want to fight with Luke about it?" he asks quietly, perhaps knowing it's a question that crosses some invisible line.

"Luke and I never really fought," she answers honestly.

"And you liked that?" There's a genuine innocence to his question that invites a truthful answer, unafraid of the judgment that typically accompanies relationship postmortems.

"I thought I needed it," she says. "But I lost a lot of myself so that I could avoid fights. Maybe now I'm realizing that you can fight and still love."

"I think that's definitely possible," he says, smiling broadly before turning away. He looks out at the ocean when he says, "Show Sylvia your paintings."

Chloe shakes her head. "No. Definitely not. Sylvia is too judgy," she says, knowing her boss is one of the toughest critics in the industry. "I'm still not sure I'm going to show anyone."

"Other than me," Wyatt says, not trying to hide the twinkle in his eyes.

"Yes, other than you. You caught me in a moment of weakness."

"Is that what that was?"

Chloe swallows. They are on an empty beach and, in that moment, it feels like they are the only two people in Florida, the heat radiating from Wyatt's body making her burn. He reaches out and brushes his fingers against her cheek and she feels the redness creep up in her face.

"I don't know what that was," she whispers.

"Are we going to talk about it?" he asks.

Chloe can still feel the way Wyatt's lips briefly brushed against hers that night. He came back to her apartment so that she wouldn't spend her birthday alone. And somehow, they ended up standing in front of her bay window, the light flooding into her living room as she revealed the artwork she'd hidden from everyone else. They opened a bottle of champagne Chloe had been saving, and after they finished that, Chloe suggested one shot of tequila. Maybe it was the vulnerability, exposing a part of herself hidden for so long. Because when Wyatt leaned down and wrapped his arm around her waist, pulling their bodies together, his familiar lips entering unfamiliar territory as they met Chloe's, she felt herself come alive for approximately two seconds before she realized what was happening. She jumped back quickly. Wyatt did the same. They mumbled excuses about tequila and bad judgment and accidental lip connections. And then they pretended it never happened.

It was an almost kiss with no discussion. No dissection the next day. Just two electrified bodies that bounced against one another. *We shouldn't*, Chloe had said. *You're right*, Wyatt had agreed. It shouldn't have felt like a betrayal after a year of being broken up, but they both knew it was.

Chloe shifts, leaning forward, and Wyatt mimics her actions, not letting their faces have more than a few inches of distance.

"Can we skip the talking?" Chloe swallows.

Wyatt lights up in a smile. "As much as I'd like to do that, we probably do need to talk."

"Have you said anything to Luke?"

He shakes his head. "There's nothing to say. Besides, I think this is between us. I'd never talk to anyone else before you, Chloe."

Relieved by his answer, she flashes a quick smile. "Wyatt, I need to work things out with Luke. Not just because it's important to me, but because it's important to the whole group. I put it off for a year. I kept thinking things would magically work out, but clearly they haven't. Luke has to be my priority this week."

"Of course," Wyatt says, and Chloe watches as his entire body alters, connection replaced with stiffness. And she returns to the mindset she's embraced all week. Regret. Regret. Regret.

"We should probably head back," he says, an automatic quality to his voice as he stands.

He extends his hand to Chloe, pulling her up. She weaves their fingers together and she's grateful for the smile he returns. Wyatt should expect more, but for now he seems to accept what Chloe is capable of giving.

Thunder cracks, forcing them to break eye contact as they both examine the sky. Up one end of the beach, the sun is bright and the sky is a cloudless blue. But the other direction is an ominous gray, full clouds melting into a purple horizon.

Standing in the middle, neither of them has time to speak before the clouds open and sheets of rain pour down.

Chloe stares upward and starts laughing. At how quickly things change. At the universe's sense of humor.

"Should we make a run for it?" Wyatt says.

Chloe shrugs. "You're already soaked from your swim in the ocean. I don't mind the rain," she shouts over the downpour.

"White was a good choice," Wyatt says, eyeing Chloe's top.

Chloe looks down, her clothes plastered to her body and on the pathway to ridiculously indecent. "Okay. Maybe we should run."

Wyatt picks up Chloe's bag of fruit, and they dash toward the house. The sand is soft farther up the beach, making a run almost impossible. She sinks and loses her footing, but his strong arm is quickly there to steady her movement. Her breath hitches at the feel of their wet bodies pressed together as they are surrounded by sheets of warm coastal rain.

By the time they reach Sloane and Alden's house, there isn't a dry spot on either of them. Chloe's hair sticks to her back, droplets pooling on the entryway floor. They sheepishly stand on the doormat, knowing that this level of wetness is probably in violation of Sloane's house rules.

Matching smirks are plastered on Wyatt and Chloe's faces as they quietly shut the door behind them.

"We were wondering where you guys were," Marianne says as she walks toward the kitchen with a mug of coffee.

"Got caught in the storm?" Alden absently asks while staring at his phone on the couch.

"Dry off. We're going to play some games." Sloane gestures toward a stack of towels in the entryway. Sloane's arms are full of every board game imaginable, from Monopoly to Cards Against Humanity. She's clearly well-prepared with a rainy-day itinerary.

When Chloe reaches out to grab a towel, she realizes she's still holding Wyatt's hand. She quickly disentangles their fingers, feeling the lingering electricity despite being thoroughly soaked. A blush creeps across her cheeks as she looks around the room, relieved to find that no one else seems to have noticed.

Chloe wraps a towel around her shoulders and walks toward the kitchen. She doesn't see Luke standing on the stairs. And when Wyatt asks if Chloe will be on his team for Trivial Pursuit, she says, "Of course."

No one notices Luke walking back to his room.

♦ 11 ♦

Six Years Ago

THE SUMMER AFTER GRADUATION should have been heart-breaking. Most friends scatter, rudely dropped into adulthood while clinging to memories of hazy college bliss.

But that wasn't the case for Chloe. Somehow, miraculously, she managed to convince everyone to stay together.

Luke had a job on Wall Street. And Marianne got a job at Teach for America in the Bronx. Even though Chloe's brother tried to convince her to come back to California, she wasn't ready. She didn't want to glom on to his life, weekends spent discussing grocery runs and toddler birthdays. She also wasn't ready for the constant tidal wave of grief that seemed to consume her whenever she went back to her parents' home.

It was easy for Chloe to get a job at a gallery. Then Sloane got hired at an interior design firm on the Upper East Side, and Alden was coding something, which he could do from anywhere. When Wyatt got an offer as an editorial assistant at a publishing house, it felt like all the pieces fell into place.

"So we're going to do it? We're all moving to New York? Together?" Chloe had squealed that spring, bouncing up and down. Wyatt didn't really want to take the job, he told them.

He wanted to write. But helping other writers seemed good enough. For a year at least. So in response to Chloe's gleeful dance, they all wrapped her in a hug and made plans for the big move to NYC.

Finding an apartment that they could afford and could fit six people was next to impossible. But by May, they'd found something doable in Murray Hill. They put up temporary walls creating rooms that Sloane called prison cells. More often, they'd all gather on the couch in the living space. It was the only room with a real window that admitted outside light. Every other room either looked out onto a brick wall or was windowless. Sloane's prison cell description wasn't actually much of an exaggeration.

They filled the apartment with thrift store finds and questionable Craigslist purchases. Sloane insisted that they all buy new mattresses, after reading one too many articles about bedbug infestations. None of them protested this mandate because buying a used, stained mattress was a threshold none of them wanted to willingly cross.

There was no design sense to the apartment, Sloane's constant complaint. It was functional and, for Chloe, full of comfort. The knitted blanket Marianne brought from home that they all fought over for movie night. The piles of Wyatt's books that they turned into makeshift side tables. The cabinet full of mugs with corporate logos that Luke seemed to have in endless supply. And the antique trunk that Sloane found at the flea market to store the *ridiculous* number of cords and cables that Alden said were absolute requirements. Maybe the comfort of the apartment had more to do with the fact that it was filled with people Chloe loved rather than any material thing.

By late August, they had a rhythm to their days. Alden slept in, after staying up most of the night coding, which meant there was one fewer body to fight over bathroom counter space. Marianne was up, dressed, and gone before most of them were awake. Chloe and Luke never complained about sharing the shower. And then it was a flurry of toasted bagels and cups of yogurt eaten on the way to the subway before Luke and Wyatt headed downtown and Chloe and Sloane headed uptown. They'd trickle home at different times, each person making sure Alden actually stood up and moved his body away from his computer at regular intervals and helped Marianne remove gum from whatever surface it attached to that day—her hair once, but more usually a shoe or, oddly, a book wedged in her giant bag.

They started carving out their own identities that year, Marianne grabbing drinks after work with the other teachers, Chloe and Sloane spending their weekends at MoMA stalking the latest exhibits, Wyatt parking himself at a coffeehouse so that he could focus on writing instead of the blue light from Alden's computer screen. And Luke, with a constant rotation of work events and late nights, so that he was difficult to pin down. But they still stuck to their Sunday dinner tradition. And they still stayed up too late, catching up on the couch, a quick conversation turning into hours of laughter. The crowded, messy, joyful apartment became the security blanket they all needed for their first year of adulthood.

So it wasn't surprising, one October evening, that Luke convinced everyone to attend a happy hour with the other junior analysts at Brother Jimmy's. The drinks were cheap, and Brother Jimmy's was close enough to their apartment that they couldn't claim it was too much of a trek to join, despite everyone's silent eye rolls at Luke's new friends. It was hard for any of them to accept someone new. They were still each other's favorite people.

Happy hour for the investment banking crew was later than most, so the girls met at the apartment and got ready together. Chloe and Marianne watched as Sloane tried on almost every dress in her tiny chest of drawers because this was going to be the night that she finally met the man of her dreams. Or so she claimed.

Sloane had a timeline, and she was running a few months behind. This year was her year to get experience working with the best interior designer and to meet the man she was going to marry. Next year, she would be engaged, move back to Atlanta, and set up her own design business, or so she claimed. Sloane's tenacity seemed to make even the most ambitious ideas seem achievable.

"I like the white one," Marianne said as she curled up on Sloane's twin bed. Marianne had the top bunk, a sleeping arrangement she agreed to on the condition that when Noah came to visit, Chloe and Luke would give up their bedroom for the weekend. Everyone paid the same rent, so they were willing to switch things around.

"I can't wear white in that bar. It's so dirty. It will stain," Sloane said.

"It's not that dirty," Chloe said. "It's just dark. And crowded."

"Have you seen it in the daylight?"

"God, no," Chloe quickly replied. "Who would go to Brother Jimmy's in the daytime?"

Sloane threw off the white dress and reached for a black slip dress. "Alden said he missed barbecue. I went to lunch with him last month."

Marianne sat up. "You ate the food there?"

"Reluctantly," Sloane said as she pulled on the dress. "It wasn't too bad. Plus, Alden seemed homesick."

"Or maybe he was pretending to miss home so that he could get some alone time with you," Marianne said, a teasing lilt in her voice.

Alden's crush on Sloane was a well-known secret. Alden had a starstruck quality whenever he was around Sloane, but he never asked her on a date or made any outward declarations of affection. Chloe occasionally caught Sloane staring at Alden or defending his brilliance to anyone who attempted criticism. Chloe wondered if Alden wanted Sloane, could he make a move and have her? But they were caught in this weird back and forth, both of them afraid to upset the balance. Chloe wasn't sure what it would take to get both of them to finally admit their feelings. But until then, Sloane seemed content to look elsewhere, and Alden consumed himself with building a mobile app.

"Alden and I are alone all the time," Sloane said, waving her hand. "Stop acting like a fifth grader, Marianne. Not everyone has a crush. Some people are just friends."

Chloe and Marianne's eyes met, not believing a word Sloane said.

"I like the black," Chloe said as Sloane turned in the mirror. With her strawberry blonde hair cut into a chin-length bob and her fair skin, Sloane could pull off almost any color. The October air was cool, but the packed bar would be stuffy, so the short dress Sloane selected would be perfect.

Chloe glanced at her outfit, a pair of jeans and a tank top. She'd be more casual than Luke's colleagues, and she thought that maybe she should change into a dress too. That's probably what Luke would prefer. Sometimes Chloe wished she were more like Sloane because Sloane was the type of girl Luke's colleagues expected. Polished. A bit aloof. Confident.

The few times Chloe had met Luke's new friends, she had felt so out of place, kind of like a fish flopping on dry land. She spent most of her days running errands for the gallery director, so she had no use for fancy work clothes. And everything about living in New York was exciting. She was too impressed to ever seem cool to anyone.

But tonight she would try. Ever since he'd started this job, Luke was dazzled by his new life. He would lie in bed next to Chloe, whispering stories about his intimidating bosses and legendary trading anecdotes. He became obsessive, wanting to get the same fleece vest that everyone else in the office wore. Concerned that if he wasn't still at his desk when his boss left for the night, he might lose some imaginary ranking among the junior analysts.

"Can I borrow a dress?" Chloe asked Sloane.

"Yes! Let's do a makeover." Sloane clapped her hands as she started laying dresses on the bottom bunk and instructing Marianne to pull out the case of makeup Sloane stored under her bed.

"You asked for it," Marianne mumbled to Chloe.

Chloe did, in fact, ask for it, and she also immediately regretted the asking. Sloane heated up a flat iron and held dresses against Chloe's chest, each of them shorter than the last. When Sloane started discussing a cat eye, Chloe realized that she was going to be spending the night playing pretend. The short dresses, the smooth hair, the presence of makeup at all, was way outside Chloe's norm. But it was squarely in Sloane's wheelhouse. And like the girls who hung around with Luke's coworkers. Chloe thought, maybe for one night, she'd see what it was like to be one of them instead of Luke's quirky girlfriend.

The primping continued, and Chloe transported herself to a place of calm as Sloane swarmed around her like one of those ambush makeovers.

"Where are you guys going?" Wyatt poked his head in their room. His bag was still slung over his shoulder. He must have just gotten home from work.

"To that party. With Luke's work friends," Chloe said. She tried to turn her head toward Wyatt, but Sloane immediately pushed it back in her direction, a very pointy eyeliner stick aimed at Chloe's eye.

"Have fun," Wyatt said.

"No," Chloe said quickly. "You have to come."

"I'll pass." Wyatt got an apple out of the fridge. Chloe could see all of this, the one advantage of a small apartment.

"Please come. Be socially awkward with me," Chloe shouted across the room.

"I'm not socially awkward," Wyatt shouted back.

"Fine. Be mathematically awkward with me. Those guys start talking about financial models and my eyes glaze over. The artists need to stick together."

Wyatt walked back to Sloane's room, standing in the doorway as he took a bite of apple. He did not seem convinced. "I haven't seen you pick up a paintbrush once since we moved here."

Chloe knew he was right. It'd actually been much longer since Chloe had picked up a paintbrush. Ever since her parents died, she'd had a hard time thinking about creating anything. It had been easy to make excuses during senior year—exams, parties, job applications—and easier still with the move. In an apartment this small, she would be taking up precious space storing paints and brushes in a drawer that could be used for underwear and pajamas. She'd paint again when she was ready. But in the meantime, could she still claim to be an artist? If Wyatt was assisting an editor of someone else's book, could he still call himself a writer?

Chloe didn't ask either of these questions. Instead, she begged. "Wyatt. Please. Luke is less finance-bro-y when you're around. Help me out."

"Fine," Wyatt said, finishing off the apple and tossing it in the trash can across the room. "But only if Alden comes too."

Alden was hunched over his computer in the corner, the makeshift office he had set up that Sloane constantly complained was an eyesore. During this entire conversation, not once had Alden looked up. He was in the zone, his fingers flying around the keyboard in a way that seemed unsustainable for more than a minute, but they all knew Alden had been there for hours and would stay hunched over like that until late in the night.

Sloane seemed satisfied with Chloe's makeup. She went over to Alden, lifted his headphones off his head, and whispered something in his ear.

Alden looked around. "Give me two minutes."

"Please take ten. You need to shower," Sloane said.

Alden left the room, and Chloe narrowed her eyes at Sloane. "Be nice."

"I am being nice. I convinced him to come so that you can have your male security blankets while you figure out how to navigate Wall Street girlfriend life."

Chloe stared at the floor, embarrassed by the accuracy of Sloane's statement.

Wyatt started unbuttoning his shirt, walking toward his room to change. "Are we meeting Luke there?"

"Yeah," Chloe stammered, looking away.

With six people living together, someone was always in some state of half-dressedness, but Wyatt seemed the most comfortable stripping down with the door open. Chloe knew there was likely a roster of girls from Mayfield who would have pulled up a bucket of popcorn for the nightly show. But Chloe felt a creep of embarrassment instead. It felt disloyal to Luke to admit that she occasionally stared at Wyatt's chest.

"Shots before?" Wyatt walked out, pulling down his clean black T-shirt.

"Oh yes," Chloe said quickly and turned toward the kitchen.

They all filed into the kitchen space, a generous term given the mini fridge they tried to share and the stove with only two burners. Wyatt pulled out a bottle of Southern Comfort, poured five shots, and they waited until Alden came out of the bathroom, towel around his waist, and grabbed his shot.

Chloe looked at Wyatt. "You should tell Riley to meet us at the bar," she suggested.

Wyatt shook his head. "Nah. Not her scene."

Chloe didn't push. Wyatt had been dating Riley for a few months but had only brought her around the group a handful of times. Chloe suspected that it was less about the bar and more about the intimidation of everyone together that wasn't Riley's scene. They were a hard group to break into.

"I'm going to throw on some clothes," Alden said.

"Yes, please." Sloane directed her attention to Chloe. "You too. I have the perfect dress."

A few minutes later, when Chloe came out of Sloane's room wearing a red bandage dress that clung to every inch of her body, her blonde hair smoothed, and the cat eye expertly applied, Alden and Wyatt were finishing their second shots.

"Wow," Alden said. "Looking good, ladies."

Chloe could feel Wyatt staring intently. "Doesn't look like you," he whispered as Chloe walked up to his side.

"Think Luke will like it?" Chloe asked.

Wyatt paused and then said, "Luke likes everything about you. He'd be crazy not to."

Even though Chloe felt uncomfortable, like this was some kind of childhood dress-up game and her mother was going to tell her to wash her face, she also felt confident. Wyatt's words had that power.

When they got to the bar, Chloe found Luke surrounded by his coworkers. For once, she didn't feel like an embarrassment. Especially not when Luke whistled as she approached. "Babe, I have no idea where you got that dress, but I cannot wait to take it off you." Luke said this loudly, so that all of his work friends could hear. Chloe blushed at the cheers and whoops that followed.

"It's Sloane's," Chloe whispered, kissing the stubble on Luke's cheek as he pulled her tightly against his chest, her feet lifting off the ground momentarily.

The red dress seemed too obvious to Chloe. In college, Luke would catch her painting in an oversized T-shirt and her underwear and tell her that's when she was the sexiest. Maybe it was because the T-shirt was so easy to remove, discarded in a corner along with Chloe's painting. The red dress would likely take as much effort to get off as it had to get on, zipped and pulled and cinched to hold her body into an artificially tight mold. But if Luke liked it, then it was worth it.

Everyone else came over to say hi. After introductions and a few minutes of small talk, Chloe watched as the groups fractured. One of Luke's coworkers tried to hit on Sloane, asking if he could see how many more dresses she had like the one Chloe was wearing. "Absolutely not" was Sloane's response and she walked away toward the bar. This was when Sloane's southern roots truly showed themselves. She expected more manners than boys in New York bars were capable of displaying.

Marianne followed Sloane to the bar. Alden and Wyatt tried to stick it out, but when Luke's coworkers started talking about changes to the management model for a potential M&A deal, Alden and Wyatt slunk away too. They tolerated Luke's coworkers because they loved Luke. But given the opportunity, they found ways to avoid extended conversations.

Chloe didn't have that luxury. She spent the rest of the evening laughing at jokes she didn't understand but watching Luke's grin grow bigger and bigger until there wasn't any space left between his dimples and his lips.

But Chloe kept looking across the room at Wyatt leaning against the wall, his encouraging smiles making her feel safer than Luke's strong hand on the small of her back. And when Luke finally told his work friends that he needed to go, that he needed to find his roommates, Chloe felt like she could finally breathe for the first time that night.

Chloe and Luke and Sloane and Marianne and Wyatt and Alden walked home together. They stopped to get giant pizza slices, passing bites of bubbly cheese and crispy pepperoni back and forth. Laughing about the guy who tried to hit on Sloane and the girl who turned Alden down. They were all exhausted when they got back to the apartment, but they stayed up, recapping their week, forming clusters on the couch, Chloe sitting on Luke's lap.

Being together was Chloe's favorite part of the night. But when Luke asked later, when they were lying in bed, her leg hooked over his hip, she said it was when Luke won the bet among his coworkers. Luke said, "Mine too," and Chloe knew she'd told the right lie.

They only lived together in that apartment for a year. Marianne and Noah would be engaged by that spring, and Marianne moved back home to Virginia where she and Noah got jobs teaching at their old high school. After Marianne moved out, Wyatt got a job offer in DC. Alden's coding project got funding and he moved to Atlanta. And even though her plans hadn't lined up exactly as predicted (no boyfriend), Sloane moved back to Atlanta too to set up her own design firm after landing a major remodel for a professional baseball player who lived in Buckhead. Luke and Chloe stayed in the apartment, taking down the temporary walls and turning it into their first home together. After his first bonus, Luke made enough money to cover the rent everyone else had paid.

Alone in the apartment, Chloe and Luke had space to spread out. She even talked about setting up an art studio in the extra bedroom, but they agreed that an office for Luke made more sense. Besides, Chloe still wasn't painting, and if she wanted to, she could always rent studio space close the gallery.

Luke worked long hours, and Chloe was often in the apartment by herself. That's when she missed her friends the most. She missed their bodies crammed onto the couch, their fights over fridge space. Because when they were living together, Chloe never once felt alone. That first year after graduating from college, Chloe would remember how, even though her family had been stripped away, it was rebuilt again by the love of her best friends.

♦ 12 ♦

This Year

"SHOPPING WAS A TERRIBLE idea," Marianne says to Chloe. "I can't afford any of this stuff."

They are in the third boutique of the afternoon, Sloane insisting that they head to one more spot because they have a new line of hand-painted plates that she thinks Chloe will love. Chloe will not spend one hundred and twenty-five dollars on a dinner plate when she can get a set of ten from IKEA for half that price. But she'll humor Sloane more effectively than Marianne.

At the first store, Sloane tries on four dresses and decides to buy two of them. Chloe and Marianne agree that the Ulla Johnson, with its bold print, is perfect for summer nights at the beach, and the Zimmermann caftan could double as a beach cover-up. When the cash register totals close to a thousand dollars and Sloane absently hands over her American Express, Chloe watches as Marianne's eyes widen.

Chloe shrugs, because of course it is a lot of money to spend, especially on a random Monday afternoon purchase, but clearly Sloane has that kind of money. It seems to bother Marianne, however, because she is constantly studying the price tags, speaking less, standing by the doorway while Sloane browses the stores.

Chloe and Sloane and Marianne used to spend hours sifting through the racks at the Goodwill store across town from Mayfield's campus. They'd try on clothes in the aisles, re-creating outfits they'd seen in the *New York Times* Street Style section. This shopping trip is nothing like that. Maybe because the equalizer of college-student poverty has disappeared. But maybe there are other reasons too.

"So what do you think?" Sloane asks, holding up the plate. It's a beautiful seafoam green, almost like the Gulf water, with a crackling effect around the edges. "Each plate is one of kind," Sloane describes. "It's a local potter who glazes and paints everything herself. Aren't they amazing?"

Chloe studies the plate, noticing the fluted edge, the subtle wave design painted underneath the green glaze. Each plate must have taken hours, from sculpting to painting to glazing to firing. One hundred and twenty-five dollars seems like a bargain, but unfortunately not one Chloe can afford.

"You should get a set for your apartment," Sloane suggests.

Chloe savors the weight of the plate before placing it back in the display stand. Last year, maybe, Luke would have whipped out his credit card and purchased a full set for their apartment. This year, Chloe's budget is her own. She made a choice and with it is a new life that is a constant adjustment. But maybe someday she'll be able to buy plates like this for herself.

"It would be so hard to fly back with those," Chloe says, manufacturing a reasonable reason instead of telling her friend the truth.

"You ship, right?" Sloane asks the store clerk.

"Of course," the clerk quickly replies and walks over to discuss the process with Sloane. Chloe tunes out the discussion and joins Marianne by the door.

Sloane excuses herself from the clerk and tells Chloe, "It's so easy to ship them. They are totally your style."

Chloe and Marianne exchange a meaningful look before Chloe admits what both of them have been thinking all afternoon. "I can't afford those, Sloane."

Sloane waves her hand dismissively. "I'll buy them for you. It will be my housewarming present."

"No," Chloe quickly responds.

"I insist." Sloane turns toward the salesclerk, but Chloe lightly touches her arm.

"I don't want you to do that," Chloe says softly.

"Oh, don't be silly," Sloane says and this seems to set Marianne off.

"Oh, my God. Enough, Sloane. We are not like you. Stop making us feel worse." Marianne says this loudly, too loudly, because everyone shopping stops and stares at the three women.

For a moment, Sloane is taken aback, but she quickly recovers. "Fine. We can stop shopping. We'll go to the Citizen and grab a bottle of champagne."

"I cannot afford a bottle of champagne. What happened to drinks in a cooler, Sloane? That's the way most people vacation. Can we just go back to the house?" Marianne walks out of the shop, and Chloe grabs Sloane's hand to pull her out too.

It takes a few minutes of brisk walking, but eventually they catch up to Marianne. Chloe acts as peacemaker, again, and suggests getting one of the cucumber refreshers at the local juice shop.

None of them speak while Chloe orders their drinks, taking them in to-go cups, but at least Marianne isn't running away anymore.

Finally, Sloane says, "When you and Luke get back together, you can buy all the plates you want." Somehow, Sloane doesn't realize how much worse this comment makes things among their friends.

It's hard calling Sloane out, because she likes to think she's always right, making the battle rarely worth it. But in this instance, Chloe needs her to understand.

"I don't want Luke's money," Chloe says. "I'm not even sure I want this kind of money for myself. This stuff doesn't matter to me." Chloe gestures down the row of high-end shops feet away from the sand, with prices high enough to justify that kind of costly rent.

Sloane bristles. "And that makes you better than me? Because this *stuff* matters to me?"

"That's not what I mean," Chloe says, not trying to hide her frustration.

"Besides," Sloane continues, "I don't really care about the stuff. I'm worried about you and Luke. Other than paddle-boarding, you two have barely spent any time together."

Sloane is right. While everyone else was playing games, Luke stayed in his room. They couldn't have dinner on the beach again, so Sloane brought the catered dinner inside, but Luke sat at the opposite end of the table and said he wasn't feeling well, going back to his room as soon as dinner was over.

"I know you're trying to help, but Luke and I are not your problem to fix," Chloe says.

Sloane shakes her head. "You and Luke were never supposed to fall apart." Sloane's voice cracks, a shocking sound for her always controlled demeanor as she says, "If you guys aren't together, what does that mean for the rest of us?"

It's a question Chloe has asked herself hundreds of times in the last year, but she didn't realize her friend shared the concern. Something about the tremble of Sloane's lip makes Chloe hesitate. "Are you and Alden having problems?" Chloe asks.

Sloane doesn't answer. Even Marianne, who was the most annoyed by the shopping trip, seems to soften, and they flank Sloane's sides.

By this point, they've made their way back to Sloane's beach house. They are standing in front of her beautiful oak door, the white stucco of the building forcing all of them to hide behind sunglasses.

"Nothing is working out the way it was supposed to," Sloane mutters.

"Look at this house," Marianne says. "Look at your life." She gestures to the giant shopping bag dangling from Sloane's arm. "I think you're doing pretty good."

"A house doesn't make a life, Marianne." Sloane doesn't go inside. Instead, she walks around the side and makes her way out to the beach.

Chloe and Marianne find her sitting with her toes buried in the sand. They plop next to Sloane, a trio facing the waves.

Marianne speaks first. "I live in a rented house we can barely afford and check my budget each month to make sure we can buy enough diapers. All of Teddy's clothes are second-hand. You're fortunate, Sloane. And you shouldn't take that for granted."

"Enough with the baby talk," Sloane says. It comes out so quickly, Chloe knows Sloane hasn't even realized the harshness of her words. But Marianne clearly notices.

"Ever since I've arrived, you've made it clear my life is pathetic now that it's focused on a child. But that's where I am." Marianne's voice quivers with hurt, and Chloe reaches out to grab her hand.

Sloane looks up, seemingly realizing the pain she's caused. "It's not pathetic," she says, but it's not convincing.

"Then what?" Marianne shouts. "Because you skipped out on Easter for *work*. And I know you love your design business, but you don't really need to work. I think you're avoiding me. Chloe had an excuse. What's yours?"

Chloe shifts uncomfortably. She hates these fights. Marianne and Sloane usually get along because they accept how different they are. But sometimes these differences explode, and Chloe hates being caught in the middle.

"I have my reasons," Sloane whispers.

Marianne shakes her head. "Not good enough. You're my best friend. This has been the biggest year of my life. Everything *is* different. It's not going as I planned either." Sloane opens her mouth to speak, but Marianne holds up her hand so that she can continue. "You've suddenly decided that you're too good for me. Your judgment of my decision to have a child and spend time focusing on that child is crushing me, Sloane." Marianne spits the words. Even though they aren't directed at her, Chloe still feels the impact.

"It's not a pathetic decision," Sloane quickly replies. "It's the best, most important decision you can ever make. I'm jealous," Sloane screams before composing herself. "And I'm not handling it well."

"You're jealous? With your multimillion-dollar home and your endless wardrobe and your ability to plan a dinner without clipping coupons? If you're going to lie to me, come up with a better reason."

Marianne storms away, and Chloe doesn't try to catch up. Because she knows, in this moment, it's Sloane who needs her more.

Chloe wraps her arm around Sloane's shoulders. "You need to tell her what's going on," Chloe says gently.

"Maybe," Sloane replies. They watch the waves and sit in silence until Chloe senses that Sloane's breathing has returned to normal and Marianne has had enough time to calm down as well.

Eventually, Chloe stands and offers her hand to Sloane, pulling her up and then pulling her close as they walk toward the house.

At the door to the back deck, after showering off their feet, Chloe says, "She needs to understand what's happening in your life. If you don't tell Marianne, you're going to lose her."

"What's the point?" Sloane says with a defeated tone, so uncharacteristic that Chloe reaches out and squeezes her hand. When Sloane looks up, there are tears in her eyes. "I've already lost everything important anyway."

Sloane goes inside. There are a million questions Chloe wants to ask. When she tries to catch up, Sloane shakes her head and shuts her bedroom door, but not before Chloe sees the tears streaking her face.

Chloe takes a moment, wondering whether she should force Sloane to talk or try to find Marianne. It's the noise in their bedroom that convinces Chloe that she should check on Marianne.

When Chloe walks into the room, Marianne is opening cabinet drawers and stuffing clothes into her suitcase, her cell phone sandwiched between her shoulder and ear.

"What's going on?" Chloe asks.

"I'm leaving," Marianne says. "The flights are too expensive. But Noah's losing his mind with Teddy, so they're going to drive down and pick me up."

"Isn't it like a ten-hour drive?"

"It's a desperate situation," Marianne says. "For all of us." Marianne tells Noah that she will call him back once she is packed and hangs up the phone.

Chloe sits on the bed, her mind spinning with how to fix this situation. She starts with a simple question. "Why are you leaving?"

Marianne looks up, her eyes seeming to judge Chloe for the stupidity of the question. "Sloane is impossible. And I miss my family. None of this bullshit is worth it anymore."

Marianne zips up her suitcase and carries it downstairs. Chloe follows, trying to change her friend's mind, something Chloe should know is impossible. "What are you going to do until Noah gets here?"

"Sit outside."

"It's eighty-five degrees. You can't sit outside all day."

Marianne's departure plans have been announced loudly enough that everyone seems to come out of their respective corners of the house and congregate in the living room.

"What's going on?" Alden asks naïvely.

"Your wife is a bitch. That's what's going on," Marianne replies.

Mild-mannered Alden, who only raises his voice when he's cheering on the Atlanta Braves, shouts, "What the hell, Marianne?"

"I don't even know how you can defend her anymore," Marianne shouts back. "Sloane's rude. And critical. And judgmental of any life that doesn't align with her view of perfection." Marianne's voice is clear, unwavering. Because she's right. That's exactly who Sloane is.

But Chloe knows there's also a lot more to Sloane. The second year Chloe was living in New York, in a particularly low moment, she called Sloane, crying. Luke was working around the clock, Chloe hadn't made many friends, she felt like she was constantly messing up at the gallery, and the grief of losing her parents came over her like a tidal wave. After years of pushing aside how much she missed them, spending so much time alone, Chloe was forced to confront her loss. She called Sloane and, through choked sobs, Chloe confessed all of these feelings to her friend. Sloane listened for over two hours, never trying to fix the situation, knowing that Chloe needed support more than anything else. When they hung up the phone, Chloe instantly felt better. She felt like it was possible to navigate the pain. But what Sloane did next was what made her truly special. Because Chloe had mentioned that Luke was working that weekend and those lonely Saturdays were the hardest, Sloane showed up on her doorstep, bagel sandwiches in hand, with an entire weekend itinerary for the two of them. By this time, Sloane had a whole established life in Atlanta, easily reintegrating with high school and family friends. But she dropped everything, booked a last-minute flight, and stood by Chloe's side because Sloane knew how to fix problems. And in this case, Sloane herself was the solution. Even though Sloane can be harsh and judgmental, she's still the fiercest, most loyal friend any of them have ever known.

But sometimes it's hard to remember the good in someone when you're confronted with their worst. Chloe's not sure how to navigate the tension between Sloane and Marianne.

Alden seems too angry to try. "It looks like you are on your way out," Alden says to Marianne. "That's probably for the best." For Alden, that's as close as he gets to kicking some-one out of his house, which, judging by the look on his face, is exactly what he would like to do to Marianne.

"Don't leave," Sloane says. At some point, she must have emerged from her room and hidden on the steps. She's peeking between the railings as she says, "I'm sorry, Marianne."

Alden goes up the stairs two at a time and crouches in front of his wife. "You have nothing to apologize for." Alden cups Sloane's face and softly kisses her lips. "You are none of those things Marianne said."

"No, Alden," Sloane whispers. "She's exactly right. I've been so focused on myself that I've turned into the worst kind of friend."

Alden shakes his head. "You didn't do anything wrong. You're remarkable."

"Honestly, Alden, you're worse than Sloane." Marianne picks up her bag and walks to the door. "All you do is enable her bad behavior. I'm sick of it."

Chloe follows, snatches the suitcase out of Marianne's hand and says, "Stop. You need to hear Sloane out."

Chloe blocks the door while Sloane stands and slowly walks toward Marianne, Alden following.

Wyatt and Luke have been silent, their eyes darting back and forth as voices and tensions rise.

"What could she possibly say that would make any difference?" Marianne asks rhetorically.

Chloe raises her eyebrows at Sloane, silently begging her to finally break her silence.

"You tell her, Chloe," Sloane says softly.

"Are you sure?" Chloe asks.

Sloane nods.

Chloe takes a deep breath, knowing that honesty is the only way to mend the break between Sloane and Marianne. It feels strange to reveal someone else's secret, but Chloe understands. The truth can be scary to admit, especially to those you love most.

◆ 13 ◆

Five Years Ago

"YOU SKI, RIGHT?" MARIANNE asked Chloe.

Chloe shook her head. "I snowboard."

"Have you ever done it on the East Coast?" Marianne bit her lip. "It's super icy."

Chloe shrugged. "We grew up going to Tahoe each winter. I'm pretty comfortable on a mountain." Chloe stood, pulling up her snow pants. "I think I'll be okay."

"What do you know about ski conditions?" Noah asked as he kissed his wife's head. "You can barely sled down the bunny hill." Marianne reached up and swept the hair out of Noah's eyes.

Sometimes Chloe thought Noah and Marianne looked more like siblings than a couple. They had matching soft, brown hair. The same chocolate eyes. The same kind smiles. But maybe that's what happened to all couples after spending so many years together. They rubbed off on one another, finding it hard to define where one person started and the other ended.

"I can barely sled because it's so icy," Marianne said as she leaned her head on Noah's shoulder. They'd been married for two months and likely hadn't been more than six inches apart in that entire time.

Over the years, Noah had joined various events—spending weekends partying at Mayfield, nights crammed into the Murray Hill apartment, joining in birthday celebrations. He wasn't exactly part of the group, but he was basically an honorary member.

But Noah usually skipped the group trips, claiming that Marianne needed time alone with her friends. The thing that Marianne and Noah seemed to understand was that meeting the love of your life at fifteen meant you had to give the other person space to live their life too. It was something Chloe admired about their relationship. The fact that Noah was a safe place to land instead of a constant tether.

But this year, Noah and Marianne got married over Christmas. They had spent a few nights in a hotel near their home but couldn't afford to take a bigger trip for their honeymoon.

When Luke's mom said she had a client with a ski house in Vermont and asked if Luke wanted to bring some friends, they were all excited to join. With two teachers' salaries, Noah and Marianne didn't have a lot of extra cash, so they decided to come along on this group trip, making it a sort of hybrid friend vacation and delayed honeymoon.

Everyone agreed to give Marianne and Noah the big bedroom at the far end of the house. Mostly because Noah hadn't stopped kissing various parts of Marianne's body since they all met up at the airport in Burlington, and it was abundantly clear that separation between multiple walls was necessary.

When they piled into the giant SUV Luke had rented and drove the hour east to Stowe, all crammed with suitcases and skis and giant puffy coats, there wasn't a silent moment. Even though they'd just been together for Marianne and Noah's wedding, two months seemed like an eternity to a group of people that functioned best as one unit as opposed to the scattered locations they found themselves in now.

The friends fully embraced the luxury of the house. When they walked inside the modern mountain cabin, everyone echoed the same gasp. Bags were dropped in the two-story entryway with its giant metal chandelier as everyone skipped through the rooms, shouting across the house about the luxuries hidden in every corner.

"There's a hot tub," Wyatt yelled.

"This bathroom has a steam shower," Sloane moaned.

Chloe let her fingers explore the home's textures, the beautiful blond wood that paneled the entry, the stacked-stone fireplace that extended the entire height of the house, flanked by giant, black-framed windows that provided portrait views of Vermont's Green Mountains. There were plaid blankets tastefully draped on the back of the matching leather armchairs. And one of those deep, long sofas, that could fit an army and swallow a person whole.

Their first night was spent grilling the steaks the house manager had already stocked in the fridge. Sipping bottles of red wine they could never afford themselves. Roasting potatoes dripping in olive oil until the edges turned a crispy brown and covering them in coarse sea salt. They all ended the night in the hot tub, the full moon illuminating snow-covered mountains as they were surrounded by steam and jets and laughter.

They awoke in their bedrooms, slipping out of giant four-poster beds, as their feet brushed against antique rugs in warm reds and blues, to eat a giant breakfast Sloane happily prepared. Frittata with mushrooms and goat cheese, leftover potatoes pan-fried with rosemary, and spicy Bloody Marys with extra horseradish.

After breakfast they were all eager to explore, to embrace the "Vermont ski vacation" that was a first for the group that usually found themselves crammed into beach hotels or sleeping on each other's couches. They were pretending to be grown up, as if they could afford a place like this, a life like this.

Once everyone emerged from their rooms, in various stages of dress for a cold Vermont winter, they began discussing plans.

"So you think you'd handle West Coast skiing better?" Noah said as he pulled a knit cap down over Marianne's eyes.

"Maybe," Marianne said, sticking out her tongue. "But I'm excited to try something new today."

"What are you guys going to do?" Chloe asked.

"We're going snowshoeing," Marianne said with more enthusiasm than anyone should ever express about walking around in clunky boots. "We'll meet you guys at the lodge after those guys finish their competitive ski expedition." Marianne pointed across the kitchen island to where Luke and Wyatt were hunched over a map.

Luke and Wyatt were up before anyone else in the house, checking snow reports and mapping out their plan of attack on the mountain. They seemed to be extra competitive these days. Now that they were living in different cities, their catch-up sessions occasionally veered into comparison battle territory. Chloe watched as the two friends, once inseparable, seemed to only focus on their differences. Wyatt was immersed in his new life in DC, throwing around insider knowledge about Hill debates none of them seemed to fully understand, while Luke couldn't help dropping obscure insights about market movements. Sometimes, when they were going back and forth like they had over cocktails the night before, Chloe wanted to scream *None of this matters*, except, she supposed, to them it did. She just didn't know why.

Chloe hoped this week in Vermont would fix whatever insecurities seemed to be lingering under all of that competitive testosterone. She sipped coffee while they continued their debate about whether they should start on the blue runs with Chloe or just skip straight to the black diamonds.

"What about you guys?" Chloe asked Sloane and Alden, who were reading books on opposite ends of the couch.

"I do not ski," Sloane said. "I'm from Atlanta."

"That doesn't seem like a real reason," Chloe said. "Luke is also from Atlanta and . . ." Chloe trailed off as she pointed in Luke's direction and he mumbled something about the best runs with moguls.

Sloane placed a bookmark in her book and said, "I was not raised by an intense mother who insisted I learn every sport where potential business deals can be negotiated."

Although Sloane was right—Luke's mother was the most intense person Chloe had ever met—Chloe never would have said that out loud. Everyone knew Luke could be extra sensitive about his family, especially his mother.

"Too harsh, Sloane," Alden said, nudging her foot on the couch.

"Sorry, Luke," Sloane said.

Chloe smiled. Because Sloane was always quick to apologize, especially when she realized that maybe the bluntness that came so naturally to her wasn't always appreciated by her audience. Chloe liked the fact that Sloane embraced who she was but also had an awareness of her faults. And Alden's role in this particular interaction didn't go unnoticed by Chloe. Although she'd be reluctant to admit it, Sloane looked to Alden as a barometer of sorts. He was usually reserved, but when he spoke up, especially to Sloane, she always listened.

"But not untrue," Luke shrugged. "I was in golf lessons at eight." He stood up and grabbed his jacket off an entryway hook. "There are going to be zero business discussions today. This is all about fun. I'm ready to forget work and ski. Can we head out?"

"Sloane, are you staying here by yourself?" Chloe asked.

Alden shook his head. "I need to get some work done. I'm going to stay back too."

"What are you guys going to do all day?" Marianne asked. "We'll be gone for hours."

"I am going to do this," Sloane said, holding up her book and snuggling deeper into the couch. "And I am very happy about it."

"Okay, we'll see you two for dinner," Noah said, ushering everyone out the door.

Driving to the ski lodge, unloading the gear, and getting everyone set up with rentals took longer than Luke would have wanted. Chloe noticed his antsy glances at his watch. The way he rocked back and forth as Noah and Marianne debated which snowshoe rental package they wanted to purchase.

"Why don't you and Wyatt go ahead," Chloe said. "I can figure out my snowboard rental and meet up with you guys later."

"Are you sure?" Luke asked at the same time Wyatt said, "We're in no hurry."

Chloe laughed. "I'm sure. I'm going to start on some of the easier runs anyway. I'll text you when I'm at the top of the mountain."

Wyatt seemed to hesitate, but Luke quickly kissed her cheek and went out the door.

When Wyatt looked over at Chloe as he slowly shuffled toward the exit, Chloe mouthed *I'm fine* and went back to helping Marianne try on a pair of rental boots.

Twenty minutes later, Chloe was starting down the first slope. There was a muscle memory to snowboarding, and immediately Chloe felt the joy of being twelve, the freedom of flying down a mountain alone, when really her father was always right behind her, watching to make sure she didn't wipe out. It made her miss her family. She pulled out her phone to take a picture to text her brother, but she had no service.

Chloe eased down the slope, quickly realizing that Marianne was right. The mountain was icy. Chloe found herself picking up speed, the crisp crunch of her board's edge cutting against the packed runs. When a group of middle schoolers cut in front of her, Chloe veered to the right to avoid mowing through a pile of kids. But she hit a sharp shard of ice and lost control. All of a sudden, she was flying into the woods, narrowly missing the trunk of a tree, as branches whipped against her face. She tried to slow down, maneuver herself away from an even worse crash, but with the slap of each evergreen, more snow fell on her head, covering her goggles. Somehow, she slowed enough to finally land with a thud in the densely wooded forest.

She sat for a moment, looking over her shoulder, and saw that she'd gone farther off course than she initially thought. She couldn't help but laugh. Even when she was first learning to snowboard, she hadn't crashed in such a spectacular manner. Chloe unsnapped her board, ready to hike back to the slope, but winced as she tried to maneuver her left foot. In all the adrenaline of narrowly missing the kids and then epically crashing herself, Chloe must have twisted her ankle.

She hoped it was minor enough that she could hobble out of the woods, knowing she had no phone signal. When she tried to stand, she immediately collapsed back on the ground. The pain was shooting up her entire leg, and she knew she wasn't going to be able to put any weight on her foot. It was too far to army crawl, so Chloe did the only thing she could think of doing: she lay in the snow and closed her eyes, trying to will away the tears. What a mess.

"Odd place for a nap," his deep voice echoed.

Chloe's eyes snapped open, and the first thing she saw was Wyatt's beaming smile hovering over her.

"What are you doing here?" She sat up and tried to brush away the snow and embarrassment.

"I wanted to join your off-road expedition." Wyatt stuck his poles in the snow and leaned against a tree.

"Seriously, Wyatt. How did you find me?"

"I was at the top of the slope. I saw those prepubescent terrors almost take you out. It just took me a few minutes to catch up to you because I didn't want to decapitate myself going fifty miles an hour through a forest."

"I think I almost died." Chloe said, leaning back into the snow.

Wyatt reached down and extended his hand, pulling Chloe back up to seated. "I think you almost hurt yourself," he said.

"No. I did hurt myself. I did something to my ankle."

"Let me check it out." He popped out of his skis and bent down to look at Chloe's feet. He gently ran his fingers around the outside of her snow boot and tried to move her foot to the side, but she yelped in pain.

"Can you walk on it?" he asked, his eyebrows bunched together.

"I don't think so." The reality of the situation hit Chloe. It was day one, hour one of their ski trip and she was injured in the forest. Not ideal.

"Alright. Leave your board," he said, stacking his skis next to her board. "I'll come back and grab our stuff. We can walk out. Wrap your arm around my shoulder."

"How far are we from the slope?"

He bit his bottom lip as he estimated. "Maybe half a mile."

She groaned. "What are we going to do when we get back to the slope?" The whole situation seemed hopeless.

"Flag down ski patrol," Wyatt said reassuringly. "You are not the first injured snowboarder they have seen."

"I'm lucky you were watching me," she said.

When he nodded solemnly and didn't reply with some sarcastic comeback, Chloe felt guilty. He seemed genuinely concerned. And although her ankle was throbbing, maybe she had overplayed the drama of the situation.

"I'll be fine," she said. "I probably just need some ice." She playfully poked his side with her free hand. "You don't have to worry about me."

"I always worry about you, Chloe," Wyatt said softly.

She felt so vulnerable in that moment. After her parents died, she had been so grateful for the support of her friends. But after a few years, her feelings shifted. She started to feel like their pet project, the sad lonely one who needed coddling. Some days she felt like she needed to convince her friends that she was strong again. Sometimes she felt like she needed to convince herself of the same thing.

"Maybe Marianne was right. I can't handle this icy New England skiing," Chloe said, hoping to deflect Wyatt's comment.

"I think you can handle just about anything. But that doesn't mean I don't worry." Wyatt's grip tightened around her waist. He lifted Chloe as they walked, her injured foot barely brushing against the ground.

"Thanks, Wyatt. You're a good friend." She swallowed as she said the words. She'd known Wyatt for years, but they rarely had these types of conversations, just the two of them. And they never had these types of conversations with Wyatt's body pressed against hers, his strong arms practically carrying her through the snowy woods.

"Yep. A good friend," he said slowly.

There was a moment of silence, that she immediately filled with an overly chipper question. "So how do you like DC?"

"I like it," Wyatt said with a small smile. "I miss you guys, but I needed a fresh start. DC feels like the place I'm meant to be."

When Wyatt ran into their apartment last year, with news of his offer at *Granite*, the political site that exploded after the last election, they all celebrated. But they also knew what that meant. Wyatt was leaving.

"And your writing?" Chloe asked. "How's that big project coming along?" Over the years, Wyatt was always working on his own project in addition to his reporting and freelance jobs. A novel? A short story? Alden and Luke joked that it was probably a collection of poems. None of them were ever sure because Wyatt was fiercely protective of his work.

"It's coming along." Wyatt said, not elaborating.

"Why don't you tell me about it? It will help pass the time for your poor, injured friend as she hobbles through the forest."

"Nice try," Wyatt said, shaking his head. "I'm not ready to share any details. But it's something that I've been thinking about for a while. And this last year has really put things in perspective. It's clear where the story is going."

"It's a story!" she said, excited about this reveal of information. "Not a comic book? Or a sonnet?"

"You guys are ridiculous." He bent down to clear a low-lying branch. "It's a novel."

"Will you let me read it?" She turned toward him, taking a break in a walk that was much more difficult than anticipated with only one working foot. "When you're ready?" she quickly added.

He took a deep breath, seeming to consider her question, before ultimately nodding slightly. "Yes," Wyatt said, and dusted some fallen snow off the top of Chloe's head.

The rest of their walk was mostly silent. Wyatt seemed somber. Somehow, agreeing to something as simple as letting Chloe read his writing clouded his mood.

When they got back to the slope, her foot throbbed and her arm tingled from its immobile position clinging around his neck. He had basically carried her the entire time, through the deep, fluffy snow of the wooded area off-trail, and his brow was damp from the effort. But not once did he complain or slow down.

Chloe and Wyatt spotted a skier coming downhill. Wyatt waved his arms to get his attention and then turned to Chloe. "I'll ask this guy to send up ski patrol. When they're here, I'll go back for your board. They should be able to wrap your ankle back at the lodge."

None of these things were revelations, but Chloe was comforted by each of Wyatt's statements. The disaster she had created was fixable. Wyatt had a plan.

When the skier approached, Chloe broke into a wide smile. As he approached, Chloe recognized his tall form shadowed against the crisp, white hill. Of course, the jacket Luke had purchased last week was immediately recognizable too, the bold blue that Chloe knew suited him perfectly the minute he tried it on in the store.

"What happened to you two?" Luke asked. He was out of breath, his cheeks flushed from a morning of intense skiing.

"I narrowly avoided a pack of children and crashed," Chloe admitted. "Wyatt helped me out of the woods."

Luke laughed. Chloe supposed it might have been funny if she hadn't just hobbled a half mile through the woods with a throbbing ankle. She managed a half smile in Luke's direction, mostly to overcome her embarrassment.

"Can you go get ski patrol?" Wyatt asked. There was zero amusement in his voice. "I'll stay with Chloe." Wyatt's hand was still around her waist, a needed support for her unsteady balance.

"Nah, I'll give her a ride downhill." Luke shuffled toward Chloe. He positioned a ski on either side and backed toward her, bent slightly.

"I don't think that's a good idea." Wyatt tried to dismiss Luke's suggestion. He gestured toward her foot as he continued, "She's injured."

"Chloe's used to riding on my back. Hop on, babe."

Chloe wasn't sure if she was even capable of hopping at this point. But Luke seemed insistent. He kept looking over his shoulder, seemingly impatient with her delayed response. Chloe knew that Luke could easily carry her down and probably do it safely. He'd been skiing since he was a toddler. She also dreaded the spectacle that a ski patrol visit would necessitate.

"Do not drop me, Luke." When Luke grinned in response, Chloe playfully poked his back. "I'm serious."

"I'd never," he said, winking. Chloe slowly maneuvered herself onto his back and Luke handed his ski poles to Wyatt. "Can you bring these down for me?"

Wyatt didn't respond other than shaking his head and looking up the mountain.

Luke gripped the backs of Chloe's thighs tightly, running his hand upward and blatantly fondling both butt cheeks. Although, through long underwear and snow gear, it was difficult to achieve any real fondling. But still, as Luke started slowly skiing downhill, balancing Chloe on his back and making jokes about sending a video to Chloe's brother, she couldn't help but laugh.

She turned her head to look back at Wyatt, who seemed to have a nervous look on his face. Chloe gave him a subtle wave and mouthed *thanks*. Wyatt replied with a tiny nod before he turned around and walked back into the woods.

By the time Wyatt made it down the mountain, carrying Chloe's snowboard, she was being attended to by two ski patrollers, who had carefully removed her boot and were icing her ankle. Luke had a hot toddy in his hands, and Marianne and Noah were ordering a fondue appetizer while Chloe was acting out a reverse-harem fantasy of having multiple men attend to her every need.

Wyatt shook off the snow and walked over and sat by Chloe. He immediately asked the ski patroller holding Chloe's ankle, "Is it a break? Should we take her to the ER?"

"Nah, just a sprain. Ice and elevate. She should be fine."

"Thanks for the rescue, Wyatt." Chloe reached out and accepted the hot toddy from Luke. She took a sip and immediately felt better. Chloe wasn't typically a whiskey person, but something about being surrounded by all the wood and stone and leather of the lodge, plus the fire, plus the injury, made whiskey seem ideal.

"She's lucky you saw her," the ski patroller said. "That part of the trail is so wooded. You can get lost in there."

Chloe took a sip of her cocktail and leaned back while the ski patroller continued wrapping her ankle. The fire was warm, the attention was delightful, and there was a hot tub back at the lodge. Despite the accident, things weren't too bad. "I am very lucky," Chloe said.

Luke sat at her side and absently rubbed her shoulders as he started sipping his own cocktail. "Want to go for one more run, Wyatt?" Luke asked.

Wyatt's eyebrows drew together. "Don't you think we should get Chloe back?"

"It's only lunchtime. She's okay hanging out, right, Chloe?" Luke squeezed her shoulder twice, before downing his drink in one large gulp.

"Yeah, I'll be fine," Chloe shrugged. "As long as Marianne and Noah share their food with me. You guys have fun."

"I think we should head back," Wyatt said.

"I'll make it quick. I didn't get to do the last black diamond, and Chloe's not going to be able to get out tomorrow. I'll be back in twenty minutes, okay?" Luke leaned down and kissed Chloe's cheek, walking out of the lodge before anyone else responded.

Marianne and Noah were avoiding eye contact, but Wyatt stared intently. Chloe didn't feel like defending Luke to Wyatt, but that's exactly what she did. "Luke's been looking forward to skiing. Work has been intense. He needs to have some fun."

"I thought being together was the fun part," Wyatt said and walked toward the bar.

Chloe sat across from Marianne and Noah, their semi-honeymoon bliss undeterred. Chloe felt the immense roundness of being a giant third wheel, unable to move with a bum ankle, trapped at a table with two people whose lips were constantly millimeters apart.

When the waitress delivered the giant fondue tray, overflowing with focaccia and pretzel bites and crusty pumpernickel, bubbly cheese, and vegetables that seemed completely unnecessary, Marianne and Noah didn't even glance at the food. They were too hungry for each other.

"Pass me a hunk of bread," Chloe shouted as she reached for a fondue fork. Like most things in life, this day was something cheese and carbohydrates could fix and Chloe wasn't going to let the food go to waste.

One hour later, after Luke's single run had turned into two more, Wyatt had disappeared into the lodge library, and Marianne and Noah had wandered off to *explore*, which sounded like a code word for something dirtier, Chloe finished off the fondue platter. By herself. Her stomach was solid Gruyère at this point. It took two trips, but they piled their gear into the rental car, and Luke carried Chloe to the front seat. She wasn't sure if it was the ibuprofen the ski patroller had given her or the hot toddy in the lodge, but when they pulled into the driveway of the ski cabin, the throbbing in Chloe's ankle was finally easing.

They expected to find Alden huddled over his computer, Sloane snuggled in front of the fire, but when they stormed into the house, Noah carrying Marianne because he wasn't going to be out-romanced by Luke carrying Chloe, they couldn't find Sloane or Alden anywhere. Wyatt walked in last, dumping gear in a giant pile in front of the door and shouted for Alden to come help with the second load. But there was no response.

Initially, they assumed that Sloane and Alden had headed into town for some shopping, but they quickly realized that was impossible. They didn't have a car, and Uber drivers were as hard to find as cell signals.

"Maybe they went for a hike?" Marianne suggested.

"Sloane avoids all physical activity," Wyatt accurately pointed out.

"Try Alden's phone," Chloe suggested. Luke went to the window, the one spot in the house where they could make phone calls, and dialed Alden's number. They all heard his ringtone and discovered Alden's phone on the kitchen counter.

Chloe hobbled toward the deck and looked outside, hoping to see tracks or some sign of them. But then she found the wet bathing suits by the back door, the hot tub cover left off, steam rising into the air.

She motioned for everyone to come over and pointed to the soggy pile of discarded clothing. Everyone went silent.

"No way," Luke whispered.

"It's not possible." Wyatt shook his head, his eyes wide.

"They're off somewhere having sex." Noah was the one to finally say it out loud.

Marianne elbowed Noah's side at the same time Luke and Wyatt burst into laughter. Then Luke pointed at the trail of water streaking across the perfect hand-hewn wooden floors. Wyatt started walking and the rest followed, somewhat in a trance. It wasn't possible, was it? Sloane and Alden?

Chloe always thought Sloane viewed Alden as more of a brother than a friend. They had a closeness that was a bit different from the rest of the group, bonded by a shared childhood in the same Atlanta orbit. Sloane gave off a protective vibe when it came to Alden, and he always seemed to have her back, even when she was acting her most questionable. But romantic? Chloe and Luke often joked about Alden's not-so-secret crush, but Chloe never thought in a million years Sloane would reciprocate.

Whenever Sloane talked about her future husband (which was more frequent than most normal twenty-four-year-olds, Chloe often thought), Sloane never described a person anything like Alden. And all her past boyfriends were the polar opposite of Alden.

There had to be another explanation. Maybe it was a science experiment that involved wet bathing suits while Alden and Sloane remained fully, completely dressed. Chloe thought there was no way Sloane was willingly naked with Alden.

"I feel like that day in sex ed," Wyatt whispered.

"What day?" Chloe replied.

"When you're ten," Wyatt continued, "and some old lady tells you how babies are made. And then you realize that's how you were made. And your parents did that. I felt queasy."

"Do you think this is the first time?" Luke asked.

"We don't know that anything has happened," Chloe tried to convince herself. But the rest of her friends looked at her like she was crazy.

"It has to be the first time," Marianne whispered as they continued, slowly following the trail of water. "They couldn't have hidden this from us."

"How bored did they get today?" Noah commented.

Marianne held out her arms, stopping the group's progress down the hallway. "Maybe it wasn't boredom." There was an excitement in Marianne's voice that Chloe immediately noted as her friend's ability to turn every scenario into a fairy tale.

"Well, on Alden's part, of course not," Luke said. "But Sloane must have been bored out of her mind."

They all stood immobile, staring at the end of the hallway and the closed door leading to Alden's room. After a series of nervous glances back and forth, as a pack, they slunk down the hallway and paused. Luke put his ear to the door and immediately pulled it back, a horrified look on his face. Wyatt pushed him aside and took his turn, and then, one by one, they all acted like snooping siblings and listened at the closed door.

The muffled sounds coming from the room told them exactly what was happening between Sloane and Alden while everyone else was on the mountain.

They tried to tiptoe back down the hallway, but it was clear they all wanted to escape the burning inferno their ears were just subjected to as fast as possible.

Chloe leaned against one of the leather barstools that surrounded the kitchen island. Everyone else gathered, forming a circle like King Arthur's council of knights.

Luke spoke first. "Slow clap for Alden."

Chloe looked at him sideways. "Stop it."

"Whatever he was doing in there was obviously well appreciated." Luke smiled.

"Alden. And. Sloane." Wyatt let his words hang in the air before he pummeled them all with the most disturbing and obvious observation. "They're naked. Together. Right now."

"Let's stop dissecting whatever is happening behind that door." Chloe turned around and hobbled toward the fridge, pulling out a selection of beverages.

"What else are we going to do?" Marianne asked, genuinely.

Chloe lined up glasses and started pouring tequila in each one. "Drink to forget."

"Done." Wyatt downed his shot first. "Brilliant plan."

Luke took his shot and winced. "Some images can never escape your brain. Sloane's wet bikini on top of Alden's bathing suit is etched forever right here." Luke rubbed the spot in the middle of his forehead. Chloe felt a shudder of sympathy travel through her body.

"It's not that big of a deal," Noah said, looking around at the somber faces surrounding the marble island. Everyone turned and stared at Noah. Because he was so wrong. For a group of friends who had delicately navigated Chloe and Luke's relationship over the years, adding another romantic entanglement to the mix was a very big deal.

Chloe instantly remembered the spring of her junior year when she and Luke briefly broke up. It had taken months for her to trust Luke again, but it had taken even longer for the group to find their rhythm again. Whatever happened between Sloane and Alden, even if it was only once, was going to change them. There was no avoiding it.

Chloe looked over at Luke, wondering if he was also thinking of those months they had spent apart. If he was thinking about how every fight they had was difficult to keep between the two of them. The side-picking was inevitable, and most of the time it only made their fights worse, but sometimes it felt like the toll they had to pay for their relationship to continue alongside the friendships that meant so much to both of them.

When no one spoke, Noah seemed to realize the idiocy of his statement. "Okay, maybe it's a little bit of a big deal."

Marianne reached in front of him and grabbed Noah's shot along with her own, downing both of them in quick succession.

"More shots?" Chloe asked. Early afternoon heavy drinking was never a good idea, but necessary under certain circumstances. Naked Sloane and Alden were those circumstances.

Luke, Wyatt, and Marianne quickly nodded while Chloe barely waited for a response before she started pouring.

Noah shook his head no. "I'm going to focus on food for you guys. Luke, hand me the keys. I'll run into town and pick up some pizzas."

Luke tossed the keys over the kitchen island, and Marianne managed a small wave to Noah before turning back to Chloe and debating when and how Sloane first lost her clothes around Alden.

"I want olives," Wyatt shouted as Noah closed the front door. Chloe could hear Noah start the car as Luke grabbed a bottle of red wine from the pantry.

Their theories diverged, Luke and Wyatt adamant that this was a one-time event, Chloe and Marianne not so sure. All of them were shocked they were even discussing this possibility.

By the time they had finished the first bottle of wine, Alden walked into the kitchen. "Oh. You guys are back. When did that happen?" Alden asked.

Chloe felt herself blush on Alden's behalf. They had told him that they'd be back in time for dinner. There's no reason Alden or Sloane should have expected them now. Chloe's injury meant they had left the mountain much earlier than expected.

Alden shifted his weight from side to side. It was clear that he wasn't sure how much they knew, and so they all stood there in an uncomfortable silence, waiting to see who was going to speak up first. Luke was more than happy to interrupt.

"We were here for the 'aahhh' and 'ooooh,'" Luke said. And then Luke and Wyatt performed their version of Meg Ryan in the deli faking an orgasm.

"Shit," Alden mumbled.

About that time, Sloane rounded the corner, wrapped in one of the luxurious Turkish cotton bathrobes that were stocked in every bathroom. She was humming. Even if they hadn't overheard exactly what was happening behind that closed door, the sound of Sloane humming would have alerted all of them that something drastic had just happened. Humming required a cheerfulness that was never a part of Sloane's default state of being. It required extenuating circumstances. In this case, Alden.

"Hello," Sloane stuttered and then immediately recovered. "I just had the most amazing bath. What have you been up to, Alden?"

"Alden seems to be up—" Wyatt started to say, but Alden cut him off before he could finish.

"They know, Sloane," Alden said.

"Know what?" Sloane walked over to the fridge and pulled out a can of sparkling water.

"That you guys just had sex," Marianne scream-whispered.

Sloane tried to muster her best perplexed face, shrugging in a shocked yet overdramatic manner. "Alden must have been watching a movie. I've been in the bath."

Luke held up Sloane's bikini top in one hand and Alden's bathing suit in the other. "Did you strip down for the bath with Alden?"

"Sloane, they know," Alden repeated. "We need to admit what's going on."

"Wait. Going on?" Chloe couldn't get the words out fast enough. "You mean this has happened before?"

"I did not want to do this yet," Sloane sighed, slumped on a stool, and reached for Chloe's glass of wine, taking a long sip.

"I know. But it's time." Alden walked around the island and squeezed Sloane's shoulder. When he leaned down to kiss the top of her head, everyone loudly gasped.

Sloane looked up into Alden's eyes. "You know what happens once we tell them."

"It's already happening," Alden said before he kissed Sloane again.

Sloane pulled her mouth away from Alden's and said, "Okay. Yes. Alden and I had sex. Who's in charge of dinner tonight?"

This wasn't new information. Chloe and Luke and Wyatt and Marianne had taken turns pressing their ears against the door. They all knew this had happened. And yet hearing this admission suddenly made it one thousand times more real.

"That's not going to be enough information for this pack of wolves," Wyatt understated.

"Are you dating?" Chloe asked.

"Have you had sex before?" Marianne added.

"Alden. Dude. Nice." Luke fist-bumped Alden. In a reflexive response, Alden reciprocated the bump, but Sloane scowled at the gesture. Like magnets, Alden's eyes connected with Sloane's.

"Sorry, babe," Alden replied.

"Babe? You call Sloane babe?" Chloe asked. "And she's okay with it?"

"Enough." Sloane opened a kitchen cabinet and got her own wineglass. She opened a second bottle, poured herself a generous glass, and resumed her seat at the kitchen island. "We are not specimens under a microscope. We had sex today. We've been having sex for months. Now, can someone please tell me about the dinner plans. I'm starving."

"You worked up an appetite," Luke said. Unrestrained chuckles escaped from Wyatt's mouth, and then they were all laughing.

"So it's a sex thing?" Chloe asked, still probing this foreign situation. "That's it?"

Alden's eyebrows jumped. Sloane rolled her eyes. "Fine," Sloane sighed. "Tell them."

"I love her," Alden blurted. "I have loved her for a very long time and I finally wore her down."

Immediately, four sets of eyes turned toward Sloane. Because sex was one thing, but love—none of them, not Chloe or Marianne or Wyatt or Luke, ever imagined what was going on behind that door was anything close to love.

Sloane smirked. "I love him too."

Marianne cheered, always ready to celebrate love, especially when it involved two of her best friends, but it took the rest of them a few moments of silence.

Because Sloane didn't love lightly. She'd *liked* boyfriends in the past. She'd expressed *affection* for her parents. But not once had Sloane ever said she loved another person. Not even when Marianne was in one of her teary drunk moods and babbling about how much she loved everyone, did Sloane ever reciprocate those words, even to placate a tipsy Marianne. The fact that Sloane had just admitted she loved Alden with such confidence and conviction, no hesitation in her statement, was the most sobering moment of the night.

If it was love that was going on between Alden and Sloane, it really did change everything. Chloe was happy for her friends. Initially, the pairing seemed strange, but the more she thought about Sloane and Alden, the idea of opposites attracting seemed to ring true.

The first night after discovering Sloane and Alden together, everyone kept staring at them. For Chloe, it was almost like studying animals at the zoo. Sloane and Alden still ate food, but strangely, Sloane wiped a smudge of sauce off Alden's lip. And then kissed him. Chloe choked on her giant gulp of wine.

The subtle changes throughout the week were the most unsettling. Each person was assigned a different night to be in charge of dinner. Usually Sloane provided printed spreadsheets, detailing assignments and demanding reports. The spreadsheet was still there, but when Sloane asked about the meal Chloe had planned and Chloe said she was going to wing it, fully expecting to send Sloane into a tailspin, she got a different reaction. Alden squeezed Sloane's hand twice, not even making eye contact, and Sloane's face changed. "Sounds good," she replied, and Chloe was amazed by Alden's powerful influence.

Sloane moved her suitcase into Alden's room at the end of the hall, and each morning they were the last to emerge. Maybe it was the infatuation of a new love, but Chloe suspected it was something else. Because Sloane wasn't waking up and preparing her green juice before consulting her itinerary for the day. Instead, she was walking around in Alden's oversized T-shirt, her strawberry blonde hair piled in a messy bun on top of her head, as she stole bites of pancake off Alden's plate. Sloane was relaxed. And Alden was so deliriously happy every moment of every day, his arm wrapped around Sloane's waist, proudly connected to a person he called his girlfriend dozens of times in every conversation.

The rest of the week was bliss. Chloe embraced the lodge life with Sloane while the rest of their friends went off on different excursions. Midweek, they all decided to rent snowmobiles and rode through the backcountry trails to a rustic inn, where they ate steaming bowls of minestrone and homemade bread before riding back to the lodge. At night, they watched movies and ate maple candy and spent hours jumping between the hot tub and the sauna, dripping all over those beautiful floors. Afternoons of cocktails in cozy bars with roaring fireplaces while Chloe tried to extract as many details of this new relationship with Alden as possible. Nights of Chloe and Luke tangled together, necessitating new creativity given Chloe's bum ankle and so many extra ears in the house.

Chloe cried on the last night, already missing her friends before they'd even left. Maybe it was because Chloe knew.

They were all growing up, getting married, starting new relationships, living in new places. But for that one blissful week in Vermont, they got to be *together*, Chloe's favorite place.

◆ 14 ◆

This Year

CHLOE TAKES ANOTHER BREATH, preparing herself to reveal her friend's painful secret. "Sloane had a miscarriage, Marianne. She's telling the truth when she says she's jealous of your life."

Marianne spins around and looks at Sloane, whose eyes haven't left the floor.

"That's why Chloe agreed to come on this trip," Sloane admits. "I told her I needed her after the last miscarriage."

Chloe looks over to see Wyatt and Luke's reaction. She had never told either of them what Sloane said to convince her to come on the trip. And by the surprise on their faces, it seems as if Alden never mentioned this news to them either.

Chloe pauses, Sloane's words echoing. "Wait. What do you mean *last miscarriage*?"

Alden wraps his arms around his wife. "You should tell them everything," he whispers.

Sloane walks over to the window, the entire room waiting for her to speak. "I haven't had one miscarriage," Sloane says. "I've had two."

Marianne gasps and Chloe instinctively moves closer, wanting to wrap her arms around her friend, but Sloane takes two steps back, seemingly needing space as she continues speaking.

"I've had two miscarriages," Sloane repeats. "Four rounds of IVF. And we're the lucky ones because we have enough money for all of these incredibly expensive procedures."

"How long has this been going on?" Chloe asks softly.

"Two years. We started trying after the wedding," Sloane replies in a monotone. She starts pacing, her voice pitching upward as she speaks. "The first miscarriage was the hardest. All those doctors. And the hospital. And lawyers. A room full of people making sure everything that's being done is legal, checking to make sure that they aren't violating a law while I'm lying in a bed, blood soaking the sheets."

Sloane slumps onto the couch and they all gather around, hanging on her every word. Except Alden. Alden is staring out the window, and Chloe sees his eyes welling with tears.

There are tears streaming down Sloane's face, but she doesn't seem to notice. After a deep breath, her voice shakes as she continues. "All of those injections and scraping and the crinkles of paper and the technical terms they use instead of saying *the baby is gone.*"

Chloe notices that none of the friends are asking questions. They are all shocked by the news they are receiving, Sloane relaying this painful memory. Personal pain that her closest friends were completely unaware of.

Alden joins Sloane on the couch. His hands weave into her hair as they stare at each other.

"It hasn't been easy," Alden understates. "But we have each other."

"Sloane. Why didn't you say anything?" Marianne asks.

Sloane straightens, her lips pulled tight as she answers. "Because it's private. It's between Alden and me. We all share so much. We know too much about each other." Sloane looks at Chloe, and she understands exactly what she means.

Chloe often wondered if her relationship with Luke had been a little more private, would it have made a difference? Or was it better to share in the challenges and joys of a relationship with your best friends? Chloe can't imagine the isolation of keeping pain like Sloane and Alden's inside.

Sloane continues. "Getting pregnant was going to be just for us. And then when I couldn't get pregnant, I didn't want to advertise my failure."

"It's not a failure," Alden says firmly.

Sloane shakes her head. "Marianne got pregnant the first month. And looked like a goddess her entire pregnancy. And the baby practically fell out. I'm a giant flaw in comparison."

"But Sloane, it's not a competition," Marianne tries to say as gently as possible.

"The only people who say that are the winners," Sloane quickly replies.

"I did not look like a goddess my entire pregnancy. I had back-ne." Marianne makes this comment in earnest. As if it would make Sloane feel better that Marianne experienced this minor, common inconvenience during an otherwise uneventful pregnancy.

Sloane is the first to laugh, and it gives everyone else permission to join.

It's a brief break in an otherwise heavy conversation, but Chloe knows that it's only temporary. There are so many questions she wants to ask. So much guilt she feels for being absent when her friend needed support.

Chloe joins Sloane and Alden on the couch. "You shouldn't have gone through that alone."

"You wanted to be alone," Sloane retorts. "You and Luke had just ended your nine-year relationship and you didn't want any of us around."

"Sloane, you can't even compare a breakup to this," Chloe says.

"Besides, Chloe wasn't really alone. She had Wyatt, right?" It's the first thing Luke has said, and Chloe hears a tenseness in his voice.

Chloe wants to let it go, but Marianne jumps in, quickly dismissing Luke. "Wyatt lives in DC. It would be ridiculous if they didn't see each other." Marianne walks toward the couch and sits on the coffee table, facing her friends.

"Both of you should have talked to us more," Marianne says, waving a finger back and forth between Chloe and Sloane. "Both of you need to lean on us. There shouldn't be so many secrets between friends."

"In my defense," Sloane says, "I did tell Chloe. That's why she agreed to come on this trip."

Chloe tilts her head. "You told me you had one miscarriage and you needed your best friends."

"So that's why you're here?" Luke asks. "Because Sloane guilted you into being here."

Chloe stares at Luke, frustrated by his comment. "Yes, because when I had only the tiniest window into what she was going through, it was enough to wake me up to my selfishness."

"That's all it took," Luke says.

Chloe shakes her head. "Another time, Luke. This is about Sloane and Alden."

"You're right," Luke agrees. He turns toward Sloane and Alden and says, "I'm sorry." But it sounds like an obligation rather than an apology.

"A lot of couples go through the same thing," Alden says. "Our doctor said one client did six rounds of IVF and then had twins." There's hope in Alden's voice that's missing from his face.

"So that's your plan? To do another round?" Luke asks. None of them have any idea how IVF works, but they want to be as supportive as possible. Because they all know that Sloane and Alden have always wanted children, and their hearts are breaking at hearing the news of their losses.

Sloane nods. "We did another round last week. I went to the doctor's office this morning."

Alden chimes in. "The blood test takes a few hours. The doctor should call us this afternoon with the results."

"It's going to work this time," Sloane says, plastering a smile on her face. "I'm pregnant. I know I am."

No one speaks, hoping there's truth behind Sloane's conviction.

Sloane turns toward Marianne. "The hormones are terrible. I don't feel like myself. I'm sorry." Marianne starts to shake her head, but Sloane continues. "I haven't been kind. I haven't been supportive. I owe you an apology."

"I wouldn't have pushed if I'd known what was going on," Marianne blurts. "I shouldn't have made you feel bad about skipping Easter."

Sloane shrugs. "You didn't know. I should have been honest."

The phone rings and every drop of oxygen in the room seems to evaporate.

Sloane looks at her phone. "It's the doctor's office."

"Do you want us to go?" Chloe asks.

Sloane shakes her head. "You know everything now. There's no point in hiding the news."

Sloane answers the phone, greeting the doctor's office cheerfully. She's a master at control, especially of her own emotions.

"Thank you for calling," she says. "I understand," she repeats twice. "Yes, we'll be in touch." Sloane ends the call with the same tone as she began it. No one in the room knows whether it is good news or bad news because Sloane's face is unreadable.

Sloane turns toward Alden and subtly shakes her head. "This round didn't work. I'm not pregnant."

Alden reaches for her hand, but Sloane stands up and goes to the kitchen, grabbing a dish towel and wiping the counters. She refolds and hangs it over the oven door handle, taking a deep breath.

"I need a moment." Her voice is even as she walks upstairs, five pairs of eyes glued to her movement.

"Should I follow her?" Chloe asks Alden.

He shakes his head. "No. She needs space when she gets this kind of news."

"How is she handling this? How are you handling this?" Wyatt asks.

"Honestly, it's terrible." Alden runs his hands through his hair and stares at the floor. "I'm worried about Sloane. She pretends she's okay, especially this week around all of you guys. But she's not."

"And you?" Wyatt asks again.

"Everything in our lives revolves around getting pregnant. I want a kid, but I had no idea it would be this hard." Alden stares at the ceiling. "It's hard feeling helpless when you're watching someone you love fall apart."

"Maybe we should give you guys some space?" Chloe suggests. "We can get a hotel room."

Alden shakes his head. "She needs you guys. I need you. It's been hard keeping this to ourselves. I would have told you guys from the beginning, but Sloane never wants to share the bad stuff in her life."

"How bad has it been?" Wyatt asks, because they all know that Alden will give them the real answer.

"After the last miscarriage, Sloane stayed in bed for a week. She hasn't really been the same since then. She insisted we try again, fixated on routines that she read about in the online support groups. She puts so much pressure on herself, as if eating pineapple and wearing a certain type of socks is going to make the difference between getting pregnant and not." Alden pauses before continuing. "I miss my wife."

All of a sudden, they hear loud noises coming from upstairs. It sounds like something has fallen, and then they hear the same sound again and again, followed by broken glass.

"What's that?" Marianne asks.

"Go check on Sloane," Wyatt quickly adds.

Alden leaps up, taking the stairs two at a time. Everyone follows, the crashing sounds increasing. The hairs on Chloe's arms stand up as they run down the hallway.

Alden stops in front of the nursery.

The door has been closed all week. Other than the peek inside during her initial tour, Chloe doesn't think anyone else has seen the space. They've all been too busy with other drama to snoop behind closed doors in their friends' massive house.

Alden pauses and then rushes inside. When everyone gathers in the doorway, they see his arms wrapped around Sloane as she sobs.

It's a mess. Sloane has wrecked the space. Tiny clothes that were neatly hung in the closet have been pulled off their hangers. The multicolored bookcase has been turned over, picture books ripped and thrown on the floor. The contents of the changing table have been dumped, the neatly arranged baskets holding diapers now strewn across the room. Framed photos of Gulf birds are broken, shards of glass lodged in the plush carpet.

Sloane screams, the high pitch reflecting her pain.

She walks over to the beautiful sconce flanking the crib and pulls it out of the wall. Wires dangle as she continues pulling, all of her hurt and anger and despair manifesting in the utter destruction of her surroundings.

Alden reaches out and grabs her hands, pinning them to her side. He rocks her, trying to soothe his wife's pain as his eyes reflect his own fear.

Sloane takes a deep breath, looks up at her husband, and says, "Call the doctor. Schedule the next round."

Alden shakes his head. "Absolutely not. We need a break. We can't go through this again."

"Yes, we can," Sloane says in between ragged breaths.

"No," Alden repeats.

Sloane tries to smooth her frazzled hair. "Next time will work." There's a manic sound to her voice that scares Chloe.

"You just ripped a light out of the wall." Alden points across the room. "The nursery you spent a year designing is a mess. And I understand," Alden says, softening. "What we've been through is terrible. You need time. We need time, Sloane."

"I'm fine," Sloane lies.

"No, you aren't," Alden argues.

Sloane's chin quivers because she must know Alden is right. Everyone in the room knows Alden is right. And yet Sloane, the strongest-willed person Chloe has ever met, stares at her husband and says, "You can take all the time you need. But I'm doing another round as soon as I'm cleared by the doctor. I'll call to book the appointment."

"No." Alden stands immobile. It may be the only time he's so forcefully denied Sloane.

"I'm going downstairs," Sloane states. "I'll clean this up later. We have dinner reservations tonight and I want to rest a bit before."

Chloe looks around. They are shocked and confused. And all of Alden's concerns about Sloane now seem vastly understated. Because a person who is ripping electrical fixtures out of the wall one moment and discussing dinner plans the next is clearly teetering on unstable ground. And not even Sloane's stoic exterior can mask this fragility.

Sloane ushers everyone out of the room and closes the door, as if she can hide what happened with an oak panel and some hinges.

"You can't keep pretending," Alden says. "You're not okay."

"I'm not pretending. I got upset and now I'm moving forward. You need to do the same."

"Enough!" Alden shouts. "Enough with the shots and enough with the medicines that steal your personality. I've watched you slip further and further away and I cannot do it anymore."

"You don't have to do anything," Sloane yells. "I'm the one this affects. Not you."

Alden shakes his head, and Chloe can see the exhaustion in his eyes. They should leave, give Sloane and Alden the space they need to grieve and process and regroup. But instead they all stand immobile, spectators intertwined in each other's most private moments.

"Is that really what you think?" Alden asks Sloane.

She nods.

Alden swipes his hand over his face. "I need to go for a walk," he says. And they all let him leave, understanding that it's impossible to stay when the person you love pushes you this far away.

◆ 15 ◆

Four Years Ago

"ALDEN, WHAT IS THIS place?" Chloe asked. A white SUV had picked them up at the Cancún Airport with a sign that read *Mr. Chandler*. During the two-hour car ride south, they all took turns referring to Alden as Mr. Chandler, but when Chloe saw the house they were staying in, she forgot all about the joke.

"It's paradise," Sloane sighed. The entrance archway was covered in bougainvillea vine, purple flowers creating a canopy for them to walk under. At the end, there was a butler dressed in white linen with a tray of cocktails and additional staff to carry everyone's bags.

"It's Rufus's place," Alden explained. "Don't break shit, you guys. I need to stay on his good side."

"You work ninety-hour weeks. Rufus has a lot of work to do to get on my good side," Sloane said.

They all knew the last year had been brutal for Alden Chandler, tech boy wonder. His app launched two weeks ago. And after the chaos of launch and the flurry of last-minute crashes and bugs, Alden looked like he was barely standing. So when his lead investor, Rufus, told him to grab some friends and hop on a jet to Mexico for a week, Alden jumped at the chance.

When Sloane called and told everyone about the last-minute plans, it took zero convincing to get the group on board. Luke hesitated for maybe a minute or two, because he was working toward a VP promotion at his investment bank, but after a quick call to his boss convincing him that this was an excellent networking opportunity, Luke packed his bag.

Marianne called in sick. And saintly Noah stayed behind to go along with the story, because they couldn't both call in sick to the high school where they taught. Chloe, Wyatt, and Sloane had creative jobs, so they had more flexibility.

"You did it," Chloe said, elbowing Alden's side.

"I did. And as soon as I've caught up on a year's worth of sleep, I can't wait to do it again."

"Do what again?" Sloane asked, her eyes narrowing.

"Kiss my girlfriend," Alden said, walking toward Sloane with a renewed energy, swinging her in the air.

"I swear, Alden. If you were telling Chloe that you can't wait to build another one of these app things, I'm going to lose it."

Alden shook his head. "Let's celebrate. We've got months of pent-up celebrating to get out."

Sloane grabbed a cocktail off the tray the butler was holding and went into the house, assuming the role of hostess and asking to see the rooms. Most everyone followed, but Alden stayed back, leaning against one of the elaborate stone columns flanking the entryway. It almost seemed like his body was too tired to make the walk through the door.

Chloe stayed behind and nudged Alden. "You missed all the fancy snacks on the private jet."

"I know, I passed out. What was the best?"

"The chocolate soufflé. I can't even make one of those in a real oven. How did they make that on an airplane?"

"Nice," Alden said, smiling, his eyes barely open, his body still not moving.

"When's the last time you slept?"

"What month is it?"

"April."

"I slept in a bed on Christmas Eve because Sloane said Jesus deserved better from me. So December-ish."

"Alden. That's terrible."

"You sound like Sloane."

"Well, she's right. You're a broken man."

"A broken man who just launched his first company at twenty-five."

Chloe smiled. "True. I cooked dinner instead of ordering takeout last week. These are the accomplishments of most twenty-five-year-olds. You're such an overachiever. But I'm proud of you. We're all proud of you."

"On a scale of one to me tripping on the stage at graduation, how mad do you think Sloane is?"

"Honestly? Zero. I know she misses you and maybe . . ." Chloe said out of the side of her mouth, "she's a little resentful of your addiction to late-night Rufus texts." Chloe quickly added, "But she's your biggest cheerleader."

Alden sighed. "I know. I'm so lucky." Alden's eyes fully opened and he nervously glanced around. "Want in on a secret?"

"Always," Chloe said, rubbing her hands together conspiratorially.

Alden reached into his pocket and pulled out a small velvet box containing an obscenely large diamond ring.

"No way," Chloe squealed.

"I'm going to propose."

"Umm . . . does this deviate from Sloane's timeline?"

"Absolutely. Screw the timeline. I launched my company. I love her. I want to get married."

"And you're doing it this week?"

"Yes."

"She's never going to expect it."

"I know. Predictions on her response?"

"Depends on your plan of execution. She's obviously going to say yes. But it could be an *eye-roll-you-know-you-were-supposed-to-wait-until-we-dated-for-a-full-year* yes, or a *hell yes*.

"First of all, Sloane never says hell."

"True."

"Second, I know her. I have plans." Alden wiggled his eyebrows.

"You can't do it in bed," Chloe quickly replied.

"Why not?"

"Because you're both going to be asked about this proposal for the rest of your lives, and I guarantee it is important to Sloane that there is a good, southern mother–appropriate story attached. This cannot be a *we had sex and I said yes* situation."

Alden seemed to consider Chloe's comment for a single second before waving his hand in the air. "The ring is too good. She's going to love it." Alden walked toward the house and grabbed his own welcome cocktail.

Chloe followed, smiling. The ring was exactly what Sloane wanted, a classic Harry Winston, emerald-cut center stone with tapered side baguettes, too many carats for Chloe to estimate. Sloane would probably know its exact clarity immediately. All Chloe knew was that the ring shone almost as brightly as Alden's exhausted smile.

Chloe also knew that this was going to be a week they would never forget.

The next morning, Sloane and Alden emerged from the giant bedroom, their lips barely leaving each other's mouths as everyone else groaned and Sloane waved around a heavy finger, bliss on her face as she plucked a slice of pineapple from the platter of fresh fruit arranged on the kitchen counter.

"Guess what?" Sloane teased, wiggling her perfectly manicured hand.

Alden blurted. "We had sex and she said yes."

Chloe threw a grape at Alden's head. "I told you not to do that."

"I considered your advice and then rejected it," Alden said, smiling.

"Why?" Chloe asked as she reached for Sloane's hand, fawning over the ring.

"Because I know my future wife." Alden bent and kissed Sloane on the lips with confidence. "Hey, Luke and Wyatt, race you guys to the beach?"

Luke and Wyatt took turns congratulating Sloane and kissing her on the cheek before the three boys took off, leaving Marianne and Chloe to get all the details from Sloane.

"You're engaged!" Marianne squealed.

"I'm engaged." Sloane said this with a faux solemnity, before breaking into a Cheshire-cat grin.

"And the proposal?" Chloe tentatively asked.

"It was perfect." Sloane walks around the kitchen, pouring a cup of coffee before settling in to tell her friends the story. "I mean, I will fabricate an entire alternate version that we will tell our mothers and future children. All of you will be sworn to secrecy about this proposal lie." Sloane picked up a piece of papaya. "I'm too excited to get derailed by minor details."

The rest of the week was bliss. Because Rufus's house came with a staff, each morning, they awoke to platters of fresh fruit, bowls of yogurt and granola, platters of eggs. A steady stream of margaritas appeared poolside each afternoon along with bowls of guacamole and ceviche and crispy tortillas still warm from the fryer. They ate dinner at a restaurant in town that had rope swings instead of barstools and returned to a perfectly clean house with glasses of cinnamon horchata and stacks of fluffy white towels next to the pool.

The boys spent the mornings trying to surf, but only Wyatt was able to ride a wave. They spent afternoons snorkeling in cenotes, riding horses on the beach, and hiking Mayan ruins, every detail of these excursions planned and arranged by Rufus's staff. Some afternoons, Luke would wander off to that bar in town, and Chloe imagined him sipping a Modelo on the rope swings and hopefully not thinking about how the market was performing. Those afternoons without him gave Chloe time to wedding daydream with Sloane and Marianne.

It quickly became clear that Sloane's wedding was not going to be anything like the simple ceremony that Marianne and Noah had. But that didn't seem to bother Marianne; they were all having fun fantasy-planning the type of affair Sloane imagined.

Mostly, Wyatt and Alden stayed out of these conversations. Wyatt read his book and Alden slept. He was doing a noble job catching up on his lost sleep.

Marianne was the one who brought it up first. As they nibbled on shrimp tostadas and sipped pale pink palomas, she asked Sloane, "In that master plan of yours, did you ever think you'd be engaged to Alden?"

Chloe watched as Alden opened one eye, eager to hear Sloane's answer.

"Maybe," Sloane said.

"Liar," Alden mumbled and closed his eyes again. "But that's okay with me. I have you now."

"It doesn't bother you?" Chloe gently asked. They'd all been friends for so long, and for so many years, Sloane very clearly described the man she was going to marry, the timeline for that relationship, and her plans for the future. Alden was not six feet tall (and never would be), he was not a lawyer or a doctor, and he did not have any Roman numerals at the end of his name. But mostly, he wasn't the take-charge type of person Sloane had gravitated to in prior relationships. He preferred leaning back and watching Sloane's expertly planned routes. Chloe didn't know if Alden ever tried to be what Sloane wanted, or if he always knew that he was what she needed.

Alden seemed to reluctantly open his eyes. "Nope. Plans change. Love does too. None of us are the same people today. We weren't right for each other then. But we are now, and that's all that matters."

Alden went back to sleep. Chloe looked around the room, wishing Luke was there. Because then he could have heard what Alden said and Chloe could have asked if he agreed.

This Year

"WHAT DO YOU FEEL up to?" Chloe asks Sloane. Alden still hasn't come back to the house. An hour ago, Luke and Wyatt walked down the beach to see if they could find him.

Chloe and Marianne are lying on the bed with Sloane, gently asking questions to fill in the gaps of the last two years while also trying to give Sloane space to process the hard news about the latest transfer. But it's a difficult task, because Sloane is robotic in her insistence that she's fine, despite the destroyed room down the hall.

"I feel like going to dinner at Pescado," Sloane says. "I rented out the rooftop. It's going to be fantastic."

Chloe and Marianne are used to going with the flow, especially when Sloane has a vision for how she would like the night to go, but this seems crazy.

"How about we order pizzas and get in our pajamas instead?" Marianne's proposal is quickly dismissed.

"Don't be ridiculous. You can wear the new Ulla Johnson dress I bought," Sloane suggests. "Now that you have a little tan, it will look beautiful on you, Marianne." Sloane gets off the bed, which is probably for the best. Chloe can tell

Marianne is still upset about the fight earlier, even if she has a better understanding of Sloane's perspective.

Chloe pulls out her phone and texts Wyatt: *Sloane still wants to do dinner at Pescado. Did you find Alden?*

Wyatt quickly replies: *Yes. We're at a bar down the street. Text me the address of the restaurant?*

Chloe shakes her head. *I don't think this is a "sandy feet" kind of place. You guys should come back and change.*

Chloe waits as dots appear and disappear. Finally, Wyatt writes: *Bring us clothes. I'll try to get Alden to sober up before dinner. Coming home right now is not a good idea.*

When Chloe looks up, Sloane is standing in her closet, staring intently. "Have you heard from the guys?" she asks.

"Yep. All set. Reminded them about the dinner plans." Chloe tries to act confident, as if things are okay when really they aren't at all.

"Good. I'm going to take a bath. See you in an hour. I'll leave the dress on my bed for you, Marianne."

Chloe waits to hear the bathroom door close before speaking. "Come help me," Chloe whispers to Marianne, pulling her into the hallway.

"I can't. I need to call Noah."

"Are you still leaving?" Chloe panics because if Marianne leaves, everything falls apart. Chloe fears that it will be difficult to ever put her friends back together.

Marianne takes a deep breath before speaking. "No. Clearly, I'm needed here. But Noah's really struggling and I've never been apart from Teddy this long." Chloe can see the wheels churning in her friend's mind. Marianne continues, "What if they get a hotel room in Panama City? The rates are cheaper and they'll be close by. I can see Teddy and then come back here. Do you think that's a terrible idea? Will it be too hard for Sloane?"

Chloe considers this question. All week, Sloane has been reluctant to talk about anything involving Teddy, trying to erase motherhood from their friendship. But all that's achieved is upsetting Marianne. "It might. But it might help too."

"I don't want to upset Sloane," Marianne says. "But I don't want to feel like I have to keep my family and friends separate."

"You don't. If you need them, tell them to come," Chloe says.

After a brief conversation with Noah that Chloe can't help but overhear, discussing the driving logistics and hotels in Panama City, Marianne hangs up the phone. She seems more relaxed.

"Feel better?"

Marianne sighs. "It's hard to say in the midst of all this." Marianne gestures around the hallway, but it's clear she means the chaos of this week. "But knowing I'm going to see my baby tomorrow makes me feel better."

"I thought Noah was driving down now?"

Marianne shrugs. "He told me he was, because he knew that would make me feel better. But he knows us and knew I might change my mind. He's going to leave tomorrow morning."

Chloe pauses, feeling slightly jealous that Marianne has a partner who knows her so well. "I still need your help," Chloe says, trying to focus on the next hour instead of the inadequacies of her life.

"With what? Getting Sloane to open up about how she really feels? Finding an emergency therapist?"

"I think those things are going to be second on our list. First, we need to get some clothes for the boys."

"Why?" Marianne asks.

"Because they found Alden at a bar and he's too drunk to come back to the house. They're meeting us at dinner."

"And you think if Alden is wearing a suit jacket instead of a bathing suit Sloane will be less likely to lose it?"

"Maybe." Chloe shrugs. "I figure it can't hurt."

Marianne stares at the ceiling as if she can't believe the ridiculous situation they've gotten themselves into. "Okay, whose suitcase are we raiding first?"

"Let's get Alden's. You can get the dress Sloane wants you to wear."

"And we're back to doing everything Sloane wants."

"Of course we are," Chloe laughs.

They tiptoe back into Sloane's bedroom. Chloe can hear the jets from the tub. Marianne reaches for the dress and her fingers slowly trail over the beautiful fabric. As much as she might complain about Sloane, Chloe knows that Marianne is secretly excited to wear something like this dress. It's fun to pretend, to imagine you could live a life like Sloane's, even if it's only for one night.

Sloane and Alden have separate closets, but Chloe needs to walk through the bathroom to access both. Chloe hesitates at the bathroom door, but Marianne marches in, clearly understanding that a distraction is necessary. She asks Sloane about borrowing shoes, forcing Sloane to sit up in the tub and turn toward her closet. Chloe quickly slips into Alden's closet and chooses a blue linen blazer, some brown loafers, a clean T-shirt, and khaki shorts. She's in and out in two minutes thanks to the obsessive organization of the closet, designed to perfection by Sloane. And as she slips out of the bedroom, she hears Sloane and Marianne debating the advantages of the nude Stuart Weitzman heels Sloane prefers versus the flats Marianne insists are more practical.

A few minutes later, heels in hand, Marianne emerges from the bedroom, shaking her head. "She's so persuasive. I forget who I am around her."

"She always means well. Even if the size of her heart is sometimes overshadowed by the bulldozer of her mouth."

"I know," Marianne exhales as she agrees. "It's unimaginable what she's been through. Why wouldn't she tell us?" Marianne asks.

Chloe shrugs. "We all put off the bad news. Plus, I think she was jealous of your life, and that's not something Sloane is used to feeling."

"I get it," Marianne says, whispering and looking over her shoulder, even though there are two closed doors separating them from Sloane. "But I don't want jealousy in my friendships."

"None of us do. You're being honest. Sloane will come around."

"I feel terrible. I never would have thrown my baby in her face if I'd known how much she was struggling." Marianne gestures toward the nursery, door still closed. They had offered to clean it up, but Sloane insisted they leave it alone.

"You didn't throw your baby in her face. You had a child and neither of your best friends were there for you the way you needed," Chloe says.

"When did we start hiding so much?" There's a sadness in Marianne's voice that Chloe understands.

"When our lives started going in such different directions."

They linger in the hallway in front of the two rooms where Luke and Wyatt are staying. "Can you get Luke's clothes?" Chloe asks. She doesn't need to explain more because Marianne turns and open's Luke's door. It would probably be faster for Chloe to pick something out, although maybe Luke's wardrobe has changed over the last year. Maybe he doesn't roll his T-shirts anymore or tuck his socks inside his shoes to save space in the suitcase. Chloe doesn't want to find out. She doesn't want to know how many ways he's changed without her being in his life.

Chloe goes into Wyatt's room and smiles at the mess. There are piles of clothes, more books than anyone should fly with on a weeklong vacation, and a disturbing amount of sand. It's a good thing Sloane hasn't seen this.

She walks over to his closet, but there aren't any clothes hanging. Chloe assumes that everything on the floor is dirty, so she searches for his suitcase and a clean shirt at least. Sloane's expectations for Wyatt are the lowest, so he can probably get away with one of his black T-shirts and a pair of shorts.

There's a bathroom attached to the room and when Chloe goes in, she finds a second closet. That's where Wyatt put his suitcase. Chloe opens it and finds two folded T-shirts, one black and one navy, and a pair of gray shorts. She takes the shorts and navy T-shirt; she decides Wyatt is going to live on the edge tonight and break out of his usual uniform, but as her fingers wrap around the waist of the shorts, she feels something solid at the bottom of the suitcase. At first, she thinks it must be a stack of work that Wyatt brought along, but she quickly dismisses the idea because Wyatt refuses to ever work on vacation.

Chloe pushes the clothes aside and her eyes adjust to what she is seeing. It's a manuscript, with Wyatt's name on the cover, a major publisher's logo, and the words *Advance Copy* in block letters at the top. Chloe sinks back on her heels. Wyatt wrote a book. Wyatt's book is being published. And he never said a word about it to any of them. The book is titled *Off Limits*. Chloe flips to the first page. The dedication reads: *To Mayfield, for giving me friends that became family.*

Chloe immediately closes the manuscript and backs out of the closet. She feels like maybe she's discovered something she wasn't meant to see, not yet at least. Maybe it's a surprise announcement Wyatt has planned. Or maybe he's waiting for the right time. Regardless, she knows she should wait. And maybe tell her friend to get his own clothes from now on.

Chloe goes back into her bedroom and grabs an oversized straw bag that she packed for the beach. She puts Alden's and Wyatt's clothes in the bag and waits downstairs for Marianne. When Marianne emerges looking like the best version of a glowing new mother, Chloe points to the bag. She's happy to avoid touching Luke's clothes, afraid his familiar scent will stir up all the memories she's trying to push away.

A few minutes before their reservation, Sloane breezes into the room and announces, "All ready. We can take the golf cart to the restaurant."

It's a short drive to Pescado, and Sloane babbles about the architecture, the celebrities she's spotted at different stores along 30A, and her favorite things to order off the dinner menu. She fills the time with discussions of anything other than the trauma she just revealed, avoiding any talk of her feelings with her friends. Chloe and Marianne go along with this, knowing it's pointless to push Sloane.

After parking the golf cart, Chloe discreetly drops the straw bag at the hostess stand before they take a private elevator to Pescado's rooftop bar.

It's one of the best views in town, the European-style roofs framing the white sand and Gulf water in the background. It's obvious these are coveted tables, and somehow Sloane has convinced the restaurant to close the place off for her friends for a simple Monday night dinner.

"I wonder what's keeping the guys," Sloane says as she flips through the cocktail menu.

"I'm sure they'll be here soon," Chloe replies nervously.

After ordering and finishing their first round of drinks, a tequila, strawberry, and lemongrass concoction for Chloe, champagne for Marianne and Sloane, Chloe pulls out her phone. There's a text message from Wyatt letting her know that they're on their way.

Chloe stares at the perfectly blue sky, wondering how bad this dinner is going to be and thankful, for once, at Sloane's luxury demands, because in this case it means they will have privacy while their friends self-destruct.

Moments later, Luke strolls in, followed by Wyatt with his arm around Alden's waist. It almost looks friendly, as if they've had some bonding this afternoon, but Chloe can tell that Wyatt is providing a necessary support when Alden trips over an invisible object. Thankfully, Sloane misses this entrance because she's busy ordering appetizers with the waiter: grilled octopus, fresh ceviche, sticky ribs, and a giant seafood tower.

They are wearing the clothes Chloe left. But apparently Alden refused the loafers because he's still in flip-flops, and maybe in their rush, Wyatt and Luke exchanged shirts because Chloe has never seen Luke in a navy T-shirt, and Wyatt is wearing a white linen button-down and seems very uncomfortable. Chloe tries to hide her grin.

Sloane is sitting at the head of the table, and Wyatt strategically puts Alden at the other end. Chloe notices that Alden is swaying, finally landing in the chair after Wyatt guides him down safely. Wyatt sits next to Marianne, leaving the only empty seat for Luke right next to Chloe.

The waiter asks if anyone else wants to order a cocktail and Luke quickly exchanges a look with Wyatt before saying, "Just water for us. We're good."

"And you, sir?" the waiter says to Alden.

"Water for him too," Luke answers, somewhat upset by the thoroughness of this waiter.

Alden leans toward Luke. "I know what I want. It's another cocktail and for my wife to give her body a break," he slurs.

Chloe looks across the table at Wyatt, who is rubbing his forehead.

Chloe hopes Sloane missed this comment, but it's obvious she hasn't.

"I don't need a break," Sloane says. "I need a child, and that requires another round of IVF, so that's what I'm going to do. I'm not giving up."

"I'm not asking you to give up. I'm asking you to take a break." Alden continues shouting with his thick tongue and broken heart. "All these doctors and shots and disappointments. It's destroying us. It's destroying you. All I want is you."

"We can discuss this privately later," Sloane says.

"There's nothing more important to discuss," Alden argues.

"What about them?" Sloane points at Chloe and Luke, who both slump in their chairs. "Those two are the ones we need to fix."

"Sloane, we've been over this," Chloe says, already wishing the dinner was over before it has even started. "There is nothing to fix."

"She's right," Luke agrees, and Chloe feels immediate relief at the uncharacteristic solidarity.

"Explain it to me then." Sloane leans forward, her arms forming a triangle with her chin resting on top. "Because one day you two are in love, planning your lives together, and the next you're done."

"It's between us," Chloe says, but Sloane immediately shakes her head.

"No way. We all know what happens when we keep secrets in this group. I should have told you about my last year. You tell me about yours."

Chloe shifts uncomfortably. Sloane isn't wrong. It's hard for Chloe to be upset that Sloane kept her in the dark for the past year when she's done the exact same thing.

"Luke doesn't want to talk about it. If he doesn't care enough to know my reasons, I don't see why it should matter to you guys."

"Oh, he wants to know. He just pretends he's okay with not knowing," Alden says with surprising clarity as he reaches across the table, grabs the second cocktail the waiter just placed in front of Chloe, and downs it in one gulp. "She'll have another," Alden says to the waiter before he leaves.

"I think you owe us an explanation," Sloane says.

At almost the same moment, Marianne says, "It might make you feel better to talk about it."

The appetizers arrive, and as everyone digs into the seafood tower, Chloe thinks she's not sure if she'll feel any better, but maybe, in order to move forward, she needs to revisit that day from her past.

Chloe takes her time, describing the day Luke proposed. Her voice is soft as she focuses on one small moment when she and Luke left the yoga studio and a woman approached Luke.

She describes how Luke's arm immediately extended around Chloe's waist as he reached for her rolled yoga mat and slung it over his shoulder. She remembers asking how Luke knew this woman. Chloe didn't know her name, but she'd seen her frequently at the Thursday night power yoga class. The way she greeted Luke suggested some familiarity, but maybe she was just a friendly person.

Chloe tells her friends how Luke denied knowing the woman. How he was eager to continue the day he had planned. But as they left, Chloe looked over her shoulder. The woman was staring, a look on her face that Chloe couldn't quite interpret. But later that day, when Luke was on one knee proposing, Chloe remembered that moment. And that's when she realized that the woman was looking at them with pity.

Chloe says it wasn't the first time she wondered about Luke and whether his naturally flirty personality ever crossed the line. She realized she didn't want to spend the rest of her life wondering whether other women were pitying the love Luke gave

Chloe. She realized that with so much uncertainty in life, in the moment when your supposed soulmate proposes, you shouldn't wonder whether the woman in the yoga studio had also felt the firmness of his lips.

When Chloe finishes the story, no one speaks.

It seems like such a small moment, a brief interaction with a strange woman the morning of Luke's proposal. That's why Chloe has been so hesitant to share her reasoning. Because she understands. There's nothing shocking, except maybe her decision to end a nine-year relationship because of a chance, thirty-second interaction with a stranger.

Chloe realizes she had pushed away tiny doubts for years, letting them build up until the moment of the proposal toppled the tower. Even understanding the full consequence of her refusal, the strain it has put on all of their friendships, Chloe knows she made the right choice. It's better to be alone than spend an uncertain lifetime together.

When Chloe looks up, she sees that none of her friends are looking at her; they are all staring at Luke. So Chloe does the same.

She turns to the person sitting at her side and is met with a face of fury.

"I didn't stop loving you, Luke." Chloe makes herself focus on Luke, even though she knows they have an audience. "I just realized that the love we shared wasn't ever going to be the love I needed."

"Are you telling me that you ended our relationship, upended our entire lives and our friends' lives, because of one irrational moment of jealousy?" Luke's voice is full of disgust, and it makes Chloe shrink in her chair.

Sloane speaks up. "First of all, Chloe did not ruin our lives. It's pretty clear that all of us kept secrets this year. And none of us trusted each other the way we should."

Luke barely seems to recognize Sloane's comment. "Chloe saw some girl in a yoga studio give me a look and decided to end our relationship. It's crazy."

This is the moment Chloe's been dreading. Because Luke is exactly right. "It wasn't just a girl in a yoga studio," she says, trying to defend herself.

"Right. It's my fault because in *college* I made out with someone else. I was a stupid kid. Don't you care about the man I've become?"

"Yes. Of course. But it made it impossible for me to trust you after that. I realized that every girl in a yoga studio was going to make me doubt how much you loved me. But it is much more my fault. Because it took me nine years to realize that I needed a different kind of love and I am so truly sorry that I let it go that long."

"You're crazy," Luke says again.

"Stop calling her crazy," Wyatt shouts.

Luke's head pivots, his tense voice now focused across the table. "But she is. She's crazy. To throw away years together because she has a *feeling.*"

Wyatt shakes his head. "Either you tell her. Or I tell her," he says.

"Tell me what?" Chloe asks.

"Wyatt, don't be an idiot," Luke says quietly. "Let's order another round."

Wyatt is staring intently across the table. "I'm serious, Luke. I'm done."

"Tell me what?" Chloe asks again.

"You're not crazy," Wyatt says clearly. "You were right to be worried about the woman in the yoga studio."

Chloe tries to process Wyatt's words. She had only hoped that her friends would understand her choice, however unfounded it may have seemed. But Wyatt is going further. He's telling Chloe she's right, and that realization makes her heart sink.

Sloane is fast in making the connection Chloe is still struggling to accept. "Did you cheat on her?" she shouts at Luke.
"What do you know, Wyatt?"

Chloe swallows slowly, the blood filling her brain making
it hard to concentrate. But she notices that Sloane is at one side
and Marianne is across the table, both of their hands holding
on to Chloe's body.

"Wyatt has no idea what he's talking about," Luke says
dismissively.

Sloane stares at Alden. "Do you know what he's talking
about? And just as important, did you know and not tell me
what Wyatt is talking about?"

Alden seems to instantly sober. "I knew about junior year.
We all knew about junior year. Beyond that, I have no idea
what's happening," Alden says. He holds up his hands in sur-
render, "I swear, Sloane. This is between Wyatt and Luke."

"Luke, just tell me," Chloe says.

"There's nothing to tell, Chloe. I promise." There's an
earnestness in Luke's voice that gives Chloe comfort. But then
she looks at Wyatt and feels panic.

Because Wyatt is furious. "Luke, I'm serious. Either you
tell her. Or I do."

The volume of Luke's voice rises. "There's nothing to tell
about some woman at a yoga studio."

"I'm not doing this anymore. Chloe deserves better,"
Wyatt says to Luke.

The entire table turns and stares at Wyatt as he speaks.
"Luke drinks and flirts. We all know this. But he also forgets
about Chloe. Not all the time. But she's right to wonder about
the woman at the yoga studio. I don't know if anything happened with that person. But I do know about the girl at the
Carlyle Hotel bar the night Luke got his first bonus. And I
know about the girl who checks him in at the Equinox

downtown. And I know about the hostess at the Standard. And I know he's called me after each time, sobbing with remorse and promising that he'll never do it again." Wyatt shakes his head, sadness flowing out of his voice. "It's possible that Chloe's *feeling* was a lot more real than Luke's promises."

Chloe's mind churns, trying to fit together this new information with the old storybook of her relationship. There have been dozens of different women working the front desk at the Equinox over the years. Maybe she remembers a hostess at the Standard who always gave them a good table. The girl at the Carlyle could have been anyone. Chloe wants to know everything and nothing at the same time. But there's one question she has to have answered.

Chloe turns to Luke and whispers, "Did you sleep with all of those people?"

"No," Luke says quickly. "Chloe, Wyatt is making this sound worse than it is. I got drunk a few times and kissed a few women. That's it. I promise."

"How can I trust your promise?" Chloe's voice cracks.

"It doesn't matter anyway," Luke says on a long exhale. "You didn't want to marry me."

Chloe hesitates, but then she says the thing that she knows will hurt him most. "I didn't want to be your wife, and now I don't even want to be your friend." She doesn't wait for Luke to respond. He's right. It doesn't matter anymore, and she is silly to think, even for a fleeting moment, that it did.

As Chloe walks away, she stops in front of Wyatt. Her voice was clear with Luke, but in front of Wyatt, it starts to crack. "You could have told me."

"I know. I should have." Wyatt's shoulders sag, but his eyes never leave Chloe's face. He's the first to see the tears stream down her cheeks.

Chloe can't figure out which betrayal feels worse.

✦ 17 ✦

Three Years Ago

"WHERE'S LUKE?" WYATT ASKED.

"Best man duties." Chloe sipped her champagne and adjusted the straps of her pale pink gown.

Sloane and Alden's wedding ceremony was opulent and dramatic, all four hundred guests sitting in gold chevalier chairs facing the grand stone stairs that led up to the historic Swan House outside of Atlanta. Dinner was under a clear-roofed tent draped with crystal chandeliers and rose arches set among the gardens of the southern mansion. And now they were sipping cocktails around the outdoor fountain while the band was setting up on the edge of a beautiful wooden dance floor under the stars.

Wyatt took a glass of champagne from a passing waiter and asked, "What is Luke's latest assignment?" All the friends knew that Sloane was going to tactfully but persistently designate tasks throughout the evening.

"As far as I can tell, dancing with Alden's little sister so that she doesn't dance with Sloane's cousin," Chloe explained.

"Why would that be a problem?"

Chloe pointed across the room to a guy holding a flask. "That is Sloane's cousin. Apparently, he was arrested last year. Sloane said it was a misunderstanding, but you know how protective Alden is over his little sister. Luke's job is to babysit Lucy."

"That seems challenging." Wyatt gestured toward Luke and Lucy. They were standing around a tall cocktail table, Lucy reaching for a glass of champagne that Luke quickly confiscated before Lucy returned to staring at her phone. She was clearly miserable and constantly making eye contact with Sloane's cousin. Luke turned and waved to someone across the dance floor, and Lucy took that opportunity to mouth instructions to the felon cousin. A moment later, the cousin slipped away and Chloe couldn't help but laugh. Unless Luke stayed by her side all night, Chloe suspected that Lucy and the felon would be sneaking off soon.

"Well, I guess that means I have a new responsibility," Wyatt said.

"What?" Chloe asked.

"Keeping you company."

"What was your old responsibility?"

"I think Sloane's expectations of me were low. I walked down the aisle. I wore a tux. She asked me to escort her grandmother to the dinner table, and now it seems like her dictator duties are focused on others."

"Poor Marianne." Chloe bit her lip to keep from laughing.

When Sloane started planning the wedding, there was no question that Marianne and Chloe would both be bridesmaids. But since Marianne was already married, and from the South, and generally one thousand times more responsible than Chloe, it was a surprise to no one that Sloane wanted Marianne as her matron of honor.

Sloane had worried about hurting Chloe's feelings and pretended that it was a hard decision. And Chloe pretended that it was a job she wanted, when in reality she was relieved not to be Sloane's maid of honor. She couldn't imagine a more torturous job than trying to make sure that someone as perfect as Sloane was having a perfect wedding day.

Marianne had spent the night scuttling from one task to another. First there were the missing cuff links that were eventually located in the men's bathroom of the hotel lobby where some groomsman had left them. Then the bridal bouquet somehow contained asters, a flower Sloane said she was allergic to but really just detested. And now Marianne was in discussions with the band about not playing the songs guests requested and instead following the set list Sloane specified. Of course, there was a wedding coordinator to handle most of these issues, but Marianne was the designated buffer between the wedding coordinator and Sloane, because even hearing reports on issues being handled would be enough to send Sloane into a tailspin.

"Did she get to eat anything?" Chloe asked.

"Not really," Wyatt replied. "I saw Marianne eating a granola bar behind the tent and then shoving the wrapper in her bra when Sloane called her name."

Chloe said, "I should go see what I can do to help."

"Or maybe we should dance?" Wyatt asked. The band had started playing, and everyone was trickling onto the dance floor. "Then we can go help together."

"You don't dance, Wyatt."

"It's a wedding. I can dance at a wedding." Wyatt held out a hand, and Chloe was about to accept when they were interrupted.

Luke frantically asked, "Have you seen Lucy?"

Wyatt and Chloe both shook their heads. "Weren't you just talking to her?" Chloe asked.

"I stopped to get a drink. When I turned around, she was gone." Luke's eyes darted around the room. "Shit. Alden's going to kill me." Luke abruptly walked away, but he called over his shoulder, "Wyatt, thanks for keeping Chloe company."

"Why does everyone think I need a babysitter?" Chloe asked the sky.

"It's your childlike innocence," Wyatt said.

"As opposed to your hardened cynicism?"

"Yep." Wyatt nudged Chloe's side. "I guess this is an official assignment now. Ready to dance?"

Chloe accepted his outstretched hand as Wyatt wove them through the crowd. The band was good, and the guests were enjoying themselves. It was one thing she loved about weddings—no matter your age or your level of everyday seriousness, when a wedding band played some classics, everyone threw away inhibitions. Who knew how much this band cost—probably more than her yearly rent, because there were multiple singers and lots of different instruments.

As Chloe and Wyatt danced, she smiled at his subtle sways, his attempts to nod his head to the beat of the music but refusing to make any steps beyond those minuscule movements. When the music slowed and couples stepped closer together, she thought that was the end of their dance. But instead, his arm wrapped around her waist and she placed a hand on his shoulder.

"This is more my speed," Wyatt said.

"I appreciate your attempt to wedding dance with me."

He smirked. "We can all be grateful those forty-five seconds of awkwardness are over."

She looked around the room at all the couples together, young and old, as her eyes landed on Sloane and Alden. It had been a joy to watch them fall in love, to see how they brought out the best in one another, and to witness the vows they exchanged. Chloe had expected a traditional ceremony, so she was shocked when Sloane and Alden decided to recite their own vows.

Chloe didn't want to spend a second of the night feeling anything other than happy for her friends, so when bits of jealousy began to bubble up, she pushed them away. When she married Luke someday, he'd probably also say that his life began the moment they met. Or a Luke version of that sentiment anyway.

"Don't let him step on your toes. He's a terrible dancer," Wyatt's father said as he danced alongside Chloe. He spun Wyatt's mother on the dance floor, and Chloe laughed.

Sloane had invited Wyatt's parents, along with Luke's and Marianne's parents. Sloane said she wanted all the important people at her wedding, and in Sloane's world nothing was more important than family. But before she did it, Sloane called Chloe and asked if it would be too hard to have everyone's parents gathered. Of course Chloe said it was fine— because it was. She never wanted her sad moments to overshadow others' happy times. And Chloe also knew she was lucky to have a friend who was thoughtful enough to ask.

"Wyatt is a terrific dancer," his mother argued. "He got it from me."

Wyatt's father shook his head. "You're going to need to practice more, son. There's lots of dancing at those political fundraisers. When you run for office, all eyes will be on you." Wyatt's parents ventured off to the other end of the dance floor before Wyatt could respond.

Chloe watched them for a moment. A couple very much in love. Wyatt was a perfect mash-up of his parents, with his father's tall frame and his mother's dark hair. But Chloe's eyes quickly narrowed in on Wyatt, staring up into his face as she asked, "Political office?"

"Can we skip over that?" Wyatt looked away. He extracted his hand from hers, wiped it on the leg of his pants, and then reached out again.

"No, we can't," she said as they continued to sway around the dance floor. "Why does your dad think you're running for office? Are you?"

"Of course not. That's my nightmare." He still didn't look in her direction. "I live in DC. He's old and confused."

"He's in his fifties and very spry," she shot back. She turned Wyatt's head toward his parents, and they watched as his dad dipped his mom in some elaborate ballroom maneuver.

Wyatt rolled his eyes. "Fine. When I got the job in DC, he may have made a couple of assumptions that I failed to correct."

Chloe feigned shock. "You lied to your father?"

"Omissions. You wouldn't understand."

She stopped dancing. "Why?"

"Because your parents loved you," he said softly, erasing the defensiveness from her body. "And supported you."

"You didn't know my parents," Chloe stammered.

"No, but I've listened to dozens of your stories about them. Am I wrong?"

She shook her head. Wyatt was an excellent listener, it was one of the things she liked most about him. She never felt like she needed to rush along when she reminisced. He liked all stories, even long rambling ones from a girl who babbled too much when she was lonely.

"How is it different?" Chloe asked.

Wyatt stared at his shoes, and when he looked up, all the fun had left his eyes. "My dad has been disappointed in me since elementary school. Sometimes it's easier to just let him think what he wants."

"I doubt that, Wyatt."

"He was a lineman at UGA. In fourth grade, I was more interested in *The Hobbit* than the Sugar Bowl. I brought books to football games and watched him scowl at his son."

"Southerners are weird about their football obsession," she tried to argue. "I'm sure he's proud of you."

"I could have a bestseller, and he'd still be embarrassed to say his son writes stories for a living. I may have mentioned that I was on the Hill for my new job, which was true. I was interviewing a congressman, and my father ran with the idea that I had political ambitions. He's too exhausting to correct. So I let him believe what he wants."

"That also seems exhausting," Chloe whispered.

Wyatt shrugged. "I figured out a long time ago that I'm never going to be the son he wants. I don't expect more from that relationship than he's capable of giving."

Chloe wished Wyatt could experience the type of unconditional love that she had always felt from her parents. But five years ago, she had learned that it was possible to live without it, especially when you had friends who filled the gaps. Maybe Wyatt felt the same.

"How's the gallery?" he asked, clearly trying to change the subject.

"Good," she reflexively replied.

"*Good* is the answer you give your aunt at Christmas. How is it really going, Chloe?"

She sighed. "The gallery is good. It's not great. I don't mind the work, but I don't love it."

"I get that." He tilted his head. "Especially since we've been conditioned to love what we do or else feel like a failure." Somehow, Wyatt summed up exactly how Chloe felt.

Being surrounded by artists could be difficult for Chloe because it constantly reminded her that some people live a life of passion and others don't.

She sighed. "I think I'm just realizing that I want my life to look different in ten years. I don't want to keep handling logistics for other artists' dreams. But I have no idea what kind of different life I want. So for now, I'm good with *good*."

"And what about everything else?" Wyatt asked.

Chloe shrugged.

"Luke. New York. Are those things *good* too?"

"You know what it's like," Chloe said to the side of the room.

Wyatt reached for her chin and turned her face back toward his. "I don't. I'm a DC man now. You have to fill me in."

It was times like this that Chloe missed the days they all lived together. They had separate lives now, and sometimes they reverted to natural fractures. Chloe talked to Marianne and Sloane the most. Luke talked to Wyatt and Alden. Chloe longed for the unit they once were.

"Doesn't Luke fill you in?" Chloe asked.

"I want to hear what you think, Chloe."

Chloe swallowed and accidentally stepped on Wyatt's toe. She mumbled an apology while Wyatt waited for her to respond. "Luke works a lot," Chloe said. "Not just hours in an office. There are events at night, and it's not my scene."

Wyatt's eyes softened as he said, "It never has been."

"I know that. And you know that. But even after all these years, I still don't think Luke knows that." Chloe said this softly, because somehow that minimized the betrayal, complaining about her boyfriend to his best friend. Chloe continued, "Luke doesn't seem to mind when I skip out of the cocktail parties early. Or ditch them altogether. But it means that we barely see each other."

"Do you think it's a phase in life or something else?" Wyatt asked.

"I don't know," Chloe answered truthfully. "Is it normal to have different definitions of fun from the person you love?"

Wyatt seemed to contemplate his answer. Chloe looked around the dance floor, and Marianne was sheepishly tapping Sloane on the shoulder. Whatever she said made Sloane stop dancing while Marianne waved her hands frantically, and they both left.

Wyatt pointed in their direction. "Do you think Sloane and Marianne have the same definition of fun right now?" Wyatt asked.

"Probably not." Chloe didn't know why, but she felt tears forming in the corners of her eyes.

Wyatt stopped dancing, but he didn't take his hand off Chloe's waist. "Talk to him. I'm sure it's important to Luke that you're having fun too. If you're just following along, you're not building a life together."

Wyatt looked across the dance floor, and Chloe followed his gaze. Luke was dancing with Alden's little sister Lucy. He must have found her and decided that the only way to keep her occupied was to force her into a dance. Luke was clearly taking this Sloane assignment seriously.

Chloe knew Luke was a great guy, the type of person who would babysit his best friend's sister when asked. Wyatt was right, he'd probably do anything for Chloe if she really pushed.

But how could Chloe tell Wyatt that she'd tried to have that same conversation a million times? She'd open her mouth to propose something different, and Luke would laugh like it was the funniest joke she'd ever told. Why would they want to try the trapeze at Riverside Park when Luke's boss was paying for drinks at the Standard? It was almost as if the lives they wanted were so different they weren't even speaking the same language anymore. Chloe was weekend trips to the Hudson Valley and a new folk artist in Lancaster County. Luke was a summer share in the Hamptons and Fashion Week after-parties.

Instead, Chloe said, "You're absolutely right, Wyatt. Luke is the best."

Then she looked away, so that Wyatt wouldn't ask any more questions, and so that he couldn't see the tear sliding down her cheek.

◆ 18 ◆

This Year

CHLOE MANAGES TO AVOID everyone the rest of the night, pretending to be asleep when Marianne returns to the room, and waking up earlier than everyone else. She grabs a granola bar and a downs a cup of coffee. When she hears footsteps upstairs, she heads into the garage to escape. There's no one she wants to talk to this morning. And two people she definitely wants to avoid.

She's eyeing the bicycles in the corner when she hears the door open. Wyatt stands and stares, waving sheepishly. Not the primary person she wants to avoid, but a close second.

"I'm going on a bike ride," Chloe announces.

"Sounds good." Wyatt walks over and easily removes two bikes from the hanging rack.

"It wasn't an invitation," Chloe says. "I wanted someone to know where I went. That's all."

"I'm sorry, Chloe. The reason I didn't—"

Chloe cuts off his apology. "There's no reason that is going to make me any less angry."

"Fair. But I am sorry. Mostly that I kept anything from you. But also that it came out like that last night."

Chloe shakes her head and takes a bicycle. She hasn't ridden one in years, but she figures she'll adjust quickly despite wobbling for the first pedals around the garage.

"Where are you going to bike?" Wyatt asks.

"There's a trail," Chloe says. "It was in Marianne's guidebook. All the beach towns are connected by the same path."

"That's almost eighteen miles," Wyatt says suspiciously.

"It's going to take me that long to burn off my anger."

"Okay. Let me grab some water." Wyatt opens the beverage fridge in the garage. It's stocked with every imaginable flavor of sparkling water, protein shakes, ginger beer, and kombucha. Wyatt puts four water bottles in a backpack he finds next to the bikes.

"You're not coming with me," Chloe protests.

"You weren't even bringing water. You clearly need me."

"I don't want to talk to you."

"Fine. We don't have to talk," Wyatt says. "But I'm not letting you bike eighteen miles alone. You get winded walking home from the gallery."

Chloe narrows her eyes. He's right, but she's not giving him the satisfaction of saying that.

"You're going to get four miles down the road and start asking strangers to carry you." Wyatt continues, "I know you're pissed. But I'm not leaving you alone."

Chloe snaps on a helmet and heads out. It's easy to find the trail, a few blocks up from the beach. Seaside is in the middle of this stretch of beach towns, so Chloe decides to head west, figuring she'll double back and finish the trail toward Rosemary Beach at the end. That's where the best shopping is anyway. Her plan is to bike all morning, spend the afternoon shopping, and then she can avoid everyone for the bulk of the day.

Even though it's still early morning, there are dozens of joggers out and several intense bikers, the kind who shout commands about moving to the right and prefer full spandex bodysuits.

The bike Chloe is riding is one of those beach cruisers with wide handlebars and bouncy seats. After a few minutes, she finds her rhythm and easily pedals along. She looks over her shoulder occasionally and Wyatt is still there, following but agreeing to her request and staying silent.

The path cuts through each town, so after Seaside, it's Watercolor and then Grayton Beach.

Most of the trail is paved, but there is the occasional wooden boardwalk and bridges that cross the coastal waterways. Chloe sees another dune lake, just like the one where they went paddleboarding, and her heart clenches. Days ago, she would have done anything to make things right with Luke. And now she feels like she spent the better part of her adulthood with a stranger.

Sloane and Alden and Marianne had seemed just as shocked as Chloe at the revelations of last night's dinner. But the person biking behind her? He knew. Chloe knows Luke's betrayal is worse. But then why does Wyatt's betrayal hurt more?

They take their first break at mile two. Wyatt is silent, but Chloe blurts out the questions that have been churning in her mind. "How many times?" and "Why didn't you tell me?" But when Wyatt starts his answer with "The first time—", Chloe realizes she can't handle hearing his response.

They take their second break at mile six, and Chloe cries from the heat and the hurt. Wyatt tries to offer a hug, but she swiftly pushes him away.

They take their next break at mile nine, and the humidity and the anger must mix too potently because when Wyatt asks if Chloe is okay, she shoves him so hard he stumbles backward.

At mile twelve, Wyatt suggests ice cream. Chloe should be furious. How could he want ice cream when he just revealed that Chloe's long-term boyfriend cheated on her for years? A fact he knew and hid for just as long. And yet, after biking for over an hour, in Florida, Chloe really wants ice cream.

Wyatt stands next to her in line, his forearm briefly brushing against hers before Chloe takes a step away. The only words Chloe says at this stop are "Peach cobbler sundae" when she's ordering and "I'm not sharing" when Wyatt tries to take a bite.

At mile fifteen, when Wyatt asks Chloe what she wants, she tells him the truth. She doesn't know.

By this point, they are back in Seaside and she can't go any farther. She cannot finish biking this stupid eighteen-mile trail that middle-aged mothers seem to finish as a warmup. She's a willowy, out of shape, heartbroken twenty-nine-year-old who just wants a shower and a cocktail and for the people she loves to tell her the truth.

When she's back in the house, everyone seems to handle her with kid gloves. Luke is suspiciously absent, and no one is quite sure where he's disappeared to all day, which makes things easier. Marianne and Sloane are rage-filled, which somehow makes Chloe feel calmer. None of them knew. Wyatt apologizes too many times for Chloe to count. Even Sloane agrees that a group dinner is out of the question.

Marianne calls Noah, who has stopped somewhere in Alabama because Teddy hates the car. It seems silly to make such a long drive for such a short stay, and Noah debates going back home. But Sloane gets on the phone and convinces Noah to join them the next day. Sloane says they can extend the visit and stay as long as they want. Marianne insists on a hotel, and Sloane says absolutely not. Chloe stays out of this disagreement.

Alden and Wyatt disappear to the basement to watch something or play something. Chloe couldn't care less. She assumes Luke comes home at some point, but keeping track of him is low on her priority list.

After two bottles of wine split between the three women, and a container of the best chicken salad Chloe has ever eaten, Marianne and Sloane convince her that it doesn't matter. Chloe and Luke aren't together anymore. And for the first time all week, Sloane agrees that's probably for the best.

But later that night, when everyone is asleep and Chloe stands in front of Wyatt's bedroom door, she realizes that she's still bothered.

When Wyatt opens the door, Chloe confronts him. "I can't believe you knew. All those times. And you never said anything to me. You're a shit friend, Wyatt."

Wyatt nods and invites Chloe into his room. "I am. I'm sorry."

"You keep saying that. But I don't feel like you really mean it," Chloe says.

Wyatt hesitates. He must have been getting ready for bed because he's wearing a pair of baggy shorts and no shirt. He runs his hands through his dark hair before speaking. "Would it have mattered? You knew about the girl junior year. You watched that with your own eyes. And you still went back to him."

"I thought that was the only time," Chloe harshly whispers.

"Did you? Because it seemed like the safety of Luke was more important than reality. I tried, Chloe. So many times."

"You should have tried harder." Chloe's mind reels, having a hard time remembering a single instance when Wyatt tried to tell her that Luke liked kissing other girls. Instead, all Chloe remembers is how Wyatt sided with Luke and kept his distance from Chloe. She feels their friendship slipping even further away. "I feel like I barely know you, Wyatt."

"You know me, Chloe. I thought I was protecting you. I kept this one thing from you because I thought that's what you wanted."

"You kept this one thing?" Chloe takes a step closer, pointing a finger at Wyatt's chest. "You're still lying."

"What are you talking about?"

"What's *Off Limits*, Wyatt?"

Wyatt's face falls. When he looks up, he has a look of confusion and something else. Panic maybe.

"I found the manuscript in your suitcase," Chloe admits.

"What were you doing in my suitcase?"

"Getting you clean clothes for the worst dinner in the history of time."

"Did you read it?" Wyatt's voice is shaky.

"No. Because I'm an honest person. I respect people's privacy," Chloe spits.

"Good." Wyatt shrugs, but there's nothing nonchalant about it.

Chloe sits on the edge of Wyatt's bed. "You finished your book. You have a publishing deal. And you don't tell any of us?"

When they first met all those years ago, and late nights were spent speculating about all the incredible ways their lives would turn out, the fearlessness of youth untainted by the reality of adulthood, she never imagined that this is where they'd end up. Hiding the most important parts of their lives from the people they are supposed to love the most.

"It's complicated, Chloe."

"Why?"

Wyatt sits on the opposite side of the bed. He rubs the stubble on his chin, a tortured look on his face. "As soon as you guys read this book, I'm afraid I'm going to lose my friends."

"That makes no sense. We know this is your dream."

He exhales and he stares at the ceiling. She waits. He's struggling to explain himself and she can't figure out why. But she's good at being patient, a skill she had to hone over years of dating Luke.

"The book is about us," he finally admits. "I tried to write something else. But I couldn't. Even though it's fiction, as soon as everyone reads it, they'll know what it's about."

"Why is that a problem?"

"Because you'll know how I really feel." Wyatt starts to shout but catches himself and ends the sentence in a desperate whisper.

"You secretly hate us or something? Is this a pretend friendship so you have content for your book?"

"No. Being a part of this group is the most important thing in my life. Just like it is for you."

Wyatt is right. Even though Chloe said she didn't want to come on this trip, and agreed only after Sloane told her about the miscarriage, Chloe knows that she did want to be here. She wants to fight for a friendship that has meant more to her than any other relationship in her life. And although her individual relationships with Sloane and Marianne and Alden and Wyatt and even Luke are important, it's the family they create together that means the most to Chloe. Especially after she lost her own parents. And yet, this week has shown Chloe that they've been clinging to memories, failing to be honest about the present.

"What did you say about us in the book, Wyatt?"

Wyatt swallows, staring directly at Chloe. "I told the truth about you."

She senses a tension building, waiting for him to explain what he means. She knows Wyatt sees her more clearly than anyone else. He studies the people around him, making it impossible to hide your flaws. He'll describe all of her messy, needy, lonely, lazy tendencies and he'll be exactly right.

"Say it." Chloe loses herself in Wyatt's dark eyes. "I've had enough secrets for a lifetime. Whatever you wrote in your book, tell me to my face."

"I'm in love with you." Wyatt's face falls and he looks away.

Chloe hears a buzzing in the room, likely a result of all the blood in her body filling her head, an overwhelming panic setting in. Because she must have misheard. Because this can't be possible.

She opens her mouth to speak, but no words come out.

He fills the silence. "I've wanted you since the first moment I saw you." He sounds guilty, as if he's just admitted stealing a pack of gum from the grocery store.

She shakes her head. "You walked into Waffle House and hated that I was there."

He tugs at the front of his hair, pushing it back before responding. "No. I hated that you were there with Luke."

"What are you talking about?" Chloe gnaws on the inside of her cheek.

"Waffle House wasn't the first moment I noticed you."

"But we'd never met before," she stammers.

"I'd seen you around campus. You were impossible to miss, Chloe."

She looks away, because of course she'd seen him too. She knew exactly who he was when he walked into the restaurant that night. But it never occurred to her that Wyatt had given her a second thought.

"You spent hours in the student union. I didn't have a class on that side of campus, but I walked that way every Tuesday and Thursday morning because I knew I'd see you," he confesses.

Her mind spins, trying to remember moments from a decade ago that are causing seismic shifts to her memories. She did spend hours in the student union, claiming one of the small round tables to read and study before and after class. She thought getting a single dorm room her freshman semester was a lucky break, but about two weeks into school, she realized it was actually incredibly lonely. She didn't talk to many people in the student union, but at least she was surrounded by the chatter of strangers.

"Why didn't you say anything?" she asks.

"The cold come-on isn't my style. I figured our paths would cross . . ." Wyatt trails off. "I was young and stupid and believed in destiny. I thought the love of your life could be discovered as easily as spotting a penny on a sidewalk."

There was a time when Chloe felt the same. But after her relationship with Luke, she wasn't so sure. She learned that love wasn't discovered; it was earned.

He continues, "For a brief moment, I saw you sitting at that table under those fluorescent lights at Waffle House and thought that destiny had brought us together. Finally. Even though we'd never spoken, I thought I knew you. But once I saw Luke's arm around your shoulder, I was so pissed I'd missed my chance."

"You were brutal to me those first few months," Chloe says, still trying to piece together Wyatt's revelations. "Why did you pretend to hate me?"

"I didn't. You were there with Luke. My best friend."

"But it took months for you to warm up to me."

He exhales. "No. It took months for me to figure out how to act around you without trying to make a move on my best friend's girlfriend. You were off limits. You've always been off limits to me, Chloe."

"We've been friends for ten years, Wyatt."

"It's been brutal." He tries to smile, but it quickly fades.

"But you've dated other people."

"No one has been you."

Chloe stands up, hoping if she moves her body, she can force herself to understand this situation. She paces in front of the bed.

He keeps talking. "I thought you were happy. I thought Luke made you happy, and how selfish would it have been for me to tell you otherwise?"

Chloe is reeling, but she manages a few stuttered words. "How could it possibly be selfish of you to tell me the truth? Don't you think I deserved better?"

"I think you deserve the world, but I thought you only wanted Luke."

She stops pacing. "Why are you saying something now?"

"Because I've known you and loved you for ten years." Wyatt stands up and walks toward Chloe. "That night, last month, in your apartment. I wasn't drunk. It wasn't a mistake."

His fingers trail across her collarbone before eventually cupping her cheeks.

"What are we doing, Wyatt?" Chloe swallows. Because as strange as this feels, Wyatt, her friend, admitting his feelings. Wyatt, holding her face. Wyatt's touch, electrifying her body. It also feels inevitable. Those moments over the years, when she'd have a fleeting thought about him, steal a glance across the room, maybe he was feeling the same.

Maybe those sins she tallied can be excused. Because she chastised herself for thinking that her boyfriend's best friend was too attractive for common society. And she savored those times when Wyatt made her feel as if the ideas Luke called crazy were actually reasonable. Wyatt is her friend, but he's also always been a little bit more.

"Something that feels very right," Wyatt whispers as his arms pull Chloe tighter.

This time, when he bends his head down to hers, their lips connecting, neither of them pulls away.

It's not the kind of kiss she has ever felt before. There's the newness of lips she's never really felt against hers, causing every skin cell to tingle. But there's the familiarity of this body. A person she's sat next to for hours, laughed with, joked with about bad dates and pet peeves. There's a familiarity in his kiss that makes her yearn for a hundred more. And an urgency like a teenager sneaking their first beer. It feels like they want to make the most of every moment, and they do.

Kissing Wyatt is like climbing into a bed with freshly changed sheets, familiar and new all at once. But once Chloe pulls back, reality floods in. Luke is down the hall. Everyone is fighting. And Wyatt's lips were just pressed against her own.

"We can't do this," she says reflexively.

He takes a deep breath. "I can," he says. "I've been thinking about this moment for years." Their eyes meet and he shakes his head as he says, "But you're right. You need to figure out why you can't."

She looks away, but he turns her head back toward his. He leans his forehead against hers as he whispers, "Figure out what you want, Chloe."

He says it like a simple assignment, but for Chloe nothing seems more impossible.

♦ 19 ♦

Two Years Ago

IT WAS STRANGE, RETURNING to a place that held such strong memories. Reunion weekend at Mayfield was supposed to be three days of slipping back into the familiarity of college and ignoring the responsibilities of adulthood.

At least, that's how Luke and Sloane pitched the weekend to everyone else. Luke was president of the reunion committee, a role he volunteered for because it was *such an excellent networking opportunity*. Chloe tried hard not to roll her eyes at his unsurprising assessment. Lately, everything needed to be a networking opportunity, especially if Luke was going to be promoted to VP, a goal that seemed more important than sleep for him these days.

Sloane offered to help Luke with the party planning, and once Sloane was involved, it became a nonnegotiable that they'd all attend. Even when Marianne complained about the expense, and Alden complained that it was a critical time for the sale of his company, and Wyatt argued that the only people he cared about at Mayfield were the five of them. All of those reasons seemed legitimate to Chloe, but she never said this out loud because she was a supportive girlfriend.

Sloane dismissed everyone's complaints, rented a house for the long weekend, and started sending Luke a spreadsheet each week, updating him on the status of events and providing alumni contacts. Chloe had never seen two people more excited to open an Excel file.

Chloe wanted to enjoy a weekend on campus with her best friends, but instead, everywhere she looked caused a pang of discomfort. A new library had been built out of glass and steel. Chloe felt sorry for the current students because they wouldn't experience fighting over the second-floor nook in the old stone building. Of course, they wouldn't have to deal with water-stained books from a leaky roof. Chloe wanted Mayfield to be the same, but it had changed like all of them.

Chloe tried to take a deep breath, but it was impossible in the tight black dress Sloan had brought for her to wear. The first night was a cocktail reception for all the alumni classes gathered, their class mingling with graduates from sixty years ago. Tonight was Mayfield's effort to assemble everyone together and raise as much money as possible so that it could continue adding more buildings that made Chloe uncomfortable.

Luke went over earlier but not before studying the alumni list for key contacts he hoped to make. Marianne and Alden were skipping the event altogether, arriving the next day. And as Chloe edged through the crowds, she kept trying to find Sloane or even Wyatt, but all she saw were strange faces and Luke's pleading eyes to join his steady stream of small talk.

If Chloe were a better girlfriend, she would have looped her arm through Luke's and smiled as he discussed his post-graduation career trajectory, peppering in compliments about Luke's dedication to whatever audience he was trying to impress.

But she didn't. She couldn't stand one more minute of listening to the false pitch of Luke's voice as he tried to sound more impressive and more competent than he really was. Or maybe the boy who used to shotgun beers in the quad really did care about the best high-yield accounts for investment returns. But Chloe certainly didn't, and she couldn't pretend for a second longer.

When Luke's eyes widened, annoyed with her delayed approach, she mouthed *bathroom* and escaped before she could feel more guilt about abandoning her responsibilities. It was easy to weave through the crowd, past the groups of classmates reminiscing, exchanging hugs and life summaries in sterilized sentences.

Chloe wasn't sure when she lost patience for small talk, when her threshold for crowded parties and surface conversations evaporated. But it was gone. The problem was that Luke's entire life seemed to revolve around these events. There was a time on this campus when their lives had revolved around each other. Chloe wasn't sure how they had spun in such opposing directions.

She found a side door and flung it open, grateful for the clean Tennessee air that replaced the heavy atmosphere from too many bodies. She just needed a moment, a few minutes at the most, to power up the fake smiles and manufactured enthusiasm that Luke expected. She sat on the concrete steps, kicked off her heels, unwound her hair from its tight bun, and immediately felt herself relax.

"There she is." The door opened at the same time Chloe heard his voice.

She was crouched like a teenager hiding their first cigarette, but she didn't feel any embarrassment because it was Wyatt. She patted the step beside her, and he took off his suit jacket before sitting at her side.

"Where have you been all night?" Chloe ran her fingers through her hair, shaking away the hair spray and formality of the prior hour.

"Hiding in the shadows," Wyatt admitted.

"What's your excuse?" Chloe asked.

"I do not have money to donate, and I do not want to discuss investment funds with your boyfriend."

"Me either," Chloe sighed.

Wyatt smiled at Chloe's discarded shoes. "You looked miserable."

"Why didn't you rescue me sooner?"

He shrugged. "I didn't know you needed rescuing."

"I didn't," Chloe lied to herself and him. "I should go back inside." She should have stood quickly, smoothing her hair back in place, adjusting her dress so that it didn't bunch at her hips. But she didn't. She sat, immobile, unable to force herself to go back into that room.

"Or . . ." Wyatt's word hung in the air, teasing Chloe with possibility. "You could take a walk with me."

"Where would we go?"

"To the old library?" Wyatt suggested. Chloe hesitated because she wanted to say yes but felt bound to say no. "Send Luke a text message," Wyatt added. "Blame it on me. There's something I want to show you."

Chloe quickly sent Luke the message, letting him know that she had stepped away for a few minutes, making false promises about hurrying back.

Wyatt stood, extending a hand to help Chloe up. She tried not to notice when their fingers clasped for a moment longer than usual. For the first time since arriving back on campus, Chloe felt a sense of comfort. That's how it always felt with Wyatt. They argued relentlessly and he challenged her constantly, but never once did Wyatt ever make Chloe feel like she needed to pretend to be something else. She was exhausted from the months of dress-up that being Luke's girlfriend had required of late, and she clung to the familiarity of Wyatt's presence like a lifeline.

As they walked along the paved paths of campus, Chloe held her shoes in her hands, unable to force her feet back into the heels.

"I wonder what they're doing with the old library building," Chloe said.

Wyatt smiled. "That's what I wanted to show you."

Wyatt opened the front door of the building and Chloe went in. She felt the cool marble against her bare feet before reluctantly putting her shoes back on. She looked around. There were signs, rooms renamed as books had been removed and replaced with crates and boxes stacked along the walls.

"Can we be here?" Chloe asked.

Wyatt nodded. "Luke and Sloane aren't the only ones with campus connections. I got a tour earlier today. The press badge gets me all the inside information."

"What are they doing with this space?"

Wyatt walked to the left, toward a dimly lit hallway. "I think the official unveiling is going to be sometime next year, but they're turning the building into a museum. There's going to be an exhibit on the history of the town, rotating displays from different departments, and a whole wing dedicated to artwork." Wyatt pointed above their heads, to an arched doorway with a prominently displayed plaque that read "The Lily Drake Room."

Chloe beamed. "She still doesn't have her name on the building, but at least she has a room."

Chloe was quiet as she stepped into the room named for the painter who had inspired her move across the country to attend Mayfield. Lily Drake was finally getting the recognition she deserved. But instead of feeling happiness, Chloe was overwhelmed with regret. None of the dreams she held as an eighteen-year-old had come true. She wasn't sure how she'd ventured so far away from a life filled with inspiration to days filled with mindless small talk in uncomfortable clothes.

"They've already hung some paintings," Wyatt said. "Look around."

Chloe walked around the room, past portraits and land-scapes and abstracts that didn't seem to have any relation to one another. There was a small selection of Lily Drake's works that she had completed while on campus, but most of the other artwork was from lesser-known artists. Chloe inspected the exhibit labels and discovered that each painting was from a graduate of a different class year.

"They're all from Mayfield students?" Chloe asked.

Wyatt nodded. "Go find our year."

Chloe slowly walked down the hallway. When she got to her graduating class, the blood rushed to her ears, shock and excitement and maybe even a tinge of embarrassment flooding her body.

Because somehow, someone had selected a painting by Chloe.

"Did you do this? Is this a joke?" she asked.

Wyatt shook his head. "I had no idea. I saw it earlier today, but I'm not surprised."

"I painted this." She was still stunned as she pointed at the river landscape.

"I know." Wyatt shoved his hands in his pockets. "It's the best piece in here. You're talented, Chloe."

It was hard for her to tear her eyes away from the wall, displaying a painting that she created almost a decade ago. It was even harder for her to believe Wyatt's words.

Wyatt cleared his throat. "I never knew you painted that day," he said.

"I never told anyone about this painting," Chloe replied.

Wyatt stepped beside Chloe, his shoulder rubbing against hers as they both stared at the wall. "You shouldn't hide the best parts of you, Chloe."

She swallowed, studying the painting of the six of them together. They were gathered at the river, and Wyatt had just swung from the rope, his body caught midair before he splashed into the water. Alden had waded in past his knees, and the rest of them were sprawled on towels, soaking up every bit of the spring Tennessee sun. Marianne and Sloane leaned together, exchanging whispers, and Chloe's head rested in Luke's lap.

Chloe painted with wide brush strokes, creating a blurry, abstract version of the scene. But the carefree joy of that hot day was clear.

"Why would they have picked mine?" Chloe asked, her voice barely a whisper.

"Because it's good. Because you capture more emotion in one of your brushstrokes than a dozen other pictures in this room."

Chloe shook her head. "They should have picked someone who became an artist."

Wyatt gently reached for Chloe's shoulder, turning her around to face him as he asked, "Why aren't you an artist, Chloe?"

Chloe had to look away in order to answer. "I'm busy at the gallery. Luke is working toward this huge promotion. The timing isn't right."

He shook his head. "There's never a good time to follow your dreams. You just do it."

"There are more important things right now."

"What's more important?"

"Luke has worked—"

Wyatt cut her off. "I don't care what's important for Luke. I'm asking you." His last word echoed in the room, the loudness of his voice surprising them both.

Chloe took a step back. "Luke is important to me. My relationships, with my boyfriend, my friends, they will always be the most important thing in my life."

Wyatt crossed his arms. "Do you think Luke feels the same?"

"Of course," Chloe said too softly.

"I see a lot of Luke in your life. I'm not sure Chloe is a priority for either of you."

"I don't need relationship advice from you." She felt her voice shake, even though she wished it wouldn't. "When's the last time you put someone's needs above your own? When's the last time you even had someone to put first?"

Wyatt's jaw moved back and forth, silence filling the gallery space as they both let Chloe's words hang in the air.

"You're the painter, Chloe. Not the canvas. Don't let Luke design a life you don't even want."

She shook her head. "You don't know what you're talking about."

Wyatt's eyebrows shot up. "Really?"

Chloe took a step forward, her finger pointing at Wyatt's chest. "You're making me sound like some pathetic girlfriend. Making sacrifices for your partner is not weak. It's love."

"Maybe," he whispered. Their faces were inches apart, and Chloe could see a tightness in his lips as he said, "As long as it's mutual. When's the last time Luke did something just for you?"

She wanted to shout a laundry list of examples. Except that's not what filled her brain at that moment. Instead, all she could think about were the times Luke had refused to stop at the art supply shop on their walk home, or when he had laughed at Chloe's suggestion that they try roller skating in Brooklyn, or when he had booked a wine tasting and she had to cancel her ceramics workshop. Stupid, small things that Chloe told herself didn't matter.

"Stop," she said louder than intended, her voice bouncing around the empty room. "I'm not defending my relationship to you of all people. You don't know us. You don't even know me anymore."

It was a lie. Chloe watched as her words slapped Wyatt's face. He stared at Chloe with an intensity that was immediately unsettling. "You're right." Wyatt swallowed slowly before speaking again. "And what a shame that is." He pointed at Chloe's painting. "Because the girl who made that—she was remarkable."

Chloe's lips trembled as she fought back tears both from the harshness of Wyatt's delivery and her immense longing to rewind time. She didn't want Wyatt to be right. She wanted to ignore every single one of his assumptions so that she could keep on pretending that she had everything she wanted.

They could hear footsteps on the marble floors, and, for the first time in minutes, Chloe and Wyatt looked away from each other, their eyes turning in the direction of this unwelcome interruption.

"There you are," Luke said, his cheerful voice immediately altering the air in the room. "Everything okay?"

"Yes," Chloe quickly replied at the same time Wyatt said, "Not really."

Luke's eyes narrowed as he walked to Chloe's side. "What's wrong?"

Chloe plastered on a smile and waved her hand dismissively.

Luke bent to kiss the top of her head as he said, "Why did you leave the party? Your message didn't even tell me where you were going. This is the third building I've been to."

"Sorry," Chloe mumbled.

"Can we head back?" Luke asked as he pulled Chloe toward the exit. "There are a lot of people we need to talk to tonight. The older couples get a kick out of the fact that we met in college. I need you."

Chloe swallowed. "I know."

"Let's go. I want to show off my beautiful girlfriend." Luke kissed her cheek, and Chloe didn't know why she immediately swiped at the spot his lips had just left.

Wyatt leaned against the wall. "Yeah, Chloe, duty awaits." His voice was thick with sarcasm that Luke ignored and Chloe resented.

Luke tugged at Chloe's arm once again. She stared at her painting, briefly wondering if Luke would notice. If he would pay attention to anything in the room except for his predetermined agenda.

But he didn't. He didn't even notice the tears in Chloe's eyes, or the fact that Wyatt stood immobile, fists clenched, refusing to join the charade of obligations that was now Chloe's life. Chloe left the room knowing that Wyatt had the smug satisfaction of being proven exactly right.

This Year

"**H**OW DO YOU FEEL?" Chloe asks.

"Like death vomited in my mouth." Marianne groans as she rolls over in bed. "And my boobs feel like lumpy boulders."

Chloe tries to be helpful and asks, "Want me to grab your pump?"

Marianne nods and sits up in bed. "How are you so awake? And sparkly? You look too good to be hungover."

"I stopped drinking around ten," Chloe says. She doesn't admit that she's been up for two hours already. She's showered and changed her outfit twice. Because she needs something to occupy her time, but she's too scared to leave the room.

"I meant to pump before bed," Marianne complains. "But I didn't. I even slept through the overnight pump. Did I drink all the wine last night?"

"You and Sloane were an excellent support system. It was wine consumed out of love."

Marianne assembles her pump parts and turns on the machine. "How are you feeling? How many people do we hate at this moment? Luke? Wyatt? Is there a hatred winner?"

Chloe shakes her head. "I don't hate either of them. I'm still sorting through those feelings." She sighs. "Actually, I do hate Luke a little bit."

Marianne shifts on the bed. "Go ahead. Sort. You might need to talk a little louder because of the whirring of this torture machine. But I'm here to listen. And for what it's worth, I hate Luke a lot right now."

There's a knock on the door, and Marianne reaches for the sheet to cover her chest. Chloe cracks the door open and sees Sloane on the other side. She has an iced coffee in each hand and a bag of something that smells like carbohydrate heaven.

Marianne moans when Sloane walks in the room. "You are the best. Please tell me there is something delicious in that bag."

Sloane pulls out a flaky croissant and a glazed doughnut.

"I will fight you for that doughnut." Marianne maneuvers the pump so that it is perched against her left forearm and holds out her right hand.

"You can have the doughnut," Chloe says.

Sloane plops on the bed. "How are we feeling this morning?"

"I am feeling very hungover, and Chloe was about to discuss her feelings."

"Skip me," Chloe says. "Let's talk about you guys first."

Sloane and Marianne both laugh. "Why do you always avoid difficult conversations?" Sloane asks.

"I don't do that," Chloe says.

Marianne tilts her head to the side. "You delayed breaking up with Luke until he was on his knee proposing."

"Maybe," Chloe mumbles. "Let me eat. You two talk first." Chloe takes a giant bite of her croissant before they can protest.

"How's Alden?" Marianne asks Sloane.

"Still upset." Sloane picks at a piece of lint on the bed-spread. "We barely spoke this morning." She quickly looks up and says to Chloe, "But he promises that he didn't know any-thing about Luke."

"I believe that," Chloe says. "Because Alden is a very good person who cares deeply about his wife and her health."

Sloane holds up her hand. "I know. But I want children. Alden needs to accept that I'm going to do whatever it takes."

"He's asking you to take care of yourself when you clearly aren't," Chloe blurts. "Sloane, what happened in that nursery was scary. You need a break. That's obvious to everyone except you."

Sloane doesn't answer. Instead, she reaches for Chloe's croissant and tears off a giant piece, shoving it in her mouth. "Let's change topics," she says, holding a hand over her still chewing mouth.

"I'm sorry. I shouldn't have said anything," Chloe imme-diately apologizes, seeing the anger on Sloane's face.

"I always hold it together. I lost it once, and now everyone thinks I'm not fit to be a mother."

"No!" Chloe and Marianne shout together. "That's not what I mean," Chloe adds. "You are going to be a wonderful mother. But you've been through so much. Give yourself time to heal before you try again."

"It's my decision," Sloane says.

"You're right," Chloe agrees.

"I get it," Marianne adds. "I was desperate to have Teddy, and if I had been through what you've gone through, I would have burned the house down. Whatever you want to do, I sup-port you. And I know Alden does too."

Marianne tries to take a bite of her doughnut, but her arm slips and the pump falls off. Her nipple seems to have gotten caught in the suction and she yelps in pain. When the half-full bottle of breast milk falls to the floor, Marianne repeats, "No, no, no, no, no."

Only a few tablespoons spill, and Chloe hands Marianne a washcloth, but she sees tears forming in her friend's eyes.

"I hate this!" Marianne yells.

"Can you be more specific?" Chloe sheepishly asks. "There's a lot to hate right now."

"I hate being tied to that stupid machine. I hate the fact that I'm going to have to pour this milk down the drain because it might have too much alcohol in it. I hate that I'm sitting here with my tits out and not in a fun way. I hate that you guys have no idea how much I hate this." Marianne sighs and sits on the floor, leaning against the bed.

"Can you stop pumping?" Chloe tries to fix the problem that seems to have the easiest solution.

But the look Marianne and Sloane give Chloe suggests that this is not an appropriate question to ask.

"Teddy spits up all the formula. It took me months of pumping to save enough milk so I could leave him, and now it doesn't even feel worth it."

"That's my fault," Sloane says softly.

"No, it's not," Marianne quickly replies. "Forget I said anything. Hangover-induced neuroses."

"I wasn't there for you. And you needed me. Talk to me now," Sloane says.

Chloe doesn't take offense at this statement. She's never been one of those people who fantasize about motherhood. It seems low on the list of identities she needs to explore in life, and Sloane and Marianne have always known that. One of the many ways they are incredible friends is because they've never made Chloe feel lesser because she's missing a maternal yearning, which is even more remarkable because Sloane and Marianne have talked about motherhood since they first met.

Potential baby names, the funny quirks about birth order, whether matching outfits are acceptable—these are common discussions between Sloane and Marianne. So Chloe understands what Sloane means. In the last year, Marianne hasn't been able to continue those discussions with Sloane. Sloane pulled away at the penultimate moment.

Marianne turns to Sloane and says, "I'm not talking about my insignificant complaints. Especially not to you."

"Yes, you should," Sloane says.

Marianne waves her hand dismissively. "It's okay. I'll be fine."

"Marianne, I'm serious. I can handle hearing about your life. I need to hear about your life, and I'm sorry I've been too selfish to realize that." Chloe watches as Sloane's earnest apology seems to work. Marianne smiles, and Chloe feels like she can breathe again.

Marianne exhales. "I think about Teddy constantly. I feel so guilty for leaving him with Noah, even though I thought I was going to lose my mind if I didn't leave. And it is so much more work. It's easier to let him nurse whenever he wants. But then it feels like my life is over. I can never wear a dress without thinking about boob access. I can never leave my kid. I'm going to be a leaky, floppy, self-serve machine for the rest of my life." Marianne stares at the ceiling and then shouts, "And I'm a horrible person for thinking any of this!"

Sloane reaches out and grabs Marianne's hand. "I think most moms feel like this. It doesn't make you horrible. It's not forever. Most kids eventually eat food."

"Sometimes it feels like forever." Marianne squeezes Sloane's hand and then lets go. She slumps forward, burying her face in her hands. "I thought this week would be good for me. I wanted to take a break. But it might be making things harder."

"Because you miss Teddy?" Chloe asks.

"No. I mean yes, of course I miss him. But I think I might miss me more."

Chloe sits on the opposite side of Marianne, all three friends huddled on the floor. "What do you mean?" Chloe asks.

"It's hard to be anything other than his mother. Even here, I'm still coming back to pump, and I'm swaying back and forth constantly because I spend so much of my life rocking a baby. I love being a mother. I've always wanted to be a mother. I just didn't realize that once I became a mother it would feel like it erased every other part of me."

"You can go back to teaching," Chloe suggests.

"I know. But I don't want to miss any moments with him. But I also want more time to myself. And I get that it sounds like those are two opposite things. And it's impossible. But that's what I need."

"Have you talked to Noah about all of this?" Sloane gently asks.

"No, there never seems to be a good time to tell your husband that you're failing as a mother."

"First of all, you're not failing," Sloane quickly responds. "Second, I guarantee the minute Noah gets down here he is going to have a whole new perspective after almost a week alone with a baby. Talk to him. You two can fix this problem together."

"Like you and Alden?" Marianne raises her eyebrows,

Sloane wags her finger. "Nope. Not my turn."

"I've talked about my boobs enough for a lifetime. Chloe, you're up."

"We talked about me last night. Over multiple bottles of wine," Chloe protests.

"No. We man-bashed Luke and Wyatt. But we didn't really talk about how you feel. Or what you're going to do."

Chloe thinks about everything that happened last night, last year, and all the secrets kept and how much they've fractured their friendships. For once, she doesn't hesitate. She wants to tell her friends what happened because she's tired of hiding the biggest parts of her life from the people she loves.

"I'm still upset, but I understand Wyatt." Chloe swallows. "I talked to him. After I left you guys."

"Did he grovel?" Marianne asks.

"Did you make him cry?" Sloane adds.

"No. He explained himself." Chloe takes a deep breath. "And then we kissed."

Sloane yells. Not a subtle, childlike squeal, but a full-body, searching for a missing person scream.

Within moments, Alden's voice is on the other side of the door asking, "What's wrong? Is everyone okay? Can I come in?"

"My boobs are out," Marianne stutters. "You can't come in. Sloane thought she saw a mouse," Marianne lies. "We're fine," she lies even more.

After ten long seconds, ensuring that Alden isn't hovering at the door, Sloane finally scream-whispers, "What do you mean you kissed Wyatt? Accidentally? Did he fall onto your lips?"

Chloe shakes her head. "No. It was on purpose."

Marianne closes her eyes briefly and then slowly asks, "How did this happen?"

"He told me he loved me," Chloe admits.

Sloane yells again. "He loves you?"

"Sloane, please whisper. They are all in this house." Chloe makes a large swirling gesture, reflecting the chaos of all the men she does not want to witness this conversation.

"Not Luke. We don't know where he went," Marianne says.

"What do you mean?" Chloe asks.

Sloane shrugs. "He didn't come back to the house last night. I peeked into his room this morning. He's not there."

"Did he go home?" Chloe isn't sure what answer she wants. She can't imagine never speaking to Luke again. But they live in different cities. Is it possible that after all of Chloe's efforts to find a way to mend their friendship, Luke is going to be the one who refuses to reconnect? And if so, does Chloe even care at this point?

"We don't know. Maybe. But let's get back to the Wyatt kissing thing. Because I need more details," Marianne says.

"Was it a good kiss?" Sloane asks.

Chloe feels her face burn. Good seems like an inadequate description. Chloe unconsciously brushes her thumb against her bottom lip, revisiting the sensation of her mouth pressed against Wyatt's. Her heart races at the memory. Because it was a kiss that kept her up all night. She wanted more, and yet she couldn't sort the confused feelings swirling in her brain.

She had two goals for this week: support Sloane and try to find a way to navigate her friendships without being Luke's girlfriend. The week is almost over and she's failed at both. There's no way kissing Wyatt makes an already complicated friendship dynamic any easier. And although this morning has gone better than yesterday, she realizes that she needs to be a better friend to both Sloane and Marianne, who are going through much more than Chloe realized.

"It was good," Chloe admits. "But it shouldn't happen again. Right?"

Sloane and Marianne glance back and forth, each of them waiting for the other to answer first.

"Why do you think it shouldn't happen again?" Sloane asks.

"Because Luke was barely talking to me at the beginning of this trip. Kissing his best friend isn't going to improve communication."

"Why do you care if communication with Luke is improved?" Marianne asks.

"Because of you guys."

"What do we have to do with you and Luke?"

Chloe pauses, slightly upset that her friends are making her say the thing they all know already. "Because you guys are Luke's friends," Chloe pleads. "I'm the add-on girlfriend. If Luke and I aren't speaking, I lose my friendship with everyone, and I don't want that to happen. It's been lonely this last year. I tried to give Luke space, but that just meant I spent most of the year without my best friends."

"Are you insane?" Sloane blurts.

"Obviously she is," Marianne quickly adds.

"None of us could figure out why you kept canceling. Making excuses to avoid us. We may have met you through Luke, but you are our friend. And so is Luke, even though I dislike him immensely right now. Our friendship doesn't disappear just because you made the obviously wise decision not to marry Luke." Sloane's voice is firm, and it's almost convincing.

Chloe rolls her eyes. "You have to say that, but don't you see how this goes? Luke and I are awkward around each other, and that makes everyone else feel awkward, so we end up doing things separately, and you guys get tired of repeating the same stories twice, so then you end up just picking the person you like more, and Luke makes better cocktails and throws more fun parties, so obviously it's going to be him."

"That was a spiral," Sloane says out of the side of her mouth to Marianne.

"You should basically move into a van by the river," Marianne says to Chloe. "Things seem dire."

"I'm serious," Chloe says, and even though she hates it, she starts to cry. "You have Noah and Teddy. A family." She looks over at Sloane, her voice softening. "And you have Alden. And you both still have your parents. And, based on your weddings, entirely too many cousins."

Chloe takes a deep breath, trying to control the emotions that have been running wild over the last twenty-four hours. "This friendship, with you two, but also with Alden and Wyatt and even Luke, is very important to me. It's everything to me. Losing my friends feels like losing a chunk of my body."

Marianne winces. "That's a disturbing visual."

Chloe groans. "You know what I mean."

"Yes. I do," Sloane says. "Because I feel the same way. I don't know if Alden and I will be able to have children." Sloane seems to stumble over this admission, as if it's the first time she's letting herself think about that possibility. "But I feel responsible for the five of you, and I'd do anything to keep us together."

"It's going to be different," Marianne softly says. "For all of us. But we are going to figure it out together, this adult life we never expected. We have to."

The three women hold hands, and Sloane starts humming "Kumbaya," and Marianne kicks her ankle. Even though there are no answers and no plan, Chloe does feel a little bit better.

"Back to Wyatt." Sloane's eyebrows jump. "Do you like him? Do you love him back?"

Chloe fumbles with her braid. "I think a part of me has always wondered about Wyatt. There's been this tension with us. And I never knew what to do with it. Other than bicker."

Marianne has a mischievous smirk on her face when she says, "Then maybe you should go figure that out."

Chloe shakes her head. "I can't."

"Yes, you can," Sloane orders. "If things between you and Wyatt are meant to be, we, as a group, will figure out how to navigate that newness in our friendship. Only losers let fear drive their decisions."

"He's a great guy," Marianne adds.

"And his body." Sloane bites her lip.

"And that hair," Marianne moans.

"We've all had our Wyatt fantasies," Sloane says. "But for us, he's untouchable. Always has been."

"He should be for me too," Chloe comments. "He's Luke's best friend. Plus, I'm nothing like the women he dates."

"You mean you smile and don't think pop culture is beneath you?" Marianne asks.

"Yes," Chloe blurts. "And I eat the whole pint of Ben & Jerry's by myself. Nothing in my closet is black. I'm five four in heels. Wyatt likes skinny, mean giraffes."

"But he loves you," Sloane scream-whispers.

"What did his stomach feel like?" Marianne asks.

"There wasn't much stomach grazing during the kissing," Chloe answers.

Sloane swats at Chloe's arm. "Please go graze that man's stomach and report back."

"Why aren't you guys more freaked out about this? Don't you feel like Wyatt is your brother?" Chloe asks.

"First, I don't have a brother," Sloane says. "Second, I'm married, not blind. Third, the more I think about this, the more it makes so much sense."

Marianne nods. "I agree. You two actually make a lot more sense than you and Luke."

Hearing his name is a reality check for Chloe. "How do you think Luke will react?"

Sloane shrugs. "I'm not sure. But Luke's reaction shouldn't be your concern. At all."

Chloe opens her mouth to protest, but Sloane holds up her hand, continuing. "He cheated on you for years. Isolated you from your friends after the breakup. You spent a decade of your life making decisions around Luke. Stop thinking about someone who doesn't deserve your time."

"Hard agree." Marianne adds. "Go kiss the moody writer. And report back." Marianne pulls Chloe to her feet and pushes her toward the door.

"Now that you've finished pumping, want to grab a mimosa?" Sloane asks Marianne. "Since I'm not pregnant, I can actually drink instead of just pretending."

Marianne groans. "I'm still hungover."

"So that's a yes?" Sloane says.

Marianne pretends to drag her feet but lets a small smile escape. "That's a yes."

"One stop before the kitchen," Sloane says. "I have a bag of stuff for you."

Marianne holds up her hand. "No more dresses, Sloane. I can't wear this stuff at home anyway. Teddy would spit up all over it."

"It's not dresses. It's the baby gifts I bought." Sloane swallows. "I kept seeing things I wanted you to have, but I was too jealous to celebrate." Sloane's jaw moves back and forth. "Teddy will have outgrown some of the stuff, but I want you to open them now."

"Are you sure?" Marianne says softly.

"Yes." Sloane answers firmly. Then she turns to Chloe. "Why are you still standing there and not kissing a man right now?"

Chloe wraps her arms around her two friends, happy to see them mended or moving in that direction at least. "The three of us make me very happy."

"The gifts are in the nursery. Watch out for all the broken stuff," Sloane says over her shoulder as she opens the door that's been closed for the last two days.

They all stand immobile in the doorway, confronted with the shards of debris from Sloane's breakdown. "I really lost it," Sloane whispers.

"What's that smell?" Marianne asks.

Chloe wrinkles her nose. "It's like fish. Or a dead animal."

Sloane waves her hand. "It's all these extra boys in the house. Don't you remember our apartment in New York? I'll open some windows and turn on the diffuser."

Marianne and Sloane go into the room, their arms wrapped around each other, and Chloe heads in the opposite direction.

She stands outside Wyatt's door for almost thirty seconds, the entire time debating whether this is a mistake or not. As she raises her hand to knock, the door opens.

Unlike last night, Wyatt is fully dressed. Same black T-shirt, as usual, a gray bathing suit, and wet hair, probably straight from the shower. When Chloe looks into his eyes, he seems like he had just as much trouble sleeping as she did.

"Hi," he whispers.

Chloe swallows. She's nervous. And she's never nervous around Wyatt. But then again, she's never been thinking about Wyatt's hard stomach, and his firm lips, and she's going to kill Sloane and Marianne for putting all of these thoughts into her head, because now she can't concentrate around Wyatt.

"Hi," she says. Her voice is strangely low. She was trying to overcompensate for her nerves by sounding confident, and instead she sounds like a seventy-year-old male smoker. "Hi," she repeats, this time in her normal voice.

"You okay?" Wyatt asks.

Chloe shakes her head. "Nope. Not at all okay."

"Want to come in and talk about it?"

"Uh-huh," Chloe stutters. She looks over her shoulder. Still no sign of Luke. Sloane and Marianne already know. And probably Alden too, because Sloane is the worst secret keeper in the history of the world. Besides, going into Wyatt's room is normal. She's done it dozens of times.

Except this time Wyatt reaches out and grabs Chloe's hand. His is warm and completely envelops her petite fingers. Chloe finds herself wishing he'd never let go, while also wondering how sweaty her nervous palm feels against his hand.

They sit on Wyatt's bed, and he squeezes her hand before releasing it. She stares at her bare feet because looking into Wyatt's eyes will likely set her on fire with embarrassment.

He runs his hand through his dark hair, mussing what was previously combed back. "I freaked you out with my confession last night, didn't I?"

She swallows and picks at a tiny string on his bedspread. "I'm feeling a little overwhelmed."

He smirks. "Understatement?"

"Maybe." She looks up. Despite the chaos in her brain, his sparkling grin immediately puts her at ease.

Wyatt shifts to the side, his shoulder brushing against Chloe's. "How about we slow things down? You're single. I'm single. Would you be interested in hanging out sometime?"

It sounds natural, a phrase Wyatt has probably uttered hundreds of times over the years. But he's saying it to Chloe, and the absurdity of this suggestion is laughable.

"I have known you for ten years. You are my ex-boyfriend's best friend. There is no simple 'hanging out,' Wyatt."

He looks at the ceiling and then back to Chloe. "I know that. That's why I went straight to the big love declaration. But now that I've scared you off, I'm trying an alternative approach."

"I have an idea," she says. "Let's best-case-scenario this."

He turns so that his whole body is facing Chloe. "Does that mean you want to put yourself in a scenario with me?"

"Maybe," she says too fast. "Yes." She swallows. "I think so. We need to talk it out first, and then I can answer that question."

"Okay. Best case scenario. You're one of my best friends. I love everything about you. Even the most annoying things you do."

Chloe scrunches her nose. "Like what?"

"You make everyone read their horoscopes, you hold up your pointer finger and thumb so that you can tell the difference between left and right, and you seem incapable of counting silently." Wyatt rattles off this list entirely too quickly for Chloe's comfort. But he's right. She does do all of these things.

Wyatt continues. "I've waited a long time for this, Chloe. Not just all those years of fighting my feelings while you were with Luke. But I wanted to make sure you had enough space and time after your breakup. If you tell me that you need more time, that you aren't ready, then I can keep waiting. Because you're worth waiting for. There's no one like you, Chloe."

She stares into his eyes. It's rare to feel appreciated by someone, but when a person knows you as well as Wyatt knows her, it feels almost too lucky.

"Best case scenario," he says. "Whenever you're ready, we love each other as hard as we can, for as long as we can, and all the friends in our lives who love us are happy that we found each other."

"But what happens when it ends?" Her voice is shaky. "What's going to happen with our friends? I don't want to lose them or you."

"I think the best case is that it doesn't end, Chloe." Wyatt's hands weave into her hair, eventually cupping her cheeks.

"I'm scared," she whispers. She takes a deep breath and stares into his eyes. "But I think I'm more scared of missing out on this."

It's all the confirmation Wyatt needs. He leans over and his lips connect with hers.

Chloe loses herself in Wyatt's arms. Any hesitation is erased the moment she feels his fingers slide underneath her shirt and up her back. It's been hours of wondering, debating, daydreaming about this moment. But if she's being honest, maybe it's been years. Because Wyatt has always been there. Always been in the back of her mind. And now he's pressed against her body. His lips teasing her neck as her heart races faster.

He lifts her off the floor and spins her around, lowering her onto the bed. As he hovers over her body, her hands moving up and down the length of his torso, he asks, "You sure?"

She smiles. "Less talking. More touching."

She lifts her arms into the air and he willingly accepts her invitation, removing her shirt before diving back down for deeper kisses and the electrifying sensation of their bare skin together.

What starts with a mutual frenzy of movements, hands groping every inch of each other's bodies, soon slows into gentle reverence.

Wyatt shows Chloe he loves her with his hands.

Wyatt shows Chloe he loves her with his mouth.

Wyatt uses every inch of his body to show Chloe how much she is desired.

And as Chloe moans Wyatt's name, she wonders why she ever thought this could be a mistake.

Afterward, Wyatt wraps his arms tightly around Chloe's body. Her head rests on his chest, listening to every thump of his heartbeat as he absently runs his fingers through her hair. All of the uncertainty of the last day disappears. Lying next to Wyatt feels right, and after so much chaos, it's the calmest she's felt. Their bodies melt into each other, and the only time he breaks their embrace is to pull on a pair of boxers and toss her one of his t-shirts, immediately returning to the bed, slipping under the blanket as Chloe wraps her leg over his side. They stay tangled together for hours, or maybe minutes, because time is irrelevant when you are finally in the right place.

But then the door creaks open.

They hear a familiar voice.

Luke pokes his head in Wyatt's room and then immediately pulls back. "Shit. Sorry, Wyatt. I didn't know you had someone in here."

Chloe dives under the covers. All the blood drains from her face, because this can't be happening. She's half naked in Wyatt's bed while her ex-boyfriend is a few feet away. She can feel the warmth of Wyatt's leg pressed against hers while the echo of Luke's voice rings in her ears.

"Can we talk later?" Luke asks Wyatt through the cracked door. "About the other night."

"Sure," Wyatt responds. Chloe is impressed Wyatt can hide the panic in his voice. For a brief moment, Chloe thinks maybe they've avoided this utter disaster. She lowers the sheet slightly, searching for Wyatt's eyes and confirmation that every decision she's made this morning wasn't a complete and total mistake.

But then Luke laughs and pushes open the door slightly, his hand waving through the opening as he says, "Sorry about the interruption." Chloe sees his hand and immediately pulls the cover back over her head.

Maybe it's the motion that alerts him. Or maybe it's her T-shirt by the door. Chloe's worn MoMA T-shirt that Wyatt threw across the room earlier, with its bold green color that stands out among Wyatt's discarded clothing.

Because the next thing Chloe knows, Luke throws the door open.

She can hear his heavy breathing. The stomp of his footsteps across the room as he brazenly yanks back the sheet. The way time seems to stop when their eyes connect, Luke staring at Chloe first, then over to Wyatt, before fury erupts across his face.

Luke screams, "Why is Chloe in your bed?"

Chloe's lip trembles as she scoots back against the head-board, bringing the sheet bunched up to her chin. She wants to answer. She wants to explain and defend and tell Luke to leave and to apologize, but she doesn't do any of these things. She's silent.

Wyatt stands in front of Chloe, instinctively creating a buffer. He holds up his hands. "Let's talk—" he starts to say.

But before he can finish, Wyatt's head snaps back as Luke's fist connects with his jaw.

Wyatt doesn't move. He rubs the side of his face. "Fine. I guess I deserve that. Ready to talk now?"

Luke clearly doesn't want to talk, because he runs straight for Wyatt, his shoulder barreling into Wyatt's stomach.

Chloe presses her body against the headboard as she watches Wyatt take two more punches in the stomach, all the while she's shouting at Luke to stop and pleading for anyone to come help.

Finally, Wyatt shoves Luke away, and when Luke comes back for more, Wyatt swings, his fist connecting with Luke's nose. Blood pours down the front of Luke's rumpled shirt.

There is a look of shock on Luke's face, as if he can't imag-ine that Wyatt hit back. And then pure rage. Luke tackles Wyatt to the floor and pins him down. He's swinging, again and again, as Wyatt holds his arms around his head.

Alden, Sloane, and Marianne rush into the room. Chloe watches as their eyes briefly dart from the two men fighting to Chloe huddled in the corner, half-dressed in Wyatt's room.

Alden pulls Luke off Wyatt. Sloane steps in between them. Marianne rushes to Chloe's side.

Everyone's breathing is rapid, eyes darting as silent judgments of this scenario bounce around their heads. Alden suggests that Luke go for a walk. Sloane asks Wyatt if he realizes the doors have locks. Marianne holds Chloe tighter.

Chloe looks around the room. Luke shrugs out of Alden's restraint and his eyes meet Chloe's. Through the blur of tears, she sees his jaw tremble before he storms away, the echo of the front door slamming filling the now quiet house. Sloane offers Wyatt a towel to hold over the cut on his left brow.

Chloe trembles as she thinks about all the different ways she could have handled this situation. She should have talked to Luke, about too many things to count. She and Wyatt could have waited. And they definitely could have locked the door. Somehow, she has taken a bad situation and made it even worse. Chloe cries in the corner, choked sobs at the realization that this is the very worst case scenario.

And yet, as terrible as this day began, Chloe has no idea that the night is going to end up being even worse.

◆ 21 ◆

This Year

THERE ARE FIREMEN AND ambulances and even more sirens in the distance. Alden and Sloane watch their dream home burn, their arms wrapped tightly around one another. Chloe's eyes keep skimming the crowd, looking for Luke. She barely notices Wyatt's hand at her back, Marianne clutching her arm, the salt water still beading on Chloe's skin from her impulsive swim.

After Luke walked in on Chloe and Wyatt that morning, they all scattered, escaping to different corners of the house, making excuses for errands they didn't need to run, so that they could lick their wounds without being overwhelmed by their collective messiness.

Wyatt left Chloe alone, giving her the space she needed, but now he's pressed so close to her body that she wonders whether she's hurting his bruised ribs.

The five of them huddle together on the fringe of the property. Chloe stares at Sloane and Alden, unable to tear her eyes away from their heartbroken faces. Chloe wonders whether Sloane is thinking about all the furniture she spent years sourcing from the high-end designers she coveted for so long. Or maybe Alden is calculating the damage to the custom equipment he designed for his home office. Or maybe their pain is about more than any single physical object; it's the utter destruction of all of their dreams.

Sloane and Alden spent years wanting and designing and executing a perfect house that they're now watching burn. No one should ever feel prepared for a moment like this, but perhaps they are better equipped than most. Because as Chloe recently discovered, Sloane and Alden spent the last year fighting for the dream of a child that only slipped further and further away. It seems unfair that they would experience even more loss. And Chloe knows that one catastrophe doesn't make others any easier to bear.

"It's gone," Sloane says as tears slide down her cheeks. Alden pulls her into his chest and rocks her back and forth.

"But we're here. Together," Alden murmurs.

Not for the first time this week, Chloe feels like it's an intimate moment that shouldn't have an audience. She takes a step away as Sloane buries her face in the crook of Alden's neck. Sloane murmurs words to Alden, and he wipes away her tears. The intensity of their conversation deepens, and Chloe walks farther away, giving them the privacy they deserve to unpack how to move forward in the face of so much loss.

Chloe can't stop scanning the house and the growing crowd of people as she searches for Luke. She was waiting for him to emerge from the cloud of smoke, but now the flames around the house are too big to hold on to that hope any longer. Instead, she looks for him in the crowd, searching for his sandy hair and cocky stride.

Chloe can't believe that just moments earlier, she was dreading an interaction with Luke, waiting for dinner to start and wondering how she was going to navigate yet another tense meal with her ex. The whole week has been a series of disasters, but no one could have predicted this catastrophe. Chloe wrings the water out of her hair as she scans the scene:

the tables of food that have been turned over, platters of grouper lying in the sand, the catering crew rightfully more concerned with their safety than Sloane's ruined dinner party.
Chloe finds her crumpled dress and slips it over her damp body
as she continues searching, her heart in her throat as she realizes she'd give anything to see Luke again.

"Have you seen him?" Chloe asks Wyatt. "Was he"—she
chokes out the next word—"inside?"

Wyatt shakes his head. "I don't think so. But I hadn't seen
him for a few hours." There's already a purple bruise under
Wyatt's left eye.

A perimeter is set up around the house, roping off the
burning building from the spectators who have gathered to
watch this tragedy. As the crowd grows, whispers are exchanged
about the house on fire, speculation rising about how it started
and whether anyone got hurt.

The firemen work, truck after truck of water being poured
onto the home, the fire slowly being contained, and then the
smoke pushing them farther and farther away, until the five of
them are forced away from the house and in search of their
missing friend.

No one has seen Luke. They are all thinking some variation of the same horror. Was Luke inside? The only time anyone speaks, it is to reassure themselves and everyone else.

"He probably went for a walk," Marianne says.

"Maybe he went to Bud & Alley's for a beer," Alden
mumbles.

"He was so mad. He's probably at the airport," Wyatt adds.

"He's fine. We'll find him soon," Sloane states.

But the guilt overwhelms Chloe. Because even though she
was furious at Luke, even though she felt betrayed, and they
spent the last few days either barely communicating or shouting painful words at each other, Luke is a part of her. She will

always love him in some way, and the thought of him being removed from her life is unbearable.

Tears stream down Chloe's cheeks as she whispers, "He can't be dead."

The five of them walk, their arms looped around each other's shoulders, past the perimeter set by the fire department.

"We need to get a hotel for the night," Alden says. "I left my phone number with the fire chief. He's going to call when it's fully out, and then we'll meet with the insurance adjuster, and I'm sure there will be a police report to fill out, and . . ."

Sloane cups Alden's face and kisses him hard. She pulls back, their foreheads leaning against one another. "Yes. We will do all of that. But for now, let's just find a place to stay."

Marianne looks at her phone. "Noah is on his way. We made a hotel reservation in case the house felt too crowded. He could probably get an extra room at the Residence Inn."

"Good idea," Sloane says.

Alden raises his eyebrows. "You're going to Panama City? To sleep in a Residence Inn? Willingly?"

Sloane shrugs. "It's high season. We're not going to find a place here. Besides, I think being together is exactly what we need."

They walk down the street, Marianne on the phone with Noah.

Chloe's eyes never stop scanning the crowds. She barely registers the gaping stares as strangers pass by. Bruised, disheveled, covered in soot, and sopping wet, the five of them are a messy, shell-shocked disaster.

Marianne hangs up the phone. "Noah got two connecting suites. It should be enough room for us to squeeze together."

Sloane nods. Chloe's eyes are too busy darting from one side of the street to the other.

"Noah is going to pick us up," Marianne says.

They are empty-handed, having fled the burning house without even a set of car keys. But Chloe and Wyatt and Marianne can still go back to their homes full of extra clothes and boxes of memories. Sloane and Alden lost everything.

Alden is on the phone with their insurance adjuster. Sloane hasn't let go of his hand once since they ran out of the house.

"Why don't we walk over to the town green to wait for Noah?" Wyatt suggests. "It's quieter away from the crowds."

They walk together the few short blocks up from the ocean and toward the center of Seaside where food trucks border the town's amphitheater. All the while, Chloe is dialing Luke's number again and again. Straight to voice mail.

"Is anyone hungry?" Sloane asks.

Chloe remembers the beautiful dinner on the beach that none of them will eat. The caterers are probably gathering trash bags to throw away the sandy, ash-covered food.

Chloe shakes her head, her stomach churning at the thought of eating anything while Luke is still missing.

But then, out of the corner of her eye, she sees him. He's standing in line at a food truck. His sandy hair shines in the setting sun, and before she knows it, Chloe is running across the green.

She's shouting Luke's name over and over again. And when he finally turns around, the first thing Chloe does is jump into his arms and squeeze his neck.

"You're okay," she screams. "You're okay," she whispers, starting to cry.

"What's going on?" Luke asks with a strange formality. He sets Chloe down on the ground and pushes her an arm's length away.

Then Chloe remembers everything that happened this morning when Luke walked into Wyatt's room. And by the solemn look on his face, it's clear Luke remembers as well.

"There was a fire," Chloe tries to explain. "Alden and Sloane's house, it's gone."

Chloe takes a step back, surveying Luke. He's dressed in his typical vacation wardrobe, a polo shirt and shorts. Clean clothes. Nothing rumpled, freshly showered. His nose is swollen and there is the beginning of a bruise on his cheek, but otherwise he's fine.

Chloe is not reassured by this fact; instead, she's infuriated. She looks at her rumpled dress, her half-wet hair, the smell of ash that is stuck to her skin, and she says, "We didn't know where you were."

"All of that smoke is from Alden's house?" Luke asks with a lack of awareness that makes Chloe even madder.

"Yes," Chloe says. "Alden and Sloane's house is completely destroyed."

"Is everyone okay? Is Alden safe?" an unfamiliar voice asks.

It's only then that Chloe realizes Luke isn't standing alone. He's with someone. A woman.

"Lucy?" Chloe asks. It's been a few years since Chloe has seen Alden's little sister Lucy, and clearly she's grown up in that short amount of time.

Chloe looks back and forth. "Does Alden know you're here?"

Lucy's eyes meet Luke's, and she shakes her head. "It's a surprise."

By now, everyone else has realized what made Chloe run. Alden and Sloane catch up, with Wyatt and Marianne trailing behind.

Alden hugs Luke and says, "We're glad you're okay. You scared us." Then Alden spots his little sister and says, "Lucy, what are you doing here?"

"I was just telling Chloe. I came to surprise you."

"Terrible timing," Sloane jokes, hugging her sister-in-law. "The house burned down and before that, these two were cage fighting." Sloane points between Luke and Wyatt.

Chloe doesn't know how Sloane can joke. How she can seem so composed and together when everything has just crumbled? But that's Sloane's superpower. She's good in a crisis and good at pretending everything is okay.

Lucy raises her eyes and says, "Well, that explains all the bruises."

Chloe looks between the two men, and it's clear Wyatt bore the brunt of this fight. There are red welts and purple bruises streaking his face. She can only imagine that the rest of his body is worse.

"Since we no longer have a home, we're staying at a hotel up the road," Sloane explains to Lucy. "Where's your stuff?"

"It's in my rental car," Lucy says. "I feel terrible. I should have called first. I can try to find another hotel room."

"Don't be silly. We'll have a girls' room and a boys' room."

"No way," Luke says, "am I sharing a room with Wyatt."

Six sets of eyes stare down Luke, disappointed and yet not surprised that he could be so petty at this moment.

"First of all, you don't have another option," Alden says. "Second, I get that you're pissed. We are all a little bit surprised by this development between Wyatt and Chloe. But you cheated on her for years. Stop being an asshole."

Luke starts to protest, but Alden shouts over him. "It's what friends do. They support each other, even when it's messy, even when you'd make a different choice, you still support the life they want." Alden stares at the sky before adding, "Plus, my house just burned down. I don't need more drama tonight."

Lucy doesn't wait for Luke to respond to her brother's lecture before blurting, "Wait. Chloe and Wyatt? Is that what the fight was about?"

Chloe looks away, still embarrassed by the situation. Wyatt answers for them both. "Yes." There's no remorse in Wyatt's voice, and that seems to infuriate Luke.

"How did you find out?" Lucy asks Luke out of the side of her mouth.

"I walked in on them in bed," Luke answers through gritted teeth.

Lucy looks around the group, and Chloe wonders what she sees. How broken and hurt they all are? The glaring signs of pain and regret and anger and sadness that are illuminated on each of their foreheads?

Lucy presses her lips together and then bursts out laughing. "You guys are a disaster."

"We know," they all answer in unison.

"Noah is here," Marianne says, pointing to the minivan parked across the street.

Noah rolls down the window and waves, then he does the universal head-tilt-on-palms-pressed-together to indicate that baby Teddy is asleep.

"No fighting in the car," Marianne instructs. "Everyone get in quietly. Do not wake my sleeping baby."

"Maybe Luke should ride with me," Lucy helpfully suggests. "To ensure a quiet ride."

Marianne gives Lucy the address of the hotel. They head in opposite directions, Lucy and Luke toward her rental car, everyone else toward Marianne's minivan.

But Chloe hangs back. Before Luke walks away, Chloe reaches out her hand and grabs his. "I'm really glad you're okay, Luke."

Luke turns to leave, but Chloe doesn't let him. For the first time in a very long time, she keeps talking and finally tells Luke how she feels.

"I'm glad you're okay. And I hate that you lied to me for so long. I hate that you didn't care enough to tell us you left and we spent the last hour wondering if you were alive. I hate that I spent most of our relationship wondering if you cared enough about me."

"Of course I cared about you," Luke says. The defensiveness in his voice makes Chloe angrier.

Chloe shakes her head. "You never appreciated me. I've made excuses for years, but honestly, you're selfish. I'm tired of trying so hard to matter in your life."

"Is that why you slept with Wyatt? To get my attention?"

"No. Your opinions don't matter anymore." Even though it's not easy to say, Chloe says it clearly and with conviction.

"Good." Luke shrugs.

His simple movement makes Chloe realize how little he cares.

He didn't apologize for the terror he inflicted on everyone with his unexplained absence. He didn't ask about anyone's safety. He didn't even express sympathy toward two of his closest friends when their home burned to the ground.

Luke takes the people around him for granted. Chloe can't imagine a worse quality.

She takes one step forward, making sure his eyes are focused on her face before she speaks. "You lost me. But if you don't fix yourself, you're going to lose all your friends too. Ask yourself if that's what you want. Figure out how to be a better person, Luke. It's long overdue."

Before Luke can speak, Chloe turns and walks away. After years of clinging to everyone around her, Chloe knows it's time to finally leave him behind.

But the temporary satisfaction is erased the minute she sees her friends. They're huddled beside Noah's minivan, Sloane's shaking shoulders being held by Alden as tears stream down her face.

"What's wrong?" Chloe asks.

"The fire chief just called," Alden says.

No one speaks, all eyes focused on Sloane.

"It's my fault," Sloane says. "I caused the fire."

♦ 22 ♦

This Year

"IT'S NOT YOUR FAULT," Alden whispers again and again as he holds Sloane.

"What happened?" Chloe asks.

Alden pauses, seeming reluctant to say anything as Sloane shakes in his arms. "It sounds like the fire started in the nursery," Alden admits. "We won't know for sure until the inspector finalizes the report, but the fire chief seemed pretty certain that's where it began."

"What does that have to do with Sloane?" Chloe asks.

"The smell," Sloane whispers. "Do you remember that rotten smell from this morning?"

Chloe nods her head.

Alden seems tortured as he continues speaking. "The fire chief said it was probably an electrical issue. He asked if we'd had any work done in the nursery. Exposed wires can cause fires."

"Burning rubber," Sloane stammers. "The wires melted the plastic insulation. He asked if we noticed any unusual smells."

Chloe shook her head. "But how is this your fault, Sloane?"

"The sconce. I ripped it out of the wall and ended up setting fire to everything." Sloane looks up at Alden. "I'm so sorry. I kept pushing and pushing, and this is where we are now."

"Stop," Alden says forcefully. "You're safe. We're all safe. Blaming yourself isn't going to make anything better."

"But it's all my fault," Sloane keeps mumbling.

It will be weeks before the fire inspector finalizes his report, proving that Sloane is right. The fire started in the nursery because of frayed wires trapped in the walls after the sconce was ripped away. But even if Sloane's actions started the fire, they were all to blame for the destruction that followed. Because those frayed wires traveled down to the basement where Alden was storing the fireworks for the final dinner celebration. Next to the storage area where Luke and Wyatt had left the extra gasoline canister for the golf cart. Beside the sea grasses Chloe and Marianne had collected on their beach walk.

Throughout the week, they'd all left tiny accelerants, unaware that their combination was capable of so much damage. When Sloane pulled the sconce out of the wall, it may have started the fire. But they all played a part in the explosion that destroyed everything.

None of them know the seemingly insignificant roles they played in turning a few sparks into a blazing building. All they know is that the fire started in the nursery, and Sloane is shouldering the blame.

"What if Luke had been hurt?" Sloane says.

"He's fine," Alden quickly replies.

Sloane seems more fragile than ever before.

The car ride to the hotel is silent. Wyatt is in front with Noah. Chloe and Marianne are flanking Teddy, Marianne's eyes focused on her sleeping baby; Sloane and Alden are in the back, Sloane slumped against his side as Alden types frantically on his phone, beginning the mountain of work required by his insurer.

They drive past a Walmart, and Marianne taps Noah on the shoulder and flails her arms to get him to pull over. They drop Marianne at the entrance and circle the parking lot for twenty minutes, afraid if the car stops, Teddy will wake.

Marianne finally comes out of the store with two giant plastic bags and zero explanation.

When they pull into the hotel parking lot, Teddy finally starts to stir.

"Alright, everyone may speak now," Marianne says as she unbuckles Teddy and immediately nuzzles his neck.

"What did you buy?" Wyatt asks.

"Toothbrushes, underwear, and pajamas. None of us had anything to wear." Marianne has a mischievous gleam in her eye. "I got matching sets for everyone."

"I'm so sorry. I've ruined everything," Sloane says, her voice shaking. "I'll replace everything you had in the house, Marianne. I know your pump was expensive."

"I'm thrilled the breast pump is destroyed. I don't care about any of that stuff. None of us do. We care about you."

"That's what I keep saying." Alden kisses Sloane's forehead.

Sloane squeezes his hand. "Let's go check in."

Alden sighs. "I need to find my sister. I can't believe she just showed up here. She's so unpredictable."

"She's young. She's supposed to be unpredictable," Sloane says.

Noah asks for extra room keys for the adjoining suites and tells everyone to get ready for the explosion of baby gear that Teddy requires. As the front desk attendant makes the keys, he tells Noah that the other members of the party already checked in.

"Luke and Lucy are probably wondering where we've been," Alden mumbles.

They all cram into the elevator and walk down the hallway toward the rooms. Marianne hurries ahead because apparently Teddy has a diaper emergency. Noah follows to assist. Wyatt and Chloe hang back from the rest.

"Are you okay?" Wyatt asks.

Chloe nods.

"Are we okay?"

Chloe nods again and squeezes his hand, willing it to be true. Chloe wants to say more and starts to speak, but they're distracted by the yelling at the end of the hallway.

Alden is screaming. This is the second time Chloe has heard him shout this week, which makes a total of two times in their entire decade-long friendship.

Wyatt and Chloe quickly make their way down the hall to the hotel room to find out what's going on.

"Why are you kissing my sister?" Alden shouts.

Luke holds his hands in the air. "Technically, she's kissing me."

"She's TWELVE!" Alden screams.

They are all crowded in the hallway, and Chloe swipes the key card, ushering everyone inside the hotel room. She barely wants to deal with this new mess. There's no reason why hotel guests should have to overhear this disaster.

"Alden, we've been over this," Lucy calmly states. "I'm twenty-three. I'm an adult. I'm kissing Luke. Get over it."

Chloe and Wyatt exchange nervous glances. Because although it is a relief not to be the center of drama for once, it is clear Alden is now on the verge of a breakdown.

Luke turns toward Lucy. "Babe, I told you I needed some more time before telling everyone."

Lucy shakes her head. "I don't need more time. And you don't either. You're afraid and so I'm doing it for you. Luke and I are dating. We like each other. Where is the wine?"

"Where is the wine?" Alden stutters. "Are you out of your mind?"

"I'm old enough to drink. I'm old enough to have sex with your best friend. This is happening."

Alden starts to hyperventilate. "Oh, my God, Sloane. Help me."

"I'm going to take Alden to get some oxygen." Sloane grabs her husband's shoulders, spins him around, and pushes him out in the hallway. Sloane is much better at managing someone else's crisis than dealing with her own problems. She seems to push aside all of her guilt about the fire and focus on Alden's rapid downward spiral. She grips his hand tighter because it looks like Alden is about to lunge at Luke, and violent Alden is the strangest thing any of them have seen.

From the doorway, Sloane says, "Lucy, wine is an excellent idea. Why don't you see what you can find in the minibar and we will join you in a few minutes."

Wyatt looks at Chloe and mouths *Are you okay now?*

Chloe looks down at the floor, her face hidden from the room. Wyatt immediately sweeps to her side, concern streaking his face as Chloe's shoulders begin to shake.

She's furious, her eyes narrowing in on Luke. "You're unbelievable. You're dating Lucy?"

"I don't have to explain myself to you," Luke says defensively. "Especially not after this morning."

Wyatt steps forward, ready to jump in, but Chloe pushes him back. "I felt terrible about our breakup. I stayed away, giving you the space I thought you needed, isolating myself from my best friends. And all that time you had already moved on? You were fine and you let me wallow in guilt?"

"I wasn't fine. I was mad."

"Well, that makes two of us." Chloe shakes her head. "Maybe more once Alden comes back. He's going to kill you."

"I know," Luke said. "It just happened." Luke runs his hands through his hair, and for a moment Chloe sees something like remorse on his face.

Lucy must see the same thing. She grabs Luke's hand and weaves her fingers with his while resting her head on his shoulder. "Alden will be fine. You're his best friend. Once he sees how happy we are, this won't be a problem."

"Seems like wise advice," Wyatt smirks.

Luke shakes his head. "She lectured me the entire drive over. You don't have to look so smug." He stares at Wyatt and Chloe, standing side by side. He gestures between the two of them. "I'm going to try to be okay with this relationship."

"Was that so hard?" Lucy elbows his side.

"Yes. It was incredibly difficult," Luke replies.

"But do you feel better?" Lucy asks.

"No. Not yet. But I'm trying." Luke grinds his teeth as he says those last words.

"Fine. Let's drink some wine." Lucy claps her hands.

Wyatt leans down and whispers to Chloe, "I think, maybe, Lucy is good for Luke."

"I hope so," Chloe says, anger still bubbling. She doesn't need Luke's permission. And she's so frustrated by his behavior. Chloe knows there's good inside him, but maybe someone else can man the search. Because it's not her problem anymore.

The door to the adjoining room opens, and Marianne walks in holding Teddy. "What'd I miss? That blowout was ridiculous. I had to shower him off."

Wyatt shakes his head. "These rooms are remarkably soundproof."

"I'll fill you in," Lucy says. "Luke and I are dating. Alden is hyperventilating, but he'll come around. And Luke and I can't wait to double date with Wyatt and Chloe because Luke is totally on board with their relationship."

"The last part is inaccurate," Luke mutters.

"But possible one day," Lucy adds.

Marianne looks at Noah. "You are changing the next diaper. I am not missing out again."

There's a knock on the door. "I ordered pizzas," Noah says. "Does that count?"

"Barely," Marianne replies.

While everyone is digging into the boxes of pizza, Luke asks Chloe if she will talk to him outside. Chloe reluctantly agrees, and they make their way onto the balcony.

"I owe you an apology," he says. "That's what I do on balconies, right?"

Chloe remembers that first fight, so many years ago, and how much has happened since then. She folds her arms across her chest. "I'm listening."

"I deserved what you said earlier." He sighs and continues, "I should have been honest. And I'm so sorry I hurt you, Chloe."

For so long, this was all Chloe wanted to hear. Some acknowledgment from Luke that her feelings mattered. It only took a year apart for Chloe to realize that her constant search for validation only made them both miserable.

"We've both hurt each other," Chloe generously says. "And I think we both realize that we aren't meant to be together."

Luke swallows. "Knowing it and hearing it out loud are two different things." He seems to hesitate and then blurts, "Can I ask you something?"

Chloe nods.

"Why did you stay with me for so long?"

It's a question Chloe has asked herself dozens of times over the years. Only recently has she been able to formulate an answer. "Because the idea of us was so good. And being alone was the scariest thing I could imagine."

"But it's not anymore?"

"No. Spending my whole life with the wrong person. That's scarier." Chloe is honest, and although it isn't her intention, her words hurt Luke. It's evident by the look on his face.

"You think it will be better with Wyatt?" Luke seems to be struggling to keep his tone even.

"I know it's messy . . ." Chloe trails off. "I don't know if Wyatt is the right person for me, but I'm open to that possibility."

"I'm trying to be okay with this." Luke shakes his head. "But I can't understand how you'd chase a possibility knowing the pain it would cause." Luke pinches the bridge of his broken nose, reminding them both of this morning's fight.

"It's new, Luke. It's hard to explain."

"Can you try?"

Chloe takes a deep breath. "Wyatt forces me to think about what I want and who I'll become. I don't always have the answers to those questions, but he makes me ask myself. There isn't another person in my life who has ever done that."

Luke looks away. "You fight with him all the time."

"I know."

"We never fought," he mutters.

"Because I never tried to be anything other than what you wanted," Chloe blurts.

Luke finally makes eye contact. "I'm sorry," he says again.

Chloe swallows. "It's my fault too. I should have expected more."

"I want you to be happy. And if it's with Wyatt, then I guess I'll have to get on board with that."

"Thank you, Luke."

Chloe leans in and gives Luke a hug, but not before waving at the four people staring at their every move. Once again, they have an audience, but for Chloe, things finally feel different.

She walks back inside and steals a slice of pepperoni off Wyatt's plate.

"Everything okay?" Wyatt asks.

"I think so," Chloe replies honestly as she takes another bite of pizza before reaching out to hold Teddy.

After an hour, Sloane returns with a slightly calmer Alden. "He's going to be fine," she announces.

Alden walks over to Luke. Everyone in the room tenses, Luke especially. Alden puts his hands on Luke's shoulders and squeezes. "Please don't ever describe sex with my sister," he says.

"I solemnly swear," Luke quickly replies.

"Never cheat on her," Alden adds.

"Of course not," Luke promises.

"I don't like it. If you hurt Lucy . . ." Alden trails off, and Sloane interjects.

"We will all kill you. Clean up your act," Sloane instructs, making everybody a little bit scared.

Alden looks around the room. The contents of both rooms' minibars are on the coffee table. There are candy wrappers and empty mini vodka bottles along with two jars of baby food. Alden picks up the pureed sweet potatoes. "Did one of you eat this?"

Wyatt shrugs. "I was starving, and Noah didn't order enough pizza."

Marianne smiles at Sloane. "While I was gone, Noah got Teddy to eat for the first time. He's sleeping now, but we all tried some and agree the peas are foul, but the pears are actually pretty good."

Sloane runs over and hugs Marianne. "I feel like we should celebrate the breast freedom."

There's a simultaneous groan from every man in the room that Sloane quickly dismisses.

"You guys have matching pajamas?" Sloane squeals.

Marianne smiles. "Walmart's finest."

"You guys look ridiculous," Alden says.

"They're surprisingly comfortable," Wyatt comments.

Everyone is wearing pale-blue pajama pants with pictures of popcorn all over their legs. The matching shirts say *Pop It Like It's Hot*. It's impossible not to dance every time you read the shirt.

Marianne hands sets to Sloane and Alden.

"Come on, Alden, let's put ours on."

Before they head into the bathroom to change, Chloe asks, "Did you hear anything else from the fire chief?"

"The house is completely gone," Alden says.

"We told him about the loose wires from the wall sconce. He agreed that's probably how it started," Sloane says softly. "I'm so sorry."

"Stop apologizing. It was an accident," Alden says. "Everything is okay. We have the important stuff right here." He smiles as he pulls his wife into the bathroom.

For the rest of the night, Sloane never leaves Alden's side. They seem to have entire conversations with the glances they exchange. More than once, Chloe thinks they should be alone, discussing the home they just lost and the futures they can't seem to agree upon. But maybe the fire erased the need for those conversations. At least for tonight. Because the way Sloane rests her head on Alden's shoulder and the way his chin quivers each time he looks into her eyes shows how much they need each other at this moment. Chloe hopes so at least. Maybe losing so much made them realize how much they still have. Eventually, they divide into a girls' room and a boys' room. But that's after they've taken turns holding Teddy and making plans for his first birthday party. Luke and Wyatt agree to wear costumes. Lucy volunteers to handle the flowers. Sloane maps out an entire menu in between bites of the leftover pizza Marianne hid from Wyatt. And Chloe sketches hand-drawn invitations.

After Teddy's midnight feeding and unsuccessfully trying to whisper through three rounds of Never Have I Ever before Alden announces that he's never playing this game with his sister again, they eventually find places for everyone to sleep.

The room is finally quiet. Chloe can hear the rhythmic breathing of her friends as they fall asleep. And she realizes that despite the chaos and anger, the secrets and the pain, this week brought them back to the place Chloe had hoped they'd return. Together.

✦ 23 ✦

One Year Later

CHLOE STANDS NEAR THE cliff, her long blonde hair blowing in the wind. The gauzy white dress whips around her ankles. She has a small bouquet of baby's breath in one hand, and Wyatt is holding the other hand. When the judge announces that they are married, Chloe drops the flowers on the ground and throws both arms around Wyatt's neck.

There's no applause. It's the smallest ceremony possible—just Chloe and Wyatt, promising to continue the life they've built together over the last year for as long as they possibly can.

Wyatt wrote their vows and Chloe said, "Ditto," because Wyatt expresses how he feels through words and Chloe does it through dozens of gestures, big and small, every day.

When Wyatt proposed last week, Chloe suggested an elopement. As soon as she said the word, they both knew it was the perfect celebration for them. The idea of being the center of attention for an entire night terrified Chloe. And Wyatt is fiercely protective of his privacy, especially since his novel was published over the summer and Sloane's viral videos of him resulted in a social media sensation.

It baffled Wyatt that a video Chloe took one morning of Wyatt sipping coffee, hunched over his computer, and then smiling in Chloe's direction could garner so much attention. Chloe only sent the video to the group text because everyone had been asking about Wyatt's book. But then Sloane posted it to her accounts, tagged Wyatt's publisher, and captioned it: *Doesn't every woman want to be looked at like this?*

The publisher did the rest, teasing their real-life romance alongside Wyatt's novel about an off-limits love. Since then, Wyatt and Chloe have been inundated with questions about their personal life. And their friends have been teasing them mercilessly.

The private wedding is exactly what Wyatt and Chloe need. The next day, Chloe plans to surprise her brother and spoil her nephew. But tonight, Chloe wants to call Wyatt her husband a dozen times and fall asleep in his arms.

"Do you miss living here?" Wyatt asks. The judge left after they finished their vows, and Chloe and Wyatt lingered by the cliff, finding a bench to watch the sun set.

"Sometimes. But I love our home," Chloe sighs.

Six months ago, Chloe and Wyatt moved into an old farmhouse in Virginia. There's space for Wyatt to write, and the upstairs bedroom floods with light, perfect for Chloe's painting. When Chloe first proposed the move, falling in love with an online listing, she expected Wyatt to protest. Or hesitate, at least. But he just shrugged and said, "I can write from anywhere. I'll live in any home as long as you're there." They moved the next week, and the cheaper rent combined with their savings allowed Chloe to quit her job so that she could focus on her art.

The gamble paid off because Chloe's first solo show is scheduled for next month, at the New York gallery where she worked after graduation. Luke and Lucy are throwing her a party, and everyone else is flying in for opening night.

"I think there are a million places I could live and love," Chloe says. "I like finding them with you." She rests her head on Wyatt's shoulder. Home is no longer a place when you find the right person.

"Are you hungry?" Wyatt asks.

"I'm starving."

"Fancy dinner or non-fancy dinner?"

"When have I ever picked fancy food, Wyatt?"

"Alright. Let's go." Wyatt holds out his hand.

"Where are we going?"

"It's a surprise."

They drive up the coast, all of the windows down, Chloe's dress bunched up around her knees as her hand weaves into Wyatt's dark hair. They are smiling broadly, singing loudly, and Chloe can't imagine a better wedding night.

A few minutes later, Wyatt pulls onto the shoulder of the highway. Chloe laughs. It's a taco truck. There are a few picnic tables, paper plates, and a menu with a picture of what looks like the best crispy pork tacos of Chloe's life. Since it's dinnertime, Chloe is surprised there aren't more people lined up. Instead, the makeshift parking area is empty.

Wyatt grins. "Come on."

When they step out of their car, a mariachi band starts playing and string lights turn on.

"What did you do?" Chloe asks.

Wyatt shrugs. "They want to celebrate with us. Sloane insisted."

Chloe turns around and sees her friends running toward her. Just before they reach her side, enveloping them both in hugs, Wyatt whispers to Chloe, "We will have all night alone in the hotel room. Do not worry." And then his eyes light up and Chloe's stomach flutters.

Marianne reaches out to examine Chloe's ring. Sloane and Alden look tanned and relaxed. They've spent the last two months in Europe, hopping around the Mediterranean. "Kid-free luxury," Sloane calls it.

Sometimes Chloe wonders how Sloane is really doing, because she is so good at pretending to be put together. But in their late-night phone calls, because Chloe is finishing a painting and Sloane can never calculate time differences, she seems at peace.

Sloane had agreed to stop IVF, at least for now. After the fire, it was apparent the physical and mental strain was too much, even for someone as determined as Sloane. Sometimes Chloe fears that Sloane is transferring all that focus from having a baby to traveling the world. She talks about all the inspiration she's gathering for when they decide to build a new home. And once, she made a passing reference to an adoption agency that a high school friend recommended, but otherwise, their conversations are mostly about the new places and foods she discovers. Chloe doesn't push because she knows that often decisions take time. Sloane would share her plans, whatever they were, whenever she was ready.

Luke hangs back, his arm wrapped around Lucy's waist.

For a brief moment, Chloe wonders if it will be awkward. It's the same fleeting thought she's had each of the handful of times they've gotten together over the last year. But just like every other time, the moment quickly passes.

Luke's been trying to rebuild trust among his friends. Marianne said he was the first to text wishing Teddy *Happy Birthday*. He crowd-sourced restaurant recommendations for Sloane and Alden from his coworkers. He was the first to buy one of Chloe's paintings. Luke's not perfect, and probably never will be, but he knows he needs to be a better friend and show up for the important stuff.

"Congratulations," Luke says, slapping Wyatt across the back and then pulling him in for a tight hug. "I'm really happy for you guys."

"I'm happy for us too," Chloe says. "All of us."

They order dozens of tacos. Luke pulls out a cooler of beer and a jug of margaritas. Sloane and Alden tell them about the cliff they jumped off of near Marseille. And island hopping through Greece. And hiking the Costa Brava.

"I never knew you were so sporty, Sloane," Wyatt teases.

"It's a surprise to me too," Sloane says. "But I like trying on different versions of myself."

Chloe likes that answer. Twenty years from now, she wonders what version they'll be on. She hopes they will have tried on several, because watching your friends turn into adults is a privilege.

"Marianne has some news to share." Sloane nudges her side.

Marianne shakes her head. "No. Tonight is about Wyatt and Chloe."

"Absolutely not," Chloe says. "That's why we didn't have a big wedding. Please share your news."

"I started my own business," Marianne beams. "The wait-list was so long for my math-tutoring clients that I decided to hire two people to help. We're fully booked through the end of the year. We might even rent some space so that we don't lose travel time driving to clients' houses."

"It's the beginning of your math empire," Sloane brags.

Marianne waves her hand dismissively, but her face is full of pride. She started tutoring students for a few hours after school rather than going back to full-time teaching. She told Chloe that those hours, when she wasn't a mother or a wife, she was just doing something she loved, made her feel alive.

Chloe smiles at her friends. She's proud of their efforts over the last year. It's not easy to fight for what you need, especially when mind-tricks like guilt and obligation try to derail desire. But it seems like Sloane and Marianne and even Chloe decided that losing themselves wasn't an option anymore.

"We have some news too," Lucy squeals.

"Are you engaged?" Sloane asks.

"Did you knock up my sister?" Alden blurts.

Lucy punches her brother's arm. "No. I'm twenty-four. I'm not getting married or having babies. No offense, Marianne."

"None taken," Marianne smiles.

"Luke bought an apartment in Tribeca. We're moving in together. He bought me a La Cornue range."

"I have no idea what that is," Marianne says.

"It's a stove that costs as much as a car," Luke says. "But Lucy makes the most amazing sourdough bread, and now she's going to do it in style."

Lucy works as a marketing assistant by day, but she spends most of her free time baking. If she wasn't Alden's sister and Luke's girlfriend, Chloe would hate her because she somehow defies physics by being so thin despite the steady stream of carbs.

Luke kisses Lucy on the top of her head and pulls her closer.

It's been strange, watching their relationship develop over the last year, but Chloe knows that they're really good for each other. Lucy has no problem challenging Luke, and Luke is constantly trying to find new and better ways to support Lucy.

Chloe used to think that it was somehow her fault that the relationship with Luke didn't work out. But now she knows, loving a person isn't enough. You have to figure out the love you need in return.

Chloe turns to Wyatt. His arm is draped behind her back on the bench, their bodies never separating for one moment tonight.

"How did you know?" she asks.

"Know what?"

"You asked where I wanted to go to dinner. What if I had said fancy dinner? I am in a wedding dress."

Wyatt shrugged. "I know my wife."

And it's true. Sometimes Chloe thinks Wyatt knows her better than she knows herself. Wyatt forces Chloe to remember that her needs are more important than keeping the peace. It's not always a reminder she appreciates, especially when she has to tell Sloane that monogrammed invitations aren't necessary for her art show or even admit to Wyatt that she hates the food at the town diner that's his favorite. Wyatt reminds Chloe that love isn't the absence of conflict. It's important to fight for the love you deserve.

Sloane leans over the table. "I was prepared for all scenarios. I made a backup reservation at a French bistro ten minutes away."

"Of course you did," Chloe says.

And then she kisses Wyatt, her husband, while the sound of their friends' laughter floods her ears. Chloe hopes she has thousands of married kisses in her future. Maybe ten years from now they'll have children like Marianne and Noah. Or maybe they'll travel the world like Sloane and Alden.

After all, everything in life is unpredictable. But Chloe hopes that wherever her life takes her, these five people will be there to watch. Because sometimes history is so deep, roots so tangled, that no matter what changes—and inevitably everything does—there's always a path back together.

ACKNOWLEDGMENTS

TWENTY YEARS AGO, I met a group of friends who changed my life. We've been by each other's sides through all the major milestones—marriages, divorces, deaths, and births—and all the mundane moments in between. None of the characters in this novel are based on them, and yet there are tiny love notes to our friendship sprinkled throughout this book. I am continually honored to have these brilliant women in my life. Thank you, Jennifer Miller, Maria Fehretdinov, Meagan Fitzsimmons, and Sara Colangelo for loving me even though I'm always the first to fall asleep on our group trips.

Endless thanks to my agent, Dani Segelbaum, who remains wise beyond her years, calm in my panicky moments, and steadfast in her advocacy for my work and career. I'm incredibly fortunate to have you on my side.

My editor, Faith Black Ross, asks the best questions and challenges me to dig deeper into each character. I'm so thankful to work with Faith and the entire Alcove Press team, including Dulce Botello, Rebecca Nelson, and Thai Fantauzzi Pérez.

One of my favorite parts of being an author is meeting so many wonderful people in the book world. A special thanks to the booksellers, librarians, book club members, reviewers, journalists, BookTokers and Bookstagrammers who take the time to review and share books with other passionate readers. I'm so grateful to be a part of this community.

I've been fortunate enough to find the best colleagues in one of the loneliest professions. My author friends commiserate about contracts and taxes, read early drafts, hype each other up when we try to make awkward social media posts, and generally understand that this industry is better when we all succeed.

Thank you to Julie Gilchrist for reading an early draft of this book and fixing plot holes while we went stand up paddleboarding.

Thank you to Meredith Kimener, my sister and first reader. This book is so much better because of her feedback and our marathon phone sessions.

I'm lucky because I have the best mother in the world. And then I got even luckier with an amazing mother-in-law. Pam Laning and Sandy Crittenden have always provided so much encouragement and childcare and love that it feels like an embarrassment of riches.

My children, Isabel, Henry, and Leo, remain my greatest inspirations and best distractions. Thank you for pulling me away from this book and into your incredible worlds.

Lastly, my biggest thanks to my husband, Jeff. I'll tell you the rest.